HORIZONS

HORIZONS

MARY ROSENBLUM

A TOM DOHERTY ASSOCIATES BOOK • NEW YORK

HORIZONS

A Tor Book
Published by Tom Doherty Associates, LLC
175 Fifth Avenue
New York, NY 10010

www.tor.com

Tor® is a registered trademark of Tom Doherty Associates, LLC.

Library of Congress Cataloging-in-Publication Data

Rosenblum, Mary.
    Horizons / Mary Rosenblum.—1st ed.
        p.   cm.
    "A Tom Doherty Associates book."
    ISBN-13: 978-0-765-31604-2
    ISBN-10: 0-765-31604-8 (acid-free paper)
    I. Title.
    PS3618.O834H67   2006
    813'.54—dc22

                                2006005726

First Edition: November 2006

Printed in the United States of America

0 9 8 7 6 5 4 3 2 1

TO JANE OTT

With many thanks to Sage Walker, Jane Ott, Alexis Glynn Latner, and Jean Lauzier for their patient help with my work in progress. I owe much to Dr. Bradley C. Edwards's extensive work on the realities of a space elevator—I hope I get to ride on it—and to Greg Bear for his generous assistance with research sources on future evolution. I also owe a debt of gratitude to the Pai family, who brought me to China as their guest and introduced me to an Asian perspective.

HORIZONS

AHNI HUANG SHUT HER EYES AS THE SHUTTLE FROM THE Elevator matched spin with the main port of New York Up. Grief distracted you, could get you killed. The Platforms were alien territory to her. She didn't know the rules. The chairs swiveled as her limbs grew heavier, giving Ahni a vivid moment of nausea before *up* and *down* settled into place. Didn't help that *down* had been *up* a moment ago. She drew a slow breath, dropping briefly into Pause until her heartbeat slowed and her biochemistry stabilized. You could control mammalian stress reactions, but like grief, you couldn't entirely banish them.

Please remain seated until docking is completed, the cool androgynous voice murmured.

All through the cylindrical cabin, seat-webs clicked and retracted and the clone-similar business passengers plus a couple of overdressed tourists smoothed wrinkles from their singlesuits and pulled bags from the storage bins beneath their seats. Ahni scanned the faces, senses heightened to the max now, watching for the telltale slide of an eye, the subtle edge in body language that would mark a hit or a tail. Her brother's assassins would expect her father to come for vengeance, but they would also be looking for any member of the Huang Family. Two natives on board. Their too-slender, almost fragile build gave them away. She watched them covertly as she pretended to fiddle with her bag.

Anticipation, resignation, fatigue, boredom . . . As a Class Nine empath, and a sensitive one, she was sure they weren't acting.

So far so good. Ahni levered herself from the padded acceleration recliner, her stomach happy with the eighty percent Earthnormal gravity of the rotating can's outer shell. She stretched, aware of the muscles cording on her small, lithe frame, wanting to go out and run for about six miles to work out the kinks from the long Elevator trip. They had a jogging path here in New York Up, but it required a Level Three tourist pass and she wasn't staying in that kind of hotel. She slung her slightly scuffed business brief over her shoulder, looking like your basic mid-level Assist running the boss's errands from the planetside business headquarters. She adjusted her body language to reflect mild boredom tinted with a bit of worry and slipped between a man with a polished gym physique and a lanky woman with natural Mediterranean genes—probably Turkey or Crete, Ahni guessed—and a taut driven face. Still on full alert, Ahni shuffled down the narrow aisle and out into Customs and Immigration.

It wasn't much more than a wide corridor with a desk and gate barring it a dozen meters from the docking lock. Just enough space for a shuttle-load of bodies. No uniforms, no stun guns, but Ahni's skin crawled with the knowledge that a half dozen beams and fields were probing every square centimeter of her skin and body cavities. Up ahead, a man with unselected Han features jolted to a halt, a look of surprise on his face that transitioned through annoyance to resignation. His com link, an earring that looked like a natural diamond, had just informed him that Security wanted to talk to him. With a small shrug, he turned and headed toward a panel that had slid silently open in the wall. A couple of people looked at him curiously. Ahni shrugged. He was innocent of anything, or thought he was. But according to Jira, the family's information synthesist, China's Dragon Home was squabbling with New York Up over tariffs. With his face, he wasn't going to get where he was going on time.

The man in front of her passed through the gate. Ahni stepped forward at the agent's nod, keeping her bored/apprehensive body language carefully in place, and adding a mental layer of worry about the LaGuardia account and the discrepancies in the inventory database, couldn't wait to get this mess untangled and get back to terra firma . . . Empaths made good money working for Security.

She stood on the painted footprints so that the security scanner could check all her vitals against her ID chip. They'd match. The ID chip she had paid so much for was top quality.

"Haarevort, Jessica, from the Free State of Singapore, Pan Malaysia Compact, on business with East Asia Biologicals, three-day visa," the cold-faced woman intoned, her eyes on the screen in front of her. "Customs declaration?"

"Nothing." Ahni gave her the absentminded and impatient smile of the "small Family" member, the seasoned businesswoman running minor Singapore Family errands that the database assured the Immigration agent that she was. She held the brief to the scanner, and it chimed in agreement that the luggage seal had been placed at the Palembang Elevator station and hadn't been tampered with.

That had cost nearly as much as her ID chip.

The agent looked up to nod her through, the hint of a flaccid sag to her muscles suggesting that she lived high up toward the axle of the orbital, not down here in the highG outer layers of the rotating can that was NYUp. For a second her eyes flickered as she focused on Ahni's face, and a small flare of indecision made her hesitate.

Ahni's face was not Dutch Indonesian at all, but rather showed an unselected mix of Taiwan aboriginal, Han Chinese, and Polynesian genes in the planes of her face and tint of her skin. When she wore her hair long, it had a reddish cast in the sun, and a faint wave to the thick, unruly mass.

The woman gave the slightest of shrugs and waved her through, although her indecision still tainted the air like a whiff of perspiration. Too bad. Ahni put tired unconcern into her posture as she hoisted her bag to her shoulder. If someone asked, this woman might remember her. Not good.

She was here to kill. The World Council had granted the Taiwan Families Right of Reply.

Still in business mode, Ahni followed the stream of passengers through the last meters of Immigration and out into the Arrival Hall. She closed her eyes, murmuring her access code to her implanted link. The screen lining her eyelids offered her a glowing map of the corridors opening into the Arrival Hall. The route to her Level Four hotel room glowed a neon blue, the others green. Fourth Level—close enough to the outer skin to have some gravity, far enough in to fit with her low-level errand-runner persona. She headed toward the elevator. Out here, on Level One, where all the tourist and business traffic came and went, the corridors were spacious, lined with shops offering trinkets—fragile crystals grown in microG, asteroid fragments set in precious metals, spidersilk clothing, food, euphorics, VR and flesh entertainment. Tourists strolled along, business travelers hurried somewhere. The thin-looking natives all wore service uniforms down here at this level. They weren't curious, nor were they particularly friendly. A lounge with a vast window offered stars and a huge, blue-green slice of Mother Earth. Ahni halted in spite of herself.

She had never been off-planet.

Enormous against the endless black of space and the hard, bright glints of distant suns, the great blue sphere held her eyes. Down there, Xai had been born. And died. Grief lay like a stone in her heart. Killing his killer would not bring him back. But this was war. Ahni smirked for Security's everywhere eyes, shrugged and turned away, the seasoned business traveler for a moment beguiled by what might have been real, but was merely a digital image on a wall screen faked to look like a window.

A slip. Grief slowed you down. Boosting her senses to painful heights she left the lounge and crossed the crowded strolling spaces to the elevator, aware of every jostling shoulder and oncoming face. In the elevator, the floor numbers increased. Axle was *up*, skin was *down*. The floor pushed against her feet, but when the large car paused, she exited slowly, feeling as if she was walking on a trampoline. The other riders scattered from the lobby, comfortable in the diminished G. They vanished down corridors, intent, busy, not looking.

A tall, skinny man in a blue singlesuit, a geneselect Masai type, hesitated, frowning slightly at a personal reader, concentrating on something slightly irritating.

A tiny shard of intent pricked through that concentration static. Ahni reacted without thought, flinging herself down and toward his feet, shoulders curling to roll. Displaced air feather-brushed her cheek as a dart skimmed past, then her roll caught him at the knees, out of control and sloppy in the lessened gravity. He flew over her back, his screen sailing to clatter against the elevator door. His head hit the wall with a dull sound. Ahni tried to continue her roll and failed. Different physics here! She slammed sideways against the wall, tasting adrenaline and blood, struggling to get her breath.

Nice setup. At this level, the elevator lobby apparently emptied quickly. Poison on that dart? No place to hide an unconscious body in these sterile residential corridors. She rolled him against the wall, tugged his singlesuit straight, arranged his limbs to suggest a nap, and strode briskly out into the corridor, her body language relaxed, senses straining. Eyes flicked past her in the hallway, not looking, not seeing, bodies brushed by. Time to disappear before Security got into the act.

He could have darted her easily, but he had hesitated. Why? Ahni ran her fingertips over her shoulder as eyes skimmed past her, unseeing. She found the slickness of the tiny pseudoskin patch, peeling it off with a sharp fingernail under the pretense of scratching a small itch. A trace of blood made her fingertips slippery as she squeezed the purchased chip from its shallow bed.

A tall woman with too-thin bones danced past her, humming to music playing in her head, naked from the waist up, a silver filigree of inlaid fiberlight decorating her full breasts, ringing her dark areoles. The naked breasts startled Ahni in spite of her homework on NYUp customs.

Holos or flat graphics decorated residential doors. The images— starscapes, unicorns, strange flowers—had the look of addresses. Not many uniforms or business suits up here, above the tourist level. Ahni turned down a connecting corridor, putting casual purpose into her posture and stride, dropping for an instant into Pause to suppress the flood of corticosteroids into her bloodstream. Without breaking stride, she pressed the pseudoskin patch to a residential doorway decorated with holographic vines. If Security looked for

Haarevort they'd find her loitering in this doorway. Ahni paused, closing her eyes to summon the map of New York Up from Data. She needed safety, time to drop into full Pause—access her personal AI—and figure out how things had gone so wrong so fast. And how to fix it. An ancient fairy tale sprang to mind, about a Muslim rabbit and an Israeli fox. About a thorn patch . . . The corridor walls up here curved into floor and ceiling without angles, covered with a fine fibered carpeting, tinted a soft, soothing green. She hadn't passed a hotel room for some time now. All residential? She'd stand out—stranger. When she reached the next service bay, she slowed until the preoccupied woman in the neon green singlesuit and natural euro-mix face disappeared into a room. Then Ahni whisked into the bay and palmed the control plate next to the service elevator. It only took a handful of seconds for the network in her palm to analyze and override the lock. The door slid open and she stepped in. They'd expect her to go down to Level One, to the safety of gravity and Security. She overrode the controls, sent the car up. Past the residential levels, past the manufacturing and storage levels, clear to the axle. The end of the line.

She'd never spent time in microG before. Rabbit in the thorn patch. The Krator clan, Xai's murderer, was an Earthside clan, just like the Huang clan. They wouldn't look for her here.

So why NYUp, where Krator had as little presence as Huang? Not even Pause had yielded an answer, but this was where the assassin's trail had led her. I will avenge you, she promised her brother's spirit as the elevator slowed and beeped at her. Xai would want vengeance. As their father did. *Secure for MinimalG.* The letters ran silver and gold across the wall in multiple languages, chasing themselves around and around the tubular walls. Not that she needed them, she was barely anchored to the floor by a shadow of *down.* Her stomach stirred, protesting, as she slipped into one of the padded harnesses that lined the wall.

Movement resumed. The harness cut into her shoulders slightly, not enough to be painful. Then . . . the downward tug ceased and she floated, held by the straps.

So far so good. Ahni slipped out of the straps. She swallowed, groping for *up* and *down,* but the featureless tube of the elevator offered her no orientation. The doors didn't open and the annoyed blip of a beep told her that she was neglecting something . . . probably a password. Her palm tingled just above the threshold of feeling as her embedded hardware dealt with the control plate. The door slid open . . .

. . . and she gasped.

GREEN

LIGHT

She recoiled, a knee-jerk primate reaction, uncontrollable. That flinch started her tumbling and she bounced off the wall. Stomach knotting, she grabbed wildly for the door frame, missed, tumbled out into the blinding glare, floundering, helpless. *Up. Down!* She struggled for orientation as the world wheeled around her. Damp air, rich with unfamiliar smells. Soft green things brushed her. Hydroponics at the axis, she remembered, and the soft brush became recognizable as leaves, but *up* and *down* still refused to fall into place. Bad choice of thorn patch! She forced her burning eyes open, struggling to bring the green glare into some kind of focus. Goggles. You had to use something up here. Would the fierce light blind her? She used Pause to quell a spurt of fear adrenaline, grabbed, feeling soft plant things crush beneath her hands. She tore free and grabbed again, palms slick with plant juices. This time the stems held and she halted. Behind her, the elevator beeped and the door whispered closed. Somebody wanted it.

So much for the thorn patch.

Still clutching handfuls of moist, bruised leaves, Ahni stretched out a cautious foot, holding tight to the anchoring plants. She felt something thick and fairly solid beneath her foot. A large column? Behind her, the elevator chimed again and she caught a flicker of movement off at the edge of vision—the door opening.

Before her conscious mind could catch up, she planted both feet against the leaf-covered column, knees bent. Her thigh muscles bunched and she shot forward, blind, arms shielding head and face, praying to all her ancestors that whoever had come down in the elevator would miss.

She felt him, intent and at ease. Sure of himself.

Her shoulder slammed hard into something that gave some and

sent her tumbling wildly, cartwheeling like a kid's pinwheel or a kite spiraling down. She curled into a fetal ball, head down, rebounded from another column, grabbed, felt stems tear in a spray of moisture. One foot landed squarely on something and she pushed again, hard. Just *go!* She rocketed forward again.

Felt something tiny sting her shoulder.

Felt his triumph.

Damn.

Vision faded and her body no longer worked. Paralysis? Or death? Her face hit something thin and whippy, then something harder, bruised, couldn't do anything. Slowing . . . vision fading . . .

Ahni tried to close her burning eyes as her body drifted. Couldn't do it.

An apparition appeared in front of her. Narrow face, like a hairless skull drawn into caricature by some art program. Weird milky eyes with no pupil, limbs too long for their thin boniness and they . . . bent. Like green bamboo. A demon. *I am dying,* Ahni thought.

The demon grinned at her, grabbed her wrist. She felt that . . . and experienced a moment of surprise, then more nausea as the demon yanked at her. *Green* and *light* fled by her and then she plunged into darkness.

"WHY?" THE VOICE penetrated a midnight sea filled with half-seen sharks. Anger rumbled in it and fear. "What were you *thinking* of? Koi, you know better."

"He was going to kill her. She's pretty. And she couldn't get around any better than a new baby. Why did he want to kill her? It . . . wasn't fair. She couldn't get away."

Different voice, high and thin like a child's. She didn't feel a child's butterfly presence, but rather a clear stillness, like a pool of water.

"Damn." The anger voice rumbled. "Now what?"

Ahni tested muscle groups and was rewarded by a whisper of response. Sank deeper into Pause. Play dead . . . or maybe get dead.

"I can take her back, Dane," the child-voice said. "Before she wakes up. I thought downsiders couldn't come up here. Look at all those muscles! I'll take her back and send her down."

"Too late. She's listening to us."

Uh oh. Another empath. Change tactics. With a mental shrug, Ahni opened her eyes and gasped, not needing to pretend confusion. The light stunned her.

"You'll be all right," the rich, rumbling voice said. "In the short term, the light won't damage your eyes."

She blinked, a major effort, struggling to sort out a kaleidoscope of images.

Plants, her brain told her. But they were too big. She had walked in the jungle preserves of Indonesia and the Amazon and that was what first came to mind. Jungle. She floated amidst a forest of tubes as thick as her leg, furred with leaves and tendrils of a dozen different shapes and styles. Pea. She recognized the tendrils suddenly, starred with white blossoms and the small scimitar shapes of forming pods. Nearby, she made out a tangle of bean vines, Chinese long beans, their skinny pods more than a meter long.

The images began to parse. Pea, bean, tomato, she recognized, eggplant, their furry leaves sheltering long, skinny thrusts of shiny purple black fruit, and peppers, green, orange, and yellow—all too large, and slightly strange. The light, turned thick and green by the dense tapestry of leaves, was tolerable. The plants grew on thick columns that vanished into a blur of green light above and below.

"Who are you and how did you get up here? This level is restricted."

She twisted toward the voice, tensed as the movement set her drifting. A hand caught her, damped the motion, and she found herself staring into the weird milky eyes and long face that she had seen as the dart hit her. The demon. Not a dream, then. She studied it. Cataracts? From the light? Not a child, but child sized, naked except for an intricately wrapped band of fabric that hid its genitals. He—not it—had no body hair she noticed, and he clung to one of the thick leafy vines with long prehensile toes. He was the source of that pool-clear curiosity. And not human. She stifled her reaction, her gut icy, looking death in the face. They couldn't let her leave now. The creature was pleased and excited, like the puppy she'd had as a kid. If he'd had a tail, he'd be wagging it.

"Meet Koi," the voice said, tinged with bitter amusement now. "You're wrong about him. And he just saved your life. He thinks he did, anyway."

He was reading her *very* accurately. Ahni tore her eyes away from the grinning kid-thing—Koi? Like the golden fish in her mother's courtyard pool? She turned toward the rumble-voice. Not old, not young, in that middle balance. Ropy muscles and thin limbs of a native, he expressed a wild mix of genes, European, a bit of North Africa, maybe some Amerind, she guessed. He wore the green and silver NYUp singlesuit, same one the officials in the Arrival Hall had worn, but his eyes were hidden by dark goggles. She couldn't read him at all. Which made him a Class Ten empath. And there weren't any Class Tens employed on NYUp. She had checked.

She dropped fully into Pause, accessing Data, scanning through it in the space of a breath for a match to the face in front of her.

Dane Nilsson. Hydroponics Plant Administrator with a degree in Botany and a Class Three Genengineer license. According to the specs, employee Nilsson was a plant waterer, a low-level gene splicer, who checked up on the automated equipment.

His smile was broader now, which *really* bothered her, because his empathic rating in the personnel file was Two. Which was slightly higher than a rock's. She blinked out of Pause.

"We need to sort this mess out," the man Dane, said, his tone cold but without threat. "Why don't you come and eat with us, get a little rest?" It wasn't a suggestion. "Your hunter gave up. He must not have wanted you very badly."

But he had and his departure bothered her. A lot. Ahni scanned the crowded columns of growing things, senses straining for an echo of pursuit. None.

"He'll be back, won't he?"

"I . . . don't know." Humiliating. And scary. So far, Krator had known her moves as if she had handed them an itinerary . . . and that wasn't possible, because she'd been making them up as she went along ever since she'd stepped into that elevator lobby on Level Four. She needed to figure out *how* they knew. But right now it didn't matter much. Only one crime brought an automatic and unalterable death penalty from the World Council. That was the dilution of human DNA with DNA from a nonhuman source. Maybe she should hope they *did* come after her. Caught between tiger and dragon? "I'll go with you," she said. As if it was a genuine invitation.

Nilsson eased closer with a complex shiver of muscles, utterly in control of his motion. He was a *whole* lot more skilled in microG than she was. She flinched as his fingers closed around her wrist.

He towed her and she went limp, letting him. The weird kid-thing followed. The ease with which the two of them moved made her think of dolphins swimming through a kelp bed. These leafy columns, as thick as her body, didn't sway the way the kelp stems did. The leaves remained still, unless you brushed them, and then their recoil was quick—a product of mass-in-motion transfer of momentum, rather than the damped sway of underwater stems. She caught a glimpse of translucent plastic tubes where plants were small, spaced to grow. Mature plants thickly furred other tubes. She identified a tube covered with beets, the perfectly round crimson roots the size of her head, the thick, lush leaves, red veined and as large as an elephant's ear. Another tube sprouted the bright green leaves and red jewels of strawberries as large as chicken eggs.

These strange versions of familiar plants scared her. As did the kid-thing who carried death in his face, and the man's cold calm. Different rules here. And she didn't know them. Dane planted a toe here, ball of a foot there, nudging them smoothly and swiftly forward, barely disturbing the leaves. Bare feet. She studied the kid-thing from the corner of her eye. He flanked her, and she had a sudden flashback to a summer afternoon swimming off the family compound at the southern tip of Taiwan when a pod of dolphins had suddenly surrounded her.

The kid-thing had the "so what" attitude of the dolphins that had brushed against her, leaped over her, that day. *Who are you? What do we care? This is our world, not yours.*

I can kill you, she thought. *With one word to the authorities. And this man, too. And he knows it.*

They were slowing, had clearly reached a destination. The tubes seemed oddly close together, forming a solid wall of green. "In here," the man said, let go of her, and slipped into what seemed to be a solid wall of leaves. Ahni hesitated, aware of the kid-thing's attention, like a finger prodding her. Well, she wasn't going to outrun them. She shrugged, which set her immediately drifting, grabbed a handful of stems, and propelled herself clumsily between the close-set tubes.

A curtain of blossoms shimmered along the walls of a small open space, bright as living jewels. The light was muted here, filtered by the wall of leaves and she realized that the tubes had been bent and spliced to form a spherical space. Anchored nets held personal items, clothes, and bedding. Clearly the man Dane lived here, among the blossoms. He pulled off his goggles, lodged them in a net full of junk and rummaged in another for a squeeze of water. His eyes gleamed like pewter, contrasting sharply with his dark skin. He sent the squeeze of water sailing suddenly toward her, and as she automatically caught it, only then became aware of her fierce thirst. "Thanks," she said, equal to equal. An honor he didn't acknowledge. She awkwardly settled herself in an empty net among sprays of purple and white flowers that looked like oversized orchids and probably were.

Dane sent a fat orange and yellow fruit zipping toward the kid-thing who snagged it with casual skill, damping his reaction with one foot, his long toes curling around the tube without bruising a single leaf. The kid cut into the fruit with a small blade and handed her a thick slice. Ahni touched it tentatively with her tongue. Blinked "How do you get mango up here?"

"Dane engineered the plants to grow small like eggplants." The kid-thing grinned at her, the tips of his teeth showing, laughing at her again. "But they have big fruit. Dane's really good with genes." He sliced more mango. "It's got a full compliment of amino acids, too. He says that makes it a complete protein. So you don't really need to eat anything else. A lot of stuff's like that now." He bit into his slice, expertly catching tiny globules of juice with his tongue.

Koi. She remembered his name, studied him. He was happy, excited, with a child's uncomplicated enjoyment of company, something new and interesting. They'd euthanize him instantly. You could do a lot with engineered human DNA—cure disease, extend life, regrow a damaged spine or a failed kidney. But bring in traits from another species . . . turn a human being into a gilled water creature with amphibian genes, or a furred little seal-girl, and you died. No appeal. No second chance. The Chaos Years had frightened all of humanity. So why hadn't this Dane person killed her?

Because he thought she was chipped, of course. He didn't know who she was—a Family daughter who didn't wear the birth-implanted ID tag, someone who had the single luxury that only power and birth could buy. Privacy. He assumed that if she died, the *where* would be on record, and so would the *how*. So she was safe. For the moment. Long enough to give her options. Ahni swallowed the sweetness of the mango. Tiny orange spheres of juice floated away from her lips. She wasn't at all good at catching them and Koi rolled his eyes at her. The tiny constellation of mango juice pearls drifted close to one of the tubes, this one planted with ruffled bells of pink and white. Ahni caught a flicker of motion, and suddenly, one of the tiny droplets was gone. Fascinated, she watched as one by one, the wayward juice drops vanished. With a jolt of recognition, she finally spotted the author of the movement. "A frog."

"Partly." Dane had finished his mango, was sending bits of the peel sailing into the greenery. "When the platforms were first built, the garden was pretty primitive. Blue-green algae, mostly, then a few plant species in the tubes. Hydroponics at its most basic, producing nutrition, but not much fun. And the plants took a lot of work. You had to pollinate, deal with fungus, and keeping the particle count down was a bear. Over the years we created a system that tends to itself."

"The gardens clean the water for the entire can," Dane went on. "It all comes here. The digester uses a sequence of aerated tanks full of tailored bacteria strains and fish to recover the heavy metals and liquify any solid organics. Then it flows slowly through the tubes. They're full of granular polymer—an artificial soil we manufacture here and populate with a thriving microbial ecosystem. The plants root in them and use the organic compounds. If you balance the variety just right, the water that comes out is clean enough to drink." He touched an orchid blossom reflectively. "I'd like to visit Dragon Home one day. They do rice. I'd like to see how."

She glanced again at Koi as his sudden alert pricked her attention. She followed his gaze and had to use an instant of Pause to quell her reaction.

Two more of the strange faces peered from the flower-wall at her. She caught only a glimpse before they vanished. They had the same features as Koi, and she retained an image of long toes grasping delicately between the blossoms and leaves.

"Yes, there's a breeding population." Dane's pewter eyes fixed on her. "I didn't create them. No one did. This isn't Earth." He leaned toward her, anchored in his hammock. "You think it is, you think that it's nothing more than another New York or Moscow, only stuck up in the sky with variable gravity as a nice tourist attraction. But you're wrong. This isn't Earth and your Earthly boogeymen under the bed don't scare us up here." He laughed softly, mirthlessly. "We have our own."

"Dane . . . I'm sorry." Koi broke in, voice low and intense. "I know not to show . . . but he was *ugly,* and not supposed to be here, and she was like my baby sister when she was born, she couldn't even drift right. And . . . she was pretty."

Pretty, again. A child's crush-bright word. She had not been called "pretty" very often.

"It's all right." Dane's assurance had the feel of summer's warmth. "It's not a wrong thing to save a life." He touched Koi's shoulder lightly, barely stirring him from where he floated. "She doesn't wear a chip, Koi. That's how come she surprised you like that. The locks won't keep her kind out. But they don't care about us." A flicker of his eyes challenged her. "They run the planet down below. We don't matter."

He knew she wasn't chipped. Ahni froze inside. She held his life in her hand, and he knew that he could kill her with impunity. If the gardens processed the waste from the entire orbital, a few more pounds of organic solids wouldn't be noticeable. "You're right," she said. "I'm a member of the Taiwan Family. My father sits on the World Council." She gave him truth, because that was all she had to offer and he would read a lie anyway. "Krator family killed my half-twin." She couldn't quite block the stab of those words, even now. "I don't know why they chose to unbalance relations like that. But they did. Our father . . . sent me to restore balance." She drew a slow breath that barely stirred her. "You're right. I don't care what you do here."

"Balance." Dane's voice was low and charged with a still anger. "Killing does not restore balance."

"I agree." She met his eyes, not trying to hide her bitterness. "But I am Xai's sister and my father's daughter and I cannot say no."

"Why not?" His eyes were cold.

The reasons could not be shrunk to a handful of words. "You're perfect up here?" she said instead. "Nobody ever kills?"

"Not often." Dane looked away.

That truth troubled him. Ahni untangled herself from the mesh and pulled herself carefully between the flower tubes, waiting for him to stop her. He didn't. The leaves and blossoms closed in behind her as she pulled herself out of his private bower. She pushed off, her trajectory erratic, steering by fending herself off the planted columns.

TWO

AHNI CURBED HER URGE TO SPRINT. THEY COULD CATCH her in a second. She pushed off from the planted columns gently, figuring out how to twist her body and change her trajectory. She wasn't sure why she still lived and had no idea where the nearest elevator down to the Level One might be. The kid-thing, Koi, was following her, of course. His bright, puppy-enthusiasm burned like an old fashioned incandescent bulb in her wake. The man wouldn't be far behind.

Moving randomly through the tubes, one eye on the trailing Koi, she searched for an elevator. Slowly, she became aware of the small hum of lives around her. It reminded her of a summer forest's life-song. That sense of . . . a living ecosystem . . . surprised her. The orbital seemed so artificial.

Ahead, she saw things moving, many things. Wary, she caught a tube coated with spirals of small green ovate leaves, holding herself still, to watch. It was too bright to see clearly, and she squinted. Many-legged robots like gray plastic spiders minced along the tubes, a slowly expanding bladder trailing behind each one. She caught a glimpse of red and shaded her eyes. More beets, she decided at last. The robots were plucking the huge round balls from the surface of the tubes. Only a single tail of root penetrated the polymer and the harvester-spiders plucked them with apparent ease. The tube healed instantly. They didn't take all, but apparently picked and chose, collecting just the right ones. Behind them, smaller robot spiders crept in the harvest-spiders' wake, four jointed front legs busy, dancing up and down as they moved slowly forward. Curious in spite of her need for hurry, she drifted nearer, because they were only robots. Planting, she realized. Each small spider left a tiny tuft of green in the space where the beet had been harvested. Ahni nudged herself gently forward, drifted over to the newly planted tube. The beet seedling sat in the center of the space vacated by the harvested beet, a tiny thread of root embedded in the translucent tube. She touched the tube, found it resilient with a sluggish give that made her think of a gel. She poked it with her fingernail and her finger penetrated it easily. Cool. Wet. She pulled her finger out and the surface healed behind her, but not before a silvery drop of water escaped. Something small and green zipped out from the leaves, scooped up the water in trailing legs and vanished into the shadows.

The intricacy of this place stunned her. Programs would do most of it, she thought. Balance harvest with planting, start adequate seeds in culture somewhere here, so that the planting-spiders could follow the harvesters. You could chart the eating habits of a million or so people, predict the trends, supply the restaurants and food shops, and clean the water while you were at it. Energy flooded in from the sun, free, ready to be turned into sugar, carbohydrates, and proteins.

This was not a hydroponics farm. This was a . . . garden. Ahni shook her head, which sent her drifting up against a tube planted with small leafy plants studded with green, unripe mangos like the one she had eaten.

"Don't get in their way. There's not supposed to be anyone down here but Dane."

She turned at the sound of Koi's voice. "You mean the spiders?" she asked.

He looked blank, but nodded when she gestured toward the slow steady scuttle of the robots. "Them," he agreed. "They've got a video link and nobody probably ever looks at it, but somebody might." He shrugged. "It's a Security link, so Dane can't fix it. Here." Koi thrust something at her. "Dane told me to give you this. He said to use them."

Goggles. The small, thick lenses were what Dane had worn out here in the perpetual flood of photons. She slipped them on, her squint relaxing as the glare dimmed, leaving headache in its wake.

Koi drifted gently closer, his curiosity pricking at her. He had pupils after all, she realized. The cloudy lenses of his eyes obscured them. "You don't need goggles?" she asked him.

"No." He blinked at her. "Dane says my eyes filter the light so that it won't damage the inside, you know? He says we're changing to fit up here. Like he does with the plants and things, only it just happens on its own in us and really fast. He called it a genetic shift, and he said that's why so many babies die—our genes keep trying new stuff and it doesn't always work." He looked away from her, gently grieving. "Like my baby sister. Why did that man kill your half-twin?" He twisted idly, upside down to her now, his long toes wrapped around one of the little mango shrubs. "And what is a half-twin? I don't understand."

Genetic shift? Ahni eyed his long limbs realizing that she hadn't been dreaming, that there was a hint of flexibility in his long bones. A pretty extreme genetic shift, even accounting for radiation-induced mutation up here. She still didn't believe it. "It's a long story," she said. Family politics didn't make for a five-minute summary. "I don't really know *why* Krator Family killed Xai." Already, economic levers were being applied, nudging small pebbles that would in turn dislodge stones, that would in turn, send economic boulders crashing down on Krator business interests. Individuals would suffer in this silent war as a vegetable business lost its loan here, a metals importer had her down-porting license revoked there, an info-service lost its creative talent. Why? She shook her head, thinking that Xai could have told her. He thrived on the three dimensional chess game of power. "He's my half-twin," she said slowly, "because we have the same father and were born together. Are there a lot of you?"

"There's my family." Koi's shiver of worry sent him drifting. "Dane's really worried. I was really bad."

"I'm not going to tell anyone, Koi," Ahni said softly. "I don't care how you came to be." She smiled at him. "This is a . . . beautiful world. And you fit it."

Suddenly, Koi's 'family' appeared all around her, as if he had called them. They darted like dragonflies and looked as fragile as dragonflies, too. She caught flashing glimpses of slender limbs, those strange, milky, blind-looking eyes. Their curiosity tickled her. One tiny female hovered in front of Ahni. She held out a hand and cool, slender fingertips brushed hers. Then the girl darted away and they all vanished.

Ahni drew a slow breath. "Can you show me a way out, Koi?"

"It's nice up here," he said wistfully. "You can stay."

He had a crush on her. She smiled and he smiled back, hopefully.

"I have to go home," Ahni said. "If you show me the elevator, I'll come back one day, okay?"

"I'll have to ask Dane." Koi pushed himself gently off with one toe.

"He's afraid I'll tell people about you. But I won't." She stretched, took Koi's hand. "I promise. It's okay to let me leave. In fact . . . it's dangerous for me to stay here. The people who want to hurt me will come back and they may find out about you."

"Dane'll be mad." Koi sighed, gave her one more yearning-puppy look, then pushed off with his long toes, gliding forward in a perfect trajectory between the thickly planted tubes. She followed, clumsy, but managing to keep up with him, although she left drifting leaves and bruised fruit and vegetables in her wake. "What do you know about the world outside of here?" she asked as he paused, pretending to consider the route. Waiting for her to catch up. "Do you have any . . . stories about where you came from?"

"Dane said we came up from down below. Where you come from. We can't ever go back. Dane says we'd die."

"Aren't you curious?"

"About what?" His surprise was genuine.

Ahni shook her head. "Nothing," she said. "How much farther is the elevator?"

"Not far." He grinned. "Real close now."

And she felt them. Coming fast. She didn't know what they had, some kind of scanner, but they knew she was there. One was the man who had darted her before. She recognized his bright hunter's certainty. The other's icy determination made her guess he was the man who had been waiting for her at the elevator. That determination tasted coppery with vengeance.

"Run," she snapped at Koi, pointing away from their pursuers. "They've spotted us." She grabbed a tube thick with ripening strawberries, spun herself around and pushed off with her foot, heedless of the crushed berries and shredded leaves. She shot forward, at the edge of control, guiding herself crudely with her hands, ricocheting off tube after tube, leaving a visible trail of damage behind her. They wouldn't need anything technical to track her. A tube thick with something round and green like guavas appeared in front of her. She pushed off with one hand, spiraled off at a tangent, utterly out of control now. Felt twin cold novas of triumph behind her, managed to grab a tube, plant her feet, and shoot away from that 'gotcha' gloating behind her. Intent on the narrow spaces between the leaves, she lucked out, arrowing between thickly leafed tubes into relatively clear space where the tiny plantlets must have been newly inserted. She soared through the narrow clearing and into the leaves on the other side, leaving no trace of her passage. Let herself slow. "Koi?" She twisted cautiously, expecting to find him on her heels. "I need another way down."

He wasn't there, and then she felt him. His terror and pain, flared like lightning in the quiet of the axle garden, with that 'gotcha' triumph.

They had been after Koi, not her.

Best choice; find the nearest alternative elevator and get out. Not her problem.

Ahni pushed off, caught a tube planted to tomatoes, kicked gently off, and headed back along her trail of damage, trying to move cautiously.

She fixed on the silver knife blade of Koi's terror. Over there. It was faint, getting fainter.

Way too fast.

She kicked off of a tube and launched herself recklessly, but it was too late. She burst from the leafy shadows of the tubes and into a wash of light that made her squint in spite of her goggles. An elevator. The wide, matte gray portal looked odd and out of place in the lush greenery. She hurtled into the wall of the enormous tube, tucking head and shoulder, rolling, and killing her momentum with her feet and knees, bruising herself but maintaining control.

They had taken Koi down with them.

As she clung to the alloy frame around the portal, something metallic and blue caught her eye. It hung in the air in the clear space around the elevator portal, turning slowly in the harsh light. Gently, Ahni pushed off and drifted closer. A bracelet. A hotel key, she realized. The new fad. A pretty bracelet to match your business singlet, but inside, the chip to open your door, turn on the lights and the enviro controls . . .

They had left the key behind.

For her.

It tumbled very slowly end over end, moving in a slow steady trajectory toward the first of the leaf-covered tubes. Ahni stretched out a hand for the bracelet as she crossed its trajectory, hesitated, thinking of all the things that could be hidden in that twisted circlet of cheap plastic. Touched it.

Nothing happened.

She plucked it lightly from the air, as if it was a poisoned fruit. An invitation? An offer? A bright puzzle-piece to toss with all the other tiny pieces that had showered around her since that hours ago trip through the Arrival Hall, like how had Krator had known her moves seemingly as soon as she did? And how had her pursuers followed her so unerringly? Why had they taken Koi?

Like bright fragments of glass, they tumbled, razor-edged in her mind, swirling microG slowly . . . to form an impossible pattern.

She knew who must have left this key.

Gently, Ahni's fingers closed over it. She slipped it into a pocket in her singlesuit, sealed it carefully closed.

Dane erupted from the leaves a moment later, halted effortlessly in front of her, didn't touch her. "Koi?"

She met his pewter eyes. "They took him."

"You and your damned war," Dane growled.

"Who's at fault here?" Rage seized her. "*You* created him. You made him into something that they'll treat like an animal. Don't blame me for this. This is your doing!"

He stretched out a hand, damped his drift to utter stillness, face shadowed by leaves. "I thought you were getting it," he said in a soft, flat tone. "When you saw his family. I thought maybe, one downsider could figure it out. That this *is not Earth*. Your rules don't work up here, don't you get it? We keep track of everybody now, but there have been some rough periods since the first space station got bolted together up here. Some people must have . . . slipped through the cracks as the orbital platforms grew. That's what I guess anyway. And they started living up here, maybe in storage space at first, stealing food from the primitive hydroponics we had up here back then. Must have been pretty grim." His pewter eyes bored into hers. "You got to wonder what it was they were hiding from, down below. But that's all I can figure out. Oh, I thought someone made them, too. Then I did a gene-scan. They're as Homo sapien as you and I are. Your brothers and sisters, downsider. I don't know what's driving the changes and oh yes, they're still changing." His eyes gleamed. "Our siblings, downsider? Or maybe . . . our successors?"

Successors. A chill walked Ahni's spine. Because he *believed* it. "So then you're safe," she said softly. "Why hide them?"

"You threw history at me a little while ago." Anger flashed in his eyes. "We have a history of hating anyone with a different face or hair. How many millions have we killed for the crime of being different? What about someone like Koi? He doesn't look different, he *is* different."

"That's in the past," Ahni snapped.

"Is it?" Dane said softly. "Rats."

She blinked at him, uncomprehending.

"That's how the last supervisor listed them in the database." Dane drifted close, so close that she could feel his breath on her face. "Temperature, humidity, crop mass, ripeness percentages, rats exterminated. It took me awhile to figure out what he meant, when I took over."

He had to be lying.

"He was probably afraid somebody would think he'd created

them." Dane's tone was coldly reflective. "Or maybe they just scared him. Because they were . . . different. He killed quite a few. I found a young boy in one of his traps, my first day here. Neurotoxins on a pretty toy. Very creative. There weren't many left. They don't reproduce well. I think a lot of pregnancies get reabsorbed, and some infants—like Koi's sister—simply die. It wouldn't take much to eliminate them all. Why do they exist?" His voice dropped to a whisper. "What are they? What do they mean, downsider? That's our question to answer, not yours. This isn't your world. I thought you understood, so I let him take you to the elevator."

Ahni took a breath of the heavy air. It smelled . . . wrong. Not like the Amazon, not like the lush tropical greenery of New Taipei. Not like Earth. "I can get him back," she said, her words leaden. "You must have a gene sequencer . . . an official model? With a time/date labeler? Uncompromisable?" No one was allowed to play with genes, unrecorded.

He was nodding. "Standard agribusiness model," he said, his eyes on her face. "Licensed and tamper proof."

She unsealed her pocket and took out the blue bracelet key. "I don't know how many traces are on this. Use my DNA as reference. I need the original hard copy. Signed, sealed, and presentable to the World Council if need be." She held it out.

He took it, closed up and unreadable again. Looked from it to her. "Do you want to give me a clue whose DNA you're looking for?"

"The DNA that isn't mine."

"I'll need a sample from you."

She held out an arm and he pulled a sampler capsule from a pocket of his singlesuit, popped it open and scraped the inside of her forearm lightly. Pocketing it, he turned, gently prodding his body around with one bare foot. "Signed, sealed, and delivered, coming up." And he arrowed away.

She followed, barely keeping him in sight. He wasn't really trying to lose her, wasn't trying not to lose her, either. She thought about Koi's delicate bones and organs that had never known even the moon's gentle gravity, much less the 0.8 Earthnormal at the Level One. Tried to ignore her estimates on his survival. When Dane vanished into an alloy-gray cluster of cylindrical pods nested among tubes and leaves—it would be the gene lab and probably the control center of the garden—she waited outside, drifting in the fierce flood of energy from Sol, nearly able to *hear* the growth of the thick, oversized spinach leaves that brushed her arms and legs lightly. Tiny lives hunted and feared and satisfied hunger all around her.

Xai waited for her on the other side of that hotel door. That's how they had known her every move—she and Xai knew each other that well. *I cried for you. I meant to kill for you.*

Why, Little Brother? Ahni watched a crystal bead of salt water drift from her face. A tiny creature like a dragonfly soared from the leaf shadows to snag the droplet in trailing legs, then vanished.

IT DIDN'T TAKE him long to sequence the sample.

"I found one major trace and a lot of contamination. Whose is it?" He tilted his head.

She was surprised he hadn't guessed. "Our father's clone." When you didn't wear a chip, you could do a lot. Cloning a child wasn't exactly legal, but . . . it happened. "I was an accident." She shrugged. "My mother was pregnant when he was implanted."

"But—" He broke off. Shrugged. "I sent a copy to your email," he said. "You should check it. This is the half-twin you said was dead?"

"Yes." She bit off the word. "His . . . body was destroyed in an accident. We identified him by . . . DNA traces at the scene." Blood. His blood. "You have the documentation?"

"The original, legally encrypted and sealed file. Suitable as evidence in front of the World Council." He held out a small data sphere and the hotel key.

She slipped the sphere into a secure pocket in her singlesuit, slipped the bracelet over her wrist. "Thank you," she said formally. "I will go get Koi now."

"I'm coming with you."

She shook her head. "The trained dogs who took Koi will let me by," she said. "Not you."

"Downsider, this is my world," he said quietly. "You need me."

She didn't have time to argue, simply hoped he didn't get hurt as he followed her to the elevator. It read the bracelet and stopped at Two. The doors whispered open and a purple arrow glowed to life in the matte blue carpet of the elevator lobby, fine as a brush-stroke. She followed the arrow and as she stepped across it, another one lighted a few meters ahead. The corridor was busy but not crowded. The murmur of emotions filled the air like whispering as Ahni followed the beckoning arrows. A vendor in a wide stretch of hallway lined with shops sold skewers of baby vegetables from a cart. She caught the scent of curry as she strode past. From the corner of her eye, she saw Dane pause to buy one, obviously not interested in her or her path. He did it well. She felt a small relief, because the dogs would be ruthless.

A North American–style coffee shop bustled, the patrons here mostly business travelers. A pair of young Asian men in cheap business singlesuits played virtual mahjong above a tiny game projector, their faces identically intent. But the smaller one with the Guangzhou face couldn't mask his reaction as she passed. Dragon Home dogs? That surprised her. Wheels within wheels here.

Beneath her feet, the arrows beckoned her left, down a side corridor lined with mid-range hotel rooms. An elegant pot of ferns decorated one entry. The purple arrow winked out as she stopped in front of it. She sensed the Mahjong players behind her in the hallway, not attacking, just watchful. No sign of Dane. Good. This was not a game for amateurs.

She didn't bother to touch the door pad. The Dragon Home dogs would have let him know.

She could feel him on the other side of the door.

It slid open and the physical reality of his round tawny face with the pure Taiwanese features—unlike her own face shaped by her mother's mixed geneset—shocked her. His hair was slightly mussed, as if she had interrupted him in a moment of relaxation. She met his eyes, closing up her emotions, her control so tight that it was nearly Pause. "You look very healthy." She said it in Taiwanese, made it an insult with her tone, watched the skin tighten over his broad cheekbones. He said nothing, simply stood aside, ushering her into the hotel room.

Banishing a twinge of unreality, she noted the basic no-frills carpeting and furnishings. Roughing it. She swallowed a sudden desire to laugh, felt the flicker of her half-twin's anger.

"I did not expect you." He turned aside to a basic kitchen wall. "Tea?"

She nodded, so polite. *He* should have come. Their father. It was *his* duty to restore the balance, to personally exact the vengeance for his more-than-son's death. Xai spooned tea into a small clay colored pot, touched a wall-set spigot to fill it with steaming water. From the garden, filtered by mangos, *mei qing choi,* and spinach? She accepted a steaming cup and it came to her suddenly—why the man in the elevator lobby had fumbled his attack. He had expected *The* Huang.

"You would have killed our father?"

He concentrated on his tea, lips tight, but he could never hide from her. Ahni set her tea down, untasted.

"There was no other way!" Xai spun away from her, flung his cup at the wall. It didn't shatter, bounced off. "He's never going to let me do anything. He just sees me as a younger, more energetic body that can run around doing what he orders it to do. I'll never be anything but a *vehicle,* a body he can use. I'm not even human to him. At least you get to be a person, my mongrel little sister."

His words stung like a slap. "You're wrong," Ahni said.

"Don't give me that empath stuff. You don't know." He turned away from her. "What am I, little sister? A spare part."

"Xai." She stared at him. "What are you saying? Our family is grieving."

"Join me." He faced her. "We can take it all away from him. We can be bigger than he will ever be."

"What about Krator Family? What about the small people who get hurt because our father thinks Krator Family killed you? *You* have gone to war with our father."

Xai shrugged. "Make up your mind, little sister."

The interview was at an end. Ahni could feel the Dragon Home dogs beyond the door. *Once we played together,* she thought. "I came to offer you a trade, elder brother." Her voice seemed a stranger's. "You give me the deformed child you took from the axle and I'll cancel the automatic send to our parents of the sealed, time-dated, and legal-encrypted DNA analysis from that hotel key. Surely you realized that a NYUp employee who was manipulating plant genes would have licensed equipment for genetic documentation in place? You touched the key, little brother."

He hadn't thought of this scenario. Perhaps he had been too sure of her answer to his invitation. His surprise that she would be that clever was revelatory and humiliating in the same instant. "It won't change anything if you send it," he said finally.

"Don't underestimate our father." She smiled, without mirth. "He's *you,* remember?"

Xai was thinking hard behind a slight sneer. There was no way out. She'd worked out all possible actions. Even if he killed her the file would go to their father.

"You can have the cripple." Her half-twin shrugged. "I take it that this is your 'no' to my offer?" He tried to mask his icy rage with a smile. "You are a fool. I don't need you."

"Perhaps." She met his stare, closed off, letting his anger beat against her.

"Ugly, that cripple." He shivered with distaste. "I won't even ask how you came to assume that debt, little sister, but it's an expensive one." He smiled, sure that he had won now, gestured with his chin. "Your creature is in there."

The suite had a second bedroom. Inside, Koi lay on the smart-foam mattress, his eyes glassy, wrists and ankles bound with wide plastic strips. His ribs jutted against his skin with each labored breath and his skin was too cool, clammy to the touch. Shock?

"What happened to him, anyway?" Her brother looked over her shoulder, his distaste dank in the room. "Radiation? Disease?"

"Yes." Ahni bent over Koi, touching his face, wondering about brain damage, spontaneous hemorrhage. She released the restraints, wrapped the light thermal sheet around him and scooped him into her arms. He weighed little, like an infant, as if his long bones were hollow, filled with air.

"Li Zhen will not be happy with me. I think he wants it for a pet." She shrugged and started for the door.

"The file?"

She reached into her pocket, handed him the data sphere.

"You are a fool." Xai pocketed it.

The door slid open and she walked out into the corridor. The dogs were back at the mah-jong board. They looked up as she walked by, stood and paid their bill.

Dane fell in beside her. "Take him." She thrust Koi's body at him. "They're after me, not you." They'd try a dart or a needle.

"Stay close to me." Dane took Koi's fragile body from her. "Don't try to run." People passed them: service staff, mostly local residents judging by their slender musculature. A small group of natives burst from a doorway, laughing and talking. Someone shouted angrily. A voice rose. Ahni glanced over her shoulder to find the group faced off with the Dragon Home dogs, voices raised accusingly.

"This way," Dane snapped, and she followed him into a side corridor. He slapped a lock plate awkwardly, and the door to a small, private elevator opened.

"How did you do that?" Ahni gasped as the elevator shot upward.

"I do favors for people," Dane said absently, his fingers probing Koi's unconscious form gently. "They do me favors in return." As they reached the bright, stunning heart of the orbital, Koi stirred and whimpered.

"I couldn't breathe," he panted. "They hurt me." A trace of blood gleamed at the corner of his mouth, and Dane rocketed away with him. Ahni followed, barely able to keep up. Koi's family flanked them on all sides, darting shadows among the greenery. She counted fifteen, maybe sixteen, sensed curiosity. No worry, no fear, just . . . curiosity. A breeding population, enough, but not too many. Changing. Shifting into . . . what?

Dane took Koi into the control center. She followed, found a bright visitor access with padded chairs with microG straps, gleaming surfaces, machines, screens, data storage tanks. A small medcenter took up one end of the space. Koi whimpered as Dane closed the unit around him, and Dane hovered over him, murmuring soothingly. She kept well back, watching him as he touched control screens, frowned, touched others. Koi whimpered again, and Dane drifted above him, his hands on the boy's face until he finally quieted.

At last Dane pushed himself away from the matte gray, coffin shape of the med unit. Koi's eyes were slitted, glassy with drugs.

"Is he going to be okay?" Ahni prodded herself closer.

"Some broken bones, minor internal damage. They weren't gentle." He touched Koi's cheek lightly. "He's in enhanced healing now. He should recover." Relief gleamed quicksilver behind his reserve. "You gave him that data sphere?"

"Yes."

"That was your ticket downside."

Ahni met his eyes, hesitated, not sure she could put it into words. "I . . . brought our war up here," she said at last. "Thinking this was just another high rise. But you're right. This is not Earth. Our war does not belong here. And I . . . believe you about Koi and his family." She bowed her head fractionally. "Li Zhen, Chairman of Dragon Home saw Koi and wanted him. My brother only saw a crippled child."

"Li Zhen?" Dane said slowly. "What was *he* doing here?"

"I don't know." She looked away. "I need to go back to Earth."

"I can give you a ride to one of the Elevators—a backdoor ride that your brother can't track."

Which just might get her downside in one piece. "Thank you," she said.

"If you ever need a place to go, this place is . . . more protected than it seems." He smiled. "You're welcome to come back."

It had the feel of a royal invitation and she thought of the crowd that had so neatly intercepted the Dragon Home dogs. "I would like to return," she said. "I would like to visit Koi again." *And you,* she thought. *I would like to know who you really are.*

For a moment, he merely looked at her, then his eyes lightened slightly, and Ahni realized that she was feeling his smile. "Any time," he said. "Come on. Let's get you out of here in one piece, before I have to deal with your brother."

Ahni followed him from the control center. This man was no low-level gene splicer. Realized he was offering her his hand. Took it.

He didn't quite tow her, but his unerring trajectories made it a whole lot easier to get around without leaving a trail of destruction in her wake. They traveled for nearly a half hour and the physical immensity of the axle began to oppress her. But it fed a small world.

"There's a microG park at this end," Dane said. "We're almost there."

"There" turned out to be a small lock, heavy and functional looking. Dane's palm and retinal scan got them into a cramped cubicle with several flaccid suits like the shed skins of caterpillars hanging on the smooth walls. Air lock? She didn't see any exit port. He touched a small flat-panel screen and a few moments later, she sucked in her breath as the wall shimmered and . . . melted.

"Smart alloy." He glanced at her, a hint of a smile in his manner.

"I know." She shook her head. "I've never *seen* it, that's all." Molecules that migrated around made her nervous and she nudged herself gingerly through the opening after him, one eye on the silvery rim of the oval gap. Found herself in a small ship.

About time we took a run, a female voice said. The ship?

"Meet Miriam, my ship-core," Dane said. "Miriam, be polite." He propelled Ahni gently into a maze of webbing that turned rather surprisingly from tangle into a hammock. Slid into a second hammock. "Head for the Pan-Malay backdoor, Miriam."

Sneaky or open?

"Sneaky."

The curved eggshell of the ship's hull . . . *melted* . . . closed and a fine hum seeped through the webbing into her bones. Suddenly she had . . . weight. *Up* and *down* struggled briefly, but there were no right angles, no straight lines to help her out.

Dane's hands moving among a three dimensional shimmer of holographic control icons. "We're heading over to the Pan Malay Elevator. New Singapore is feuding with Dragon Home over a smuggling matter, so that may slow down Li Zhen's dogs. And I'm licensed to use one of the private docks."

Ahni clung to her stomach, retreating into Pause to damp down the biochemical upheaval in her bloodstream.

Your passenger is about to urp, Dane. You clean it up.

"Enough, Miriam." Dane gave Ahni a sympathetic glance. "We're almost there. Hang on."

Like to see you get off the Elevator at sea level and walk, Ahni thought, as they finally docked. She swallowed sourness and released herself clumsily from the hammock as the wall melted open . . . in a different place this time . . . to reveal another lock much like the one she had just left.

"I'm assuming you can handle whatever security you run into?" Dane clung to the webbing, looking down into her face. "You can get down okay?"

"Yes." She drew a breath, suddenly reluctant to propel herself into that lock. "I . . . Taiwan Families have no quarrel with the Pan Malaysia Compact. I'll be fine. I . . . Thanks," she said. "For showing me your world."

"Thank you for Koi." He touched her cheek lightly, his eyes dark as a cloudy sky on Earth. "One day . . . I hope you come back up. I think you'd fit."

"I'll try." And she meant it. She pushed off, suddenly reluctant to leave, sailed through the oval emptiness that had been a wall, too fast, hit the far wall of another cramped lock with the same caterpillar skins of suits hanging on the wall. Grabbed one as she rebounded. "Goodbye," she said, but the wall had already gone solid. A tiny change in pressure told her that the lock had sealed and a green light filled the chamber.

Good to go. She blinked briefly into Pause, summoned the specs for this Elevator, found a route from the service corridor beyond the lock door to the main tourist plaza. Laid her palm against the plate in the lock.

She stifled a sudden pang of regret as the door opened. Straightened her singlesuit. Time to go home and face their father with Xai's betrayal. Grimly she headed down the corridor.

THREE

THE TOWN MEETING WAS FULL TONIGHT. AND SEETHING with emotion. Dane lounged at the fringes of the crowded public square, perched crosslegged on a bare table that would be crowded with scarves or jewelry or the tools and parts of a service trader come market day, but served as a good vantage point. In the center, a fountain bubbled and leaped with the abandon of the marginalG up on this residential level. A dozen kids splashed in the water, paying no attention to the adults. All around him, eyes fixed glassy on eyelid screens, adding to the Con, the weave of live-chat conversation that rippled 24/7 through every level and corridor of NYUp. Everyone attended townplazas, either in person or by Con.

"Noah?" Dane spoke softly over his com link. "What do you hear on the Con?"

"Running just under forty percent, I'd say, for immediate secession." Noah's young voice sounded loud in Dane's ear. "That's up two percent in a week. Why the change, Dane?"

"I don't know." Dane paused, frowning, watching a skinny kid toss handfuls of water into the air. He had the disproportionately long arm and leg bones that were showing up in this generation.

Like Koi. "It bothers me, Noah. It's too fast, too soon. See if you can pinpoint sources, will you?"

"Like hunting for a molecule in an atmosphere," Noah said, "but I'll get a few people in to help. Got to quit now. They're serving dinner. I'll keep on it while we're dropping. Sorry, Dane. Bad time to go downside."

"Family comes first, Noah. Just do what you can do. Thanks." Dane broke the link. He missed Noah. Noah was the most skilled at reading the Con. The perpetual chatter online had proven to be a very accurate predictor of events. He'd set Noah up to monitor trends with a powerful AI. This new increase in secession fever worried him. And Laif was late. Not good, tonight. Dane suppressed a frown, blinked his own eyelid screen to life, the crowd vanishing behind a blue virtual wall, lines of speech scrolling down, threads of conversation flowing . . . With practiced ease, he skipped across a dozen threads, adding a word here, a comment there, but mostly reading, taking the pulse of NYUp.

Noah was right. The Con had a fever tonight. No major nexus . . . lots of small hot spots . . . story about a rude downsider here, an accusation of theft in a skinlevel hotel there. Small irritations, but more reaction than usual? Like an allergy—a few molecules and you're itching. NYUp was itching. Dane opened a visual link to the control center and Koi, still in Enhancement. Another six hours. He watched the boy's eyelids shiver. Dreaming. He thought of the strange downsider, Ahni. Wondered if she had made it back all right. Nobody had tried to look for her in the axle. Which might not be a good sign.

She really had understood about Koi and his family. Too bad she was a downsider. He put that regret aside as Laif arrived.

"Sorry to be late." The Administrator's voice carried across the townplaza, larger than life, as he was physically. Dane watched him thread his way through the crowd, his mahogany scalp rising well above those around him, his grin flashing, the emerald in his left ear scattering shards of green light. An afroamerican-amerind-euro mix with a longtime resident's elongated bones, he greeted even the pushy complainers with an easy manner and steel competence that always managed to find balance in any situation.

He needed that talent tonight.

Dane sat up straighter as the crowd parted ahead of Laif, revealing glimpses of the grass carpet and mosaic paths of the townplaza, giving him respectful space. A woman had been making the most of the crowd, selling iced fruit juice from a heavy plastic thermos hung over her shoulder. Laif paused to speak to her. The silver tracery of lightfiber decorating his naked scalp reflected glints of the emerald's green as he bent to listen to something she was saying. He laughed, his head tossed back, his face so alive with the *essence* of laughter that people around him laughed, too. Even some of the grim faces, couldn't help themselves, although they laughed grudgingly.

Laif unclipped his big personal mug from his belt and presented it to the juice seller with a flourish. She grinned, poured ruby colored liquid into the mug, offered the reader at her belt for his thumbprint. Grinned wider as he bowed and imprinted it. Dane smiled grimly. Laif scores again. The mood in the crowded townplaza had lightened, and when Dane blinked into the Con, the spinning conversations were lightening, too: *laif does a good job, not his fault the heavyweights keep milking us, he does his best to keep their grubby downsider paws where they belong, and did you hear about that kid, some heavyweight tourist hit with a cart, why they need carts when they can go up a couple of levels where we live or maybe lose some of that heavyweight flab . . .*

In a heartbeat the Con had recast Laif from stooge for the downsiders to beleaguered hero. Not bad, even if it didn't chill the secession fever. Dane lifted a finger in a quiet salute, one that Laif didn't acknowledge, although Dane was pretty sure Laif had spotted him. He might act casual and hurried, the overworked Administrator rushing in from his screen, but he would have scoped the crowd through the security cams first, surfed the Con, and counted the members of NOW in the crowd. Like Dane. He leaned forward as Laif made his way to the podium set up for the meeting.

"All right, let's get it over with." He swung himself casually up onto the podium. "Don't want to make you all start throwing stuff. Costs to clean up, after, so we'll just cut to the yelling."

"Well, hey, I'll start." A small man, round-faced, with native muscles, waved. People around him withdrew politely, giving him floor. "What the hell joke is this Security tariff all about?" Arms crossed on his chest he stared up defiantly. "Security for who? Who is Earth keeping us secure *from*? We're the ones in the Arrival Hall scanning the scum that comes up here. They let anybody get on the damn Elevators. I mean, my sister, she had these two guys just walk out of her shop the other day, ate a full lunch, didn't pay. And for that, she's gotta pay extra next time she boosts realmilk cheese up here?"

"So how come she can't use soy like the rest of us?" The juice seller spoke up, her half-empty jug sloshing as the crowd gave her space. "If she wants downsider cheese, fine, let her pay their 'security' skim. Me, I like the local stuff. She too good for it?"

"She's on the skinlevel, got to feed the customers what they want."

"Maybe the customers should learn to like something different. Or stay home."

The crowd cheered at this and the man flushed. "You sell what you want, you . . ."

"You've both got a point." Laif's drawl cut through the rising voices and the crowd hushed expectantly. "Yeah, we need to buy upside when we can, but on the other hand, the downsiders bring their credit up here with them. If they want a little Earthside cheese on their local salad, hey," he spread his hands, winked. "I'd rather boost a little realmilk feta up here than see them bringing their picnic lunches and leaving trash instead of credit." He paused as laughter and applause, along with a few whistles of disapproval, rippled through the crowd. "But I came here tonight to bitch about the new security tariff right along with the rest of you." He leaned forward now, the emerald flashing, his smile fading. "That caught me blindside, made me feel like a fool, I can tell you. I've been screaming about it all afternoon. We do our own security up here, and it's a whole lot more effective than anything the North American Alliance puts on the ground, at least if you go by the crime stats."

"So why didn't you just tell 'em no?" Dane unfolded his legs, rising to his feet on the table, looking over the upturning faces below to fix his stare on the Admin. "Tell 'em we don't have to pay for what we don't use."

"It's more complicated than that. Don't try to oversimplify

things for your own purposes, Nilsson. You're good at that and we all know it." Laif faced as the crowd moved back to reflect the line of tension between the men. "I walk a damn fine line between telling the Alliance downstairs what they can't do and kissing butts. I don't know about you, Nilsson, but I hate kissing butts."

Nervous laughter skittered through the crowd.

"But I do a hell of a lot more of it than I want to do. If they yank me out of here, the next Admin is gonna dance to their tune, you better believe it. I've pissed off too many people down there. They won't make the same mistake twice. They'll put somebody in here who not only likes to kiss butts, but takes orders, too."

"And we appreciate the butts you kiss, believe me." Dane's earnest tone brought more laughter. "But we need to talk about this new tariff. I don't know about you, but a bunch of folk I've talked to, the ones who still have to boost stuff up here, are really hurting. We're on a thin enough margin already. What does the NAA want? Is it out to bankrupt us all, repo the can?"

Cheers erupted, some whistles, but not that many. The crowd buzzed, anger and agreement sweeping his senses like a hot wind. He blinked into the Con for a few seconds, did a quick surf. Yep, it mimicked the townplaza tone pretty closely. Little less enthusiasm from the skinside merchants who depended on downside traffic, more from the service level folk who had local businesses on the side, like the juice seller.

"Yeah, they probably wouldn't mind if they could repo this place." Laif raised his voice. "We're a pain in the butt up here. They'd love to do away with the lifetime leases they handed out back when nobody wanted to live long-term up here. Then they could stick a bunch of nice obedient tenant-farmers up here, like New Singapore has." His face grew grim as the crowd quieted. "But I don't plan to go along with that. I've been pressuring them to let us impose that tariff on the refined metals and spider silk they're so hungry for down there—collect on all that stuff going down the Elevators. Told 'em it's to pay for more rock jocks out scouring the skies for falling stones that might mess up the cities down there." He waited for the applause and clapping to fade. "They're listening. Falling rocks scare 'em."

"What do we use as a lever next time, Admin?" Dane crossed his arms, his body language challenging, despite the smile on his face. "And the time after that? It's gotta stop some day. If we ever want to start expanding on our own, we gotta stop hemorrhaging raw materials *and* credit down there!"

Cheers bigtime, solid enthusiasm, only a couple of whistles, but then the ones who didn't want independence for the orbitals mostly didn't show up in person at the townplazas. *It's in your court, Laif,* Dane thought. *We need a good slam here.*

"Jeeze, Nilsson, I don't know what game plan I'm going to run until I know what the game is." Laif shook his head tolerantly, but anger flashed in his dark eyes, bright as the emerald. "Why don't you get yourself appointed to my job for awhile. See how well *you* walk this tightrope, huh?"

"I'd rather stand down here and ask the questions." *Not good enough,* Dane thought. *Come on, Laif. Cancel that percentage we're seeing.*

"I got a question for you, Admin." A small taut man appeared as the crowd gave him space. "Why walk that tightrope of yours. huh? You're right. It's gotta be a tough job. Gets you a paycheck, sure. But that doesn't seem like a whole lot of payoff for a tough job." The crowd fell silent. The man was a stranger, small and mixed-euro with a narrow face and a fanatic's eyes. Fringer? Dane watched him, senses alert. One of the extremes who were ready to go to war with the planet? Dane didn't recognize him from the NOW meetings. New here?

"We pay the tariffs on stuff we haul up and they make sure we have to haul it up, so it's a sweet deal." He turned his back on the Admin, his voice rising, body swaying with the cadence of his words. "Only way out, I see, is to tell the heavyweights the rules instead of saying 'yessir' and standing around in crowds like this, blowing air. Wow, our Administrator might get us some credit on a few pounds of metal going downside. Who cares? They own us and they know it!" He turned and pointed at Laif—the rude gesture eliciting a murmur of disapproval. "I think you're getting paid to help 'em own us."

The crowd erupted again. Some whistles, too much applause, the anger back, just like that. Damn.

"Now hold on." Laif strode to the edge of the podium, his anger radiating, real this time. "You walk in here and accuse me of being on their downsider team, then you better be ready to back it up," he boomed. "You want to do that?"

"You bet, mister Administrator." The small fringer stood alone in a wide space now and the crowd fell instantly silent. "What about those investments you made this week? Downsider companies. I've been watching for that sort of sneaky backdoor type of deal, and hey ho, Mister On Our Side, I sure found it. You bought a nice slice of a pretty profitable sea farm off China. Profits go into a downside bank, and they're nice profits. Retirement fund? Pretty sweet deal, boss man. Don't want all your eggs up here in the basket with us, huh? They sure must pay you a good salary if you can buy something that pricey."

Shouts of outrage, applause, and whistles filled the plaza. Laif was saying something, yelling. Dane hopped lightly down from his perch, merging with the throng, nodding, shrugging, agreeing, shaking his head as he worked his way toward the fringer. He caught a hard thread of a cold, calculating satisfaction as he neared the site where he'd seen the man last, but if the emotion belonged to the agitator, he couldn't tell, couldn't spot him in the surging crowd.

"Do you believe him?" A woman stepped front of him, her chest heaving with anger, her euro-latino face pale. "Laif's on our side. He wouldn't sell out."

"Why say it if it's not true?" A smaller mixed afroamerican-asian man pushed between them. "We can check and—" his gaze went vacant as he checked the Con—"Oh, gods, it is true. It's all over the Con. He bought the shares, he's selling us out, can you believe it?"

Dane froze just for an instant. Bad. He glanced toward the podium, but Laif was no longer there, was down on the floor, gesticulating, not losing his cool but damn busy right now. They weren't giving him much space, either. The afro-asian wasn't the only one who had checked the Con.

Dane made his way through the crowd, watching for the agitator. He was good. He was a stranger. Might be a smart idea to invite him to the next little get together of NOW, get a handle on where he came from, what he was up to. He blinked into the Con.

Yeah, a few hundred people had found the new purchase made by Laif or at least by someone with credit registered to Laif Jones-Egret and hidden just enough to make it believable. If you didn't think about it too hard.

Dane skipped across a half dozen Con threads, dropping comments into the raging torrent of words. *Dumb move for someone as smart as Laif. Pretty easy to really hide your tracks. Stupid to leave the evidence just sitting there, waiting for some fool to stumble over.* Dane skipped here and there, using the various solid personas that Noah had hacked up for him, slick enough to fool even Con security. Bit by bit, his planted questions began to ripple through the outcry.

Without warning, his implanted link buzzed, tickling the skin on his shoulder. An alarm. He blinked his link open. Someone was trying to get past the security lock on Elevator 3B.

Which wouldn't be a big concern except that Koi lay locked into the med-unit in the core, and 3B was the closest elevator to the core. Which suggested that someone was after Koi.

Good luck, Laif, Dane thought as he headed fast for the corridors and the nearest elevator bay. *You're on your own.* As he reached the corridor he felt someone's pointed attention on him, but when he looked around, the corridor was empty.

Damn.

This had the feel of a very well-planned set-up.

Dane pushed himself into a skimming run, taking the long flat strides that lowG allowed. He took the closest service elevator, thumbed in manual control and sent the bare unit up at max speed. He shot out of the door as it opened, pulling goggles from his belt clip, even as he soared through the aisles of 'ponic tubes. A couple of Koi's people flanked him, worrying. *Hide,* he told them silently. *Just in case.* They vanished instantly. He slowed as he neared the control room, checking his link. According to his security system, the intruder hadn't managed to disable the lock on 3B yet. Dane killed his momentum on the side of the control center, slung himself into the lock and eyeballed the inner door open. He glanced at Koi's glazed and dreaming face, then opened the main control field, one toe tucked under the grab bar in front of the main console as the icons blinked to life.

Nothing. Dane stared for a long moment at the security read-out, then shut down the field, pried loose an access panel in the control wall, and slid his hand in behind a tangle of wires. Removed a small lethal-grade stunner. For a moment he stared down at the palm-sized gray oblong, then he slipped it into his singlesuit, and grim faced, let himself out through the lock.

Salad vegetables surrounded Elevator 3B, spirals of red, green, and yellow lettuces and leafy plants, herbs, tomato vines trained around the 'ponic tubes. Dane slowed, drifting to a halt at the elevator entry, eyeballed the control scanner and paused, his eyes on the door.

If Li Zhen opened the door?

Dane slipped the stunner from his suit, thumbed the control to non-lethal. Killed the security lock. Then he pushed off, drifting away from the light, fading into the leafy vines of a tomato's sprawl where the heavy crop of orange, ripening fruit would camouflage his NYUp uniform. The elevator whispered to a stop. Dane drew a slow breath, relaxed his muscles, stunner aimed at the door.

It sighed open.

The empty compartment yawned at him.

With a shrug, Dane pushed over to the elevator and sent the car back down. Frowning, he headed back to the control center to up the security levels for all access points. It would be a nuisance because he'd have to okay every shipment going down, but that was his only option right now.

Thoughtfully, Dane kicked his way back to the control center. There, he reset security, okayed the shipments scheduled to go out in the next shift, then turned to Koi. He touched the boy's face and for an instant, Koi's glazed stare sharpened into focus. He tried to smile.

"You're just about finished here," Dane murmured. "I think I'm going to let you out a little early. You can finish the job on your own, okay?" The fractures were 90 percent solid and the organ damage had already finished healing. He'd be okay kicking around and a whole lot safer than he was tied down here. Dane overrode the med-unit's program and ended the healing protocol.

Drifting, he watched Koi's eyes brighten as the unit sent drugs down the microtubing implanted in his veins, banishing the heavy soporifics that kept him immobile for the enhanced healing, shutting off the stimulation protocol that kept muscles and tissues healthy and toned while healing progressed. Koi blinked as the microtubes and catheters withdrew and the unit opened to release him. He moved a shoulder and drifted upward with perfect control. Yawned and stretched, without drifting a hair.

"Did she come back?" Koi's cloudy eyes glowed with memory. "The pretty one?"

"Ahni?" Dane shook his head. "I hope she's safe." His smile disappeared. "The people who took you tried to come back up here."

Koi shivered. "It hurts down there. I can't breathe." He pushed himself off with one toe, drifted toward the refreshment panel. "The ones who took me . . . they hurt me. But the one down there, he looked at me for a long time. Took blood out of my arm, but he didn't hurt me, like they did."

"I think it was Li Zhen, the Chairman of Dragon Home. I sure wonder how he fits into this." Dane closed his hand gently around Koi's fragile arm. "You need to stay invisible. It's really important."

"We will." Koi gave him a sideways look. "How come we scare them?"

"You scare them, because you're different." Dane let his breath out in exasperation. "The downsiders, I mean. The people up here . . . they'll get used to you. Later. When the downsiders can't do anything about you."

"Stupid." Koi pushed off delicately with one toe, arching into a slow and perfect back somersault, his body supple as an Earth-ocean dolphin. "I don't want to live down there anyway."

"You're right, it is stupid, and it's really a downsider fear," Dane said patiently. "Right now, we've got some other things to fix."

"Uh oh, is Laif in trouble again?" Koi rolled an eye at him. "He's always in trouble isn't he?"

"Not really." But Dane had to smile. "It's a tough job, trying to run the orbital from our end of the Elevator and from the North American Alliance's side at the same time. But we need him."

"Okay." Koi pushed off harder this time, arching into another perfect somersault.

The chip in Dane's shoulder tickled, and he pushed over to the control desk, brought up the field. "Laif 's on his way up. Let's go meet him." He snagged an extra pair of goggles from a gear hammock, pushed off for the lock. Koi drifted along beside him.

"You take it easy," Dane told him sternly. "I let you out early. Get wild and those bones might crack again."

"I'm not going to get wild," Koi said loftily.

"Noah's going to need your help," Dane told him. "Somebody bought an expensive aqua culture farm Earthside. They did it with credit registered to Laif. It's a frame, but we need to know who did it and how, and Noah's stuck downside for a few days."

"No problem." Koi spun effortlessly, his trajectory wobbling not at all. "That why you woke me up early?" He smirked at Dane as he shot ahead of him.

"I woke you up so you wouldn't be a gift-wrapped prize for someone walking through Security," Dane snapped after him.

"Sorry, Dane." Koi slowed his momentum with a complex shiver of limbs. "If somebody made that downside buy so easy, I bet I can track 'em back, if Noah's busy. He says I'm almost as good as he is, now."

"I hope so." Dane killed his momentum on a tube planted to Asian eggplant, placing his hand carefully between the narrow, black fruits. What had Noah said of Koi? *A pain to teach, but really creative.* A shred of blossom drifted away from the tube and one of his frog-flies darted out to seize it, ricocheted off the next tube, vanished back into its sheltered niche on the eggplant tube. The small creatures he had created had adapted so effortlessly to microG. Within a single generation, many of them—phenotypes shifting radically, genes expressing in surprising ways.

Like Koi and his family.

The elevator doors opened and Laif drifted out, squinting in the brilliant light. He looked . . . battered. Dane pushed off. "Here." He shoved the spare set of goggles into Laif 's hand. "Sorry I had to cut out. I had an intruder down here, and not an accidental one either."

"That's all we need." Laif pulled the goggles into place, his voice weary. "A legal fuss about Koi's folk would be the last straw right now."

"I sort of thought of that," Dane drawled.

"You know, you and your family are a great big pain, kid." Laif had drifted clear of the tubes, stalled now, out of reach of anything to push off of. "Damn, I'm bad at this. Koi, gimme a hand." He held out one of his long-fingered hands. It engulfed Koi's but instead of pulling Laif in closer to a tube, Koi pushed off, gave Laif's arm a sharp downward jerk and spun the tall Administrator into an ungainly somersault.

Laif yelled.

Doing a neat somersault turn off another tube . . . without bruising a leaf . . . Koi snagged Laif by one wrist and stilled his spin with impressive precision, then shoved the Admin face first into a tube planted with tomato vines—just hard enough to squash the fruit—and arrowed away into the green light.

"Damn!" Laif sputtered, wiping red tomato juice from his face. A cloud of frog-flies darted about him, scooping up the drifting droplets and fragments of pulp. "Double damn." Laif waived at them. "Good thing you didn't make them bite. Everything up here is better than I am in microG. What did I say to piss him off?" Laif wiped his face on his arm. "You got a towel somewhere? I need you to find out who planted that fake purchase. I had hell's own time getting up here without anyone seeing. Everybody wants to ask me personally about that. If I ever get hold of the SOB who did it, he's airlocked."

"You called Koi's family a pain in the butt, Laif. And whoever that was down there today, he sure stuck it to us." Dane regarded the Administrator thoughtfully. "Come along and clean up. Tell me how bad it got after I left. I did manage to seed some questions about that 'sale' into the Con. Dunno if it did any good. Haven't had time to drop in again. Noah'll tell me."

"I guess it worked. Last time I sampled—on the way down here—people were wondering just when I got so stupid. Something I wonder almost daily, but we won't tell anyone." Laif's laugh sounded loud, even down here in the vastness of the garden.

Dane smiled. "Only you could laugh right now."

"Beats screaming and crying and tearing my hair . . . which I don't have. Slow *down* will you?" Panting he caught up to Dane, leaving a trail of damage behind him about as bad as Ahni had done. "So where did that asshole come from? Is he one of your crowd?"

"No, he's not a member of NOW. Not yet." Dane slowed as they approached his home, waited for Laif to catch up to him. "I think I'll invite him though. If I can find him. He's an outsider. New to me. Makes me wonder."

Laif grunted, made his way through the twined tubes that made up the shell of Dane's living space. "We need to know who holds his leash. According to his entry data, he's an NAA citizen, recently employed as a contract code writer for some little manufacturing. That's crap. Made up story."

"I thought so, too." Dane pushed across the spherical space, retrieved a towel from a storage hammock, sailed it toward Laif. "I think he's a pro, doing a job. Did you get my forward of Noah's report?"

"Yes." Laif snagged the towel, scrubbed his face. "Two percent is bad. We can't go to the Council yet. That pricey synthesist we hired downside tells me it's a ninety-two percent certainty that an autonomy motion on behalf of the platforms would go down. I don't get it. People up here have been getting increasingly unhappy with NAA control, but it's been a steady curve. How come it's heating up now?" He wadded the stained towel into a ball. "It's the edge of violence that bothers me. Where the hell did this come from?" he growled. "We're not a violent folk up here! Except on the Scrum field."

"Dragon Home." Dane said.

"What about it?"

"I'm not sure," Dane said thoughtfully. "Li Zhen was prowling around here recently. Unofficially. Noah says the hot threads in the Con are starting out with people he hasn't seen before. I doubt Noah is the only person capable of hacking up a fake persona that can pass Security."

"What in nine hells is Zhen up to? He's ambitious and has his own agenda, everybody knows that. And China is a power-hungry loner, up here, and downside on the World Council. Why us?"

"I don't know." Dane frowned at the orchids blooming along

the curve of the inside wall, touched one perfect petal. "I ran into a wildcard up here. Private war from downside, I gather, but Zhen is involved."

"Who?" Laif snapped, his emerald earring glinting.

"Name is Xai Huang. Taiwan Families." No need to mention Ahni. He wondered if she had checked the DNA sequence he had done for her. "I don't know what Huang's agenda is."

"I'll get an image of him, plug it into Security. I hate wild-cards." Laif scrubbed his face again, glowered at the stained towel in his hands. "We're so damn close," he said softly. "If we increase the resident population just a little . . . within the current living-space limits we'll tip the balance. We'll have a stable economy. Pro-ducers and consumers. It'll be tough, but then we can start expanding for real. And we won't *need* Earth. We can run our own show, make our own rules. Put our interests first."

"*If* we can start dropping rocks down here." Dane shook his head. "We can't do it if we have to depend on the asteroid miners refining up in the belt. Darkside figures they own the moon and they're willing to fight for resources. Rocks make Earth nervous— as you so aptly pointed out this evening. I think you're underesti-mating downside opposition to that. They've got the weaponry to shoot at us and hit us, Laif."

"Hey, you're the leader of the secession group, what's with this pessimism?" Laif stilled his sudden drift with a grab at a nearby vine. "The Council can be swayed. We're spending every spare credit we can scrape up to sway them and we all know better than to talk rocks at this stage. Meanwhile, a wildcard war is not what we need up here right now. They're messy."

"I think it might be more than that," Dane said slowly. "Huang family doesn't have any interests up here. I checked. I'll keep all my ears open." He pushed himself away from the Admin-istrator. "And I've got a list of favors I need from you. A couple of subsidized loans, some jobs, and a couple of 'get out of jail free' cards."

"Not too many, I hope." Laif sighed. "All I need is a corruption charge from some whistle-blower."

"No more than usual." Dane sailed a data sphere his way.

"Will do." Laif snagged it. "Now I'd better find Koi and apologize."

"Yeah, you'd better apologize." Koi stuck his head through the wall of leaves. "You know, a six-month-old baby gets around better than you."

"I believe it." Laif gave Koi a lopsided smile. "Okay, I was an asshole and didn't think about what I was saying. Didn't mean it either, was still kind of fried from getting my butt whipped at that townplaza this afternoon. But you stuck it to me proper, so how about it we call it a tie? Or a truce, anyway?"

"Tie? I won. You looked pretty stupid with tomato all over your face."

Dane swallowed a chuckle, turned it into a cough.

"Okay, fine." Laif sent Dane a sizzling glance. "I cede the game, kid. And you're not only better at me in microG—*way* better—you're better in the Con, too. So please find out who scammed that fish farm purchase for me, will you, so that I can airlock the bastard?" Laif held out a hand. "Don't throw me this time, okay? I might break something of Dane's."

"You might." Koi grabbed his wrist, vaulted past Laif's head, rebounded from the far wall and came to a perfect halt at eye level and upside down in front of the Admin. "That was a dirty trick," Koi said. "I'll find out who did it."

"Thanks," Laif said and nodded. "You're impressive, kid. If this is how we're gonna evolve, I guess it could be a lot worse."

FOUR

HANDRAILS LINED THE CORRIDOR BEYOND THE LOCK IN
the Pan Malaysian Elevator. Ahni blessed them as she pulled herself
confidently along, trying hard to look as if she belonged there.
Painted a soft and boring green, lacking the protective resilient carpeting that lined the tourist areas, the corridor clearly handled service traffic. At the end of the corridor she halted herself, and
drifting, dropped briefly into Pause, calling up the specs for this Elevator.

She located the service lock where Dane had let her off, traced a
route to the travel plaza, the main arrival and departure areas where
the climbers docked. Most of the retail trade clustered around the
travel plaza. She wondered how long it would take Xai's dogs to
check this Elevator once they realized they had lost her trail on
NYUp? The door in front of her wasn't locked from this side and
opened to the touch of her palm.

A dense plush carpet in a soft blue-lined floor and walls contrasting with a pale, carpeted ceiling. If tourists bounced off the
walls, they wouldn't even bruise. The Elevator interiors were still
founded on the right angle, unlike the upper levels of the platforms,
and a part of Ahni's mind found the corners where wall met floor

comforting. The corridor was moderately busy, full of tourists still awkward in microG. Few even glanced at her.

Ahni found she blended nicely into the mostly Indonesian and Indo-Pakistani crowd, her tawny skin and black crop a bonus. A dress shop offering microG-spun spider silk caught her eye. Ahni stepped into the shop, nodded to the shopkeeper's smiling bow, waved away her offer of assistance, and browsed quickly down the display of scarves, sheathes, singlets, sari-suits, and even full saris. She chose a full sari in a shimmering salmon embroidered with gold, and found a creamy undershirt to match it. The shopkeeper was nearly beside herself with delight as she floated gracefully to a high shelf to retrieve a packaged model. Ahni could certainly understand her enthusiasm as the shopkeeper totaled the purchases. Tourist prices, she thought sourly, but the spider silk was lovely, shimmering in the light, finer than real silk to the touch. "Don't wrap it," she told the woman as she started to fold the sari. "I think I'll wear it right now."

"Oh, what a marvelous idea!" the woman gushed. "You'll look lovely in it and it's quite secure in microG with the hidden closures. Are you headed to a Platform?"

"Dragon Home." Ahni nodded and palmed the milky oval of the reader set into the counter. It chimed completion of her purchase as the woman scooped the sari and shirt into her arms. "We have a fitting room here."

Ahni followed her into a curtained alcove lined with mirrors and hangers for garments. She stripped awkwardly, even with the woman's deft hand to keep her from drifting, pulled the shirt on over her head, and let the woman wrap the sari around her. Hissing softly to herself, the shopkeeper tucked and arranged the drape of the fabric to her satisfaction, fastening it into place so that it wouldn't float too freely. "You can open the fasteners when you reach Dragon Home," she said as she pushed herself away to eye Ahni critically. "It looks even better on you than I expected."

It looked lovely, Ahni thought absently. She stretched her senses, searching for a hunter's cold purpose, felt only the white noise of a crowded travel plaza—weariness, expectation, nausea in microG, and annoyance. The woman continued to gush compliments, hands clasped, her smile as bright as the ruby fiberlight inlay on her fore-head, shaped to resemble a caste mark. Ahni studied her reflection briefly. The sari would confuse her pursuers briefly. She bought a scarf on the way out, pinned it into her hair, sloppily so that it drifted across her face. Waved away the shopkeeper's clucking attempt to fix it. Many Moslem women wore decorative head scarves and it added to the distraction. The shopkeeper graciously packed her discarded singlesuit into a shopping bag with the shop's logo prominently glowing in fiberlight script, handed it to her with a bow.

Leaving the woman reciting blessings on her health and future, Ahni proceeded down the corridor, senses alert, feeling less conspic-uous. She passed a string of offices, a flower seller's shop, a small tea and coffee bar featuring Turkish pastries, and exited into the main travel plaza, her senses alert.

Passengers emerged from an arriving climber, while others waited to board for the trip down, or purchased tickets from the many kiosk screens scattered at all levels about the room. Ahni made her way to the nearest screen, her body language hesitant and awkward, a tourist, unfamiliar in microG. She touched in her ticket purchase, using an anonymous cash card. She received her Econ-omy Class ticket and struggled across the crowded plaza along the guiding handrails, pausing to bend over a small, wide-eyed child and smile, a doting auntie to any onlooker, a tourist on her way home from a first time in Near Earth, bringing souvenirs for those at home.

Ahni let hurrying families haul themselves along the handrails past her, scolding their playful children, slowing her down, getting in her way, leaving this timid auntie confused and blinking as the shimmering holo clocks blinked closer to departure time, a look of helplessness and mild dismay on her face. She hesitated, pretending to rearrange a fold of her sari. Almost time . . . A couple of hurry-ing latecomers scurried through the gate and entered the car.

Now.

Lifting her head, she pulled herself forward, ignoring the uni-formed attendant who pushed off to stop her. He raised his voice, his irritation hidden behind a polite face, thinking her deaf, or stupid and she gave him the confused, obedient expression he expected, used his instant relaxation to duck around him, grab the bar, and fire herself through the entry port. The closing doors hissed, halted, opened for her, then closed again, right in the face of the pursuing attendant.

He could stop the climber, hold up the trip, but that would affect the schedule and she had a valid ticket. She waved it in front of the scanner. Sure enough, the departure chime sounded and the car shivered. Ahni grabbed on to one of the ranked handrails forming a semicircle around a vid window that would offer a stunning view as the climber ascended or descended. Now it allowed her to see into the travelplaza. A young couple waved. Ahni scanned the crowd and spotted the dogs immediately. One was the man who had darted her in the axle. The other was unfamiliar, an unselect northern chinese. They stared at the departing car, their faces revealing no emotion. She frowned, wondering what allied Li Zhen and her brother. The picture blinked, and now the window showed the diamond brilliance of a million distant suns and the dwindling crown of lights that was the Elevator platform. She turned away from the window and made her way to her seat, pulling herself along by the handholds along the rows of recliners. A single attendant cruised up—a downsider, she guessed from his body mass—and offered help.

She found her seat, a relatively luxurious recliner, she supposed, but not a welcoming prospect for the long drop. Especially since significant gravity would be a long time coming. They wouldn't achieve 50 percent Earthnormal until they down-climbed to the 2,600 km level. With a sigh, Ahni pulled herself into the seat and snugged herself to the cushions with the mesh netting provided. Coming up, she had traveled Business Class and her grief had distracted her. Her smile twisted and she banished it, putting on the face of mild confusion that went with the sari and her act in the travel plaza. She was not about to underestimate her brother again.

She stowed her shopping bag in the bin below her. The seat sprang to life, elongating, cushioning her head, back, legs. It occurred to her that it was probably made of the same stuff as Dane's ship with its melting walls. Next to her, a lanky man with a unselected celtic face hunched over a portable holodesk, his fingers flying among the cryptic icons. Orbital native, she guessed, assessing his lanky build and lack of muscle mass, a bit younger than her, maybe early twenties. A fiberlight inlay circled his wrist, emerald green, in an intricately woven pattern. He glanced her way, no hint of curiosity in his face, looked quickly away and back to his desk.

Ahni closed her eyes, at full awareness in spite of her relaxed posture, searching for any predator hint among the passengers.

What were Xai and Li Zhen up to? Leaving her senses alert so that she would notice any focused attention, she shifted into Pause. Methodically she sorted through her memories of her brother's recent activities . . . up to the moment of his apparent assassination. From this perspective, they reeked of stealth.

I do not really know my brother. The thought troubled her. A lot. It made her vulnerable.

SHE SPENT THE first twenty-four hours of the down-climb awake and aware, pulling herself around the Economy level of the climber, brushing up against passengers and crew, making eye contact whenever possible—the best, if most dangerous, way to startle a revelation from someone shielding their intentions. At the end of that time, exhausted, she decided that she was safe enough, unless one of the absent crew members tending to First Class or Business was in her brother's pay.

She decided to assume not—that would be farsighted even for him—and finally dropped into Pause to induce sleep. She slept without waking for twelve solid hours. When she finally waked, she could discern a *down,* a slight sense of weight that slackened the mesh net holding her into the recliner. Gratefully she released it, yawning, wincing as her muscles protested the long slumber in the confines of the recliner. The minimal lights illuminating only the aisles between the recliners suggested that this was night, by local Earth time. Sure enough, the digital clock displaying Elevator time told her it was three AM at its midocean base. She pulled her gaze away from the windows and stretched again, realized that the man sitting next to her was awake and surreptitiously glancing at her.

Adrenaline flushed into her blood and she came alert, feigning another relaxed yawn as she probed for any threat. Found only curiosity, a trace of hostility, and a hint of lust. That's right. The platform natives didn't look at people directly. She relaxed slowly, gave him a slight smile. "Insomnia?"

"Different time here." He shrugged, the lust component of his attention sharpening. "I sure can't imagine living down under all those clouds where you can't see that view. No wonder downsiders are so shortsighted."

"Not everyone is shortsighted," she said mildly. "You can see the stars on Earth, you know."

He waved that observation away. "The attendant was going to wake you up, tell you dinner was served. I chased him off. You looked pretty beat when you conked out."

"Thanks," she said, checking a flash of irritation at his patronizing manner. "I needed sleep more than dinner." But now her stomach reminded her that except for the fruit Koi had handed her . . . how long ago? . . . she hadn't eaten since her climb up here. Her stomach immediately contracted with hunger, so strongly that she stilled an urge to double over.

"I was just gonna flash our guy for food," the orbital native said. "Can't help it if they keep the wrong time on these things. Mostly downsider food, but they offer a few decent choices for snacks. You can call up the menu on your screen."

She thanked him politely and touched the control that extended the small flatscreen mounted on her recliner arm. It unfurled and stiffened, and she selected refreshments from the screen menu. Thai and Japanese influences predominated. Lots of seafood. The food would be nuked for shelf-stable storage, not fresh. She passed on the sushi plate, selected tofu Pad Thai instead and a cup of seaweed salad. Those items could take life as a shelf-stable package and still remain edible, she thought wryly.

When the food came, she noticed that her seat mate had chosen a grilled cheese sandwich—one of the few non-Asian offerings on the menu. He eyed the small golden longan fruit that accompanied it skeptically as he removed the cover.

"They're good," she said, and showed him how to peel one.

"Dragon's Eye," she said. "Sort of like lychee, but better, I think. Which platform are you from?"

"NYUp. Good!" He sounded surprised, began to peel a second longan. "I wonder if they'll have that where I'm going. Edinburgh," he said, before she could ask. "My great-grandfather wants to see me before he dies and refuses to take the Elevator. But the old boy's a hundred and forty two, so I figure I can climb down." He laughed, made a face. "I'm his only male descendent. I guess the family runs to girls. So he made a big fuss about meeting me once before he dies. Even sent the credit for the trip." He shrugged. "Bad timing, it turns out, but who knows? The old boy thinks he won't live much longer and I might never get down to Earth, otherwise. Might as well see what it's like."

That casual statement, his total dismissal of Earth, rather shocked her. No regret, no sense of moment . . . *I might never get down to Earth* . . . No big deal. "Aren't you excited?" she asked, curious.

"About Earth?" He took a big bite of his thick sandwich, made a face as he chewed and finally swallowed. "Cheese tastes weird. I don't think I'm all that excited." He tilted his head. "Yeah, I'm excited to see someplace new. Like I said, I've never been down the Elevators before. Costs a lot." He tried another bite of sandwich. "But not because I'm going back to Earth or anything, if that's what you mean," he said finally. "That's something you downsiders don't get. You always ask it." He peeled another longan. "If we don't miss the Earth, I mean. What's to miss? Never been there, never really wanted much to go. You weigh a ton down there and you can't see the stars." He popped the sweet, white globe of fruit pulp into his mouth. "Wonder if we could grow this on NYUp?"

"Ask Dane," Ahni said absently. It had never occurred to her that upsiders wouldn't miss Earth.

"You know Dane?"

The change in his tone snapped her out of her reverie. "Yes," she said cautiously.

"Cool." His smile warmed a bit, and his edge of hostility vanished. "That's really cool. How'd you meet him?"

Ahni ran potential answers through her mind. "I got to know

him this trip," she said. "His garden is quite a place." She wasn't reaching him. Thought about what Dane had said, about the future, took a gamble. "I'm pretty impressed with what he wants for the platform. I think he has the right idea."

"Yeah, no kidding." Her companion's face relaxed, and his smile was genuine this time. "He really sees pretty clear. Clearer than the heavyweights, that's for sure." He jerked his chin toward the floor. "We're just a cash cow to them. That's all. All that stuff about it not being safe to drop rocks down to Near Earth? That's stupid. We're a whole lot more vulnerable to crap upstairs than Earth is, and we make darn sure none of it hits *us*. We're sure not gonna let it hit Earth. Hi." He offered her a hand, as if they'd just met. "Name's Noah." He made a face. "Mom's joke. Don't ask"

"Ahni." She gave him her real name because that's the name Dane knew. "Could the platforms really survive on their own, without stuff coming up from Earth? The media made a big fuss about how it wasn't possible." And the World Council had solidly voted an independence discussion right off the floor, two years ago. China had been one of the strongest backers of that vote, along with the Taiwan Families, of course.

"Well, we could, but it would be really tight for awhile." He was frowning. "We need a ten percent minimum expansion in population. Then we'll have enough people to make a self-sufficient economy work, balancing producers and consumers, even if the tourist trade stops for awhile. Dane has been increasing the productivity of the garden so that we can eat, but life will be pretty spare. Until we really get flying." He made a face. "That's what the people worry about who aren't behind it . . . they like their little downside treats, I guess. But we can survive." His eyes sparkled. "And pretty soon, we won't even miss the stuff that comes up the climbers. We'll do just as good."

"I'm already impressed," Ahni said, thinking of Dane's garden. This is Dane's religion, she thought. The future he sees for his strange children. And wondered how many orbital natives shared this particular religion. The downside politicians didn't realize that this fervor existed up here.

And her brother? Connected? She shook her head. Too many

questions and no real answers. "So what do you do in NYUp?" she asked, alert for his response to this question.

He shrugged, his emotional spectrum relaxed. "I do system traffic . . . keeping the Con moving. Takes a lot of people to keep it flowing. The Con is the constant chatter on the net," he answered her blank look. "The Conversation. Want to know what's going on? Jump in and surf the threads. Everybody talks about everything all the time. Fun job though . . . but you gotta like code. You think on your feet, do some quick patches when things heat up, keeping the flow evened out so you don't get a jam. But we only work one six-hour on, two off, so I got time to slack out. And I crunch some data for Dane. Keep him in the picture."

Ahni nodded, projecting comprehension, although he had lost her.

"I just can't handle the taste of this cheese." He dropped the un-eaten sandwich half onto the tray with the longan peels and covered it. "Feed it to the plants. Or whatever they do with the recycle here." He slid it into the disposal port on his recliner and it vanished with a slight sucking sound. "You get to the axle free-park while you were here?"

"No." She shook her head.

"The tourists all go." His sneer flavored the air. "But they keep downside time, so you go when they're not there. Next time you're up, look for a pickup game of scrum. That'll give you some exercise." He chuckled. "And a few bruises. But hey, it's a great way to loosen up, you know?"

"Scrum?"

"You got two teams . . . however many people you got divided in two . . . and you got a ball and a couple of goal buckets anchored wherever. You just go at it. You can run with the ball, play defense, be a shooter or do cannonball, see if you can take out the runner so that your runner can get the ball and score . . ." He went on to regale Ahni with the details of what sounded like microG mayhem. She suppressed her amusement, thinking that maybe good old primate aggression had to have its outlets, even in orbit. She hadn't seen a single hostile confrontation between natives in the corridors, aside from Dane's little intervention. Maybe you could rid yourself of a lot of it slamming into your buddies like a bunch of sentient pool balls. Apparently broken bones happened. No big deal, according to Noah.

For the rest of the long climb down, she managed to maintain her "insider" status in Noah's eyes with a bit of adroit evasion and some lucky guesses. An attack of lactose intolerance brought on by his cheese sandwich made with milk cheese rather than soy cheese, actually kept Noah pretty busy and pretty miserable for the next twenty-four hours. But in spite of his physical distress and general frustration with all things Earth, he was a fount of information on NYUp politics, and the social climate of NYUp.

She filed the information for future use, enjoyed the slow and steady return of gravity, and spent her time thinking about just what Xai and Li Zhen were up to.

And what her father's reaction would be to the news of his clone-son's survival.

Slowly, the faint glitter of lights on the dark, distant ball of Earth gleamed brighter, until the view of the planet was breathtaking. Light dusted the continents and spangled the ocean where the big pontoon resorts and Elevator cities floated amidst their houseboat communities and the tethered icebergs that provided water and recreation. As the planet grew larger, Ahni noted with amusement that Noah's confidence dwindled proportionately. By the time they began to descend through the atmosphere, he was spending most of his time lying back in his recliner, a pair of VR glasses on his face, immersed in the distress of increasing weight and changes in pressurization.

Even after only a few days upside, Ahni noticed the pervasive discomfort as she neared sea level. Noah seemed to have been flattened by a giant and invisible hand, uninterested in food or even the special electrolyte beverage that the attendant tried to persuade him to drink. As they approached docking, Ahni visited the galley and returned with a container of the orange-flavored electrolyte. "Drink this," she said, touching the control on this recliner to bring it to full upright.

He jerked out of his doze with a snarl, jerking off his VR glasses, his glare moderating as he focused on her face. "I don't want anything." He fumbled with the glasses.

"Oh, knock it off." She snatched them from him, shoved the

container into his hand. "They know what they're doing on the Elevator. If you get stubborn, you're going to spend your first twenty-four hours downside throwing up. Your choice."

He glared at her, glared at the orange liquid in the container, then popped the lid and drank it down. "Awful." He dropped the container into the disposal slot. But his color improved noticably and he seemed to be less indisposed as the Elevator sank to its landing site on the huge ocean platform.

The First Class and Business passengers on the lower levels disembarked first. In Economy, passengers collected personal items, breaking camp, as it were, after their long climb down. The pressure changed as the doors unsealed and then they slid open.

A wave of sea-scented air wafted into the cabin. Noah drew a shallow breath. "Smells," he muttered under his breath.

Better than NYUp, Ahni thought. She and Noah fell into the flow of people. Everyone hurried now, a destination in mind, places to go. They exited into the Arrival Hall. Noah looked lost, staggering a bit as if he was drunk, his legs refusing to do quite what he asked of them.

He looked as if he was going to throw up any second. Ahni slowed her pace, touched his elbow which made him start violently, pointed her chin at the single line for arriving orbital residents. Returning tourists queued up at several other desks that separated them according to travel class. Ahni stayed in line with him, since it didn't much matter which line she chose, thinking he was going to need a steadying hand while he upchucked any moment now.

But he made it past the official, his expression grim. Ahni shook her head, then smiled for the uniformed young woman manning the scanner whose eyebrows rose just a hair. She was new, Ahni guessed, hadn't run into many of the elite, yet. "You'll need to get a retinal," she prompted the woman, who gave her a quick smile, blushed, and swung the scan arm her way.

Ahni rested her face lightly against the mask, staring at the small green dot glowing in darkness, withdrew as the scanner chimed.

"Welcome back, Miss Huang," the woman said with an overly bright smile. "I hope you enjoyed your visit to the Platform."

"I did," Ahni returned the smile. If someone finally noticed that she had managed to take a one way climb down from the platforms without going up, she would be long gone. With no luggage, she headed out across the huge hall, ignoring the carts offering fresh seafood, flowers, personal services, escorts, bodyguards, tours, and leisure services. On the alert, because instructions traveled much faster than a climber, she stretched muscle groups as she wove through the crowd, assessing her mobility. She was readjusting to full gravity quickly.

Good thing. She spotted them on the far side of a flower seller, nearly invisible behind the bank of greens and bright tropical blooms. Hired dogs. Unselect malay types, a man and woman dressed as economy tourists, their focus prodded her like a sharp fingernail.

Nobody had told them about her empathy rating. She altered her course just enough to angle her away from the flower stall, but not enough to alert them that they had been spotted. From the corner of her eye she watched them change direction, their casual stroll on a course to intersect her path where the arriving passengers swirled and backed up around the various travel kiosks. He carried a small holo camera, she carried an embroidered shoulder bag. Needle attack, Ahni guessed. Quick stab, quick acting poison. By the time people realized it wasn't just a heart attack, they'd be long gone. And she'd be dead.

Death was their intent. This was too public for anything else.

Outside, in the open air plaza in front of the Elevator, she could snag a cruising freelancer, a skimmer or an air car, ride it to one of the travel companies that wasn't willing to pay the exorbitant use-fees for operating directly from the Elevator compound itself. That should throw a bit of random into this little plan.

If she could make it outside in one piece.

They were closing fast, their movements languid in spite of their speed, drawing no attention with any sign of chase, but fast as sharks driving in for the kill. Ahni wove quickly through the throng, zig-zagging, heading always for the huge portals that opened onto the plaza. She could feel them now. They had split up, were closing from both sides, making use of her evasion tactics. Smart to send a pair.

The damp, salty air brushed her face, heavy as wet silk as she exited, seabirds crying overhead, crowds and chaos. Skimmers hovered at the edges of the platform, fan-jets idling at a whisper, poised on wheeled skids to launch themselves into the swells that slapped up against the distant edge of the vast platform. Air car would be faster. She looked around, but all the cars were loading passengers, felt that "gotcha" of the final attack, spied an empty skimmer a few dozen yards away and ran.

Ahni almost missed the third one coming at her out of nowhere. Damn. *Three* of them! She hesitated for a second, assessing distance, realizing that she had lost, if she dodged this one, the others would reach her.

A tall skinny figure burdened with a large out-of-style tote lurched from beyond a chattering group of Japanese tourists, slammed full tilt into the third attacker. Both went down and she recognized Noah! He was on top, apologizing loudly, even as his knee jerked up between the man's legs.

Her attacker jerked, gasped, snarled a curse in Malay.

Ahni grabbed Noah's arm, hauled him to his feet. "Run," she snapped and yanked him, stumbling, along with her. The skimmer pilot had the door open, his round Straits-Born face bright with delighted curiosity. Ahni tumbled in, hauling Noah in after her. He still clung to his damn tote. It hit her in the shoulder hard enough to bruise. The door hissed closed and the skimmer launched, fast enough to throw them both against the rear cushions, its right ski lifting as it veered around a slower craft. The lip of the platform appeared, hurtling toward them and the skimmer launched arcing out over the wrinkled blue skin of the water, down—"Brace!" Ahni yelled and grabbed Noah who still didn't seem to have quite caught up to the moment.

The skimmer slammed down onto the sea's surface with the impact of a car dropped onto asphalt. The force of the landing nearly tore Ahni's grip from the safety strap and her arm felt as if it had pulled half out of its socket as Noah's weight lifted from the seat. A curtain of water fountained up on either side, and the skimmer rocked wildly for a second, slewing half around before the pilot straightened it out and hit the throttle.

The little craft lifted on its extending legs, gaining speed, hull totally clear of the water.

"Hey, Hollywood getaway!" The pilot chortled, throwing a delighted glance back over the seat. "Fine for speeding, three thousand Peoples Republic of China dollars."

He wasn't quite right about her nationality, but close enough. She told him off for that bit of thievery in very precise Beijing Mandarin, which impressed him, then told him exactly what the local fine for reckless launch actually was, which made him think she was an upper level bureaucrat, and impressed him even more. Then she told him that she would certainly pay the fine, even though he had committed a major violation of the personal safety laws by not requiring them to secure their safety harnesses before launch, and if she chose to pursue the matter the fine for *that* was three times the fine for reckless launch from the Elevator deck.

Crestfallen, he thanked her very stiffly in polite, if lower-class school boy Mandarin, then switched back to the Straits-born dialect to tell her with a sly look that if she wanted her arrival at a travel float to be unknown, his ID system just happened to have a bad connection and it shorted out from time to time. Everybody knew about it. Nobody worried. Which meant he payed a hefty price to smuggle blind.

Before he could name a price, she told him that was worth five thousand PRC dollars, payable in cash when they disembarked safely and without further interference. That was more than he had dared to ask, and she watched him up her status from bureaucrat to something much greater. He bowed to her, his respect smirched a bit by his panting hunger for her business. Asked which float they wished to use, did she wish anything, any comfort, did her passenger wish anything?

She wondered what Noah's reaction would be if she explained to him that their taxi driver regarded him as sort of a large pet? Not really human, but valuable because he belonged to her? Decided that it would not be a nice thing to do. And probably, she would occupy that particular set of shoes upside, if she was up there with Noah as guide. "Global Express," she told her fawning pilot. They cost, but you could go anywhere on the planet from any base, and if you had . . . special needs . . . they did their best to accommodate you, local laws notwithstanding. Plus, they did business with the Huang Family regularly.

The pilot bowed again and turned back to his controls. Acceleration squashed them into their padded couch and Noah grunted.

"Relax," she told him. "It'll last only a few seconds at the rate he's going. Then you can breathe again."

"Want to explain to me—what just happened?"

"Someone wants me dead."

"I got that part," he growled. "How come?"

"Call it a dysfunctional family feud." She didn't try to mute the bitter edge to her voice. "And thank you very much for getting in the way." She regarded him soberly. "That was risky."

"I didn't quite mean it to happen that way, but I saw that they were attacking and figured I'd mess that up anyway." He blinked. "I guess I always wanted to do the hero thing."

"Saw them?" She blinked. "I figured you're an E-eight."

"Empath? Me?" He laughed. "Hey, if I was, I'd be working Immigration and making a ton of money in a cushy station in the Arrival Halls. Nah." He shook his head. "You could just see what they were up to, you know? How come nobody else did anything?"

Clearly the orbital natives were a whole lot more aware of body language than the average Earth resident. "They didn't realize what was going on," she said absently. Because they hadn't been obvious about their intent at all. Except to an empath. Or to Noah. The orbitals might not look at you directly, but they might be a whole lot more aware than she had assumed. "You're headed to Edinburgh, right?"

"Yeah, I guess so. Although I'd rather take the next climber back up," he grumbled.

"Hopefully, the rest of your stay will be less . . . eventful." She looked out the glassteel canopy as the skimmer slowed for its approach to the Global Express dock. The hull sank gracefully to the water, the bump of its immersion barely jarring them. Good piloting. She upped the amount of her tip.

The pilot whisked them in through the arched entry port to the domed travel plaza, brought them to a perfect stop at the carpeted dock and leaped out to offer a hand as the canopy opened. With the other hand, he offered the charge tablet.

Ahni smiled, upped the balance due with a tip that made his eyes gleam and eyeballed her signature to the charge. Noted his call number and filed it in short term memory. When she had time for Pause, she'd drop it into her data file. Never knew when you might need a fast, no-questions ride somewhere. He'd drop what he was doing and show up, after this.

The main desk, well staffed, faced the dock. Ahni greeted the small geneselected Han woman behind it in brisk business Mandarin, booked a First Class fare to Edinburgh with custom delivery to destination and an open reservation on any of the Elevators. She booked her own fare to the Huang Family compound. The facilitator realized immediately who she was, Ahni noted with approval. She would have a scanner field covering the customer space in front of the counter so she knew Ahni didn't wear an ID chip, and would of course have memorized the faces of the Elite families the company regularly served. She nodded, acknowledging the woman's professional service, made a note of her name, to email with approval to the supervisor here. Ahni accepted the twin trip cards from her and handed Noah his.

"What's this?" He eyed the card skeptically.

"Give it to anyone wearing a Global Express insignia." Ahni smiled up at him. "They'll take you to your grandfather's door. And when you're ready to leave, you can contact the service and someone will come pick you up. You have an open reservation on any of the Elevators for your return trip."

"Wow." He looked at the card, then at her. "Who are you, anyway?"

"My family has money." She shrugged. "They owe you as much as I do."

He was shaking his head. "I don't know—I mean this seems like too much. It's a lot of credit—"

"It's just money." She touched his arm. "What you gave me was life. This isn't enough, but it's something I can do right now."

"I still have a hard time getting my head around people just running up to someone and killing them." He hunched his shoulders. "I'll be damn glad to get back to civilization."

She smiled and offered her hand. "Thank you, Noah," she said. "If you need assistance while you're down here, contact Ahni Huang."

"I'll remember." He clasped her hand and smiled, his face relaxing briefly. "I just hope these people speak English," he said.

"They do. They speak twenty-five languages." She nodded to the waiting porter. "He'll take you to your shuttle."

"Thanks again." Noah waved and almost grabbed for his tote as the Malay man hefted it, but the porter whisked it out of reach, grinned at Noah, and beckoned. Ahni waved and followed the uniformed woman to the small private skimmer-jet that would take her to the family compound. Her smile faded as she boarded. Time to face her parents.

FIVE

AHNI LEANED BACK AGAINST THE PADDED SEAT AS THE skimmer-jet circled down to land just offshore from the Huang Family compound. Security had already swept the skimmer and cleared it to land, but she knew that a couple of defensive lasers targeted it. Just in case. The red tile roofs of the large rectangular compound gleamed bright amongst the lush green of the tropical forest that surrounded the compound on three sides. On the fourth side, white sand and rocks offered swimming and the tide pools of her youth.

The skimmer touched down and settled into the long low swells with barely a jar, drifting precisely up to the family dock. The sun roof had polarized to cast some shade, but it was open to the hot, humid Taiwan air. Ahni hopped out, offered the pilot a cash card. The woman refused with a bow, climbed back into the craft and touched it to life as Security hurried out to meet her. The hard-eyed Captain offered a welcoming bow, greetings, and a careful observation of the skimmer.

Ahni returned the woman's greeting absently, her eyes on the pale brick walls of the compound. Built in the classic old-northern courtyard style, the family apartments, roofed with the traditional red tiles, enclosed a central garden. No weather canopy kept out the rain or heat, by her mother's decree. This time of day and season, sun poured into the courtyard, turning the still air beneath the leaves of bananas and bamboo and carefully pruned plum trees steamy hot and rich with the smells of home. Ahni drew a deep breath, reaching for calm.

Beyond the family compound beach grasses carpeted the low shore with emerald. Here and there, remains of ancient Buddhist gravesites poked above the tall grass, red tile roofs and pink and cream facades, ornate, sheltered alters where families had once gathered to leave gifts on appropriate dates. Many of them had been abandoned, but the Huang family paid to keep the walls freshly painted and the roof tiles repaired.

Here, along the sweep of coast dominated by the family compound, time seemed to have stopped centuries ago. A small fishing village occupied the end of the perfect half-moon bay, an ancient concrete dock jutting out into the water on its jetty, dozens of its small blue and white boats clustered along tie-ups, bare chested men tossing handwoven and plastic baskets of silvery fish and crabs up onto the dock itself, children in shorts and thongs running and shouting, dogs fighting with the gulls for scraps. The sloped temple roof of the fish market was white with gulls and a dragon kite sailed overhead. But solar or clean-fusion powered the boats now and you could safely eat the shellfish from the bay. The fish in those baskets were counted and the harvest carefully controlled. At night, a hundred public cleaners scoured the old dock. The oceans were healthy again, and that had taken a planet-wide cooperation, spearheaded by the aggressive Gaiist Movement.

Taking a deep breath, Ahni turned away from the view, calming her breathing, gathering her awareness to a fine point. "Are my parents in residence?" she asked Security.

"Your mother." The woman bowed. "Your honored father will return later today." She ushered Ahni through the arched main gate and into the steamy courtyard.

Ahni bowed her head in thanks, walked down the narrow path thick with blossoms to her mother's private sitting room, the scent of jasmine heavy in the air. She ducked beneath a bower twined with the glossy green leaves and white sprays of jasmine flowers, paused and picked a sprig.

White. The color of death.

The wooden shutters had been folded back from the broad windows, and a tiny bird hopped up onto the sill from the room within before fluttering away. Even in typhoon season, her mother rarely activated the weather screen or closed the shutters unless a storm threatened to come directly onshore. Now the faintest of breezes stirred the intricately knotted hangings of linen thread and carved jade beads that hung as a screen in the open windows. Ahni slipped off her sandals and ducked through the strands of silk and carved jade that curtained the door, the stony clack of the jades an echo of childhood.

Her mother stood at her loom, knotting an intricate tracery of fine silk thread and jade beads in shades of pink and white and palest green. Her simple sheath of polished cotton in a creamy tan contrasted with her tawny skin. Behind her, a vid window shimmered with constantly changing images of ocean and beach above the polished stone slab scattered with unfinished pieces of jade and the laser carving tools she used. Framed panels of antique fabric, intricate piece work in rich colors that had once been a treasured family heirloom passed from mother to daughter, perhaps a tunic or a wedding coat, hung on the walls. Intent on her weaving, her mother's face might have been carved from golden jade by a master crafter, her high cheekbones shadowing the strong lines of her face. Her long dark hair, untouched by gray, hung in a thick tail to the middle of her back, caught at the nape of her neck by a strip of green silk. As the jade strings clacked and rattled behind her, Ahni's mother stepped from behind her loom and came to greet her daughter, hands outstretched, dark eyes fathomless pools above her welcoming smile.

"You're back. Daughter, I have missed you!" She hugged Ahni briefly and hard. "Tea?" She turned away, ushering Ahni to the end of the long room furnished in carved teakwood covered with hand-woven raw silk cushions. An antique Ming teapot already steamed on a tray with two cups and a wooden bowl of dried fish and nuts. A plain white bowl of salted plums accompanied the savory snacks and Ahni smiled. Trust her mother to offer her favorite childhood treat. "A new project?" Ahni nodded at the half-finished hanging.

"An invitation from a London gallery."

"I saw one of your hangings in the NYUp Arrival Hall," Ahni said. "Your fame extends beyond the surface of the planet."

"All women have woven, forever."

The bitterness behind her mother's words narrowed Ahni's eyes, but her mother's face betrayed no emotion as she handed Ahni a cup of tea, both hands cupping the fragile bowl. Ahni breathed the rising steam and saw Xai in that NYUp hotel room, offering her tea.

"I did not know that your father sent you in his place. It was his duty to risk himself. Not yours."

Ahni reached for a salted plum. Fear lay beneath her mother's anger. Why fear? "I could not do as he instructed," she said carefully.

Her mother leaned forward and set her cup down very carefully on the teakwood table. "Tell me," she said.

"Xai is . . . not dead." Until this moment she had not been sure how much she would say and how much she would leave out. But under her mother's steady gaze she recited the details of her encounter with her half-twin, her eyes fixed on the plum staining her fingertips red.

When she finished, her mother was silent. Angry but . . . not surprised. She already knew Xai lived, Ahni realized with a sense of shock.

"He has chosen his own path," she said finally. Birds called and chirped in the quadrangle and somewhere, someone closed a door with a muted thump.

"What is going on here?" Ahni asked.

"Your father is drunk on DNA." Hatred edged the words. "He is a smart man, but when his precious DNA is concerned, his brain turns to water and seeps from his pores. And he has created Xai in his own image. He had no use for you, or for any other child we might have. Your father and Xai deserve each other!" She rose, back rigidly straight. "You will not tell your father that his precious clone-self lives."

"What?" Shocked, Ahni rose to her feet. "How can I not?"

"Xai has chosen to walk his own path." Her mother stood

straight, her head up. "I was a bed for him and nothing more. A breast. There is none of *me* in him. And I have watched your father lose clarity of sight. Because of that strand of his DNA that I nurtured." Her eyes gleamed, cold and polished as the jade stones she carved and wove. "I have groomed you to be your father's heir. You are a better heir than his dream of immortality. You *are* his heir and we will make this so. *You will not tell him.* I did not give up my life to see him throw away the family for the love of his own image."

Ahni stood, her mind bruised by these cold-stone words. "*Xai is not dead*. Mother."

"He has chosen to die to his father." Her mother looked at her for the space of three heartbeats. Then, to Ahni's horror, she fell to her knees. "I gave up my life." She looked up at Ahni. "This will make it a trade of value. If you do as I ask. Ahni, it is the right thing."

Ahni looked down at the blue and white tea bowl in her hands, regarded the pale sheen of bone in her knuckles, and wondered that the eggshell-thin porcelain had not cracked. Very carefully she set the Ming bowl down on the carved table and fled her mother's apartment.

Her feet carried her along the raked gravel of the path past the carefully maintained plantings, treading an automatic path. When she reached the path to her door, she hesitated, then turned instead to her brother's rooms.

Wooden shutters closed the windows, painted a dull glossy red, the color of drying blood. She put her hand on the door, waited while it analyzed her biochemistry, skin texture, and vitals. It swung open and she walked into shadow. "Light," she said and blinked, her eyes dazzled by the multiple broad spectrum lights that flooded the room with artificial sunlight. Where her mother let in the world, Xai preferred to create his own. Beyond thick glass, an aged, albino Ball Python reared a thick, pale head, it's tongue flicking, disturbed by the light. In the huge herpetarium a half dozen snakes lived, thrived, and sometimes ate one another. The Ball Python had been his first and favorite, a gift on his fifth birthday. A rabbit nibbled on greens in one corner. She looked around at his neatly made bed, the holo-desk in front of the near wall, the dustless perfection of every surface. She had not been in this room since the day she had heard the news. "Why?" she whispered. "What have you done to all of us?" But he had not done this, she realized in a moment of clarity. This path had been laid for him from the moment of his implantation. And her own path?

The python struck silently, thick coils wrapping the rabbit in a heartbeat. It shrieked once, high and shrill, then it's eyes bulged as the coils tightened and crimson blood burst from its quivering nose.

Ahni turned away.

Something was missing. She frowned, glancing around the spotless room. Something . . . She closed her eyes, calling up a vision of her brother's room from the past.

The medallion.

She blinked, turning to stare at the space where it had hung above his bed, a small circle of silver, the highest academic award bestowed by Taiwan after its annual Exams. Their father had received it at the public ceremony in Tai Pei, had hung it beaming around Xai's neck. It was the ultimate symbol of The Huang's pride in his self-son. "Fan," she said aloud. "Would you come here, please?"

A handful of moments later, Fan Fujin appeared in the doorway, her broad Northern face apprehensive. "Is something wrong Elder Sister?" she asked. A peripheral relative, she lived and worked as maid in the Huang compound. "I cleaned this room just this morning. Did I do a poor job?" She drew herself up, prepared to be affronted.

"It's spotless. As usual." Ahni shook her head. "Xai's medallion is missing. I wonder when he took it down. Do you remember?"

Fan's eyes flicked instantly to the wall, and she froze, her distress a sour smell on the afternoon air.

"I . . . It was here only this morning, Elder Sister." Fan bowed deeply. Frightened. "Or perhaps I was not observant and failed to see that it was not in place."

She reeked of fear now, and Ahni remembered that she had an only son in the top engineering school in Beijing, only there because he was a member in good standing of the Huang family. His future was assured upon his graduation. But if his mother was disgraced . . . She sighed. With the limits required in order to keep the planet clean

and healthy, career choices were often restricted, and family connections counted. "Have the staff search for it," she said. "If it is returned
promptly, I will not need to bring it to The Huang's attention."

"I . . . will make sure it is found." The woman flushed darkly. She
bowed so deeply she nearly fell, then fled the room, stepping quickly
into her sandals at the threshold.

Who had taken it? This small theft threatened to destroy her
self-control.

She left her brother's rooms, cut across the end of the courtyard
to her own room. The weather shield was on and the air inside was
deliciously cool and arid after the thick moist heat of the courtyard.
Ahni pushed through the carved latticework doors and into the spacious simplicity of her room. Handwoven rugs covered the tile
floor and a vase of flowers stood on the low wooden table in the
middle of the room. Pale yellow lilies, she noted absently. Her favorite flowers. But they looked strange, as did the room. *It is the
right thing,* her mother had said. *I am a stranger here,* she thought. *I
am a stranger to myself.* A bowl stood on a carved stand backed by a
silk embroidery. She picked the bowl up, turned it over in her hands.
It wasn't the perfect curve of the Ming tea bowls in her mother's
rooms, but a bit lopsided. The colors of the painted decoration—a
simple mountain and village in browns and greens—was faded, as if
mist shrouded the landscape.

Four thousand years ago, someone had shaped this piece on a
primitive wheel, squatting perhaps beneath a rough shade-roof of
poles and thatch. What had that long ago man thought about? The
rains to come? A marriage, a birth? She ran her fingertips along the
rim of the bowl and for a second felt the ghostly touch of his fingertips against hers as he shaped that rim. And Koi? She smoothed
a tiny roughness where the glaze hadn't fired perfectly. What would
he feel if he touched this bowl? Anything? Would those millennia
of lives matter to him at all? Would they even be real to him? Un-
bidden, Dane's face appeared in her mind. They were his children,
Koi's people. She suddenly wished she could tell him everything
that had happened here. He might see what was so hidden to her.
He might understand her mother's cold rage.

Feeling utterly alone, she stripped off her singlesuit, wrinkling her nose at the smell of travel. Dropping it into the split-willow basket in the corner she walked into her bath. The soaking pool at the end of the room wisped steam into the air, screened from a thick planting of grass bamboo by lacquer latticework. "Local windows open," she commanded and the rich green scent of the garden rolled over her as the weather shield shut off.

She stood under the wide shower head, the water washing away the grime and adrenaline sweat of the day, sluicing it across the ochre tiles. She sank into the soaking tub, closed her eyes with a sigh, not wanting to think about Xai, about her mother's terrible, cold words. She heard the outer door open, the whisper of feet on the carpet . . . came halfway out of the water, muscles tensed before she recognized . . .

"Tania?" Ahni gasped, then laughed aloud as arms went around her neck, and a river of tawny hair smelling of coconut and ginger tumbled around her face.

"Boo!"

Just like . . . the old days. Ahni's heart leapt at that English syllable, but there was pain in that leap, too, and confusion as this moment and the last time this had happened overlapped, folding months and years between them. "What are you doing here?" She twisted around to smile up at Tania's broad, unselected Dutch Indonesian face. "I didn't know you were here! My mother didn't tell me." She used English because Tania had always been better with English than Mandarin and couldn't handle Old Taiwan speech at all. "Did you quit the monastery?"

The words spilled from her heart, and the moment they emerged she regretted them. "I'm sorry." Ahni looked away. "I—it was automatic. It's just . . . I haven't seen you in . . . years."

"You know where I live." Tania said the words with a determined lightness. "You're still soapy." And she shoved Ahni's head under the water.

Ahni came up sputtering. "Ha. Even a Daughter of the Gaia can get wet!" She reached up and tumbled Tania into the pool, her shift ballooning around her, filled with trapped air as Ahni caught her on her hip so that she didn't bruise herself on the pool's edge. Tania laughed and tried to duck Ahni, got ducked herself and came up laughing, her fair hair plastered to her face, a wave of warm water sloshing over the edge of the pool, splattering like rain onto the grass bamboo beyond the screen, startling the small ground-scratching birds there. For an instant they were kids together again, wrestling breast to breast, the thin wet cotton of Tania's shift the only barrier between them. Tania's nipples, dark as her eyes, hardened beneath the thin gauze and for a moment, as her eyes met Ahni's, her arms tightened around her, her belly and breasts hot against Ahni's naked skin.

Ahni tensed, then turned away, Tania's hands falling from her shoulders.

"I've missed you." Tania sat back in the pool, pushing wet hair the color of old straw out of her eyes. "I was sorry when you left to oversee the European concerns."

"I've been back here to visit." Ahni stepped out of the pool, water sheeting from her onto the tiles to drain away into the bamboo garden. "Did you come to see your father?"

"I came to see you," Tania said softly. "Your mother told me. That you were in danger."

"My mother?" Another newness here. Ahni reached for one of the soft cotton towels hanging on the wall. "I . . . am surprised."

"Oh, we're friends, Ahni." Tania laughed as she stripped off her wet clothes and perched naked on the edge of the pool. "She knows I'm no threat, now. Did you kill him? The person who killed your brother? The one your father sent you to kill?"

"No." Something was wrong here. Ahni threw the towel onto the floor near the pool, crossed to the closet and pulled out two silk shifts, one blue, one sea green. She tossed the blue one to Tania who now stood arms akimbo beneath the blast of warm dry air from the dryer. "Xai's not dead." Her voice quivered in spite of her control as she pulled this shift over her head. "My mother . . . I don't understand."

"Tell me." Tania's arms went around her and this time, they offered only comfort.

The words tumbled out. Xai. Her plea.

"You don't see it, do you?" Tania murmured, her cheek against Ahni's hair. "What your mother gave up?"

"What has she given up?" Ahni pushed away, wiped tears with her forearm. "She's one of the best-known artists on the planet."

"She gave up power, Ahni." Tania stroked Ahni's hair back from her face. "Before she married your father, she was nearly his equal in the families. But after . . ." Tania shrugged. "The Huang has a very traditional Chinese ideal of 'wife.' Do you really think artistic success would outweigh loss of her power?"

Ahni recalled her mother's bitter words. "I never considered it," she said slowly. "She never seemed . . . unhappy. How did you find all this out?"

Tania laughed and shook her drying hair back from her face. "I wanted to find a reason for blackmail," she said. "To punish her for coming between us. Instead, I found a woman I could admire. She understands our goals, Ahni."

Our. The Gaiists.

Ahni sighed and ran both hands through her cropped hair. "Let's not go there."

"We're changing things, Ahni. *Us.* The Gaiists." Tania came up behind her, put her hands on Ahni's shoulders. "You don't hear about it in the media because we don't want you to hear about it. But we are. What is your father doing but making money? I know you think we're a bunch of ostriches with our heads in the sand but that's just because we don't draw attention on what we are doing. We—our planet—came close to the edge a couple of generations ago. The sea was dying, the land was dying. And now we pat ourselves on the back about how much progress we've made, but it's not enough. We still pay attention to our human wants first. *She* must come first, the Mother who gave us birth."

Tania drew a slow deep breath, her nipples brushing Ahni's shoulder blades. "Humanity hasn't really evolved. We came down from the trees as apes and our technology froze us as a species, even as it made us comfortable. We have stopped, Ahni. We are a dead end. If we want to move beyond that, we need to be in balance with our Mother. We help the process along, help Her, one small act at a time. The oceans are coming to health again and the animals are coming back. Bird watchers have reported loons in Canada, and lions walk the savannah in Africa. They were extinct, Ahni. With Her power we brought them back to life. Six years ago, when I left for the monastery, you almost came along. Do you remember that?"

But not because I believed. Ahni looked away. *Because I loved you.*

Fanatic. It was so easy to dismiss her, but Ahni thought of Dane, the fervor behind his words when he spoke of Koi's people. "So what should I do, Tania?" Ahni closed her eyes. "What do I say to my mother?"

"Xai chose his path." Tania's breath tickled her ear. "Let him walk it. Become your father's heir. You will be a better leader for the families than he is. You will give your mother back the life she gave up for you."

Ahni shivered as Tania's lips brushed her neck. "Don't," she whispered. Shivered again as Tania's tongue traced the corner of her jaw. "That's over, Tania." She stepped from beneath Tania's hands.

"Ahni? Daughter, are you there?"

Her mother's voice. Urgent.

Tania sprang back, was examining the antique bowl as her mother appeared in the doorway.

"Your father has arrived." In the wash of moonlight and floods tuned to simulate moonlight, her face looked taut and expectant. "He flew directly back when he . . . was informed of your arrival. Tania, please excuse us? This is a family matter."

"Of course." Tania bowed and a look passed between the two women.

"At least you had time to wash and dress." Her mother took her arm and escorted Ahni along the paths of river-polished stones.

To Ahni's surprise, a dinner waited, not in his private dining chamber, but in the banquet hall, normally reserved for visits and special occasions. Her father waited, hands clasped behind his back, head tilted back to study a scroll from the Forest of Stone Tablets in Xi'an, a hand rubbing from one of the stone texts kept there, blackened with ink, a chiseled archive of the evolution of Chinese writing over thousands of years. History, she thought. What would we be without its weight? Thought again of Koi.

Ahni studied her father's rigid shoulders, seeing Xai in the curves and planes of his flesh, aware of her mother's tension.

"Your daughter is here," her mother murmured.

Ahni bowed.

He returned her formal greeting briskly. At his nod, one of the house servants began to carry food to the table. "We'll eat," he said, and it was a command.

The kitchen had done a very good job on short notice, Ahni thought absently. She nibbled at the small dishes of bamboo tips with sauce, fresh green soy beans, and tiny fried fish with chilis. It wasn't banquet fare, but the steamed fish sliced artistically and layered with thin squares of fried bean curd, and the dish of braised pork with white fungus were special for a family dinner. Ahni, starving an hour ago, picked at her food, her appetite vanished. Her mother ate calmly, she noticed, her eyes fixed on her food. The meal ended with clear lotus seed soup, seasoned lightly with sugar. It was only then that he pushed his bowl away, drank some tea, and faced his daughter. "Have you fulfilled the task I gave you?"

Ahni looked down at her tea cup, aware of her mother's attention like a prodding fingernail in her back. "I did not kill my brother's killer," she said carefully.

"And yet you returned." His palm slammed down on the table. "You have turned your back on our family honor. You are worthless. Less than worthless."

His rage would have stunned her, only days ago. She had seen, felt, that same rage as her brother flung his cup across the orbital hotel room. Anger scalded her. *My mother is right,* she thought. *This is between you and Xai.* She had not decided about what she would and would not say. She decided now, pressed her lips together and bowed her head.

"I have not prepared you adequately." Her father's voice shook with anger. "This is my failing. But I will make amends for this lack on my part. I am posting you to our southern station." The Huang rose to his feet, staring down at her. "You will leave for our main factory ship, *The Soo Li,* in the morning. I will contact our manager there. You will replace him to oversee the krill harvest. He will return on the flight that brings you there."

Ahni studied his face, struck again by the feeling that she was a stranger here, an outsider, meeting these people for the first time.

Punishment, she thought. And humiliation. The krill fleet was a mainstay of the Huang Family fishing business. For him to send her, a novice, to manage the operation and remove the experienced manager at the same stroke, ensured failure on her part. And a significant injury to the family income if she failed spectacularly.

"May I be excused to go prepare?" she murmured in formal Mandarin.

At her father's curt nod, she rose from the table and left the banquet hall, passing the carefully averted gaze of the servant who was bringing in a plate of fresh melon, on the way out.

Tania waited at the door to her chamber, her face expectant.

"I am sent to ruin our krill fishery," she said.

"Don't worry." Tania put an arm around her. "He is angry and needed to hurt someone. Your mother will change his mind when he calms down." She smiled. "She has had a lot of practice at that, remember?"

Ahni dropped onto the low couch with its embroidered silk cushions. "Tania, I need time . . . to think."

"I understand. You are exhausted." Tania leaned down to kiss the top of Ahni's head lightly. "Sleep well, and don't worry."

Ahni listened to her steps fade. She could read Tania, Easily. And she had read . . . triumph. A battle won? *What war is this?* she thought. She was a player, like it or not. She remembered the nested boxes her grandmother had had. Each time you opened one, you found a smaller one inside. And the battlefield for this war seemed to be NYUp. What would Xai destroy before it played out? *You are right, Dane,* she thought bitterly. *We brought a war up to your world.* "I do not know enough to play your role, Mother," she whispered.

Ahni stood. "Room, video record," she said. A silvery chime told her that the room was recording. "Honored father." She bowed. "Before I gratefully undertake the task you have set me, your lowly daughter, I must fulfill my duty. To fail in this would be to further fail the Huang family honor. I will return when I have carried out that duty. Room, end record. Email to The Huang at 9 AM local time tomorrow."

Tania's wet clothes lay tangled on the floor beside the pool. Automatically, Ahni picked them up. Something metallic clattered on the tiles. Ahni picked it up. Xai's medallion. She stared at the silver oval inscribed with her brother's success. How had Tania entered Xai's room?

And why take *this*?

Frowning, she pocketed it, less certain than before of what lay behind this day's events. "Security," she murmured over her private link. "I want a skimmer at the service dock immediately. Private departure."

Security affirmed. Only The Huang himself would be able to access the log to determine when she had left and how. If she was a player in this war, so be it. She would not play from the sidelines. The battlefield lay in NYUp. This was her war, too, even if she had no idea whose side she was on, or what the sides were.

SIX

MEETING TIME WAS SCHEDULED FOR THE FOURTH SIX-
hour, this day. They rotated the times so that everyone could make
some of the meetings, no matter what shift they worked. Dane
drifted near Elevator 3B, watching the swift rise of the car on his
handheld security link. Already a half dozen NOW members talked
or watched the Con on their com links, keeping up with the flow of
NYUp's conversation with itself. Beside him, Kyros yawned, his
odd eyes, one brown, one green, speculative.

"Politics." He ran a freeze-scarred hand across his naked scalp.
"Good reason to stay out in the Belt. Got to say though, would be
more fun to drop rocks down here than balloons full of ice. Ain't
gonna happen, though, Dane."

"You might be surprised," Dane said mildly. He scanned the two
men and two women who kicked out of the 'vator and drifted toward the thickly planted tubes that surrounded the column. "Ripe
tomatoes a couple of tubes that way." He raised his voice, pointed
with a subtle jut of his chin that barely stirred him. "Help your-
selves. No strawberries right now. The harvesters went through yesterday."

"You're a good host, Dane." One of the women, Kani, a small

business owner with a square, blunt, russky face and the long skinny body of a native, flashed him a grin. "That's why we keep electing you."

"For you, I have a few strawberries." He led her down an aisle, plucked a huge, ruby berry.

"Lovely." Kani bit into it. "Sweet, Dane."

"You know, Jaret's complaining that your juice sellers are squeezing him. He's a solo operation."

"Hey, Dane, that's commerce." Kani shrugged, stilled her drift on a tube. "If I can sell cheaper . . . too bad."

"You're not selling cheaper in other neighborhoods." Dane selected another berry. "Just in his turf."

Kani shrugged.

"If we're gonna make this work, we have to keep our backs together, Kani. Your business is making a good profit. You don't need the few credits you're squeezing out of Jaret."

"Look, Dane, it's not your business." But she looked worried.

He examined the fat strawberry. "I heard Sheila might have some money troubles. She might have to call in that note of yours she holds. How much do you still owe her?"

Kani flushed, looked away. "I'm not pulling my sellers out of Jaret's neighborhood."

"Just keep the price fair." He held out the berry.

Kani glared at it, snatched it from his hand. Bit into it. "This one's sour."

"Sometimes they are." Dane followed her back to the elevator.

"Keeping the population in line?" Kyros eyed him.

"You might call it that." The elevator sighed open on its final trip and Dane narrowed his eyes as Raj and Kurt, two fringers, kicked out, followed by a small, taut man with a narrow, mixed-euro face followed them.

The troublemaker. Good. He'd gotten the word he was invited, then.

Dane nodded to him, received a grudging tilt of the man's head and a quick, challenging stare in return. The man had kicked off a bit too hard and had to spill his forward with both hands on the nearby tube. Shredded leaves drifted and frog-flies darted from the surrounding foliage, scooping the ragged bits of drifting leaves from the air.

"Shit." The newcomer recoiled. "What kind of bugs are those?"

"They don't bite." Dane lifted one shoulder. "Nice to meet you, stranger. Name's Dane."

"Sharn."

Dane faced the loose scatter of NOW members. Some of them sucked on tomatoes, catching drips of juice with the ease of practice, others hung in the bright, humid air, waiting. "This is Kyros. Belt miner. Ice." Dane nodded in Kyros's direction. "He's been around a long time, knows folk out there. He's been asking around, keeping his ear to the ground." He hooked himself backward, giving Kyros space.

"Yeah, I talked around some, listened a lot." Kyros scanned the scattered group of drifting natives with his mismatched eyes. "Ain't no re-pre-sent-ta-tive ya' know." He drawled the word out. "You repr'sent yerself out there mostly. But yeah, sure, most of us'd be happy to sling rocks down to ya. Long as you catch 'em and pay us for throwin' 'em."

"You want pay, you ride 'em down." Kani, the juice seller, lifted her chin at him. "Hand 'em to us."

"Then you pay for our climb back out, sweetlips." Kyros smiled at her, his grafted-in teeth gleaming neon blue in the harsh light.

Kani didn't lower her chin. "Catching's the hard part."

"You got rock jocks. They stupid, or what?"

"Look, we'll work out the numbers and who does what when the time comes." Dane kicked forward just enough to end the confrontation. "What you're saying is the miner's will back us on this?"

"Some of 'em." Kyros's shrug didn't move him a millimeter. "Most don't care who pays. You, Darkside, or the mudball. Doesn't matter to us."

"We've got plenty of rock jocks out there sweeping for the spitballs," Dane swept the crowd with his eyes. "We can increase the teams, get the rocks into stable orbits, then do the refining close to home here." He grinned. "Darkside doesn't field rock jocks with all that nice protective moonscape for a shield, so they can buy from us. That'll pay for the extra teams. I finally got the last of the numbers from Maria and Florez," he nodded his thanks. "We crossed the line a month ago. We got the numbers, we got enough supplies tucked away thanks to our network of hoarders to make it for two years if we live lean and work our butts off. By then, our economy should begin to balance. We've got refined metals, some local microG manufacturing that should be well competitive with the big corps that lease space here—after we impose our tariffs." Dane grinned. "Add in the luxury and art trade and even before tourism gets going again, we can get by." He let his eye travel from one to the other. "We can do it," he said quietly. "It's just a matter of *when*. We need to focus on that, now."

"What about the other three platforms?" Sean, small and moon-faced, downside born, twined his fingers together nervously. "Dragon Home dances to China's tune. Heck, the Admin over there, or Chairman or whatever you call him, is the son of the Chairman of the People's Republic. He's not going to do anything he's not told to. New Singapore is nothing but a prison and a bunch of tenant farmers." He lifted both shoulders in disapproval. "They won't join us."

"You're probably right about New Singapore," Dane said thoughtfully. "We left them out of the equation. Dragon Home is a guess." He frowned. "We need three of the four platforms going in on this." He paused. "But we've made some overtures to Li Zhen and he hasn't said no."

"Con in Dragon Home is all over the place." Zero, a random amer-mix, bone thin and a druid of an info wizard, spoke up. "Euro Two is a sure starter, just waiting for us to do the leap. If they get impatient, they might start the show first. They know our numbers and their own are better than ours for supplies." He made a face. "The euros stuff extra into every crevice in their can. Squirrels."

"We may have to carry New Singapore for awhile, if it comes along after all." Dane shook his head. "That'll make things real tight, but we can do it."

"I don't think they'll come along." Zero looked down his long dark nose, on the verge of insulted. "I told you seventy-three percent probability they wouldn't."

"Three out of four orients to me," Kani said. "I'm betting

Dragon's gonna be right on our heels. My cuz has been skimming their Con and compiling for me." She tilted her head at Zero. "You're not the only info wizard around."

Zero lifted one shoulder a milimeter.

From the corner of his eye Dane caught Sharn, the agitator, shoot Raj a glance.

"So we're all set up here, and we're gonna do what?" Sharn pushed himself away from the tube he had anchored to, leaving bruised leaves in his wake. "I guess maybe you need to spell this out for me, cause I think I'm lost. We're waiting for what?" He wore arched eyebrows, a face of innocent confusion. "Permission? I mean . . . so who tells us that we're allowed to say we're on our own?"

"Nobody said anything about permission," Zero snapped.

"You got four platforms to coordinate. Well, three without the Malays." Kani retreated a hair as Sharn pushed into her space.

"Yeah, I mean, we can't just say we're on our own." Raj threw this in. Out of character. Dane looked at Sharn, because this was a set-up and Raj had just tossed Sharn the ball.

"Why not?" Behind his mask of confusion, Sharn's eyes gleamed. "I mean, we could hold our butts for what . . . years? Waiting for the 'right time'? Who benefits from that?" He faced Dane directly, chin up, his stare direct. "Our Admin is busy skimming a little sweetness for himself up here. Any chance you're getting a taste of that cream?"

Silence. A frog-fly made a tiny creak that seemed loud in the sudden stillness. Dane smiled, because yeah, this creep or somebody working for him, had tried real hard to plant just that, the way they'd planted the fish farm purchase that had scorched Laif. But Koi had spotted it and Noah had fixed it. "If I was doing that, I bet you'd have found it by now." He made his lips smile, locked his glance with Sharn's. "You want to show us that link?"

"Doesn't mean it's not there." But Sharn's glance faltered just a hair.

"Get out of the way." Kani made a rude noise. "Admin might skim, not Dane. You want me to believe that, you better show me something that Zero here couldn't do himself. Then I'll believe it."

"I'd have found it first." Zero was looking hard at Sharn.

"Wondered how come you got to that little game of Admin's when I missed it." He pushed forward, into Sharn's space. "You scammed that? You're not bad."

"Get off." Sharn flexed, pushing off the tube behind him, stiffened fingers aiming for Zero's groin. But Dane had been waiting for that. He shot forward, caught the agitator just off his center, killed his forward as he spun him. Kyros, silent in the shadows, arrowed forward just right to deflect Sharn's spin, sent the man spiraling, flailing gracelessly for control. Gently, precisely, Kyros drifted back to his place in the shadow of the leaves. Dane drifted less than thirty centimeters from where he had kicked off.

Kani snickered.

Zero raised an eyebrow, nodded at Dane.

Smiles, and quiet chuckles wave-fronted across the group. Sharn had finally halted his tumble, kicked back to the group, wearing a tight smile. "Nice schoolyard trick." He nodded deeply to Dane. "I'll watch my back."

And with that act of humility, with tone, and his words, he . . . changed . . . the actions of the past moments. Suddenly, *he* was the victim and Dane the bully. Dane watched derisive smiles falter and grow thoughtful.

He was a pro, Dane thought sourly. He realized suddenly that Sharn had set him up for just this. "So what do you think we should do." Dane retreated slightly because he had to now, gave him space. "What is your take on our next step?"

"You don't *ask* the downsiders, that's my take." Sharn gave Dane a measured look that didn't quite conceal the glint of his triumph. "We throw every one of 'em off the platform, rough some of 'em up, tell 'em if they want to come back up here they ask pretty please. Let 'em shut down the climbers. Who cares? Didn't you just say we don't need stuff anymore? So how come you're all standing around? If they want to manufacture up here, come screw in microG, they pay rent. And tariffs for shipping down. We're *up* here and we call the shots, it's our turf, and they can damn well say please when they talk to us."

"That's what we're doing." Dane kept his eyes on Sharn, but

noticed the furtive nods here and there among the other NOW members.

"So how come we're standing around here?"

"The Con. You notice it?"

Sharn shrugged.

"It's ugly. We start that—shut the platform down, and send the downsiders home—and people are going to get killed."

"So?" Sharn held Dane's stare. "A few bodies just make the point better."

"It'll be more than a few. Then what?" Dane pushed forward ten centimeters, another ten. Aware of the low murmur behind him. "What do you think the downsiders will do? Cave? Roll over? The four major powers never have trusted one another up here. They've got the military platforms to watch us and they're loaded with weapons that could take us out. What are we gonna shoot back with? We do it our way and we get a World Council vote, not missiles and Council Security Forces." He pushed closer. Sharn would have to back up or react.

For a moment, their eyes locked and Dane relaxed his muscles, ready for the first twitch of movement.

Then, Sharn laughed. "Fine. Finish your scout meeting!" He had drifted too far from his anchor and had to work his arms gracelessly to get himself moving. Which detracted a bit from his exit, but he did his best to compensate for it. "I thought we were after the same thing. But I think I was wrong." He made it to the 'vator. "Don't get too old waiting for tomorrow." The door whispered open and he pulled himself inside, followed by Raj and Kurt. Kurt turned, his pale scalp white in the glare of light, and gave Dane a cold stare. Then the 'vator door cut off the view.

"I don't know." Kani was staring at Dane, challenge in the set of her shoulders. "Why not his way, Dane? We got to push if we're going to start the rock moving. Maybe he's right. I'm so damned tired of downsider attitude."

"They don't." Zero spoke up, legs tucked up into a modified lotus, his frown thoughtful. "They don't think about us the way we think they think about us—"

"Speak English will you?" Kani snapped.

"You dip into the Con and the heavyweights are throwing it all around up here. Pushing kids around, spitting on us, farting all over the plazas. But . . . you see any of that? Huh?"

Kani lifted a shoulder. "Wrong place, right time."

"Wrong place, *no* time!" Zero rotated slowly upside down. "Kani, *nobody* sees this stuff happen because it doesn't happen. I tracked a bunch of threads back and you know what? Somebody's friend, somebody's cousin got spit on, pushed, farted at." Zero looked to Dane. "You get what I'm saying?"

"Yeah, I do." Dane let his gaze travel from face to face. "I've been unraveling some of those threads, too, backtracking. Know something? Somebody is putting a hell of a lot of code power into hacking all kinds of Con. And it's all about the downsiders. Acting like heavyweights!"

"Gossip." Zero curled his lip. "Con is full of it."

"Nah." Dane shook his head. "Not with this kind of spike. It's an attack."

"I was right, huh?" Zero looked pleased. "Like somebody planted that stuff about Admin. They were good. I didn't spot the mock up 'till I went in after and started looking for the patches. I figured I couldn't have missed it, cause I look for that kind of stuff all the time."

"They were good." Dane nodded. "Same operator tried to set me up, too. Make it look like Admin was paying me off."

"Shit." Kani, pushed forward, her earlier anger forgotten. "Who the hell is doing this? That creep?"

"Dunno."

"Bet it was." She lifted her chin. "He thought he could walk in here and take over."

"We're off topic." Annie Devereaux, who contracted cleaning services in the upper levels, pushed forward. "When do we shift this rock? Dane, it's ready to move! The can'll be on fire in an hour once we start."

"Didn't you hear me?" Dane pushed forward, into the midst of them, scattering them backward. "We start pushing now and it's going to get out of hand. We need China to back us up at the Council. We're walking a fine line here. We get seen as terrorists and all the old ghosts from the last century are going to pop up. They'll shoot holes in the can and figure they'll clean out the bodies and rebuild later. We want to shift the rock, not smash the can with it. We want to shut things down, make it clear to the people downstairs that they can't conduct business as usual up here if we don't cooperate, but we've got to keep bloodshed out of the equation. If we start that . . ." He let his glance travel among them. "We'll lose. If we let the media label us monsters, the planet'll back whatever the North American Alliance tells them they need to do to us. Which means we need to be the good guys, no matter what it costs us. This is a media war. We got to look good on the Net. We're going to get arrested, and some of us are going to get hurt. We need to be the victims, the underdog. Then, we'll win. We'll force the World Council's hand. Because it's not going to cost the average downsider anything personally to let us have our independence," he said softly. "Most of them won't care either way, and if we're a good story, they'll back us. But if we scare them . . . they won't." He looked at each of them in turn, reading reluctant agreement. "We need to calm things down. Then . . . we shift this rock."

They left, two or three at a time, expressions thoughtful, body language not quite as positive as when they had come up here. They had been working toward this point for years now, some of them for a lot of years. Hard to wait, knowing it was almost time. Kani lingered after Zero left.

"Where did this guy Sharn come from?" she asked. "I never saw him around before."

"I don't know." Dane frowned. "I've tried to find out."

"Everybody heard me being pissed at you. I may have a change of heart about your policies." Kani's eyes glinted. "After all, you levered me."

"Watch yourself." Dane shook his head. "This guy is a pro. He's going to expect that."

"I'll distract him. He was giving me the eye, earlier." Kani winked, kicked lightly off the tube next to Dane and arrowed neatly into the elevator, the door whispering closed behind her. Dane watched it drop.

"He's not a native." Kyros drifted gently from his shadowy

station. "No matter what he looks like. He's not good enough in micro. But he's sure good with people. You should have let him double that kid over."

"I should have." Dane let his breath out in a sigh that sent him drifting slowly. "He set me up, there, and I fell for it. Someone's paying him. I can smell it."

"You should have stayed out in the Belt." Kyros laughed and kicked himself into motion. "You got yourself all tangled up in this politics thing. What do you care who runs this can? It's still a can."

"You know why." Dane sighed.

"Yeah, those damn kids."

"Who, us?" Koi zipped by them, followed by two of his cousins.

"By all the hells." Kyros's flinch sent him off his trajectory. "Yes, you. Watch your clearance."

"I missed you by a mile." Koi somersaulted off a tube to drift along with Kyros, matching his pace perfectly. "You're better than Dane in here. Not much, but a little."

"He goes skinside sometimes. I don't. Any new kids in the family?"

"Nah." Koi somersaulted, toed himself back into a parallel course with Dane and Kyros. "Laif is in the control center. Waiting for you." He planted one long-toed foot on a tube and shot away like a missile, his two playmates flanking him.

"Uh oh, I'm out of here," Kyros said. "Let me know when you're ready to start your little revolution. Us miners'll stay out of your way and sell to the winners."

"Miner loyalty."

"Call it survival." Kyros kicked off. "I got plenty of ice for another miner in the patch I'm working. Less stress, Dane."

"Watch yourself out there, miner." Dane angled off a tube newly planted to fennel and headed for the control center, flanked by Koi and his friends.

Koi peeled off, somersaulted off a tube planted with small perfect pineapples and killed his forward on another tube beside Dane. "Laif's mad." He blinked at Dane. "Just so you know."

Damn. Koi was upset. "Thanks." Dane smiled for one of the girls who had spun back to join Koi. She greeted him without words. They didn't talk much. Had the ability, just . . . didn't.

Sure enough, Laif was inside the control center, webbed into a hammock, fingers stabbing into the icons dancing above his holo-desk.

"Bad timing." Dane killed his forward on the autodoc and faced Laif. "You need to take this guy seriously. Sharn's his name, by the way. He already tried to set me up like he did you."

"I saw that. Good thing you were on top of it. Sharn Smith. Talk about a spit in the face, that name. A little challenge huh?" The Admin grinned sourly. His left eye squinted, swollen and dark.

"What happened to you?" Dane snagged a hammock, pulled himself into it. "You need the autodoc?"

"Nah." Laif started to shake his head, grimaced. "I got in the way of a little . . . altercation on the skin level." The tension in his face belied his light tone. "Dane, there just happened to be a free-lance eye wandering around. Downside media."

"Just happened to be."

"Yep. Look." He stabbed fingers into the holofield, and a scene shimmered to life in front of them, soundless, a scene of a skinny native with an angry face and blood red scalp inlays slugging a young, well dressed tourist. Inset, a geneselect scandanavian media-head spoke wide-eyed, her expression suggesting outrage.

"Must be a slow hour downside," Dane drawled, but the obvious slant dismayed him. "What's her voiceover?"

"Increasing incidents of violence. Hostility." Laif sighed. "He was out of control. I bounced him off a bulkhead. Turned out he had a couple of friends. Didn't see 'em in time. They're house guests of NYUp right now. Blood tests say they'd all been doing some of that mushroom juice those guys are growing in storage, one level down. I guess we're going to have to shut them down."

"That's just a psilocybin mutation." Dane frowned at the screen. "If anything, they should be too busy watching the pretty lights to bother anybody. It's not the mushrooms, Laif. It's the Con."

"Well, it's cranky." Laif shrugged. "Damn bad timing if you ask me. How come that freelance just happened to be wandering the halls?"

"Good question. You ask him?"

"Her. She didn't want to talk to me. In a hurry to sell her scoop." Laif winced again. "Damn, my head hurts. You think those bozos set that up for her?"

Dane shook his head. Maybe, but he doubted it. Laif didn't see the power the Con had, didn't spend much time on it. He had his info people keep tabs on it for him. Your ordinary NYUp resident, working in manufacturing, or a little self-business, or cleaning rooms for the skinside hotels . . . they plugged in all day, scanning or listening with audio, heads filled with the whispered conversations. "Back in the old days," Dane said slowly. "Back in the Terror Years, you wanted to take out a city, you poisoned the water system."

"You worried about the water system now? Who the hell is gonna poison it and how? It's so monitored now, you couldn't drop a molecule in there without shutting down the system."

"Not the water." Dane shook his head, hiding his worry. "The Con."

The newsfeed holo now showed a rolling vista of green hills and a line of hikers. Some human interest/eco story. "Video off," he said aloud and it vanished.

"So what did you hear tonight?" Laif closed his eyes, long legs taking up a lot of the room in the small space. "You were gonna tell 'em about the numbers." You could hear a ghost of New York in Laif's voice when he was tired.

"Yeah." Dane scowled at nothing. "The numbers work, but now . . . I don't know. This isn't the time. They don't want to hear that."

"*I* don't want to hear that." Laif glanced at him sideways. "We wait too long, Dane, they're gonna yank me, put my so-well be-haved Admin Assistant in my place and his first move is going to be to stuff you out an airlock."

"You'd do that." Dane gave him a crooked smile. "Boone doesn't have the balls."

"Be glad." Laif glared. "You're running this show, and I'm glad you are, but are you sure that putting this on hold is the right way to go? We're set to go here. We're at the peak, opportunity-wise. It's not going to get better."

"I thought we were." Dane levered himself lightly out of the hammock. "But . . . things have changed." Ever since Ahni Huang had bolted out of that elevator, right into Koi's arms.

"What things?"

"The Con."

"Don't give me that." Laif pulled himself out of the hammock, considerably less gracefully than Dane. "The Con is a bunch of chat. That's *all*. And those bozos tonight, they were doing mushrooms and the pretty lights weren't enough for 'em, and I'm going to shut down our boys with the fungi farm and make sure the downside media gets it as a bigtime story." Laif pulled himself toward the door. "Look, Dane. I sure don't want to go up against you, but I don't think we can put this off."

"I'll let you know." Dane called up security and checked the elevators. Nobody had tried to come up here since the meeting started. He followed Laif out into the harsh light of the axle. Koi arrowed past, gave a thumbs up. All clear. "Take the backdoor down, okay?"

Laif waggled his fingers in acknowledgment, and pushed off, heavily, flanked by Koi, who made a point of zig-zagging across the Admin's trajectory in perfect slices, doing precise somersaults off the tubes, stirring barely a leaf.

It was lost on Laif, but Dane smiled, caught Koi's mental wink.

He pushed off, himself, heading for his room, wanting to eat some dinner, curl up in his hammock and see if he would think his way to insight on this strange attack on the Con. It mattered.

A lot.

He needed to figure out what was going on here before they shifted this rock wrong.

SEVEN

WAKING IN HER FIRST CLASS RECLINER ON THE NORTH American Alliance's climber, Ahni winced at her stomach's instant protest. On day five, they had passed from Earth's gravitational tyranny to the sense that gravity wasn't such a tyrant after all. Two young children traveling from Toronto with their parents, had spent the last day entertaining all with their hands-on exploration of their diminishing weight and its limits. Smiling in spite of bruises, they made everyone smile.

Ahni tried to enjoy their antics, but her anxiety over what awaited her on NYUp oppressed her. Her mother had commanded her to return, then pleaded. Not once would she admit that she had known Xai was alive when Ahni gave her the news. That was a lie and it made Ahni wonder what other lies hid here. It would be dangerous to face her brother, but by now, he must know that she had not revealed his presence to their father. He would be curious and curiosity had always been his weakness. With luck, he would reveal a glimpse of the larger picture she knew lay behind these small lies.

Her mother had, at least, ceased calling her. Through a crack in the privacy curtain which enclosed her First Class recliner, Ahni caught a glimpse of the two children, Donya and Kelly, swinging down the aisle between the curtained recliners, Tarzan-like, from handhold to handhold, pursued by the resigned attendant who probably looked forward with longing to the arrival of the climber. Ahni checked the screen on the arm of her seat. Less than an hour to arrival. She stretched, wrinkled her nose, wanting a long soak in the hotel in comforting gravity. And she wanted to see Dane again—needed to talk to talk to him, *wanted* to see him. Revelation there. She smiled in spite of her worries.

"Hey, we're gonna land soon." A face thrust through the curtains, interrupting her thoughts. Nine-year-old Donya grinned at her, the natural mix of North African, Mediterranean, and Spanish genes a perfect blend in her oval face. "Kelly already has his spot staked out. And I know they're not real windows, don't you tell me, *too*." She made a face.

"A window is something you look at to see the outside," Ahni said gravely. "I call them windows."

"Well, they *are* just a digital image," the girl stated with a child's solemn attention to getting the details right. "But I suppose your definition is broad enough so that you may call them windows."

"It is. I was careful to make it so." Ahni laughed and released the webbing that kept her safely in her seat. Gingerly she pulled herself to the aisle sliding the curtain back along its guide rail, one hand on the hand grip. She noticed that Donya had already mastered the art of flying. She couldn't match Koi, but she learned a whole lot faster than the adult passengers with their less-fluid inner ears who pulled themselves laboriously around the climber or clutched white knuckled at hand grips, their eyes glassy with anti-nausea drugs. They would appreciate that Level One gravity on the platforms.

"I looked at the welcome vid in the climber's library." Donya grabbed the guide rail to keep herself from flying past Ahni. "They have a really cool park. It's in the center of the orbital and there's no gravity, and people play all kinds of games there and race and—I can't wait." She ran out of breath finally.

Ahni spared a glance for Donya parents who belonged to the glassy-eyed white-knuckled set. "You'll be living up here for a while, right?" Ahni joined her at one of the big "windows." "So you'll have plenty of time to find friends to go with you to the park."

"You're right. *They* won't want to go." She gave her parents a disappointed look and shrugged. "I wish it was going to be longer. I want to get good in no-gravity, shave my head, and get a lightfiber tattoo. Or do you have to be born up here to do that?"

"I think it's just fashion." Ahni smiled, thinking she and Koi would hit it off. "I never heard there was a law."

"The Administrator has a tattoo. He's quite dark and it looks really cool. We met him last year when Father brought us up here to see. Mama didn't want to come up here to stay, but Father said it would 'round out our life experience'—one of those things parents say, you know? And I'm glad. I didn't want to spend the winter in Montreal. Snow! Brr!" She shivered. "I miss Ankara but this will be so much more fun!"

Ahni smiled. The vid camera had shifted its view and now they seemed to be passing close to the matte black cannister that was NYUp, although the terminus of the Elevator was actually some distance away.

"Oh, look at the lights!" Donya crowed. She tried to bounce up and down and Ahni caught her as she rocketed away from the window, hauled her back.

Gripping the handhold beneath the window, she looked briefly up at Ahni. "I know you're going to be very very busy up there, but if you don't have anything to do sometime, and you want to go to the park—"

"I'll call you." Ahni smiled at her, distracted from her worry. This girl, child of an upper-class family who moved in global circles, had had no casual childhood, school, friends to hang around with. "I really will," she assured Donya, who had put on a polite face that Ahni guessed was her response to adult lies.

THE FIRST CLASS section disembarked at the terminus, hauling themselves directly from their cabins to the shuttles that would take them to their destination with only the barest nod from Security. Most of them were headed for NYUp, although a few scattered to other shuttles. Donya kept up a bright commentary all the way, while her brother kept his eyes fixed on the vidscreens offering various views of the looming platform with its forest of solar arrays, telescopes, radar dishes, and all the other devices that cluttered its skin. The parents were clearly holding on to their stomachs.

Ahni finally saw the last of the irrepressible Donya in the Arrival Hall, as they passed through the First Class aisles and out into the plaza. Tired from her forced inactivity, the cramped sleeping space of the recliner, and her restless worries about Xai, Ahni followed the lavender arrows that lighted beneath her feet, leading her to her hotel.

It wasn't far from the Arrival Hall, so she didn't bother to hire a cart, even though she had reclaimed her large suitcase and now lugged it along with her small bag slung over one shoulder. In the sub-Earth gravity, it wasn't a particularly heavy load. But before she had passed more than a Tai Pei block down the busy corridor leaving from the Arrival Hall, she hesitated.

It . . . felt different here.

Normally, once she had the feel of a place, whether it was the family compound, the streets of Tai Pei, or a strange hotel, the emotional static from the people around her faded into a blur like white noise. Only the unexpected or extreme emotional spike stabbed her attention. So this time, barely two weeks away from the corridors, she should have felt at home.

She didn't. A simmering—anger—tainted the air like the smell of burning wires. It wasn't like this last time. A uniformed woman carrying a static cleaning wand stepped around her with a flash of irritation that startled Ahni as much as a slap would have done. The woman gave her a direct stare as she stalked past.

How rude. Ahni walked on, resolving to drop into Pause in her room and consider this change in mood up here. The sour tinge of anger in the air nagged at her as she followed the lavender arrow down the thickly carpeted aisle. The arrow led her left, then right, then vanished beneath the feet of a doorman with the muscular look of a gym rat and red hair braided into neat cornrows. He glanced at a wrist mounted link and leaped to take her bags, his wide amer-mix face fixed in a smile. "Welcome, Ms. Huang. Nice of you to stay with us this trip." He hoisted the big bag as if it was filled with feathers. "I'll show you your room. Is there anything you'd like? A massage? It helps after all those hours in one of those climber recliners. I think they were designed by chiropractors hungry for business." Chatting on glibly, leaving just enough pause to allow her to answer, but not so much that it was obvious that she wasn't answering, he escorted her through the doorway.

It led to a small square plaza. Ahni stopped still, startled by the vista of blue sky and puffy clouds overhead. A trio of birds winged across it, vanishing into a belt of trees beyond green lawn and a distant brook. Beneath her feet, grass carpet so real that she stifled the urge to lean down and touch it enticed her to that distant stream.

"Pretty realistic isn't it?" Her guide laughed. "It helps the visitors who have claustrophobia problems."

"No kidding." Ahni laughed, too. Yes, it was a ceiling, not endless sky, and you could just make out the line where the grass carpet met the rolling lawn of the virtual landscape. Nice projection, she thought. Very dimensional. Top of the line software and hardware both. Rustic white fences—real ones—kept patrons from walking into the walls.

"This is your suite." He led her across the "grass" to a door in what seemed to be a neat row of small cottages. More projections. With a flourish he palmed the lock and threw the door open. "Now I've opened it, it won't respond to my hand anymore. If you'll just stand here a second," he indicated a faintly darker circle in the carpet, "the vitals scanner will record you and then the room will take your personal security from there."

Ahni stepped onto the dark carpet and imagined that she could feel the Security program recording her bioelectric field, her image, body temp, muscle synergy. It would now recognize her without further ID. The room itself was of typical Hong Kong or Tai Pei size, she decided, small for American or European hotels. A single room, the sofa converted to a bed. A table and two luxurious chairs took up the rest of the floor. Drawers and a closet lined one wall, entertainment screen and holo-desk the other. A refreshment panel and the door to a private bathroom filled the other wall. An enormous vase of white lilies and pink orchids stood on the single, small table.

"The controls." With a flourish, the man touched a watercolor of a grassy valley and it shimmered into a control screen. "There's a separate one in the bathroom for the functions there. Window—" He touched the screen and instantly the entertainment wall vanished, showing her blackness and the scattered diamond dust of a million stars

Ahni stilled an urge to grab for something solid, as if she might be sucked out into that freezing, beautiful void. "Nice," she said dryly. "How often do you have to get out the defib?"

The doorman chuckled. This was clearly his private perk, his little test of his visitors. "Good reaction," he murmured.

Ahni merely scanned the control panel. "Everything else looks pretty routine. I think I can find my way around the bathroom, thanks." She slipped a cash card out of her pocket, handed it to him. The LCD displayed the amount on the front.

"Thank you, ma'am." He grinned. "If there's anything you want—"

"Did the hotel provide the flowers?"

He looked at them as if he had just noticed them, eyebrows rising. "I don't think so, ma'am. Doesn't look like our usual supplier. I could try to find out."

"Please do." She smiled at him.

He bowed his head to her. "Right away, ma'am."

Ahni closed the door behind him. Quite the step up from the little cheapie hotel on the main corridor she had booked last trip. Cautiously, Ahni walked over to the table, circled it, staring at the flowers. Her assiduous doorman had placed her bags on a wide shelf in the closet, leaving the sliding doors open. She retrieved a small hand-held security scanner from it, checked the flowers. No contact toxins, explosives, hardware of any sort. Just flowers. No card. Xai?

She leaned close. The scent of the lilies pervaded, but a delicate trace of rotting meat threaded the flowery sweetness. This particular species of orchid depended on carrion flies for pollination. Bemused she straightened. Sweetness and rot. A comment? Warning? She touched one creamy lily petal, its flesh crisp and fresh beneath her fingertip. Grown here? In Dane's kingdom? She turned her back on them, touched open her suitcase and surveyed the contents Fan had helped her pack. Time to go make herself available. And to watch her back. She smiled, mirthlessly.

————

SHE DRESSED IN the "orbital chic" she had seen in the corridors, loose and elegant. Out in the corridors, she sauntered along, looking as curious and mildly bored as the genuine tourists she had noted. The main corridors here were wide, crammed with shallow shop fronts, vendor carts, and strolling tourists. Ahni pretended interest in the same styles and designers you could get for the same price on Earth. That undercurrent of anger nagged at her. She shook her head at the skinny little androgyne, intricately tattooed with light, who offered her faceted pieces of polished gemstones set in hairfine wire. Then she looked twice, because he . . . she . . . reminded her of Koi. Ahni bought a skewer of fresh fruit chunks from a native-boned girl with wise eyes in a gamine face. For all her nonchalance, Ahni kept her awareness honed, searching for an echo of Xai. She needed to contact Dane, too. Her surge of anticipation was—revelatory. Maybe he could see a pattern in Xai's actions.

She entered a shop selling spider silk clothing, fingering the delicate tissues of gold, soft green, peacock blue, and rich crimson that hung on the racks or draped artistically about surrealistic mannequins seemingly carved from ice. The shopkeeper, a round-face mixed-euro with blonde hair and fair northern skin, followed her, her manner a perfect blend of helpful and polite, her eagerness humming behind her careful unobtrusiveness. "I like this color." Ahni selected a fitted blouse with short, loose sleeves in a soft green and gold flower pattern that made her think of the axle garden.

"It suits your skin tones. Visiting from China?" The woman led her to a mirror and a shimmering privacy curtain instantly surrounded them in the tiny shop. "Do try it on." The shopkeeper withdrew to the other side of the privacy curtain. "This style flatters your figure."

"I will try it on." Ahni smiled at the woman's adept sales technique. "I'm from Taiwan. This is my first visit up here." As herself anyway. She stripped her singlesuit down to her waist and pulled on the top. It had a slight stretch and the woman was right. The fitted waist and loose sleeves, ending well above her elbows did flatter her boyish figure. It would work in microG, too. She bought it, and a pair of loose formal pants to go with it, chatting with the woman about affairs downside and up here.

"A bunch of folk want to see us go independent." The shop-keeper looked down at the clothes as she folded them. "They're crazy. How could we get along up here? I mean . . . I came up here because I could own a shop and it was just . . . there was too much red tape in Lucerne if you wanted to start a new store. You had to wait until someone gave up a place and the waiting list—" She shook her head. "I do okay up here, but how does NOW expect us to survive if the tourists stop coming? They're crazy. Downsiders don't all look down on us. But that's all you get on the Con these days." She flushed, smoothed the folded silk she'd wrinkled. "Let me bag these for you. I didn't mean to be bothering you with our silly local politics."

"What's the Con?" Ahni eyeballed the charge screen as the woman slipped the clothes into a bright bag.

"Oh, it's just a local thing." The woman laughed a bit awkwardly. "Sort of an ongoing gossip session—but everyone does it all the time. It's kind of a mess if you're not used to it. People just talking about their day."

That's right. Noah worked on it. Traffic cop, he had said, or something like that. Ahni thanked her and left the shop, continuing her aimless tourist wandering. No tours to the garden, although the park Donya had mentioned advertised a view wall into it. On a whim, she took an elevator upward a few of levels. This particular elevator let her out in a retail area, one that obviously didn't cater to tourists. No angles. Walls, floor, ceiling curved into one another. The shops offered basics and a few luxury items. And she didn't be-long here. Ahni's skin prickled with attention as she wandered among the natives, stepping carefully because she felt as if she had springs on her feet. Most of the natives didn't look at her, but here and there, someone stared rudely.

She pretended not to notice them. Maybe she'd made a mistake. Unobtrusively she scanned the pale mauve arch of corridor, looking for security eyes. Saw a few, not many. Meanwhile, she noticed that two men and a woman were following her. They stared at her. Ahni stifled a prickle of apprehension. They were between her and the elevator plaza. Ahead of her, the corridor widened into what seemed to be a small park.

Grass-carpeted space offered complex climbing equipment for children and a scatter of natives sat or sprawled on the carpet, alone or in small groups, eating, looking at readers, watching small portable holodesks, or listening to music. Some had stripped naked in the summer-afternoon light that filled the space and splashed under a towering fountain that seemed to fall back to the pool in slow motion droplets, curving a bit from the spin of the platform. Behind her, her shadows closed in.

Ahni headed for the center of the park. Here, strolling vendors sold food from backpacks, mostly cold sandwiches and stuffed buns of various types, or poured beverages from shoulder-carried plastic jugs into mugs that natives wore clipped to their belts. One vendor with pale skin and a buzz of black hair looked vaguely familiar. Ahni drifted closer, watching him plant the single pole leg of the grill on the carpeted floor, brace it with one foot, and stir fry a handful of mixed vegetables and tofu for a customer, tossing the food high with a drama that could never work in full Earth gravity. With a flourish, he scooped the hot stir-fry into a rolled cone of thin flatbread, fished a squeeze from his pack, squirted sauce onto the veggies, and handed it to the buyer in return for a couple of small, bright orange disks.

A fiberlight inlay on his wrist, a green Celtic design confirmed her recognition. "Noah?"

He looked up, grinned, his manner easy, pleased. "Hey, Ahni. How cool. I just got back last night." He offered her a hand. "Wow, what a ride back up! Privacy and everything. Thanks a lot." His hand closed briefly about her wrist, and tense as she was, she almost knocked it away.

"You don't want to shake like a heavy—like a downsider. Here." He grabbed her wrist firmly, his little grill leaning safely to the side. "You grab mine. Like that." He nodded as her fingers closed around his skinny wrist.

"Good job." He squeezed her wrist hard, let go. "Now you shake like an upsider." His grin widened. "'Cept your muscles give you away. Too thick, even for a gym rat."

Her shadows had vanished. "Noah, do you mind walking back to the elevator with me?" She smiled up at him. "Do you have a couple of minutes?"

"It's right over there." He gestured with his chin. "You lost?"

"No." She started to put a hand on his arm, stopped, because she realized that she hadn't seen any natives touch one another in the corridors. His eyes darkened and narrowed as she told him about her shadows and their intent.

"I'd say you were mistaken, 'cause that kind of thing never used to happen. But lately—" He shook his head, wiped his grill down with a cloth, slung it over his shoulder with his pack. "Where are you headed?"

"Back to my hotel room. It's on the skinside level, so a convoy to the elevator is all I need."

Without a word, Noah took her arm. It had the feel of an important gesture and again, Ahni felt *attention*. Bemused she walked with him to the elevator, unsteady because he moved a lot faster than her coordination would have let her do. "Door-to-door service." He winked as he followed her inside.

"You didn't stay down long," she said as they dropped.

"No." He bit off the word. "I didn't . . . impress my grandfather. And . . ." He lifted one shoulder. "I needed to get back up here fast."

"Do you see Dane often?"

"Yeah." Noah followed her out of the car. "All the time, why?"

"I'm not sure how to get in touch with him. Informally, I mean. I couldn't find his name in the access directory."

"Probably not." Noah laughed. "I'll tell him."

"Thanks." She didn't want to draw any more attention to Koi and his family by sneaking up to the axle again. Someone might notice.

"Thank you," Ahni said, as they came within sight of the doorman, a different one this time. His flicker of instant disapproval tickled her. "Noah, what did it mean? That you took my arm up there?"

"Nothing—Well, no, that's not true." He blushed. "It means . . . you're my friend. Just so . . . people up in the neighborhood know."

"Thanks." She smiled. "I appreciate it."

"I work the mealtime crowds when I'm off. A little extra to add to my regular pay." His smile gleamed in his eyes. "Come on back up and I'll show you how to play scrum." His eyes dimmed briefly. "I'm sorry about those jerks. The Con has gotten nasty. Dane thinks it's hackers, but I don't know." He shook his head. "You probably shouldn't go wandering around on the upper levels right now by yourself. But my neighborhood's safe now, so come back up, okay?"

"It's a deal." She smiled and he walked away with a flip of his fingers that she translated as a wave.

Her room door opened at her approach. Lights glowed on as she stepped over the threshold and the scent of the lilies almost made her dizzy. *You have an urgent message,* the room told her in a gentle female voice. *Would you like to hear it?*

"Yes!"

Ms. Huang, my greetings! I'm Laif Jones-Egret, the Administrator for NYUp. I'm honored to have a premier member of the Taiwan Families as a visitor to the platform, and I'd like to extend an invitation to you for dinner. If you have no plans, I'd be honored by your attendance tonight at 700 hours. If you'd like me to call for you, just say 'yes'. I hope you can make it!

Intrigue or protocol? Ahni tossed her bag full of spider silk dress up onto the bed. 'Yes,' she said clearly. Two hours to prepare. Plenty of time.

Wonderful! His recorded answer sounded almost real. *You'll find a cart and driver at your door at 700 hours on the nose!* And with that quaint turn of phrase the message ended.

Something had certainly started happening up here in the week that she had been away. Her hindbrain tickled her with the suggestion that it involved Xai.

Proof?

None. She needed to talk to Dane. Ahni explored the bathroom. It was adequate—shower stall, double sink, mirrors, dryer vents. The wall dispenser in the shower offered her usual shampoo and conditioner, the brand to be found in her personal file along with the toothpaste she preferred, the type of breakfast she favored, and her favorite colors. Sometimes she thought that a hotel database held more personal information than a Council Security Force snoop file. She turned the shower on full and hot, the six sprays swiveling to evenly bombard her body with water.

It felt . . . strange in slightly diminished gravity. Water didn't behave normally. But the heat and steam relaxed her and she decided to find a bathhouse where she could pay for a good long soak tomorrow.

She found the refreshment wall stocked with her preferred brands of tea and ordered a pot. The pale liquor soothed her as she took her time dressing. First impressions had value. From the tone of the message, she guessed that this Administrator was waiting to be impressed. She would not disappoint him, she thought as she put on the spider silk evening pants and top, then donned a lacy cap of silver beadwork hung with strings of pale jade that drew attention to her fine-boned face and slender neck. She finished a careful job of makeup just before 700, and not five minutes later, the room voice spoke to her. *Ms. Huang, a private car is waiting for you. Would you like to reply?*

"I'll be right there," she said, slipped on a pair of real-leather sandals and left the room.

One of the little electric cars she had noticed in the corridors waited outside the gate to the inner courtyard. A small, native-boned woman with an unselect-hispanic face sat at the controls. She smiled at Ahni, nodded approval. "You look great." She patted the twin facing seats behind her perch. "It's all yours tonight, help yourself. I'm Doria."

"Ahni." She seated herself facing forward, relieved at the friendly greeting. "So where are we going?" she asked lightly as the car surged forward with a subdued whine from it's electric motor. "The governor's mansion?"

The woman clearly didn't get that reference

"To the Administrator's official residence?" Ahni amended.

"Sort of." Doria grinned, weaving the little cart through the increasingly crowded corridor with deft precision. "It's sort of the official hall. Sometimes guests have dinner there, sometimes we have work parties there." Her grin widened. "Sometimes we just party there. Like on Christmas and New Year's, and E Day. That's

Elevator Day, the day the first climber hit the platform. That really was the start of the orbitals as a place to live I guess. That was a long time ago. I think my grandmother was a little girl then, or maybe not even born yet." She shrugged and cranked the little cart around a tourist group spread out across the corridor, kids darting about, moms hurrying belatedly after them. Doria shook her head, irritation tarnishing her bright mood. "They just don't get it—that we have to go places, that this corridor isn't just for them."

Doria guided the little cart into a doorway large enough to admit it. The double doors whisked sideways, revealing a tiled atrium decorated with rocks and water. Perhaps ten people stood around the tiny, splashing fountain, drinks in hand, the air already thick with cocktail hour levity veneered over purpose.

"Ah, Ms. Huang." A very tall man with a mixed afro-amerind face separated himself from a pair of women and strode to meet her, light fiber tracery glowing on his scalp, a huge emerald glittering in one ear. "I'm so pleased that you accepted my invitation."

"I would hardly say no." Ahni took his hand—like a downsider would—and let him help her climb out of the cart. He was *big*. She had seen his image on the media, but there had been no point of reference to prepare her for someone that tall. Tall, big . . . he didn't seem to fit up here. She looked up . . . up . . . met dark twinkling eyes, and an easy smile that did an excellent job of masking his very intent focus and an edge of tension. Uh oh. The name *Huang* meant something. "Do you invite all new visitors to dinner? How very welcoming."

"Oh, he rarely invites us downsiders to much of anything." A small, stocky woman with spiked purple hair and out of fashion cheek and eyebrow art sashayed up with a half-empty drink in her hand. "I haven't been able to pry the real reason for this red carpet unrolling out of him. Why don't we join forces?" She looked Ahni up and down, her lust like the moist lick of a tongue on Ahni's skin. "I think he's gathering the faithful in the face of the oncoming storm."

She was drunk. "What storm is that," Ahni asked politely.

"What can I get you to drink? Wine, liquor, one of the euphorics?" The Administrator steered her away from Spike Hair. "The bar is well stocked. We have juices, too, if you'd prefer. Fresh."

"I'd like to try one of the local beers." She had done her home-work. "I'll try your local brandy another time, thank you."

"Light? Dark?" One eyebrow rose. "We have a nice IPA."

"I'll have the IPA, please." She accepted the wide glass he handed her and tasted the beer, hiding her attention in that small ritual of sipping, considering, and praise.

The younger woman—geneselected Hindi with the muscles and grace of a dancer—looked bored. She was clearly Spike Hair's lover. Four other guests arrived and the Administrator greeted them easily and made introductions. Ahni filed the names in short term mem-ory. Santos, the Argentinian businessman looked vaguely familiar. He had his young, decorative wife in tow, a platinum haired geneselect Scandinavian type. The other couple, both amer-mix men in their early thirties, seemed to be business partners rather than bed mates.

Interesting selection.

A couple of natives in plain blue singlesuits circulated with plat-ters of small pastries and decoratively sliced fresh vegetables stuffed with herbed soy-cheese. Ahni nibbled and listened, hovering at the fringes of conversation. Complaints. Irritation. Service was poor, people were rude, shipments were being held up by disabled equip-ment and mistakes. The overall theme was . . . *change*. And not for the good. The business pair backed the Administrator up against the bar, complaining that their spider silk plant had dropped in pro-duction recently. They suspected theft among the native employees. Spike Hair was saying something about an epidemic of miscar-riages and deformed infants up here. Ahni pricked her ears and drifted closer, thinking of Koi, but the wife-in-tow latched on to her, looking out of her depth and desperate and Ahni got to listen to a litany of small inconveniences and discomforts suffered on this, her first trip upside.

She didn't know *why* her husband had to come up here person-ally. He usually handled this sort of new business on the Net.

That, too, was interesting. When you went from routine Net ne-gotiations to personal conversations . . . there was always a reason. "Your gown is lovely—I'm jealous. What business is your husband in?" she asked with an admiring smile.

"Oh, he downports computer hardware. You know . . . the kind that they manufacture without any gravity. Boring stuff." She rolled her eyes.

And that industry not only provided the current economic underpinning of NYUp, but was entirely controlled, she had discovered in her research, by a single downside corporation through several well disguised satellites. That fact . . . an economic vulnerability here . . . had caught her attention.

The other two downported spider silk and also represented Earth-based companies that leased space and local labor. And the Administrator had invited her when Huang downported nothing. Thoughtfully, Ahni followed the small assemblage as the Administrator ushered them to the table set up at the far side of the large space. The in-tow wife claimed a seat beside Ahni.

"I went walking in one of the quaint parks." She shook out her napkin and leaned close to Ahni. "These . . . children ran past. They said . . ." She blushed delicately and Ahni wondered if hubby had married her for her perfect, porcelain skin. "They said something very nasty. My friend said everyone was so nice to her, when she spent two weeks on the Indonesian platform. She didn't have to lift a finger the whole time she was there. I don't know why we had to come here." She sounded aggrieved.

The wait staff served a delicate tomato broth as a first course, filling wine glasses with a cool crisp white wine without waiting to be asked. Ahni raised her glass to her lips, tasted it, and set it down again. Very nice California vintage. She noticed that her nearly full glass of beer had vanished, and that the staff topped up glasses as quickly as they emptied.

Ahni realized that the Administrator's attention was on her and she lifted her full glass in a tiny salute. His lips curved briefly, then he turned to Spike Hair who was tapping urgently on his elbow with one perfectly inlaid and polished nail.

The soup had been removed and plates of sauteed fish and baby carrots lay before them accompanied by a salad of tiny greens. Ahni thought of the spider-like harvesters creeping along the tubes, their busy feet selecting, plucking . . .

"What about these rumors that the secession movement is getting out of control?" One of the silk manufacturers spoke up. "Our manager says that skilled employees are getting harassed—told they should be working for our competitor because he's local. I've lost a couple of talented design and dye-chemistry people." He paused while the silent server refilled his wine glass, seized it. "I can't just bring up downsiders. You got to run spider silk in microG modules. You bring people from down below and about the time they get good in micro they quit. My best designer and top chemist quit. It's pressure. From these NOW people." He gulped half his fresh glass of wine. "They're running off my best people. What are you doing about them?" He glared at the Administrator. "Why the hell are you letting this get out of hand, Jones? Where the hell's your Security?"

"Busy keeping track of the criminal element." The Administrator smiled, rocking one long, dark hand gently in the air. "I did respond to your complaint if you remember, Mr. Terrington. Your designer left of her own free will and applied for a job with Star Silk Co-op. There is nothing illegal about that. And your chemist is married to the designer. Are you surprised she followed her wife?"

"Bullshit!" Terrington stared morosely at his glass. "Yushi would never have deserted us. She was the creative talent that put us at the top of the market. She got leaned on."

"That's not what she told me."

"They're going to kick us all out." Spike Hair's drawl silenced the table. "They're going to start a revolution, herd us all into the climbers, or hell, maybe they'll just push us all out the locks. Won't they, Mr. Jones-*Egret,* dearest?"

"Oh, my God, you're kidding?" In-tow clasped her hands together charmingly.

"She's not even kidding." Her husband reached for his wine glass. "She's drunk."

Spike Hair's decorative companion rolled her eyes and went back to poking food around on her plate with the tines of her fork.

"There's absolutely no worry about that." The Administrator smiled reassuringly at the woman. "We have excellent Security up here."

"And you have the North American Alliance's military platform with those great big guns that they put up there expressly to shoot anybody up here who might think about doing anything they didn't like," Terrington's business partner murmured.

"Of course." Jones-Egret smiled. "So you're perfectly safe."

Terrington's partner and in-tow's husband were paying very close attention to this conversation. Interesting. Ahni blinked their faces into short term memory. She'd run a search on them later.

"There is some . . . feeling that the orbitals should be independent. That's true," the Administrator was saying. "But it's just a lot of hot air . . . people venting. The media on Earth is blowing it out of proportion."

"Bunch of terrorists." Terrington glared at his empty glass, transferred the glare to a woman who leaned over him to refill it. "I say send the CSF up here and clean the place out before those terrorists start dropping rocks on us."

Silence gripped the table.

"How could rocks hurt?" In-tow asked.

Ahni thought she was playing the dumb blonde act a bit hard. She looked up and found the Administrator watching her, but he shifted his glance away quickly. Terrington was explaining in graphic detail just how rocks could hurt Earth and In-tow was doing a very nice job of shrinking in horror which seemed to please both hubby and Terrington equally. The other businessman, meanwhile, was carrying on a quiet conversation with Spike Hair. Ahni had realized some time ago that she wasn't drunk at all. Good acting. For whose benefit? By now the delicate crème brulee served for desert had been finished and the wait staff removed the plates.

The Administrator invited the guests to relax in a loose semicircle of comfortable smart chairs surrounding an actual open fire pit, although the logs were fake, Ahni noted. Brandy was served here, but the peak of the evening had passed and the businessman and his wife started the exodus. Terrington also stumbled off, complaining that they needed CSF up here to teach these spoiled hicks manners. Spike Hair's bed mate also left, her demeanor sulky and feline.

Ahni, Terrington's partner, and Spike Hair settled in with their brandies.

"You were very quiet tonight." The Administrator smiled at Ahni. "I hope we didn't bore you?"

"Oh, not at all," Ahni said lightly. "I don't know anything about the platforms so it was all very interesting."

"You traveled on the climber with Mr. and Mrs. Santos." He contemplated his brandy. Did you have a good trip?"

The connection finally closed. Santos was a Small Family member of Pacific Fisheries, the huge NAA conglomeration. He had had dealings with Huang Family.

"I did have a good trip," she gave him a bland smile. "But of course, my brother dealt with Senor Santos. I never actually met him."

"Of course." The Administrator swirled the brandy in his glass, his eyes fixed on the climb of the amber liquid up the curve of the glass.

Everyone's attention was fixed on their brandies.

She didn't know the password here. "I think it's time for Huang to look up," she said lightly. "My father has been stubborn about avoiding commerce with the platforms. But I am more . . . open to new connections."

Clean miss. Their collective lack of response made her wince. Damn.

"You'll have to forgive me." The Administrator gave her an apologetic smile that hid irritation. "I have not met your brother. But I'm delighted to hear that Huang Family is interested in exploring a trade relationship with us up here." He shifted his glance briefly to Spike Hair.

"Great dinner you put on. You guys are doing better and better with the hydroponic stuff." The woman drained her brandy snifter and stretched. "I'd better be off. I've got business in Europe to deal with and their morning comes pretty damn soon now. Nice meeting you." She nodded to the spider-silk manufacturer and to Ahni. "See you around."

The Administrator rose, too, and so did the spider-silk manufacturer.

Meeting adjourned. Ahni let the Administrator usher her out to the entrance and the cart that waited to transport her to her hotel. Spike Hair had already vanished, but the spider-silk manufacturer hung back as Jones-Egret handed her into the cart. Everyone made pleasantries, and as the cart did a U-turn and headed down the corridor toward her hotel room, Ahni saw the Administrator and the manufacturer step back into the room. The meeting hadn't been adjourned after all. Ahni wondered if Spike Hair would return, too.

Ahni rode in silence to her hotel, slipped a generous cash card onto the driver's seat as the woman hopped down to hand her out. Her doorman with the red cornrows was back on duty. She caught his spike of attention as he recognized her, loitered a bit as the cart wheeled away.

"Your flowers," he said softly as he bowed her through the door. "Dragon Home by a private courier."

Ahni nodded without speaking, slipped a cash card into the man's hand. "I would like to know the identity of anyone interested in me." She didn't wait for his nod, passed through the door and crossed the inner atrium, beneath an Earthly full moon and Milky Way. Northern hemisphere constellations on this platform, of course. Her door opened for her, warm yellow light filled the room, and soft cello murmured in the background. Someone had turned her bed down, left a single tiny rosebud and a chocolate on the pillow. She sniffed it, smiled at the pheromone load. Laced with a transitory chip so that the hotel could keep track of her. She dropped it into recycle, left her sandals near the door and sat down crosslegged on the dense rug, the spider silk whispering against her skin. Dropped into Pause, the room vanishing. Searched for a public access for Li Zhen. Found one. "Honored cousin, Li Zhen, I wish to thank you for your so very lovely flowers," she said in precise Beijing Mandarin, using all the traditional flourishes of antique etiquette. "You do me much more honor than my worthless self deserves. I humbly wish to express my gratitude to you in person, and perhaps chat about your friend, my esteemed brother Xai Huang. At your convenience. And again, I humbly thank you for your lovely gift of these flowers."

She ended the link, then began to research the platform secession movement. Too bad she hadn't guessed the open sesame for the meeting this evening. She would like to be a fly on the wall right now. Negotiations for post-secession trade? The orbital lobby for independence had been gaining ground with the World Council. What did it have to do with Xai? Too tired to think anymore, she let her clothes puddle around her feet, climbed under the silk comforter and pulled it over her. Before she could even turn over, she was asleep.

EIGHT

IN THE MORNING, AHNI WENT BACK TO THE PARK WHERE she met Noah. Time to take him up on his invitation to play games in microG, where there would be witnesses if Xai or Li Zhen showed up. It was too early for the lunch crowd he sold to, but he was there, playing a thready melody on a small flute, his portable grill propped against a spreading oak tree. Too large for the space, Ahni thought and realized as her fingertips brushed the rough bark that the crown and branches were holo, that only the bottom part of the trunk was real. Birds even flitted among the branches and a fat gray squirrel chittered at her.

"Hey, you're up early." Noah scrambled to his feet, pocketing his flute. "Did you get some breakfast yet? I've got half a melon. Real nice one."

"Thanks," she said, and took the thick orange slice he handed her. "Are you working, or can we sneak off?" She wiped juice from her chin. "I really want to try your ball game."

"Let's go." He bounded to his feet. "People off this six-hour have had breakfast if they're just getting up, or they're done with dinner, and the park'll be filling up. I was just about to head up there. Cleo—my girlfriend—she'll already be up there, getting together a good pickup scrum. She's an addict." He chuckled as he leaned his pack up against the tree beside his grill and scrubbed his hands on his singlesuit. "I bet you'll pick it up in a sec."

"You just going to leave that there?" She nodded at the pack.

"Yeah." He looked puzzled. "Why not?"

That said a lot right there. About this world up here in her sky. She smiled. "Why not."

They took the elevator upward and when it beeped at them, she slipped into the padded straps as if she had done it every day of her life. This time, when the door slid open at the axle, she squinted automatically, but it wasn't necessary. The air was bright, with a harsh brilliance that the 'sunlight' in the park and the light in the corridors didn't have, but it was quite bearable. No green here, no planted tubes. Instead, thick cables crisscrossed the space. Lots of room to fly and that's what people were doing.

Off to her right, a woven lattice offered hand and toe holds along a string of kiosks selling squeezes of juice, tea, and water, skewered snacks, and bright nylon backpacks with small directional air jets for propulsion and steering. "For the tourists." Noah's lip curled. "You got cables all over the place."

The brightly colored cables seemed to crisscross randomly at first sight, but Ahni noticed that they enclosed several large spherical patches of clear air. In the one just beyond the kiosks and elevator terminal, five skinny figures darted about like thrown spears. Fascinated, Ahni anchored herself with one hand and watched the game. Sure enough . . . they used a ball, although it had two grip loops attached. A stiff mesh bag hung not too far from where she drifted. One of the players grabbed the ball by a loop, her foot twined around a cable, gave the ball a two handed jerk that whipped the man gripping the other loop head over heels. He lost his grip and she was off in a second, kicking off the stiff cable and soaring straight for the bag, the others angling in on trajectories to cross hers.

She snagged a bright blue cable as she sped by, whipped around it, and shot off at an angle, feet first, toes pointed, evading her closing pursuers neatly and earning a hoot of frustration from the closest, who grabbed, missed, and spun out of control, grabbing for cables just out of his reach. The ball handler spun 180 degrees around another cable, but this one gave too much to her pull and sent her spiraling, close to out of control. The opposing players were on her now, yelling as they arrowed in, deflecting the ball handler's teammates who hurtled in to run interference so that they went tumbling, grabbing for cables to kill their momentum, rebounding as they slammed into cables and one another. No helmets, Ahni noticed and winced as a player connected face first with a shoulder at full speed. Rough game.

With a whoop, Noah launched himself on a flat, shallow trajectory that would take him past the bag. The ball handler caught a cable, whipped around it, and used her momentum to shoot the ball on a perfect intersecting trajectory to Noah. He snagged it, somersaulted around another cable, spilling a lot of momentum, and spun himself feet first toward the bag.

Yelling, two of the other team hurtled toward him, certain to deflect him before he connected.

Ahni shrugged, grinned, and kicked off hard from the cable she'd anchored to. It was stiffer than she had guessed, with less give, and she rocketed forward, almost out of control but not quite. Her aim was good and the pair of interceptors weren't watching for her. She tucked her head, hit the first one hard with her shoulder, heard his yelp as he spun, momentum transferring, caroming off her like a cue ball on a pool table. She'd imparted enough of her force that he hit his teammate. Not hard, but it deflected his trajectory and there was nothing for him to catch, to correct it. Yelling, he missed Noah by a handful of centimeters, writhing wildly as he tried to close that tiny gap.

With a howl of victory, Noah slammed the ball into the bag and tucked into a series of diminishing somersaults. The other players had spilled their momentum and rescued floundering teammates. They converged on Ahni now, radiating satisfied aggression, pleasure, and curiosity in equal amounts.

"Cheater, Noah! You weren't playing!"

"Neither was she!"

"Would have been if you'd waited." Noah grinned. "And Cleo was short, so I figure she'd pick me. I told you!" Noah reached Ahni first, arrowing back to spill most of his momentum on a nearby cable and kill the rest with a resounding slap on her back that sent her tumbling, out of control. "This is Ahni. A friend of mine. Not bad for a downsider, huh?"

Ahni sensed what was coming and tucked herself into a roll, just as a pair of hands connected and shoved.

She shot away from the push, felt another, less powerful connection that this time that sent her spinning sideways. Initiation? She closed her eyes as blue and green cables spun around her and nausea spiked in her gut. Waiting to see if she panicked? Flailed? Another contact, this time from someone in motion, so that they shared the momentum and she spun off in a new direction. Her stomach protested and she squelched the sensation. How to win? She cracked her eyelids, focused on fleeting glimpses. A cable coming. If nobody hit her . . .

Fingertips brushed her, but the pusher had misjudged the trajectory. Now! She flung out her arms, back arching, her straightline path wavering, momentum faltering a hair. The cable slapped her palm and she clamped her fingers around it, readying herself for the jerk on her shoulder joint, her muscles flexing with it, taking up the shock. She whipped around, momentum spilling, and grinned. "Cool." She laughed. "You do this to all the new kids on the block?"

The skinny rope-and-bone girl who had headed for the basket laughed with her, diamond inlays glinting in her teeth. "Next game, she's on my team!"

"I brought her here, Cleo. She's mine." Noah drifted up beside her, grinning, totally pleased with himself. "Okay, beer is on me. Tell Jacques at the stand." He winked at Ahni, offered her a hand. "Nice save. You sure you never saw scrum before?"

"Sure I have." Ahni grinned and grabbed his wrist. "It's called 'pool' downside. And we're not the balls."

Noah laughed, planted his foot against the cable, swung her into a sharp arc and launched her.

Ahni had the presence of mind to let go of his wrist and look ahead to see where she was going. Right toward the kiosks, with the rest of the scrum players in a loose scatter around her. She had a moment or two to watch a couple of them deftly grab cables, spinning around them to increase momentum, then arrowing off precisely toward the next cable, zig-zagging feet-first toward their goal. She tried it, did a sloppy launch on the first one, barely had enough momentum to reach the next cable, did better there, and managed to reach the kiosk under her own power, if not as neatly or as quickly as the rest. From the corner of her eye, she caught a glimpse of a couple of young kids playing tag . . . maybe ten years old. They darted like fish and looked sort of like Koi.

"Your downside shows," the diamond-toothed Cleo said when Ahni caught the guiding cables that fenced the kiosks. "But you do okay for all that."

"Ah, she needs practice, is all." A skinny man with a fuzz of bright red hair and freckles handed her a squeeze.

Ahni looked for the kids, but they had vanished. She stuck the spout of the squeeze in her mouth. "Good," she said, swallowing rich, bitter beer.

"Friend of ours makes it, sells it here." The redheaded man poked his chin toward one of the kiosks. "I'm Paul." He gripped her wrist.

"Ahni." One by one they introduced themselves, gripped her wrist. Cleo, Noah's scrum-addict girlfriend, worked the Con, too, along with Illie, the other girl, a near albino with lavender eyes. Paul made and sold fruit wine locally, the other two players, Jose and Von, worked in Security, one in Customs and the other on patrol. They carried their beers to one of several loose hammocks of netting strung around the kiosks, perched there, one ankle woven through the mesh, orienting in the same direction.

"We're here every day," Cleo told Ahni. "Just hop on up. You gonna be here for awhile?"

"I don't know how long I'll be around." Ahni grinned. "But I'll be back. That was fun."

"Good way to do some bump and bang, you know?" Illie spoke up, her voice a rich, jazz-singer alto that didn't go with her snow-queen color. "Get rid of it when you're about ready to hit someone."

"Some of these creeps heating up the Con oughta come up here more," Von wiped sweat from his ebony face with the front of his singlesuit. "Energy level is getting hot, down at the skin."

"That stuff's not all for real." Noah sucked the last drops from his squeeze. "Some of it's ghosts. Whole bunch all of a sudden." He shrugged. "Some wise ass dicking around."

"Ghosts?" Ahni finished her own beer.

"People hacking a fake persona, pretending to be real in the Con. You can do it, but the system catches you eventually. Too hard to create really solid ghosts. Keyboard patterns, word use, syntax—they all give you away eventually, and your real name starts showing up. We've got a couple of real virtuosos playing hide and seek in there, though."

"So who cares?" Cleo made a face, flashing her diamonds. "You know the type—got to prove they can get around the game—they got a bigger dick than you do. Kids and hormones. Doesn't have anything to do with people getting ticked off skinside."

"Well, we're sure having a lot more trouble with the tourists." Von stuffed his squeeze into a recycle slot on the side of the closest kiosk. "Everybody's touchy and I don't know how many complaints we got just this last week. From silly stuff to a couple of actual fights—like punches, right there in public space. Heavies don't have *any* manners." Shaking his head, he waggled his fingers. "I'm off. On shift in a couple of hours. Stuff to do." With a precise thrust of his foot against the webbing of the hammock, he arrowed away toward the elevator.

"I think you just got sort of a compliment." Illie winked at Ahni. "He forgot you're a downsider."

"I figured." Ahni made a face. "I'd better go, too." She disposed of her own squeeze. "Thanks for the intro. Next game I'll buy." She pushed off and headed for the elevator, looking vainly for the kids she had seen earlier.

HER CORN-ROWED DOORMAN was on duty and watching for her. "A private courier from Dragon Home is waiting for you," he told her. "Would you like me to inform him that you are back?"

"Urgent?" Ahni raised her eyebrows.

"Didn't say so." The man shook his head. "The hotel would have contacted you if it had been a bonded, urgent message."

Probably not. Ahni hid her smile. Since she hadn't eaten that very enticing chocolate on her pillow. "Fifteen minutes," she said, because she could smell herself after that brief stint of aerial soccer and she wasn't about to greet a messenger from Dragon Home stinking of sweat. Hurrying now, she crossed the atrium to her room, the door opening to greet her. The faint film of scented powder—right where an intruder would be sure to step into it—was unmarred. The other articles she had left in precarious and strategic locations hadn't been disturbed either. Good. She stripped out of her single-suit, wincing at a host of small aches.

Rough sport. She stood under the multiple shower jets finding the beginnings of tomorrow's bruises as she quickly washed. Great way to work off aggression in a closed little society like this one. Dry, she hesitated, then selected a long, elegant pant dress with a fitted bodice and a high collar, a hand-woven silk brocade in a rich forest green with delicate gold thread embroidery. Very Chinese. Very imposing. This was the time to look the part of The Huang's daughter. "Send the courier," she told the room.

He's on his way, Miss Huang.

A handful of seconds later, the door flickered and seemed to vanish, revealing a small, compact man with a Cantonese face standing in front of the door. "Huang Ahni," he said in English, "I am here to offer you an invitation from Li Zhen to join him for tea." The Courier Union glyph glimmered on his right cheek, a bolt of scarlet lightning in a pearlescent circle that guaranteed safety.

"Open," she said, and the image vanished as the door slid open. "I accept with pleasure."

The Courier bowed again and ushered her to one of the small rental carts available for tourist use. He touched the screen to life, selected a destination, and climbed in beside her.

"I have a shuttle docked here," he told her as the cart took off, threading the crowded corridor at a rapid pace, its sensors whipping it neatly around strolling tourists and hurrying service personnel. He wore a loose, full length jumpsuit, and she eyed it, searching for the cutting edge weaponry that each Courier was required to carry. It was well hidden. He guessed her interest and his internal smile glimmered like quicksilver for an instant. He had the skinny, ropy body and gravity-thick bones of a long-term resident born downside.

They entered a small docking facility that required a vitals pass and a retinal scan before an inner lock admitted them. He led her along a corridor to a numbered door, palmed it open to reveal a small craft stuffed into a closet sized space that barely fit it. It looked like an old fashioned bathtub with a top, Ahni thought. Ugly. The top folded up like wings, to reveal two recliners inside with space behind for minimal cargo. At the Courier's nod she climbed down into the craft and pulled the webbing harness across her. It tightened and lights glowed as the hatch winged closed. "I'd like to see out," Ahni said mildly.

The Courier nodded. Instantly the upper hull vanished, leaving Ahni with the disquieting feeling that she was indeed sitting in a bathtub. At that moment, the dock port irised open and the little shuttle zoomed backward into the void.

Eerie to move and feel no wind, no rush of passage. Not to mention that they were floating in vacuum that would wring them to dry husks in an instant. Ahni drew a deep breath, damping the rush of adrenaline into her bloodstream, using a moment of Pause to control her reaction. Caught that quicksilver glimmer of a smile as the Courier whipped the little craft around and booted it away from the huge hulking curve of NYUp's outer hull.

Damn, that thing was big. Acceleration pushed her into her seat with its invisible palm.

And then . . . Earth came into view. Huge. Blue and white. So close that she stiffened, prepared to fall *down* to it, clutched by its steel arms of gravity. Draw a slow breath. Another. Better. Aware of the Courier watching her, gauging her reaction. "What . . . did you do before you were a Courier?" She managed the voice of calm if not internal tranquility.

"I was an asteroid miner. Got tired of the belt. I have family on Dragon Home."

"What's it like out there?"

"The Belt? Alone."

Alone, not *lonely*. Ahni nodded slowly. "Did you mine metals?"

"Ice." The shuttle tilted and stars swung across Ahni's field of vision, so that she had to swallow hard. Damn her stomach anyway. "Look." He gestured with his chin.

At first she couldn't figure out what he was pointing out. Then she saw it, the matte black of a ship shape trailing a lacy veil that glittered as it caught the light.

"Solar flare due tomorrow . . . X class," he said. "That'll help keep your genes good for the next generation."

"What is it?" She squinted, spied one . . . no, two more of the dark ships trailing lace.

"Ice crystals. Melt the ice, spray it out. Makes a curtain to shield the platform. For awhile." His grin tinged his words. "Steady job, ice."

Up ahead, another vast shape obscured the stars, began to eclipse the sun. Dragon Home. Indistinguishable from NYUp, it rotated slowly, majestically, just fast enough to give skinside residents a good percentage of Earthnormal gravity without creating a problem for the fragile primate inner ear. Small craft zipped around it, glittering in the sun, vanishing into the darkness of its shadow. Silver balloons garlanded it. "What are those round things?" Ahni asked.

"Storage bladders. You fill 'em with ice or refined metal, drop 'em down the gravity well to your catcher out of Darkside. You stay up there and keep mining."

She felt an echo of that *alone* in his voice.

"Saved my credit, wanted to bring my sister up here, and her daughter. She's a professor and my niece could be one. There are no jobs down there and we could use her up here." An edge of bitterness threaded his mild words. "Can't do it. All those years I saved, they don't matter."

"Why not?"

"Too many people. Dragon Home won't take new resident families. Neither will Euro Two and NYUp. We've hit the limit unless we expand."

"Why not expand?" Anhi flinched as they dove beneath the garlanded balloons. They were big . . . everything was bigger than it seemed. Perspective didn't seem to function up here. "Why not just build a new platform if so many people want to live up here?"

"Money. Numbers." The Courier shrugged. "We're saturated with downside corporations. They don't need more space up here. We can't afford to lift downside material for expansion. Not for residential space. You need to drop big rocks down here if you want to have enough resources to build big. Darkside doesn't want us mining the lunar and they're backed by the military. Earth's not gonna let us drop rocks down. Just the refined stuff. We can't refine enough out there to expand."

Another piece to this puzzle, but she had no picture yet. Ahni stifled a gasp as they closed on Dragon Home. It loomed and her brain wanted that to be *up,* screamed at her that it was going to topple over on them, crush them. She closed her eyes, did Pause to still the chemical panic, breathed deeply. Opened her eyes just in time to see a lighted opening in front of them.

The shuttle dove into it, walls sliding past, making her realize just how fast they had to have been moving out there. The Courier halted in a narrow bay nearly identical to the one she had just left, only here, the miscellaneous labels, warnings, and instructions were in Chinese. The Courier touched his invisible controls and after perhaps a minute, the winged hatch folded back and he leaped out, turning to offer her a hand.

She scrambled out, straightened her dress and ran a hand over her short crop. Stepped toward the door at the end of the little dock at the Courier's gesture. It irised open as she approached.

The man standing on the other side was thirty-three, she knew, but Li Zhen looked no older than Xai. Slender with high cheekbones and a long, lanky northern build, only son of China's current Chairman, he smiled at her, bowed slightly as she stepped out of her sandals. "Huang Ahni," he said in upperclass Beijing Mandarin. "Welcome to Dragon Home." He gave her another shallow bow—you are not my equal it said, but you are my guest—and ushered her through the doorway and into the room behind it.

Woven carpets in shades of gold and black accented with lacquer red covered the floor and several chairs of carved wood covered with embroidered cushions circled a low table. An antique square of silk, exquisitely embroidered, hung on the eggshell colored wall. A carved screen hid a refreshment wall. This must be his private dock, she realized. This would be where he greeted visitors, perhaps offered them tea if they were not important enough to deal with in his private rooms.

"So what is your impression of life above the sky?" he asked as he ushered her through an arched doorway. "Your father has never been interested in the orbitals."

"My father keeps his eyes on the ground," Ahni agreed. Polite chit chat, tea, then real talk. They passed through a small garden with a cloudless sky above, all gravel paths and neatly pruned bonsai, with a pool full of gold and silver fish. Koi. She glanced at them. "I find this world . . . fascinating," she said slowly. "It is not Earth."

"You are perceptive."

He was curious. And wary. He would know that she was a Class Nine empath. He himself was a Class Five. Sensitive enough to benefit him as a leader, not sensitive enough to read people clearly. "Have you tried a few games in micro gravity?" He smiled but his eyes glinted with a razor hint of mockery.

"I have indeed." She smiled. "I enjoy exercising the wings of flight. And I envy those born here with such talent to fly." It was a pleasantry, so his spike of reaction surprised her.

She had touched a nerve with this casual comment. Why?

"I rarely have time for childish games," he said crisply. "But then you are on vacation, are you not?" He stood aside to usher her into the room beyond the garden.

This was his private chamber. More rugs covered the floor and the furniture was of lacquer, inlaid with mother of pearl, antiques lifted from Earth. An intricately carved and inlaid screen decorated one corner and a small bamboo plant grew in a celadon pot. Sofa and chairs with heavily embroidered cushions grouped about a low table with an inlaid surface. A tray held a round, imperfect pot and two cups. Ahni seated herself on the sofa, realizing that this furniture was genuinely old, certainly more than a thousand years. Her grandmother could have told her which dynasty had produced it, who the emperors were, and why it ultimately failed. And then she would have rapped Ahni on the knuckles with her fan for not knowing these things.

"Tea?" Li Zhen was already pouring and Ahni realized that the pot was very old, perhaps from the Qin dynasty, shaped on a primitive wheel. How had it survived? Buried in some noble's tomb?

Dug up by looters, perhaps used by some peasant family who bought it cheap in the bazaar because it wasn't perfect and had been in the ground with the dead? Ahni accepted the cup of golden liquid that Li Zhen handed her, murmured thanks. The tea was flowery and delicate, delicious. She sipped it, bowed her thanks. "Very nice. From Earth?"

Li Zhen nodded. "But we grow good tea here. In our internal garden. Much like the one in the North American Alliance platform that you visited. Have you an interest in micro gravity gardening?"

First thrust. "Not really," she said. "I am more interested in those who garden."

"I see." He looked up as a teenaged boy bearing a lacquer tray entered the room. He set several small dishes of tiny dumplings on the table, placed a pair of chopsticks before each of them along with a small plate. Bowed and departed. He looked like Li Zhen.

"Your son?" Ahni asked.

"No." That spike of reaction flared again. "My cousin's son. Please." He gestured at the table. "Help yourself."

Ahni picked up her chopsticks, selected one of the plump dumplings. It burst in her mouth, the tender skin releasing a flood of delicate broth and a filling of chopped pork and green onion. "Excellent." She smiled at him, wondering about those spikes. "Your cook is better than the best dumpling shop in Tai Pei."

"He was a chef in Beijing." Li Zhen took one, gestured at the dish. "These are filled with duck," he said. "Very good. How is your father these days?" He gave her a brief sharp look as he popped a dumpling neatly into his mouth.

"You are right." She smiled. "The duck is very good. My father is . . . concerned about his son. As you perhaps know."

Li Zhen laid aside his chopsticks, sipped his tea thoughtfully. "Friendship is a very complex thing," he mused. "One may amass a certain amount of . . . obligation. And when the time comes to discharge it, one does. It would be distressing to find that one's friend had used that obligation to dishonor his own family."

"Particularly his father." Ahni selected another dumpling.

"But it may be, that one is not aware of the use to which one's assistance may be put."

Ahni nibbled at the dumpling. "Very nice," she said. "Is the spinach from your garden here?"

"Of course. I will give you a tour of our rice paddies if you wish."

"I would like that, another time." She made her tone apologetic. "Alas, I need to speak with my brother, and I must concentrate on finding him first. Do you know where I might contact him?"

Li Zhen deftly selected another dumpling and put it on her plate. "You must try this sweet one. It's a specialty of my chef. I cannot tell you where your brother is." His tone was apologetic.

He was lying, but Ahni made her face reflect resignation. "I am disappointed. I had hoped to . . . restore the situation. You're right. That was excellent." She laid her chopsticks crosswise on her plate. "Your chef is very skilled."

Li Zhen bowed his head fractionally. "Please give your brother my regards when you speak to him," he said. "I would be honored to entertain you both in Dragon Home. Since you have not visited the platforms before."

"Perhaps we will do that." She was tired of the polite circling. "The flowers you sent me were lovely. I enjoyed them."

He acknowledged the point with the slightest hint of a smile. "A gesture of apology," he murmured. "For my inadvertent cooperation in less than honorable behavior."

"I found the combination of scent to be . . . intriguing."

"Ah, the richness of life is always tempered by the knowledge of the grave is it not?" He smiled gently at her.

"How true." She picked up the teapot, poured tea into his cup, unasked. "A pair of assassins stalked me on Earth recently. The threat of the grave is always there, is it not?" She smiled at him. "We cannot spend our lives fearing it."

Li Zhen got up abruptly, crossed to the wall beside the carved screen. At his approach it suddenly shimmered and seemed to become transparent, showing Ahni a layered landscape of corridors above, people, parks, busy manufacturing floors, and finally, the green and hot light of a garden, all overlaid like transparencies one atop the other. "What do you see?" he demanded.

Ahni feigned consideration. Not a test, no. Genuine question.

A tin can? Her father's perspective, a floating outpost in a waste-land above the ground, of no real consequence. She looked with Dane's eyes. She studied the corridors, the ant sized people, the man selling stems of fresh flowers, the woman applying a fiberlight tat-too to a customer from a one-legged table that reminded her of Noah's grill, the rich greens of the garden. "I see a world," she said softly.

"Yes." His eyes lighted as he looked at the bustle of life on the wall. Then he faced her, his eyes holding hers. "I am dismayed that your brother has caused trouble for your family. And I regret that I cannot tell you where he is. I have no argument with Huang Fam-ily. This world—as you so aptly named it—is my entire concern. I encourage you to remain here as my guest, for as long as you wish. This world up here . . . its future is worth contemplation, Huang Ahni."

Genuine invitation and . . . something more? "What is the fu-ture of this world, Zhen Li?"

"It is our tomorrow."

A tickle of cold made the hairs rise on the back of her neck. "My father does not share your vision of tomorrow," she said softly. "Nor does my brother. I think he may have misled you."

"This is a possibility, of course." He lifted the empty teapot from the table. "Take this as my gift." He held it out to her. "It from the tomb of Qin Shi Huang." He smiled, his eyes enigmatic, his emo-tions mixed enough to be unreadable. "You will appreciate it."

"I am honored." She bowed as she took the pot, stunned at the gift, aware of the *age* of it against the skin of her palms. "I thank you for this treasure," she murmured and meant it.

"I will be honored if you accept my invitation." Zhen's eyes were on her. She felt the gaze without needing to lift her eyes from the ancient porcelain in her hands.

"Thank you for inviting me," she said. "I will . . . consider it." The teenaged son of a cousin had appeared at the door, and her visit was obviously at an end. "And thank you for this gift. I will treasure it." Which was truth and she let him hear it.

He didn't answer, merely inclined his head. The son of a cousin led her back through the small reception chamber and her Courier was waiting for her. He didn't say anything as she webbed in and the small dock opened. The hull was still transparent and she almost asked him to opaque it. But she didn't, and on the trip back, cradled the pot in her lap. Qin Shi Huang. More than two thousand years ago he had unified the many warring states into one country, had given them a single currency and language and legal code. From his name, Qin, had come the name of China. He had died at age forty, leaving behind an army of pottery warriors to guard him that still stood watch. And China was whole, still.

Priceless, this pot. She touched it, wondering if that long ago emperor had ever touched it, picked it up with his own hands to pour tea for an honored guest. Beyond the seemingly transparent walls of this mobile bathtub, the blue-white ball of Earth shimmered, partially eclipsed by the dark mass of NYUp. And she tried to feel the connection between this ancient piece of fire-hardened clay in her hands and that planet before her.

She could not, and that troubled her.

NINE

NO SOONER HAD THE BOY USHERED AHNI FROM THE
chamber than part of the wall shimmered and thinned to reveal an
arched doorway, and a bed beyond, covered with a raw silk coverlet.
Xai stepped through the door, threw his head back and laughed.
"My little sister!" He grinned at Li Zhen, threw his arms wide, the
long tail of his midnight hair knotted with ruby strands of fiberlight.
"She is so determined! And the pot. I really think she believed it was
from the old emperor's tomb."

"It was." Li Zhen turned away from him, staring at the layers of
life that still covered the wall.

"Waste of a valuable antique then. She'll cuddle it all the way
back down to give it to Father." Xai's face twisted briefly. "You
know, listening to you, I wonder if I can really trust you, my longtime friend?" He smiled, but his eyes glittered. "You sounded like
some driven monk, talking about tomorrow."

"You have your tomorrow in hand," Li Zhen said mildly, his
eyes still on the wall. "I have mine. They happen to converge for a
time." He turned to smile at Xai. "I would rather your little sister
stay on Dragon Home until you have finished."

"I would rather she did not." Xai stared at him coldly. "Do not interfere with her. I will take it personally."

"Your sister will do exactly as she wishes. Has it occurred to you to ask why she did not reveal your deceit to your father?"

"She wants to be his heir." Xai grinned. "Let her."

"I think you underestimate your sister's subtlety. Remember that you will not kill her, up here." Li Zhen frowned. "How is the slow fire in our sister city?"

"I will not kill her if she is no threat. It is ready to explode." Xai threw himself down on the sofa, rolled onto his side to snatch Ahni's chopsticks from her plate and help himself to a dumpling. "Hire the right person, and your path is made easier."

"How soon?" Li Zhen looked at the door. "Wait."

A moment later, the young cousin's son appeared with a tray and a new pot of tea with two fresh cups. Took away the cups Li Zhen and Ahni had used.

"No antique for me, cousin?" Xai picked up the white pot, tipped it to pour, the stream canting slightly into the cup, a visible reminder of the spin gravity that gave them a *down*. "As to how soon, I don't have that much control. The right incident will take place with the right people in attendance. Already there have been several small . . . skirmishes. And the camera-eyes I tipped off are prowling for blood." He grinned broadly. "You will look so virtuous, cousin, as you humbly step in to save them all. They will worship you and you will have your empire to build your tomorrow in."

"I am not interested in worship." Li Zhen poured himself tea, sipped it reflectively. "Just the Council vote. Where did you find your point of access?"

"Would you give me that information if I asked it of you, cousin?" Xai smiled and crossed his arms behind his head. "There is always a back door and always a key to it that may be purchased. Let us say that my father's money has been well spent, as has my own. The latest word is that a motion is on the table in the World Council to send the CSF to NYUp to maintain order."

"It won't pass." Li Zhen prowled across the chamber, blanked the view of the orbital's many levels. "The Pan Malaysian Compact will vote for the intervention because they are in a quiet trade war with the North American Alliance and would like to see it discomfited. So will the Estados Latinos, simply because they always vote against the NAA unless they have a pressing agenda of their own. Of course my father will vote for it. As will the Taiwan Families, yes?" He raised an eyebrow at Xai.

"Honored Father always votes with the Tiger." Xai grinned. "He is very predictable."

"That is not enough." Li Zhen seated himself, frowning at the bright gleam of the fiberlights in Xai's hair. "You stand out quite nicely in a crowd," he said absently. "Is that clever?"

"Everybody wears light fibers in NYUp." Xai shrugged impatiently. "It's the fashion statement of the moment."

"The vote will not pass." Li Zhen shook his head. "The NAA will vote against it of course. The North Americans have never tolerated outside intervention at all, and the EU always backs the NAA. The Black Sea States always vote against the Pan Malaysian Compact because they are very anti-Muslim." Li Zhen shrugged. "We need two votes. The Black Sea States have two votes."

"Some things have more power than religious intolerance." Xai rolled lithely to his feet. Bowed. "I will see what I can discover by way of my "back door." He hesitated. "There is one complication. The local faction that promotes autonomy on NYUp—NOW—is led by a very strong and charismatic individual."

"Dane Nilsson, the Chief Botanical Engineer for the hydroponic system there." Li Zhen inclined his head. "We have not met, but he has contacted me in the past, wearing the cloak of their secessionist movement. Do not underestimate him."

"I don't." Xai nodded, grinned again, showing the tips of his teeth. "He is in my way. I plan to remove him. Permanently."

"No."

Xai's eyes narrowed at the Chairman's tone. "Why not? He conceivably could complicate matters. He has a large and very loyal following there."

"Precisely." Zhen folded his hands, unsmiling. "If you kill him, he becomes a martyr. It is dangerous to create a martyr. They are immortal. And untouchable. Better to destroy the man before he becomes a martyr."

"And just how do you plan to do that?"

The Chairman smiled slowly. "I have an arrow that will destroy the man and his chance at martyrdom."

"What arrow?"

Li Zhen smiled. "You gave it to me."

Xai scowled. "Just shoot that arrow soon, will you? I can fine tune the moment when events proceed, but only so far. Nilsson may be able to stop it."

"The arrow has already left the bow." Zhen rose to his feet. "Do you need transportation back to the orbital?"

"No." Xai gave him a brief hard glance. "I do not. I hope it's a swift arrow."

He left unceremoniously, and for a long time Li Zhen stared after him, frowning thoughtfully.

TEN

THE COURIER DROPPED HER AT THE SMALL DOCKING BAY where he had picked her up. Ahni frowned as she exited the dock to find a glowing lavender arrow on the floor beneath her feet. Damn. The hotel had managed to sneak a chip into her after all. Well, it didn't really matter. She wasn't trying to hide from anyone.

But it still annoyed her, because usually she was canny enough to avoid house-chips. She blinked up the schematic for this level, deciding to walk back to her hotel. The visit with Li Zhen had left her troubled. He had not been lying the entire time, but he was connected to Xai for all his protest of innocence. The conversation made her think of an iceberg, the lethal mass invisible beneath the waves, only the white, picturesque tip gleaming in the sun. It had to do with the secession movement. She was sure of that. What did Xai stand to gain here?

Gently she touched the fragile curve of the pot. And what was the subtext here?

One did not give away a priceless heirloom to a casual guest.

Before she had strolled more than a dozen meters from the dock, the tension in the air penetrated her awareness, banishing her contemplation of the pot. Ahni paused in front of a closet-sized shop front displaying microG manufactured personal electronics and offering right-now implantation. Casually she studied the passersby. The tourists were oblivious, but the business folk walked with shoulders slightly hunched, their steps hurried. They felt it, too, or maybe they were just noticing a change in attitude.

It hit her suddenly what she was noticing . . . staring. And crowding. Not all the natives, but enough that she noticed. And she also noticed that the natives who were *not* staring and crowding were noticing it, too, radiating dismay, or disapproval. Or approval and mimicking it. She saw quite a few people pass a crowder, notice, approve, and then crowd the next tourist they passed. Up and down the corridor tourists were walking a crooked path, taking unconscious little sidesteps as a native swerved too close.

One man marched down the hall, body language erect, pushy, radiating challenge, pushing every tourist coming toward him a half step off course. A native woman approaching him, a very dark afro-mix, noticed and her approval sparked bright in the air. As she passed, she aimed for a Korean businessman approaching. The poor man, clearly sensitive, took nearly a full step sideways and stumbled, obviously not adept in the less than normalG.

The tall pushy man's response flared.

Score!

Ahni nearly turned to look at him, stilled her automatic reaction. He was doing this on purpose. Enticing others to do it, too. A memory prodded. Noah's girlfriend—what was her name? Cleo. Ahni drifted on a few meters to watch a skinny boy getting his nails inlaid with gold. Cleo had reacted to something Noah had said about ghosts, about fake personae in the Con. And then she had said that it had nothing to do with the tension. But what if it was coupled with people like the alpha she had just seen? Start provoking downsiders and sooner or later someone would react.

A shape flung itself at Ahni. She pivoted, ready to defend herself, recognized the dark hair and oval face of Donya, the child on the climber, and wrenched her response under control.

"Ahni, Ahni, Ahni!" The girl leaped up against her chest, arms around Ahni's neck, slender ankles locked behind her back. "I looked for you everywhere!"

Ahni smiled for her, shaky with aborted violence. The tension here was affecting her. "Donya!" She managed a cheerful tone. "You shouldn't startle people like that. Are you enjoying your stay?"

"It's boring." Donya pouted. "Kelly is doing this intern program with some engineer or other and he's being a butt. I'm just a little kid and he doesn't have any time for me at all. And my nanny has to go with me everywhere and she's not a native and Mama won't hire a native because she's convinced I'll get kidnapped or raped or something. I want to go fly." She gave Ahni a sly smile. "You know how to do that, right?"

"Yes, I do." Ahni smiled. "But I think maybe . . . not this trip. Your parents are right. This isn't a good time to wander around on the upper levels."

"Ahni, that's not fair!" Donya's face took on a stony stubbornness. "You promised me."

"I did not." Ahni held her gaze until the girl looked away.

"Well, okay, you didn't promise. But . . . Oh, never mind." She turned away, sulky. "You're just like all the other grownups after all."

"What would your parents do to your nanny if she let you do something they thought was dangerous?" Ahni asked gently. She watched Donya think about that.

"Yeah, you win." She gave Ahni a narrow look as the worried nanny charged up, frightened and scolding. Donya smiled. "See? I wasn't lost. I was talking to Ahni. See you later!" she called, waving, as the frustrated nanny dragged her away.

What a handful. Ahni smiled absently, then focused on the issue at hand. Time to find a safe way to visit the axle. The hotel chip complicated matters. Thinking hard, Ahni returned to her hotel to dress in clothes that looked more like local garb and didn't shout "tourist." She rode the elevator up to Noah's park, jumpy in the confined space as the tourists vanished. Not even the business travelers seemed willing to brave the upper levels. Ahni made her body language as unassuming and invisible as she could, but was aware of hostile attention as people got on and off.

Noah wasn't at his plaza, so she took the elevator clear up to the axle park. A few tourists floundered around amongst the criss-crossed web of colorful cables and Ahni noticed uniformed Security lounging nearby, obviously watchful. She had seen no Security yesterday. As she pulled herself toward the scrum fields, a small dark girl kicked off and soared toward her.

Donya! Ahni recognized her this time, winced at the bright flare of her triumph.

"Catch me!" The girl flung out her hand as her trajectory took her past Ahni. Clutching the nearest cable, Ahni grabbed her wrist, swung her into a tight inward spiral.

Donya grabbed the cable and got herself stopped. "Now the nanny won't get in trouble," she crowed, grinning.

"What the hell are you doing here?"

The girl met her glare with an innocent smile. "You were right. Nanny couldn't risk taking me places my folks don't want me. So I gave her the slip."

"So she's still in trouble."

"Well." Donya lifted one shoulder in a perfect native shrug. "It was really easy to slip her, so maybe she deserves being fired. I mean . . . what if someone really had kidnapped me?"

Ahni rolled her eyes and Donya's smile blossomed.

"So come on! Look!" She spun and pointed. "They're playing ball. Have you done that?"

Sure enough, Noah and his friends were at it, zooming like mis-siles across the open space between the cables. Without waiting for Ahni's reply, the girl planted both feet against the cable and pushed off, hurtling through the maze of cables and smack into the center of the playing zone. "Look out, kid," the red haired Paul yelled as he hurtled by. "Get off the field."

Donya made a grab for the ball, missed and yelped as Noah shot past on an intersecting trajectory, one lean wiry forearm clamping around her waist. His trajectory wobbled and faltered, but still took him out of the play zone, the yelling Donya clamped firmly under one arm. Ignoring her shouts and pummeling fists, he snagged a cable, planted one bare foot, and shot straight over to Ahni.

"Does this belong to you?" A smile glimmered beneath his severe tone. "You need to keep it on a leash."

"I am not an 'it' and if you let me play, I bet I can do really well." Released just out of reach of the cable, Donya floundered, glaring. "I saw other kids out here playing."

"Yeah, but they live here. Sweetheart, you have the guts for it." Noah nudged himself lower, so that he faced her on eye level. "And you can sure play, but you need to practice first. It's not fair to bust up our game and if you do something we don't expect, you'll get hit hard and we could both get hurt."

"Yeah." She looked down and away. "Sorry. I was rude. But I . . . just want to play so much and nobody will *let* me. I really *am* sorry."

"S'right." Noah gave Ahni a wan smile. "I was gonna take a break anyway. I'll give you a few pointers, okay?"

Ahni swallowed frustration. She needed to talk to Dane but she couldn't leave this kid to wander around on her own. Noah had tugged Donya into motion, was instructing her on how to push off and regulate her speed, how to change her trajectory in flight and use the cables to increase or spill momentum. While she waited for him to finish his lesson, Ahni dropped briefly into Pause and called up demographics on NYUp reproduction. Donya had made her realize how few young children she had seen, even on the upper level she had visited.

Interesting. The birth rate was significantly lower than normal for the overall downside population. Radiation? Less family orientation? She wondered how many pregnancies ended before term. Hacking medical information wasn't easy, cheap, or safe. She emerged from Pause as Noah and Donya arrowed back to her, Donya radiating disappointment.

"Come down another time," Noah was saying. "And I'll give you another lesson. You do really well for a downsider." He gave Ahni a lopsided smile. "Your relative?"

"Not mine." Ahni fished a cash card from her singlesuit, handed it to Donya. "You want to get yourself a squeeze of juice?"

"Thank you." Donya took the card and made her way speedily if not quite accurately, to the refreshment kiosk. "I hope she doesn't get beer." Ahni sighed, and examined Noah from the corner of her eye. Something was bothering him.

"Noah, I have a question for you."

"Sure." He drifted closer, his eyes warming as he looked after Donya who had landed safely at the kiosk. "Nice kid. What's up?"

"In all honesty . . . how difficult would it be for someone to jack their way into the Con in a big way? Maybe replicate a large number of ghosts? If money was no object?"

The hot slash of his response nearly made her flinch. Outwardly he didn't move, merely stared at his hand, closed white-knuckled around the nearest cable. "What difference would it make it some-one did?" His tone was flat, even. His emotions were not. "Sure they could plant some misinformation, but you start talking to peo-ple, you find out the truth. It isn't really going to do any harm."

He was asking her.

Donya was on her way back, sucking on her juice squeeze, ex-perimenting with motion and the cables. "If there were enough ghosts," Ahni said softly. "And they were . . . say . . . spreading anger . . ."

"You couldn't do that. You can't just make people . . . feel dif-ferently." Noah kicked off and zoomed back into the rough game.

Thoughtfully, Ahni watched him collide hard with Jose, heard the security guard's exclamation as he went tumbling off course. Too late to ask him if he'd told Dane she wanted to see him. Shook her head. "Okay kid." She turned her attention back to Donya. "I've aided and abetted you enough here. Time to go back and face the parents before they call Security out to scour the whole can."

"You know they're never going to let me out of our hotel room after this." The girl regarded her morosely.

"Probably not."

"They think there are weird people up here. There are weird people everywhere. Well, at least I got to fly." Donya shrugged, sto-ically. "And he said I was good."

Ahni laughed in spite of herself and caught hold of Donya's wrist. "Okay, kid, let's go. If I get arrested for kidnapping, I hope you'll set them straight before they throw me in jail."

"I will," Donya said cheerfully. "Don't worry."

"Now that the game is over, you might want to link and leave them a message that you're alive," Ahni suggested as they reached the elevator.

"I did that while I was waiting for the juice." She rolled her eyes. "They didn't even know I was gone yet. Nanny's probably still out looking, poor thing. I told Father that he should let her know it was okay to quit and that it wasn't really her fault. I'm very clever. They know that." She gave Ahni a sideways look. "Father didn't blame her too much. He says sometimes that if he believed in demons he would worry about me." She smiled, warm with smug certainty. "He doesn't really mean that, but he wasn't too mad."

"Your father is a wise man," Ahni said dryly. She shrugged into the padded straps in the elevator. Only natives got on at the first few levels as the elevator dropped. Ahni pretended indifference and sorted through the emotional tone. How would it go? You hear a hot bit of gossip about a nasty little encounter, another heavyweight putting down a shopkeeper, harassing a cleaner, spitting on a clumsy aide, maybe even rape. And you get angry. And you talk about it with your neighbor, your coworker, your lover. Did you hear about . . .

Stones tossed into a pond, she thought. Toss enough stones and you have a choppy, stormy sea. You could buy stones. You could buy someone to toss 'em. Noah had run from her.

They exited on the skinside level, the harsh reek of hostility muted here. The scent of sizzling olive oil wafted from a little sit-down restaurant. Donya dragged her feet, sniffing like one of Tai Pei's protected feral dogs, down on the docks. "I told Father that I wanted to stop and eat lunch." She looked hopefully at Ahni. "He's got my chip under surveillance, so he said it was okay. I'm really not making that up," she said, without a whole lot of hope.

Ahni smiled at her. "I know you're not."

Donya got it instantly. "You're E-rated. That's so *cool*." Her eyes widened. "Are you really high? A ten? So what am I thinking right now?"

"You don't know what people *think*." Ahni steered her firmly into the little restaurant. "You've seen too many vids. But I know when people tell the truth. Or when they lie." She hid a smile as she watched Donya cast back over their conversations. The place served a nice vegetarian menu. Grilled vegetables. Tofu in various forms as well as a classic gardenburger with realmilk, upported cheese, according to the menu.

She ordered a salad with smoked tofu while Donya ordered the gardenburger and grumbled about the lack of meat. Father wouldn't let her order it. Too expensive. Five little round tables crowded elbow to elbow in the tiny space, each with a vase of opalescent vacuum glass holding a single pink rose. Ahni hadn't seen roses in Dane's kingdom, but she bet they were there somewhere. They took their cycleware platters to an empty table, collecting utensils and drinks on the way. Donya had loaded her burger up with sauces and greens until it resembled a small urban tower and threatened to succumb to gravity in a soggy mound. Ahni forked up her salad noticing that the greens lacked any sort of onion and no garlic flavored the vinaigrette dressing. Odor?

At the next table a young couple held hands, natural Mediterraneans both of them, newlyweds or new lovers to be sure. She smiled at the drift of pheromones slowly filling the small space. He leaned forward to caress her hand, his skin the color of honey, his dark eyes sparkling as he lifted her hand, turned it palm up and lowered his head to kiss her wrist. Her long fingers with their lacquered and inlaid nails curved to caress his cheekbone, the dark fringe of her lashes brushing her tawny cheek. Every person in the restaurant shifted and sighed and Ahni smiled into her salad. Only Donya seemed oblivious.

He pulled her to her feet. She wore her hair long, parted in the middle and swept back to an intricate knot at the base of her skull. A tiny pale lizard perched on it, ruby eyes blinking slowly, throat pulsating, its scales like slices of pearl.

"Oh, look, she has one of those jewel lizards." Donya bounced in her seat, the sloppy ruins of her burger abandoned. "They're illegal in North America. I wonder if she got it up here."

At that moment, a narrow-faced native in a grimy singlet pushed past the couple, bumping into the woman hard enough to press himself briefly and quite explicitly against her. She recoiled with a gasp of shock. The native quite openly grabbed her breast through the gauzy fabric of her shift. She squeaked. Her husband thrust himself forward, trembling between action and inaction.

The native said something to him in a low voice.

The Mediterranean threw an awkward, looping punch. It was a joke, Donya could have ducked it . . . but the native went down, knocking over the nearest table. Dishes flew, splashing two native women at a nearby table who shrieked and scrambled out of the way. On the floor, splattered with food, he groaned.

Crimson blood blossomed on his face and this time, the Mediterranean woman screamed, a shrill nail-rake of sound in the tight space. Diners were on their feet now, mostly natives, Ahni noticed suddenly. Only she, and Donya, and the honeymoon couple were tourists.

"Wow." Donya pushed forward. "He didn't hit him that hard."

"Keep your damn fists to yourself, heavyweight." A broad native with a lot of lanky muscle shoved forward. "Who the hell do you think you are, coming up here, pushing us around, eh?"

"He . . . he assaulted my wife." The man had gone pale, took a half step back from the native's out thrust face and hunched, threatening shoulders. "I didn't hit him that hard."

"Someone call Emergency," a petite woman at a nearby table shrieked. "He's bleeding to death!"

Faces gathered at the door, the news got yelled back, out into the corridor. Ahni peered through the small window, her gut cold. Where the hell had the crowd come from, and so quickly? Ahni grabbed Donya's arm as the girl pushed toward the fallen man and the tourist who was now the center of a shouting knot of diners.

"He's dead," someone screamed. "Oh my God, he killed him."

Which was patently false. Ahni could see the heave of his chest from here. She quick-blinked into Pause, scanned the local schematics, blinked out. "We're out of here," she hissed in Donya's ear. "Right now."

"But—" Donya tried to pull away, but Ahni twisted her arm just enough to wring a gasp and compliance from her, aimed her at the narrow door to the kitchen. Back door, service alley, fast way out before this blew up. Behind her the woman screamed again, long and loud this time, fear piercing the air. "That way. Go!" She shoved the uncooperative Donya summarily toward the kitchen.

And felt Xai.

He was out there. Behind her. In the corridor. She hesitated, almost turned back. But to get out there meant going straight through the knot of seething violence in the center of the restaurant. The woman was screaming wildly now and red violence fogged the air. Where the hell was Security? "Go!" She shoved the girl so hard she stumbled, burst with her through into a flash-image of crowded space, heat, steam, food smells, blank, stunned faces and wide eyes, shock, surprise, and fear. Pushed on through, leading with her shoulder, dragging Donya now, who kept trying to turn and look back.

Back door, service alley. Ahni erupted into it, looked both ways. Delivery pods, sealed recycle bins coded for processing.

"Did you see that? Did you see what was going on? People were bleeding!" Donya trotted with her down the corridor, breathless with excitement. "How did you know that this was back here. Are you a spy? This is so *cool*."

"You want to go back and join the fun?" Anhi snapped as they approached the intersecting corridor that would take them to an unmarked door into the man promenade not far from the riot. "You can bleed, too."

"I'm a kid." Donya sniffed. "Nobody hurts kids. Wow, cool." She peered into the distance as they exited into the promenade between a massage station and a small luxurious food store. "We can go back and see what's going on."

"No way."

"Look, there's Security." She pointed at a narrow wedge of uniformed people penetrating the mob around the restaurant.

Good. Ahni paused, one hand clamped around Donya's arm, stretching her senses for Xai. Yeah, that way. Right through the middle of the riot and out the other side. And he was moving away from them. She cursed softly, voicelessly. "Hey!" She spotted another trio of Security headed in the direction of the riot. Waved. "We need help!"

The threesome, intent on the violence ahead, nearly didn't stop. She was dressed like a native, not like an Elite. "This tourist girl nearly got hurt in the riot. She's lost."

"I am—"

"Shut up," Ahni hissed. "This is bigger than you. Help me."

One of the threesome peeled off, reluctantly, giving her distracted attention. He was young, like Jose, the scrum player. "She got separated from her nanny," Ahni said breathlessly, helplessly. "Her folks are up here doing consulting work for NYUp. She's scared!" Pinched Donya's arm. Hard.

"I don't know where Nanny went!" The girl, bless her, did a wonderful sniffle and scared-little-girl voice. "I don't know where she's staying."

The Security guy had whipped out a scanner. Blinked at Ahni. "You're not chipped?"

"Huang, Taiwan Families," Ahni said impatiently. Only up here would someone even ask. "Will you take charge of her? It would be ugly if something happened to her, I'm sure."

He cast an anxious glance toward the riot. The crowd was already thinning, the action clearly over. "Yeah, I'd better." He reached for Donya's hand. "Come on, little girl, let's go see if we can get you safely back to Mom and Dad, okay?"

"Thank you," Donya murmured demurely, giving Ahni a "you owe me" look.

Ahni winked. "Thanks so much, I was so worried." Then she turned and hurried off, ignoring the Security's call for her to wait.

Focusing, she reached for her brother, found a trace of him, faint, fading rapidly. Damn. The crowd was dispersing, most people hurrying away, others standing around in small, huddled groups, talking or speaking into personal links. Con will be buzzing, she thought. The emotional fog in the corridor was bad enough. She spied a media cam, his forehead camera eye fixed on the door of the restaurant. Oh great. She pushed past two women in business suits who barely glanced at her, their conversation intense and threaded with worry. The corridor was clearer here, and she broke into a trot, ignoring the startled and disapproving looks she got. Straining, she groped for her brother, touched the merest whisper of his presence, halted as she reached an intersecting corridor. Which way? Stretching her senses to the limit, trying to pinpoint the origin of that faint tickle, she took a few hesitant steps down the corridor.

Gone. He had moved out of her range of perception.

She turned to go back to the main corridor when a shadow moved at the edge of her vision, someone hiding in a shallow service bay. Ahni spun, ready to strike.

"Dane!" She halted, trembling. Twice in one day. If she wanted a barometer of the mood in this place, this was it. "Oh, I am *so* glad to see you. I've been looking for you. Did Noah tell you?"

"Noah finally remembered to tell me. We need to talk, Ahni."

"Where?" she said. "My hotel room is on this level."

"Up at the axle. That's safer."

"I'm carrying a hotel chip. That's why I didn't come up there."

"Not a problem." He smiled faintly. "I can deal with that."

"How's Koi?"

"He misses you." Dane searched her face. "Why did you come back up here, Ahni?"

"To stop whatever my brother is doing." She held his pewter gaze.

Dane's eyes softened. "I'm glad you came back." He leaned forward suddenly and kissed her lightly on the mouth. She caught her breath, mouth opening, heat flushing through her, tasting him, the corridor, the riot, fading in an instant.

Reluctantly, he pushed her away. "I'll see you at the axle," he said, his voice husky. Then he stepped into the corridor and vanished into the thinning crowd.

Dizzy, Ahni searched for any hint of Xai, found nothing but the crackling static of a lot of upset people. Her blood pulsed with the aftermath of that kiss as she plotted her way to the nearest elevator. As she entered the main corridor, she found a cordon of Security keeping people back, their emotional signature jagged.

Two members trotted a lightweight gurney down the corridor. A sheet covered the body on it.

ELEVEN

THE ELEVATOR RIDE UP SEEMED TO TAKE FOREVER. ONLY a scattered handful of men and women got on and off the elevator as it rose. They didn't look at her at all, their focus inward, or fixed on eyelid screens. The Con, she guessed. Buzzing. The last one exited as they reached the final "open" level. From here on up you had to have access. This time, she didn't have to override the security.

The warning chimed, she donned the straps, and felt weight vanish from the universe. The door finally irised open and that familiar green wash of light flooded her. Almost before the door had completely opened, Koi shot through it, handed off into a perfect backward somersault from the wall beside her, killed his momentum in a rebound off the ceiling and ended up perfectly still and upside down facing her, eye to eye, his grin so wide it threatened to split his face.

"You have lovely molars," Ahni said, peering into his mouth and trying vainly to hide a smile. "Nice to see you, too, Koi."

"I knew you'd come back, no matter what Dane said." He shivered and drifted sideways, ushering her out the elevator door. Then, with a whoop, he kicked off from the side of the elevator and arrowed away, looping and rolling, deflecting his momentum with the merest stretch of a limb or touch to one of the tubes. The scrum players had seemed incredibly skillful, but now she realized that they weren't a whole lot more skilled in microG than she was. Not compared to Koi.

His family joined him suddenly, perhaps a half dozen slender shapes, echoing his rolls, twists, and loops. One of them shot down to spill her momentum precisely and without flourish, ending up eye to eye with Ahni.

"Hi," Ahni said, regarding those strange milky eyes. Good adaptation for the light, she thought. "Do you talk?"

The girl, her face flower-delicate and feminine in spite of her hairless skull smiled at her.

And greeted her.

Ahni blinked, because that's what it was . . . a welcome, a hello, glad to meet you. Only . . . no words. None. Nothing that could be called a "word" by any stretch of the imagination. But a greeting, none the less. "You do talk," Ahni said, her mind whirling. "Where's Dane?" Thought of Dane, his dark hair, strong face.

The girl smiled again, turned and pushed off. Ahni followed, noticing how she matched her speed to Ahni's. Koi zoomed past.

"Hey!" He somersaulted, twisted, looped around her, angry with a child's "you ignored me" pique, arrowed straight at the girl.

She rolled instantly. Made a quick grabbing gesture that must have connected although Ahni couldn't quite make it out. With a yelp, Koi shot off on a tangent, caught himself on a tube.

Ahni laughed, couldn't help herself. "You are so *good* all of you." She clutched her knees, somersaulting slowly, her stomach for once cooperative. "You make me feel like a dodo on precivilization Earth. I'm stuck." She waved her arms, fingertips brushing the leaves on adjacent tubes, not moving at all. "I need a tow."

Both Koi and the girl arrowed in, stalled neatly in front of her, offered simultaneous hands. "So you understand English?" Ahni asked, her eyes on the girl's milky one.

Assent. Surprise?

"Sure." Koi's gaze tickled Ahni. "Dane uses words, so we do, too. I just say 'em out loud is all."

"Oh." Ahni seized his wrist, native style, so that he could propel her back into motion, concentrated briefly on straightening out her trajectory. "Can anybody else in your family . . . speak out loud?"

"We all can. Why?" Genuine puzzlement.

Why indeed? "Most of the people on the orbital probably aren't . . . as good at hearing you as Dane and I are," Ahni said.

Koi's shrug was something Ahni felt rather than saw. *So what?*

What was it like to share . . . what? Images, feelings, sensations, needs? You really wouldn't need words, Ahni thought. "So how did you learn to talk in words?"

For a few moments, Koi drifted silently beside her. "I guess my mother died . . . right after I was born. Dane raised me," he said at last. "He talks out loud."

They really were his children, Ahni thought. The girl swooped off and as Ahni looked after her, it occurred to Ahni that the planted tubes looked familiar. Sure enough, there in the middle distance, the tubes curved to create the small sphere where Dane lived.

He emerged as she drifted close, pushing off to richochet off of the nearest tube, spinning back toward the spherical globe of grafted tubes, offering her a hand as he drifted by. She caught his wrist, native style, earned a silent chuckle, and let him tow her deftly to the bower.

"She's better than she was last time," Koi announced, flanking her.

"Noah taught me to play scrum."

"I'll forgive him for being an idiot and not telling me you were here." Dane shook his head, smiling. "He said he met you on the Climber." He ushered her into the familiar orchid-clad space. "Ahni—" His smile vanished. "Are you sure you did the right thing, coming back here? Your brother tried to kill you."

"I know." She caught one of the hammocks, hooked her leg through and caught the squeeze Dane sailed her way. "I think I'm under Li Zhen's protection. Dane, what's going on up here? Everyone is so *angry*."

Dane frowned. "I'm pretty sure your brother and Li Zhen are trying to start a secessionist rebellion up here."

"Ghosts!" Koi made a rude sound that set him drifting slowly. "All through the Con. Dane says it's making people crazy."

"Noah said something about that." Ahni eyed Dane unhappily.

"The World Council will just send CSF troops up here." And what would happen to you and Koi's family then? She wondered. "Can you stop them?"

"So far." Dane's attention prodded her, dark with worry. "I wish I knew what their ultimate goal is. Do you?"

"Li Zhen is more your ally than you both realize, I think. He is," she answered his skepticism. "I saw the same look in his eyes when he talked about the future up here. His father is very powerful and I doubt he'll share that power with Li Zhen. I think . . . Li Zhen sees this unrest as a way to force secession on the Council and to gain personal power up here. China swings a lot of leverage in the Council." She shook her head. "I don't think they have enough votes to pass independence, but that has to be his goal. How this unrest comes in, I can't quite see." She sailed her empty squeeze across the space in frustration. "And I can't figure out what Xai gets out of this. Li Zhen will want to run the show up here and Xai has never taken orders well." She sighed. "There's a piece missing here, Dane. And I can't see its shape."

"You've seen a lot." Dane caught the squeeze, tucked it into a net. "Thanks. That insight about Li Zhen helps. I haven't been quite sure about his interest in secession. It opens some possibilities." A smile glimmered in his eyes. "Do you think you can get me a meeting with the Chairman? Before things blow up?"

"I can try," Ahni said slowly. Li Zhen would never meet with a low level gene splicer. "Who are you really, Dane?"

"Head of NOW."

"The secessionist movement? I wondered, but when I researched it, I couldn't find your name associated with it." A handful of her puzzle pieces clicked into place. "You run this platform from behind the scenes don't you?"

"Well, not entirely on my own." Dane's amusement warmed her. "Let's say I get things done for people. And they are grateful."

Ahni thought of the silk manufacturer's complaints about lost talent. Nodded. "I'll see what I can do about Li Zhen," she said. "I suspect he already knows who you are."

"Probably." That amusement surfaced in Dane's eyes. "A lot of people do. I want to talk to him. We might be able to work together—if you're right about his goals. As to your brother," Dane said softly, "Ahni, we need to stop him."

"He was at the riot today," she said in a low voice. "Someone died. I saw the body on my way up here." Winced at Dane's reaction. Drew a deep breath. "I came up here to help you stop him. However we do it."

Dane reached for her hand, drifting toward her. "Thank you," he said softly. "I'm sorry." He turned to activate a holofield.

Instantly an image formed, a handsome woman with a square, serious face, and blonde hair speaking rapidly, unsmiling. "One of the Euro media links," Dane said absently. The image faded into a man with a long mohawk threaded with green fiberlight threads, his mouth moving rapidly, then into a woman with a perfect face and athlete's body. "North American Alliance media group," Dane said.

". . . killed in a violent riot on the tourist level of the New York Up orbital platform," the woman said, her voice charged with excitement. "Turkish nationals, the newlywed pair were honeymooning on the platform, when the incident took place. According to bystanders, a pair of orbital residents assaulted the young woman and when her husband tried to intervene, they stabbed him. He died at the scene and the resuscitation team arrived too late to reverse the death." Her wide eyes and arched eyebrows underlined the shock in her voice. "This is the worst outbreak of violence to date on the platform. Travel and tour agencies everywhere are cautioning vacationers that a low gravity outing may not be the best choice for the family right now, although Ralph Gearheart, Toronto native and spokesman for the Alliance refuses to admit that the situation has reached emergency status on the platform." The image shimmered and resolved to a long faced man with the air of well-tended middle age, smiling wearily yet earnestly into the video eye.

"There is no cause for serious alarm or a change in travel planes." He spoke in a reassuring voice. "This is a small incident that has been blown up out of proportion by the media. We are in touch with the Administrator of New York Up and extra security measures have been implemented in order to assure that this sort of tragedy never occurs again."

The spokesman's face faded to be replaced by a succession of images; the crowded corridor outside the restaurant, angry faces, a couple marked with blood, the gurney crew in an island of space, that sheeted body in full view.

"The camera eye sure made it look like a war. How fortunate that the vid-jockey just happened to be there at the right time," Dane said dryly. He sighed and snapped his fingers, banishing the vidcast. "I wonder if Laif knows he's being consulted?"

The tone in which Dane used the Administrator's name spoke volumes. Ahni raised an eyebrow thoughtfully. "That's not the way it happened. I saw it."

"How *did* it happen?" Dane pulled himself closer.

"Some guy bumped into the man's wife and grabbed her breast, and when her husband started to get angry, he said something that really set him off. The husband threw a punch and the agitator played victim." Ahni shrugged. "Then everybody started to get into it. At least a couple of people were part of the set-up. I don't know how many people noticed the upsider touch the woman. It was pretty quiet until her husband started swinging."

"Sounds like our pro." Dane looked at Koi, who touched an icon in the holofield.

A narrow face shimmered to life in the glowing fog, mixed-Euro genes with a fanatic's eyes. "That's him." Ahni nodded. "He's the man who started the whole thing. I don't know what he said to the husband but he sure got a reaction."

"He's very talented." Dane scowled at the image. "I would really like to get an ID on him, but it's like searching for a small moon in the center of the Milky Way. If we knew who he was, we could find a way to lever him out of here."

Koi was getting restless. He somersaulted off the wall and slipped out of the bower.

"Dane, what are they?" Ahni looked after him. "A mutation?"

"No." Dane crossed his arms behind his head, frowning. "That was my assumption, although the entire can is shielded and we're smack in the center up here. "But I've scanned DNA from most of the members of the population. There are no more mutations on the alleles than the ordinary platform-born resident. What do you know about lateral transference?"

Ahni blinked briefly into Pause, summoned the word. "A dramatic shift in genetic expression causing an altered phenotype in a single generation." She opened her eyes. "Only references I can find were to low level organisms, though. No mammalian species at all."

"What happens when you do that?" Dane was looking at her curiously. "You feel as if you're asleep."

Ha, a first. He hadn't admitted to his high E-rating before now. "It's new technology," she said. "New this generation, because you have to implant the original nano-ware in the early stages of fetal development. It's like I have . . . an onboard AI. It uses cellular structures for storage, wireless technology. All nano stuff." She shrugged. "Some of the more useful nano-ware to come out of all the hype. So Koi and his family—just evolved? Is that what you're saying?"

"I can't find a better explanation." Dane shrugged. "We still don't completely understand what triggers some DNA to express while other segments seem to have no function. That's why so many clone attempts fail. Look back in history to the Cambrian explosion." He looked after the vanished Koi. "I think we're seeing what happens when those unexpressed alleles express. Don't forget, we're starting our second generation of kids born without any planetary influences—tidal forces, Earthnormal gravity, the planetary electromagnetic field, and probably factors we don't even realize are important."

"Non Darwinian evolution?" Ahni shook her head.

"Come up with a better theory. This is the best I can do."

"But if it's the environment—why aren't kids like this showing up in the rest of the population?" Her eyes widened at his silence. "They are," she said softly. "I think I saw a couple."

"They're not as extreme as Koi's family, for the most part. But by Darwinian standards . . . this generation shouldn't be showing the skeletal, neuromuscular, and biochemical changes that they are. Natural selection is a long slow process."

"Let me guess," she said softly. "The big push for secession is mostly from the . . . native born?"

"Bingo." Dane nudged himself away from the control panel with one toe, drifted slowly across the space. "I'm not even sure that the majority are aware that they are different. They just know that you smell wrong, move wrong . . . don't seem like them. Body language, facial expressions, body odor . . . you're *different*. Not tribe. It's tenuous in Noah's generation of native born, seems to be stronger in their kids. But they're young, yet. I don't think we've lost the tribe/not tribe hard wiring," he said thoughtfully. "That will . . . cause problems. We're going to turn into aliens."

Aliens in our sky. She shivered.

"You get it." Dane nodded. "That's why we need to be separate . . . and soon . . . but peacefully separate. Cooperative. Linked in some way that is greater than our 'mutual humanity'. Friends and trading partners. Or we're going to be at war."

"Race . . ." She had started to say that race was no longer an issue to humanity, stopped herself. It didn't cause bloodshed in big wars, like it had once. But it was still an issue. In a global economy, with access to business partners on every continent, her father mostly did business with . . . Chinese. Sometimes Koreans or Cambodians. Rarely Europeans or Latinos. And he was not the exception. If anything, the vanishing barriers of distance and physical isolation had increased the racial divides rather than healing them.

You didn't have to do business with your physical neighbor. You could do business with someone like you, a continent away. Her family mostly did business with other Asians. Casually, race no longer mattered. Deep down, it did.

"That's where the anger is coming from." She reached for a delicate white blossom, snapping its fleshy stem. "Natives are seeing the tourists as the 'aliens'."

"That's only part of it." Dane's tone reflected his suddenly grim mood. "We need to shut those ghosts down."

"I thought my brother might contact me." She studied the flower, noting the tiny veins in each perfect petal, delicate, pale green, a symmetrical lacework that made the most expensive jewelry look coarse. "I don't think he's going to. I think Li Zhen needs to talk to you as soon as possible." Although Dane had no lever to move him. He would be a supplicant, and she doubted Li Zhen would respect a supplicant. She looked at Dane. "If CSF troops come up here . . . they'll find Koi."

He was silent for nearly a full minute and the rippling palette of his emotion shifted and changed too rapidly for her to follow it "I think Koi and his family are the blueprint for where humanity will go. I'd like to see them live rather than die. Koi's mother was . . . killed by a hunter." A hard darkness charged the air between them again. "The man here before me sold hunting rights. For the 'rats'. It was a . . . private club. It's pretty easy to dispose of a body down here."

Ahni closed her eyes against the images that kept forming in her head, thought of the girl with the milky eyes and her wordless greeting.

"He was a newborn. The . . . hunter was going to dispose of him along with his mother's body. I guess he thought nothing had changed when I took over. He found out."

His tone sent a shiver of ice down Ahni's spine. Dane didn't run things through favors only, she thought.

"That was the last hunt." Dane's shrug sent him drifting this time. "I did some work on Security to make sure. But the others wouldn't show themselves, and I didn't know how many there were, or if any of them could nurse Koi. So I . . . kept him." Dane's expression didn't change but a remembering smile warmed him. "We did okay . . . much to my amazement." That warmth faded as he met her gaze. "They will be the casualties if we take Earth head-on. It won't stop what's happening . . . but Koi and his family will be dead or in a lab the minute the downside media discovers them."

And you will be dead, too, she thought. "You're a zealot."

"I am." He met her eyes, smiled. "You sure you don't want to take the next climber down?"

"No," she said softly. "Sometimes . . . the universe needs zealots."

He drifted closer, touched her arm, sending shivers through her. They hung motionless in the bower, face to face, a handspan apart. Ahni focused on the heat of his palm and fingers as his hand closed around her wrist. She closed her eyes and drew a breath that shuddered into her lungs as he pulled her gently toward him. Felt the pulse leaping in her throat.

His lips touched hers and he pulled her against him suddenly, fiercely, his arms around her, his mouth on hers, all sense of flesh boundaries, of *you* and *me* dissolving, vanishing. She ran her hands down the lean muscles of his back, over the flat curve of his flanks. He touched her face, fingertips tracing her cheekbones, sliding featherlight along her throat, burning hot and tingling like ice. His excitement matched her own and Ahni laughed deep in her throat, sucked in her breath as his lips moved down the groove of her neck. She shrugged her singlesuit over her shoulder, shivered as his lips followed the spare swell of her breast, her hands on his hips, now, reaching for him. "How do you *do* this?" she asked, her voice hoarse. Laughed. "This is what the tourists come up here for, right?"

"If you want to get pregnant you use straps. Elastic." Dane touched one of her nipples with the tip of his tongue. "If you don't want to get pregnant there are . . . other things that work better here."

She didn't need to ask for details as he left a burning trail of kisses down her flat belly, groaned as he slid his fingers inside her. She was content to follow the dance. She knew what she wanted and wanted to do, and it worked, she found, quite well in microG. There came an exquisite moment when sweetly scented blossoms brushed her face and shoulders as she cried aloud in pleasure. He groaned when he came, gasping out her name.

After, they drifted, arms and legs entwined, wrapped in a sweet lethargy. Absently, Ahni noticed the tiny frog things zipping out from the shelter of the leaf wall, snatching up the droplets that drifted like miniscule pearls in the air around them, before they vanished once more into the leaves. Dane's body comforted her, warm against her naked flesh, rich with a sense of *shelter* that went beyond the physical. "What was it like?" she asked drowsily. "When you came here? Koi says you did all this."

He was thoughtful for a moment. "The infrastructure was the same. Except for this." A smile suffused his tone as he reached languidly to brush his fingertips across the wall of leaves and blossoms that surrounded them. "I needed a place to live and I was tired of small artificial spaces."

"When did you come up here?" she asked, her head against his shoulder, watching the gray of his eyes change like a cloudy spring sky. "Where did you grow up?"

"I was born on Earth. I came up to the asteroid belt with my brother. I was about ten. I mined for awhile. Got tired of it after my brother died in an accident. Did some online education and applied for this job. You have to live here and not many like microG full time." His shoulder, the one against her cheek, moved in a shrug. "I just stayed."

He was silent for a moment. "We were born in the refugee camps left over from the Terror Wars. My brother was a lot older than me. He traded a lot to get up here to Darkside. I never saw much of a future for Earth. Just more of the same. Up here . . ." He touched her cheek lightly, tracing the curve of her jaw. "Up here, we can leave the past behind. I think we need to do that."

"Koi," she said.

"They aren't us. Maybe they won't have to make the same mistakes."

Ahni pulled him close, savoring the feel of him. The permanent camps still existed, housing the survivors of the wasteland that had been the Middle East, and their descendents. *They have been forgotten,* she thought. The camps were not kind places. She bit him lightly on the neck, then harder, felt his darkness fade, warming into passion. For awhile, they were too busy to talk about anything.

"HEY, YOU GUYS." Koi's bright energy intruded as they drowsed among the leaves and blossoms. "You done yet?"

Ahni jerked awake.

"I guess we are now." Dane was laughing in spite of his mock-severe tone.

"So are you going to visit Li Zhen?" Koi eyed them with the head tilted curiosity of a dog watching primate antics. "Right now?"

"I have to get him to invite Dane, Koi." Ahni looked around for her singlesuit, discovered it snagged among leaves a couple of meters away. She pushed off from Dane, collected it, and pulled it on with all the casual dignity she could muster. Her nakedness didn't seem to attract any particular focus from Koi, never mind that he certainly did seem to have a crush on her. She thought of what Dane had said about the second generation upsiders. Smell and taste were a big part of sexuality. Maybe Koi's 'crush' was something that had little to do with sex, unlike the Earthly version. Certainly he wasn't reacting much to the obvious evidence of recent sex, she thought. Well, he was, but more the way he might react to a new game that hadn't included him.

Interesting.

And a bit chilling, too.

"Are you really sure Li Zhen has your brother on a leash?" Dane—still naked—nudged himself over to drift beside her. "Would you like to stay here?" His pewter gaze held hers. "I'd be . . . happier. Security up here, I'm sure of."

She wanted to. A lot. She shook her head, mildly annoyed when the gesture sent her drifting, clutched at Dane's hand to still her drift. "I can't. I need to contact Li Zhen through formal channels. And . . . I'm your only link to my brother," Ahni said slowly. "He may still contact me." Or try to kill her if she was wrong.

"Bait." Dane twined his fingers through hers. Not happy.

"Yep." She kissed him lightly, lingeringly. "Very wary bait."

"She'll be careful." Koi somersaulted impatiently. "She's not stupid, Dane."

"Thank you for reminding me, Koi, I had forgotten," Dane said dryly.

"I'll go back to the hotel." She suppressed regret. "I'll ask Li Zhen to see me, and I'll try to arrange a meeting between you."

"I can't see a better alternative." Dane sighed, still unhappy. He accompanied her as she left the bower.

"I'll be okay," she said as they reached the elevator. "You don't need to do guard duty." He merely shook his head, and to be honest, she was glad. The seething, suppressed anger of this place was really getting to her.

"I'll set a shadow to watch you," he told her as they rode down to the open levels. "You won't see them, but they'll be there." Locals got on and got off. Some of them looked at her with anger or curiosity. Some of them noticed Dane. Their eyes connected Ahni to Dane and they made a note of it. Interesting that only a few of them actually greeted him. The others pretended they didn't know him. But they did. She could tell Li Zhen with truth that Dane ran this platform, not the NAA. Li Zhen would respect power, especially when it was self-created.

Nobody said a negative word to her. When they reached the skinside level, Dane exited with her, and walked beside her, his posture casual, although he was on the alert.

Her doorman was on duty. He knew Dane, too. Ahni caught his brief sharp sizzle of attention before his face went bland and bored, and he bowed them past with the unseeing smile of the well-trained servant. "Your status shows," she murmured as they crossed the inner courtyard together.

"Hush." His lips barely moved. "They record all guests here. Focused mike."

"That's okay." She twined her fingers through his. "Some of my embedded hardware takes care of that. They will get visuals." She gave him a sideways look. "Do you mind?"

"We should make it worth someone's time." He halted, arm sliding around her waist, swinging her around to face him. "Keep them awake."

Their mouths met and she caught her breath, the oxygen insufficient here suddenly. She twisted away from him, his arm still around her, led him to her door, which opened for them. "My world," she said as they crossed the threshold. "Gravity."

"My world once, too." He smiled. "I don't miss it."

The door whispered closed behind her and automatically she scanned her small tell-tales to see if anyone had been in the room.

No one.

Good. She put serious thought aside and attended to what mattered here and now.

TWELVE

THE DELEGATES TO THE WORLD COUNCIL SCHOOLED LIKE nervous fish on the sea of bright mosaic tiles that floored the World Council's Atrium. The floating island that was home to the Council belonged to no nation, protected by its own elite Council Security Forces, the world's top employer of the offspring of the lower classes, backed by state of the art technology and satellite protection left over from the Terror War. The buzz of conversation in a hundred languages and dialects swelled and ebbed as the assembled members sipped beverages and nibbled on snacks that represented the delicacies of half a hundred cultures. Robes swept the polished tiles, sandaled feet shifted nervously or planted aggressively, trousered legs and skirts clothed both genders, native dress being the fashion of the moment. Hand-woven camel hair and cotton brushed against supple seal skins and vests shimmering with ap-pliquéd parrot feathers.

Flowering trees and shrubs growing in hand-shaped pots per-fumed the air. The equatorial sun streamed through broad win-dows, the harsh light softened and tinted by subtly tinted panes, so that the chamber was filled with the comforting hues of rose and gold and clear yellow. Servers, young men and women wearing the sky blue and white of the World Council circulated, offering trays of refreshments with a smile and word or two in the member's own language or dialect. They alone seemed oblivious to the air of tension that permeated the spacious chamber, although rumor said that they were all Class Nine or Ten empaths, sampling the emotional nuance and reporting back to the Chairman and his staff, so that the Chair would know what to expect.

You didn't need to have a significant empathic rating to feel the tension circulating in the room.

The Session warning chimed through the atrium and the tension spiked, voices rising in pitch as the human schools fragmented and regrouped. Members made their way toward the door that led to their seats in the amphitheater-like Main Council Chamber. One by one, they were greeted by Security and ushered down the narrow, white-walled hall while every cell in their bodies was scanned and checked against their biostatistics. No one, not even during its nascence in the Terror Years, had ever managed to bring violence into the Chamber.

Wen Huang, The Huang, strolled through the bath of scanning beams, alongside Chou Zhen, the Chairman of The China Republic. The air tingled with anticipation and he allowed himself the tiniest of smiles as he and Zhen made their way down the familiar aisles to their adjoining boxes. Each member-country had a private box, a spacious room with a transparent wall overlooking the dais with the President's desk and the holodesk podium, made of a single sheet of indestructible glassteel. Inside, Taiwan's box had been decorated with wool rugs and embroidered silk panels imported from Northern China. A suite of antique lacquer furniture faced the small holodesk in the middle of the floor. Huang touched an icon and scanned for recent email. His trace of his renegade daughter had led clearly and directly to a hotel on New York Up. She was still there.

He would give her this chance to atone, in spite of her disobedience. He blanked the screen and took a seat in the custom recliner. A moment later, a page entered, bearing a steaming pot of tea on a tray, along with a dish of tiny dried fish, seaweed, hot peppers, and rice crackers. Bowing silently, the young page, a geneselect Scandinavian type, set the tray on the small table at Huang's elbow and left.

On the podium platform below the boxes, the Council President, the small brilliant head of the Pan Malaysian Compact, Dr. Suri Kurichatam, sat down at her desk with its data center and surveyed the members in their boxes, her expression coldly serene. This was her second term as Council President, and the fact that she had won the most recent election easily was a testament to her even handed and unbiased administration.

The morning session had dealt with small issues . . . trade and ocean resource disputes, mostly concerning species taken across national fishery boundaries. All of them had been dismissed or sent on to the World Court for adjudication. Business as usual.

Crucial issues were brought to the floor in the afternoon session. Huang couldn't see Chou Zhen in the box adjacent to his but a slow smile crossed his face. Rumors had circulated wildly during the break. Chou Zhen's absence from the atrium had been noticed. Rumor was a useful tool. A small push on the correct stone and you could move an entire hillside.

He was looking forward to the afternoon.

"The Council Meeting is now in session." Kurichatam's voice sounded as if she sat across from Huang on the lacquered sofa. "Is there any New Business to bring before the Council?" She glanced down at her panel. "I recognize the Chairman of The Republic of China, Chou Zhen." She nodded toward his box. "Your issue, Chairman Zhen?"

On the dias, the holodesk shimmered, and the image of Chou Zhen, dressed in the historic high collared jacket of the Chairman, appeared. Somewhat small and dark for a Han, a trace of Mongolian blood showed in his round face and the squat muscular body. His son had not taken after him, Huang thought. Li Zhen looked pure Han. Banishing a pang of grief for his own dead son, Huang clasped his hands and waited with anticipation for Chou Zhen to speak.

"My issue is the current unrest in the orbital platform settlement of New York Up." Chairman Zhen's precise, Mandarin filled Huang's box and the Chairman seemed to be looking Huang in the eye. "We have understood from the very inception of the orbital expansion the dangers inherent in permitting such settlements to become inhabited by long-term residents who would eventually evolve a divergent agenda. Until now, we have not had to face a threat to world safety from our skies. However, the growing unrest in the New York Up orbital settlement and the unwillingness of the North American Alliance to bring it under control, fills me with grave concern."

Down on the dais, Kurichatam's expression was severe as she eyed her desktop. Huang permitted himself the tiniest of smiles. The NAA First Delegate, the President of the United States, as usual, would be shrieking by now. America had always elected their presidents the way they cast actors in their movies, he thought. Lots of good looks and stage presence. Not much substance, and of course the Americans had always believed that they were the center of the universe. Not that the Chinese were much different. Huang's smile broadened. But history—several thousand years worth—was on the side of the Chinese rather than this upstart country who had come late to the world scene and had never really learned to think of itself as a member of the world community.

The United States was entirely too full of itself, Huang thought with disdain. It considered its interests as representative of the NAA. Canada was easy to bully, as was Mexico with its unfortunate economic reliance on American markets. Now, ostracized by the Estados Latinos, it had no choice but to remain part of the NAA and support America's swaggering.

The recent disdain with which the NAA's Ambassador of Trade had dismissed the proposal by the Taiwan Families for an exchange of the Families' excess eco-credits in return for minor offshore fishing rights had insulted Huang personally. Who did these people think they were, that they could snap their fingers when they wanted something and ignore the needs of others? He sat back, his smile broadening, as the President, with a resigned expression granted the North American Alliance member from the United States the floor.

"I beg to question the esteemed First Delegate from the China Republic!" The figure of Harold Warner, President of the United States, replaced that of Chou Zhen, his handsome face quivering with indignation. "There is no cause for any sort of global concern here." His words came to Huang's ears in perfect Mandarin. In real life, he spoke it with a terrible accent. The Huang smirked.

"The media, once again, has been capitalizing on the sensational-ism of a minor incident or two. The actions of a handful of disaf-fected misfits is being blown all out of proportion, and . . ." The First Delegate's holographic eyes seemed to bore into Huang's. "The entire trivial situation is being twisted to suit political agendas."

In the privacy of his box, Huang smiled and nodded watching the Council President from the corner of his eye. She was frowning at the screen embedded in the podium in front of her. Obviously the NAA First Delegate's statement had roused a storm of response.

"Recognizing the First Delegate from the Estados Latinos." The Council President's expression gave nothing away. Even handed, Huang thought. The Latino states opposed the NAA at every turn. He leaned forward as the woman with the bold Mayan features and graying braid wound around her head replaced the NAA delegate on the box holo deck.

"The Council convenes to consider events from a global per-spective," she began in a low, melodious voice. La Presidente of Guatemala, newly elected as First Delegate by Los Estados Lati-nos, was an unknown quantity, but so far Huang had been im-pressed, in spite of her gender. He leaned forward now, idly sipping at his tea, still hot in its thermal cup that mimicked fine porcelain.

"When we began to assemble the Platforms and embraced the new frontier of Low Earth Orbit, we embraced equally a share of responsibility and risk. We have pooled our resources and shared our grief for those who died in their building," she went on in her soft, compelling voice. "This has been an effort by humanity to col-lectively push our borders, to expand our horizons beyond the boundaries of gravity and the surface of our birth world." She smiled into Huang's eyes. "It has been a shared undertaking. For most of us. But not for all. From the origins of our low orbit ex-pansion, the first International Space Station, the United States was a reluctant participant. And even now, as a member of the North American Alliance, the platform New York is in reality, if not in name, a U.S. possession. I say that it is time for the United States to step into the world community. The threat of hostility originating from orbit has brought the rest of the world together to ban all satellite weaponry other than that maintained by the World Council's Security Forces, but note that it took serious pressure to force the United States to yield its satellite defenses to CSF control, and that only under the threat of global conflict."

Huang smiled to himself, imagining the foam flecked rantings of the NAA delegate at this moment. The man had a photogenic charisma, but little self-control. Sometimes, the Council rule of a single speaker at a time made for a dull session.

The Estados Latinos delegate had finished her oration. Huang touched the arm of his recliner and a holo-field shimmered to life, morphing into a three-dimensional model of the dais and the surrounding boxes housing the delegates from the countries and alliances. Each box glowed a color that ranged the spectrum from red to violet. Red meant a positive response to the current speaker's words. Violet meant negative. His own box on the holo shimmered the sunny yellow of neutrality. For now.

The NAA First Delegate had the floor again, his face contorted with a childish outrage that he made no attempt to conceal. Huang watched him with disdain. Such a poor choice of First Delegate. He had had personal dealings with the Canadian Delegate when they negotiated a long term trade policy concerning Taiwan's carefully bred and controlled giant shrimp. The Canadian delegate was a canny player on the global field and was a much better choice than the spoiled and egocentric U.S. Delegate. Huang watched the shifting spectrum of color on his holo, noting the dramatic deepening from yellow through the greens toward violet.

But personal inclination did not mean votes. At his last count, it would be a close issue when Chou Zhen proposed the vote. Patiently he waited through the speeches of the various other Delegates as they expressed their official opinions either for or against revoking the NAA's control of its platform. The speeches had more to do with pending trade deals or eco-credit negotiations than it had to do with the issue at hand, but that was an unavoidable aspect of World Council debates.

A soft note chimed through his space—a request for private

speech. Huang glanced at the glowing icon that appeared in his holo-field. Sri Lanka, one of the small independents, like Taiwan, but allied to no particular coalition at the moment. "Greetings," Huang said, acknowledging the Delegate's request. The Sri Lankan Delegate shimmered to life beside the gesticulating image of the NAA First Delegate.

"You will vote with Chou Zhen?" Chai Somkeet, a small, taut man with a round Buddha face dressed in a perfectly tailored cream colored suit addressed Huang briskly. "He believes that this call for intervention will succeed?"

Sri Lanka had been courting NAA trade lately, but last Huang had heard, the negotiation wasn't going well.

"Chou Zhen is concerned for the safety of citizens of the planet," Huang said earnestly.

"Don't play games with me." Somkeet's eyes snapped. "This is a move to rub the NAA's nose in their own arrogance. They will be angry if it succeeds and even more angry at those who supported it, if it fails."

"You cannot serve two masters," Huang said smoothly.

"Don't give me those old platitudes." Somkeet's fists clenched in a very un-Buddha like pose. "If I fling pig dung in the NAA's eye, I do not wish to do so alone! What is to make up for the trade agreement that will not happen if I join you in this vote?"

Huang picked up a small antique jade carving from the low table near his recliner. The amber tint of the white jade marked it as a tomb item, recovered by looters or archeologists as they later called themselves, a thousand years or more after its burial. The tiny clawed dragon . . . the symbol of his clone-son's birth year . . . seemed to smile. "I feel, as does Chairman Chou Zhen, that order must be maintained in such a dangerous location." He regarded the First Delegate of Sri Lanka. "What is the World Council for, if not to maintain order?"

The First—and only—Delegate of Sri Lanka grunted and vanished.

Barbarian, Huang thought. He had no manners. Council votes were not a chicken in the market place to bargain over. He and the NAA deserved each other. And besides, Somkeet had nothing he wanted.

The last Delegate yielded the floor, and Huang could almost feel the shiver of anticipation that swept the assemblage. Even the Council President seemed to stand straighter, her shoulders tense. Then something on her podium caught her attention and she frowned, her polished and inviolable calm fracturing ever so slightly.

Right on schedule. Huang sat forward.

"The assorted news media are featuring a live-cast direct from the North American Alliance's orbital platform, New York Up." Her tone was flat, noncommittal. "As President of the World Council, I choose to exercise my authority and set aside our rule about the exclusion of media feeds entirely from the chamber. The incident in progress seems to bear specifically on our ongoing discussion. It is appropriate."

Huang touched his controls. The holodesk shimmered and formed the image of the First Delegate of the North American Alliance. The U.S. President sat upright in his own recliner, his face betraying anger only, without expectation. He does not know what he will see. Huang smiled. He shifted his eyes to the glassteel wall as it opaqued, then shimmered with image.

People crowded a corridor. The vid angle showed mostly shoulders. Uniforms, Huang noted. The New York Platform's security? Others seemed to be bystanders. A woman half turned, her pale, northern European face ugly with fear. Then, as if a hand had parted them, the bystanders moved aside. For an instant, the vid focused on a stretcher, more uniformed figures lifting a limp body of a man onto the padding. The man's head lolled, slack and pale, streaked with blood. For an instant the assemblage had a close up view of the man's dead face. He was young, Huang noted with approval. Mediterranean in phenotype. Excellent choice. The Black Sea States voted with the NAA.

The medical people weren't working on revival, although a tangle of equipment suggested they had tried it already. A media announcer was speaking in a tight, excited tone. Russian, Huang thought, before his translation program took over and dubbed it into Mandarin.

". . . today, for no apparent reason. Unrest has been increasing on the platform, and apparently the attack was unprovoked . . ." The sound ended as the Council President deleted it.

The NAA First Delegate had gone white, clutching the arms of his recliner.

"I move that we send Council Security Forces to the North American Alliance's platform!" Huang recognized the First Delegate of the Black Sea States. "This is an outrage!" The man's voice shook. "The situation is out of control!"

"This is no longer a matter for a single member to settle," the Delegate of Los Estados Latinos took the floor, her voice cold. "We cannot tolerate further outbreaks of violence against world citizens."

"Is there a second to the motion?" the Council President asked calmly.

The NAA's First Delegate was on his feet, mouth working. Huang smiled at him, then touched a control. "Taiwan seconds the motion," he said clearly.

"The motion has been moved and seconded." The Council President's tone was matter of fact, but her face betrayed the strain of the moment. "All those in favor . . ."

Huang narrowed his eyes as the images of the other Delegates acquired a halo of either red or green. His own holo and that of Chou Zhen, China's First Delegate, glowed bamboo green. Those of the NAA Delegates glared ruby red. One by one, the other Delegates glowed with color. No abstentions were allowed here. His eyes narrowed as he kept count, then slowly, a smile spread across his face.

Yes, the Black Sea States had tipped the balance. Huang touched the controls, and Chou Zhen's image shimmered to life in the holofield. China's Chairman nodded, accepting Huang's request for personal communication. "I applaud your second, First Delegate," Chou Zhen said smoothly.

"I admit that I was surprised at the motion proposed by the Black Sea States." Huang nodded. "They have been uncooperative of late." Meaning that they voted against anything that China and the rest of the so-called Asian Axis voted for.

"I heard a rumor that the murdered young man was the son of the First Delegate's brother." Chou Zhen's face was unreadable. "What a terrible coincidence. Of course, personal feeling did not account for the decision of the Black Sea States to make a motion for intervention. It is the only appropriate action to take."

"Of course." Huang agreed. He sat back as the communication ended, and smiled thoughtfully down at the Council President as she announced that World Council Forces would be dispatched to the North American Alliance orbital platform of New York Up to assume control. The NAA First Delegate's image replaced that of Chou Zhen. He sat rigid in his expensive real-leather covered recliner, his expression one of cold rage . . . and defeat.

Huang sat back and touched in an order for fresh tea and a bowl of noodles.

The North American Alliance had lost a lot of political ground today. The effect on trade would be . . . fortuitous. The noodles and tea came, delivered by a female page with an air of suppressed excitement. This was an auspicious day, Huang thought, as he picked up his chopsticks. It was important now to press the advantage, and quite possibly to reduce the NAA's standing in world politics for years to come. He slurped up the noodles with their topping of fermented tofu and green onions, drank some tea. Chou Zhen would have a plan for pursuing this advantage.

He was sure of it.

THIRTEEN

"WAIT A MINUTE. THIS IS INSANE!" LAIF JONES-EGRET bolted to his feet. "Are you interested in what is really going on up here, or just the media's version? Since when has anyone believed the media?"

"It's a little late to worry about PR, Jones." The holo of the tall, thin-faced Quebecoise stared at him, her expression icy. "Your little riot ended up broadcast live in the World Council chamber yesterday just as they were discussing the topic of World Council intervention on your platform."

Your platform. Usually it was *our platform* with the implication that it was really *her* platform. Besides, he was just there to do as he was told by Madame Fournier, chairman of the North American Alliance's Committee for Orbital Affairs. As she frequently reminded him.

"We are far from pleased with your handling of the situation."

"It was just that . . . a *situation.*" Laif hung onto his temper with both hands. "It was one man . . . an agitator we've had trouble with for the past few weeks. He shows up, starts trouble. He's a *professional,* Fournier. This whole 'rebellion' rumor is somebody's doing, and intervention was what that somebody is after. So who wins when the Council intervenes?" He met her cold blue stare, keeping his voice flat and calm with an effort. "*You're* down there in the sea of world politics. Who has a stake in this mess?"

"This is not a matter of global conspiracy." She looked down her long Gallic nose at him.

"Crap, it's not."

"This is a matter of local unrest, fomented by the misfits who regularly gain citizenship on New York Up and are allowed freedom by your lax security policies. We have pressured you for years now to institute a narrower window of tolerance, something along the lines of the strict immigration policy instituted by the platform of New Singapore."

"Now *there's* a platform that's on the brink of explosive rebellion," Laif snapped. "It's as repressive as any dictatorship in Earth's history. The Prime's jail cells are listed as hotel rooms on the stats, and from what I've heard, some people go back downside without benefit of the elevator."

"And it is *Madame* Fournier to you," the committee head went on as if he hadn't spoken. "Give me a good reason why we should not simply recall you and appoint your Administrative Assistant as your replacement?"

"Because within a week you'd *really* have reason to call in the CSF." Laif gripped the back of his chair, struggling for calm. "You don't know what's going on up here. You don't know how things work up here. This is not Toronto. This is not Washington, DC. This is a different place with its own rules and its own type of people. My . . . assistant doesn't understand this world. I have no idea why he wants to be up here, or why you think he's competent for the job."

"I am surprised that you bring up the topic of competency." Fournier gave him a Montreal-in-January smile.

"Damn it, you need to look beyond me for the cause of this problem, and you need to do it *now,* because someone has an agenda up here, and you'll do just what they want if you recall me."

"I expect to hear that you have the situation under control before the CSF arrives. They are on their way, thanks to you. Good day, Mr. Jones." She vanished, leaving only the shimmer of an empty holo-field.

"Damn!" Laif lunged to his feet, his chair toppling. "Damn, damn, damn!"

"What happened?" Barachat, his young aide stuck his head in the door. "Is the system down?" He peered anxiously at the holo shimmer.

"Yeah, the system is down, and no the holo-field is working just fine." Laif stalked across the tiny cubical. "I'm about to get recalled, Bar. They're going to put Arlin in charge here."

"You're farting, right?" Barachat, with the slender, supple build of a second generation upsider raised his eyebrows. "Are they nuts? He's as downside as you get. He'll have the Con blowing up in a day. Maybe it'll take two days if he stays shut up in his room and doesn't do anything."

"They don't know what's going on up here and damned if they're going to listen to me." Laif leaned on his desk. "This is a set-up. Who the *hell* is behind it? It's costing someone big-time to plant as many talking heads in the Con as you say we've got."

"Yeah, no kidding." Barachat shook his head, his dark eyes thoughtful. "They're hard to spot and harder to shut down and it's a big operation. Somebody paid a lot for state of the art. There's big money behind this."

Laif straightened, feeling tired, feeling *old*, damn it, and he wasn't that old, not really. "Where's a communication failure when we need it?" He looked up at the ceiling. "Like something to cut us off for a bit, before I get my orders to go downside and the pet spy-eye gets promoted to replace me? Which is going to happen any minute now."

"Yeah." Barachat rubbed his chin thoughtfully. "That kind of thing doesn't happen too often. There is one nice little bottleneck that can really shut down all our communications. Course there's a backup." He inspected his fingernails with a contemplative expression. "But we're only required to test the backup yearly and that was about nine months ago. Who knows? It might fail."

"Bless you," Laif murmured under his breath. "Just don't leave any traces."

"I'm better than that." With a flip of his fingers, Barachat left the cubicle.

Well, that bought him some time, but not much. Just until the CSF showed up. He shook his head and left, hoping that Barachat was right about not getting caught. In all likelihood, he, Laif, wasn't going to be in any position to do much for him if he did. Leaving the administrative offices he strode down the quiet back corridor, stopping to greet the few people in sight. The small private elevator was about halfway down the hall, next to a public restroom and shower. He slowed his pace, surreptitiously watching the few people in the corridor. If you weren't close, you couldn't tell if someone entered the elevator or the shower. Casually he palmed the lock and stepped into the 'vator. Sent it up to the top. "Nilsson, you'd better have some options for me," he murmured as it shot upward. "Or we're both in trouble."

The CSF would have to come up the climbers and shuttle over. If Bar was right about being able to crash the communications for awhile, he'd still be Admin when they arrived. The 'vator slowed and beeped and he grabbed for the dangling straps, locked one around him.

The damn kid was waiting for him. They gave him the creeps, all of them, with their weird, blind-looking eyes and bones like plastic. Laif pushed out of the 'vator, flipped the kid a few fingers. He'd seen the DNA analysis on these things, knew they were as human as he was, knew Nilsson was probably right in his guesses but . . . he still didn't like 'em.

Which meant Nilsson was probably right about what would happen to them, too.

He was usually right. "Okay, where is he?" he hollered at the kid.

"In the control center. Come on." The kid did a series of complicated tumbles.

Designed to show Laif just how lame he was, Laif thought sourly. He didn't need the kid as a guide to the control center, managed to get there without stranding himself between handholds, too, even though they crossed a big stretch of bare, newly planted tubes. No way he was going to ask that thing for a tow.

Nilsson was waiting for him, drifting in front of the control center bulk. "You look grim." He narrowed his eyes. "What happened."

The man's intuition was impressive, Laif thought. He'd checked his stats and his E rating was low, but he'd swear sometimes that the man was at least a Class Eight or Nine empath. "The Council voted to take over and send up CSF. They're on their way." He bit the words off, anchoring himself on a tube planted to purple and white flowers.

"They should have been two votes short." Nilsson's face gave nothing away. "Who changed sides?"

"I don't know. They didn't release the voting details. I suspect that by now, I'm already formally relieved of my duties," he said. "But we have this communications problem, so I can't find that out right now." He checked his watch. "I figure we've got about twenty-four hours to find out who's behind this."

"China."

"What?" Laif stared. "Come again?"

"This mess is going to cost the NAA politically," Dane said. "China is their main rival. And Li Zhen is involved in the unrest."

"Huang!" Laif slapped his forehead, grabbed for a handhold. "That damn wildcard bitch. I wondered why the hell she was playing tourist up here."

"Not her." Nilsson snapped. "Her brother Xai Huang."

Blood was thicker than water, Laif thought. "I'll get Security on it. We'll pull a visual from the media and watch every vid eye in the can. If he uses a public bathroom, or sticks his nose into a corridor we'll get him. Keep in touch, okay?" He pushed off, not waiting for Nilsson's reply and kicked back to the elevator. Connected on his private link to Barachat. "Get Security. We've got a wildcard staying in a hotel here. Huang is the surname. Female. Pick her up right now." It was a start. She knew something that would lead to her brother and by all the gods he'd know who was doing what for whom and why before the CSF blew down the door.

DANE WATCHED LAIF push awkwardly toward the private elevator. Everything they had worked for was about to come apart. He had to talk to Li Zhen. Their only hope was that China could—and would—back the Council off. Dane pulled himself into the control center. Koi was waiting for him, his distress bright and abrasive in the air. "Get Ahni for me, will you?"

"You want me to tell her Laif's gonna send Security after her?"

"Yes," Dane said bitterly. "He didn't listen to me." He scowled as the empty holo-field remained just that . . . fog.

"I overrode her mail filter with an emergency code." Koi sounded puzzled. "Her hotel majordomo should have waked her up by now."

"Damn." Dane clenched his fist. "Laif guessed I'd warn her." He let his breath out in a sigh. Born in the sub rosa street culture in downside New York Metro, Laif had learned trust late in life . . . and it was a veneer he shed quickly under stress. "Damn," he repeated softly. He was not doing well, right now, not making good guesses.

FOURTEEN

AHNI SAT UPRIGHT IN BED, WAKING FROM A NIGHTMARE about Tania.

Are you all right? The room voice queried her in a feminine, motherly tone. *Would you like me to call someone? Would you care for a calming tea? I have several in stock.*

"Green tea." Tania had kissed her, then bitten her throat with vampire fangs. "Has Li Zhen replied to my message?"

No.

Ahni swung her legs over the side of the bed. The mug of tea already steamed on the refreshment bar. She crossed the room naked to get it, caught a trace of Dane's scent on her skin as she lifted the cup to her lip. How was Tania involved in this? Ahni remembered her sense of triumph after Ahni had left her father's banquet room. Perhaps she should have stayed another day, confronted them both. She had let her emotions drive her up here. With a jerk of her shoulders, Ahni stalked over to the built-in wardrobe, pulling open a drawer for clean clothes. A glint of gold caught her eye. Xai's medallion. She had kept it with her, tossed it into the drawer with her underwear. She pulled it out now, inspecting it. Why had Tania taken it? And how had she gotten access to

Xai's private rooms? She and Xai had always competed, teased each other with barbed words.

A tiny imperfection caught her eye . . . a dark speck revealed by the angle of the light above the wardrobe, it gleamed with an odd matte sheen. Ahni peered at it. A data dot. Someone had glued it to the back of the medallion. Probably a homily recited by some famous poet or scholar urging the young recipient to greater honors. She started to drop the medallion into the drawer, hesitated. She had been at that ceremony and had no memory of anyone saying anything about a holo as part of the award. Frowning, she dressed quickly. Dane would have equipment to read it. Secure equipment.

You have visitors, the Room announced.

"Who?"

Security. Apologetically. *I have to let them in.*

Which meant they had a warrant. Ahni slipped the medallion into her pocket as the door opened and two uniformed young women with narrow, wary eyes slid into the room, looking everywhere all at once. The first one in the door carried a small stun pistol openly in her hand. It didn't quite point at Ahni.

"Ahni Huang?" The smaller of the two women, with a native's lithe build took a half step forward.

"Yes." She drew herself up. "You waked me."

"We have a warrant for your arrest."

"For what?" Ahni didn't move.

"Questioning." The other security guard spoke up. "That's all." And she stepped back, urging Ahni toward the door with a twist of her shoulders.

Ahni decided to play this game out. "Fine, whatever. I hope you have a good reason for this." She didn't make it too much of a threat because the woman with the stun gun looked hopeful.

A small cart waited outside, emblazoned with the NYUp logo and painted the same blue as the Security uniforms. Her doorman was on duty and he pointedly did not look as she marched past him, flanked by her escort. Ahni climbed in beside the taller woman, wondering just how often they took guests in for questioning with weapons.

They navigated the tourist corridors and it struck Ahni that they seemed quite empty for this time of morning. "Where is everybody?"

The woman did the one-shoulder shrug.

"What's it like to be so rich you don't have to wear a chip?" asked the one with the stun gun.

Ahni shrugged and settled herself to wait. They passed through a plaza lined with expensive shops. The small tables set amidst the garden boxes planted to real flowers and blooming trees were deserted. They turned suddenly into a narrow side corridor, then into another. A door slid open at their approach and the cart whipped inside. If this was town hall, she thought, it wasn't too impressive. The cramped space barely gave them room to exit the vehicle. The driver had relaxed, but the other one still waited for an excuse. Ahni didn't give her one as she followed the driver to a small door that opened for them, closed behind them. The guards ushered her down a corridor with the right-angle corners of the tourist level and into a small, featureless room less than two meters square. It was cold inside, not quite refrigerator cold, but chilly, containing no furniture at all, just walls colored an off green that made her feel slightly queasy.

The door slid closed behind her, leaving her alone.

A cell? Ahni looked around, her breath fogging in the cold air. A small ventilation grill near the ceiling hissed with a rising and falling sibilance that Ahni found annoying. She had never heard a whisper from any ventilation system anywhere on the platform. Combine it with the temperature that had already raised goose bumps on her arms, the ugly color that definitely affected her stomach, and you had a deliberately unpleasant environment. And she smelled vomit. Nice touch, she thought and sat down with her back against the wall opposite the ventilation grill, as far from its trickle of cold air as she could get. She was obviously not here as an honored guest. The floor was cold, too, as was the wall. She shifted to a squat, arms clasped around her knees, grateful now to the hours spent in her grandmother's garden, squatting beside the raised beds with her, weeding. Grandmother did not tolerate a sloppy western sit.

No one had searched her for weapons. Ahni looked around the room. That meant they had scanned her thoroughly at some point in her journey. Probably here, she decided. They'd know by now what she was made of right down to the bone marrow. She was starting to shiver. Ahni blinked into Pause, electing to constrict external blood vessels, reducing heat loss, conserving her core temperature. She shut down the shivering response, too. That would cost her some warmth, but would make whatever confrontation was about to happen a bit more even. It was hard to negotiate well when your teeth were chattering. Finally, she shut down her pain response, felt the creeping chill fade, and dropped into waking sleep, slowing her heart rate, reducing metabolic function to minimum.

The door whispered open and two people burst into the room. Ahni blinked out of Pause as a man with a medical insignia on his sleeve caught her by her chin. "I'm fine." She brushed his hand aside . . . forcefully . . . and stood up. "Hands off."

He didn't answer, had whipped out a handheld bio-scanner was staring fixedly at the readout. "Damn." His eyebrows rose. "I've read about people like you, but it's impressive to see it in the flesh." He looked up from the display, his mixed-latino face crinkling into a smile. "How far can you shut down?"

"Pretty far." She returned his smile, noticing the platform's Administrator behind him. He was angry and getting angrier, so she smiled even more sweetly at the medic. "I can make someone believe I'm dead if they don't happen to have a scanner or a high E rating."

"Wow." The man was shaking his head. "That's really cool. I've only seen that in the teaching vids. I'd love to see you do that sometime."

"Out, Seguro!" The Administrator glared from her to the medic. "Nice trick," he said as the man left regretfully. "I should have read up on your kind more."

"Yes, you should have." She kept her voice and manner sweet because it was irritating him enormously. "Before I contact my family's legal staff, would you care to explain this illegal detention? And the physical conditions?"

"This isn't an upscale hotel. Sorry about that, but the rest of us live a little differently."

Oh, so it was going to be like that. She tilted her head, taking her time, studying the Administrator's dark face, lightfiber tattoo, and earring, smiling at his building fury. "Not many people with a 32°C body temperature are comfortable in a 10°C environment," she said at last.

He shrugged and clearly came to some decision. "I don't have time for games and I'm already in a corner so threats about lawyers and lawsuits aren't going to get you anywhere. I want your brother and I want him right now, and I'm going to do anything it takes to get him."

"And when you find him, you can tell me where he is," Ahni said. He was very stressed, and it occurred to her that she had played the wrong tile, here. "I don't know what my brother is up to, or why he's causing trouble up here. I am looking for him for personal reasons." She met the Administrator's eyes. The sharp edge of his desperation chilled her more than the temperature.

"You can help me find your brother and I am going to do whatever it takes to get your cooperation." He bared his teeth at her. "The stakes are a lot bigger than you know. And don't think your Elite physical games are going to help you out here. I can shoot you full of enough drugs to override anything you can do with your expensive nanoware. Think about it. I'll give you fifteen minutes. That's all the time I have." He turned on his heel and left.

His back was to the wall. He meant his threats. Ahni looked after him, cold bothering her again. The temperature was dropping. A little more coercion. For the first time, a bleak fear began to seep in around the edges of her calm. What had happened?

Ahni squatted, conserving heat, dropping into a low metabolic state, her awareness focused on the door. In spite of her physical adjustments she was shivering continuously by the time it opened again.

"Damn!"

She didn't need the sound of his voice to recognize Dane, and the flare of his anger was almost enough to warm her. As she blinked to full awareness, he dropped to his knees beside her on the floor, his hands hot as fire on her throat and face, which only made the shivering intensify.

"Sometimes Laif has the brains of a lizard. Maybe less." Dane pulled her against him. "Ahni, are you all right?"

"I—I am. Actually." Her teeth were chattering now and she struggled to control the shudders that racked her. "I can stand up. I'm just cold is all." The temperature in the room was increasing rapidly. Felt like Taiwan. She drew a deep breath of humid, blood-warm air, but had to drop into Pause again to finally get the spasms under control. He had his arms around her, steadying her, and she luxuriated in the heat of his flesh.

"Damn, it's my fault. I should have realized he wasn't going to believe me. I know Laif. He just forges ahead when he thinks he's on the right path. And then I had a couple of fires to put out, and I couldn't get up here. I'm sorry, Ahni."

"I'm okay." She looked up at him, steady on her feet now, *so* glad for the warmth. "Dane, what happened?"

"Council intervention. CSF are on their way up here."

Ahni bit her lip, thinking of all that meant. "How soon do they arrive? And . . . what's going to happen when they do?"

"A lot, I'm afraid," Dane said heavily.

"How much time?" She closed her eyes, still holding the shivering at bay, trying to think.

"About eighteen hours." Dane's arm tightened around her. "They're coming up at emergency speed. Let's get you out of here."

"Laif's going to let me go?"

"Oh, yeah. He damn well is." This last he addressed to the video eye overhead. The door opened silently and she exited gratefully, still leaning on Dane.

The Administrator stood there and he didn't look pleased at all. "So since we're all on the same side now, want to tell us where your brother is?"

"Same answer as last time." Ahni gave him a level stare.

"Knock it off, Laif." Dane's temper was simmering again. "Now we have less time to find him." He turned his back on the Administrator. "Ahni, any word from Li Zhen?"

"Not at the time Security picked me up." She stared at Laif, accessed her link. "Nothing there now. I'll have to try and drop in on him. Wait." She groped in her pocket, a bit surprised at its metallic warmth when she still felt so cold. "This belongs to my brother. There's a data dot on it—probably a copy of the award, but I didn't have time to look at it—" She gave the Administrator a brief, cold stare. "Before I ended up here."

"Where's the reader, Laif?" Dane held out his hand and Ahni dropped the medallion into it.

Dane pried the dot up with a fingernail, dropped it onto a scandisk and sealed it down.

Without a word, the Administrator took it and dropped it into a scanner. Almost immediately, the machine emitted a silvery chime. *Encrypted data,* a silvery voice murmured. *I'm afraid you do not have access. If you are an authorized reader, please enter your personal bio-ID.*

"So much for an award," Ahni murmured, her pulse quickening. Ah, older brother, she thought. Did you make a mistake here? At last?

"Who do you have who's good with encryption?" The Administrator glared at Dane.

"Noah." Dane nodded. "I'll send him up here. While Noah's working on that, Laif, we're going to go visit Li Zhen."

"I need you here." The Administrator's face darkened.

"That's our only option right now."

He stayed close beside here when they left and took her hand in the alley, his grip tight. "I thought you were on opposite sides," she said as they reached the end of the alley way and turned right, toward the main tourist promenade.

"Officially." He gave her a sideways look, a crooked smile. "We share the same goals."

They reached the tourist promenade, turned toward her hotel. The wide corridor was fairly crowded. Dinner time, Ahni realized, and her stomach immediately cramped with hunger. She hadn't eaten since the evening before. Caught the wafting fragrance of grilling fish and managed not to drool. "Dane, I have to eat something or I'm going to fall down."

"Sorry." He looked startled, then concerned. "What else am I missing? Do you need anything else? I'm not thinking very well right now."

"Food will do." The vendor offered an assortment of vegetables and fresh tofu, which she was stir-frying quickly in a small pan and serving in rounds of thin bread, topped with spicy sauce. When the woman handed it to her, Ahni could barely restrain herself from wolfing it.

As she ate, she began paying attention to the people around them. She had become accustomed to the level of hostility in the platform corridors, and here, on the main promenade, where most of the people were downsiders and the rest were the vendors and service staff who catered to them, that hostility wasn't extreme. Hadn't been.

It was now. She blinked, scanning the wide promenade, realizing that it had risen to an intensity like that of the upper levels. Dane's hand closed on her arm and she swallowed the last bite of vegetables and tofu, following him as he wove through the crowd, deftly avoiding contact with the tourists. Worry—anxiety—spread down the corridor like ripples in a pond. Someone had dropped a stone into this one, all right. Ahni thought of the restaurant and hurried to catch up to Dane.

The tension and anger grew, and Dane's face was grim. Up ahead a knot of bodies swirled in the corridor and tourists and vendors were hustling away in both directions, their anxiety a bright metallic overlay to the dusky eddies of anger and aggression filling the corridor. Dane slid through the packed bodies effortlessly. She followed much more cautiously, afraid of provoking someone, making the situation worse. Natives, she thought, as she searched for space, squeezed through. Most of these people were natives, young, second generation, with the skinny, supple bodies of the scrum players. The bodies around her parted unexpectedly and Ahni found herself on the inner edge of the crowd.

She took in the situation in an instant. Three downside tourists and a handful of natives had squared off, trading insults. The tourists, three gym-muscled men in expensive singlesuits, had clearly been doing something recreational, either alcohol, Ahni thought, or chemicals. Testosterone-agression edged with flight/fight tension clogged the air. Dane was speaking to the native onlookers, a quick word here and there, a chin-jerk, radiating authority. And the natives were listening. One by one they stepped back, some of them reluctantly, blending into the crowd. The spectators were also thinning,

Ahni noticed, slipping away, leaving the braver tourists behind. But these people were beginning to simmer now, too.

One of the intoxicated tourists, a small, compact man with the muscles of a dancer, farted. Loudly.

A growl swept the crowd and the ring around the men tightened. One of the natives facing off with them said something sharp. The offender laughed. "You monkeys are all pussies," he said, loudly enough for every spectator to hear. "You'd never make it in the real world." And with one fluid and totally unexpected move, he punched one of the natives in the gut.

It caught Ahni totally by surprise, not even the faintest whisper of intent had leaked out. The native doubled over with a choked cry, dropped to his knees, and vomited. The stench drifted across the crowd, and the wave of shock and surprise that gripped the onlookers erupted.

Bodies surged forward, sweeping Ahni with them. Someone clawed at her shoulder, twisting back and down as if to pull her off her feet. She twisted, ducked with the pressure, stabbed with stiffened fingers, and heard a grunt as she connected, caught a flash of a euro face, eyes round with shock.

"No!" Dane's yell filled the corridor, and the whip-crack of authority halted the crowd briefly. Ahni whirled just in time to see him grab the offending tourist.

Drunk or stoned as he might be, the downsider clearly knew how to fight, and Dane's slight, upsider muscles weren't going to be much of a match. Ahni started forward, shoving intervening bodies aside, but there was no need. As the man swung, Dane ducked it in a fluid motion that seemed more dance than combat, sidestepped and grabbed the man's arm and the top of his singlesuit, adding to the momentum of his swing so that the tourist staggered forward, too fast in the less than normal gravity to catch himself. Dane gave him a little extra help so that he slammed chest first onto the corridor flooring, knocking the wind out of himself.

His buddies surged forward, but from all sides, nearly a dozen natives leaped on them, pinning arms, restraining the men as they swore and threatened, spittle spraying as they raged. The two-toned chime of Security sounded and Ahni realized that the crowd had nearly evaporated, that the natives were leaving fast, some of them even breaking into a run. But Security cars, a bit larger and more powerful than the shuttles she had seen in the corridors, converged from all directions, cutting off escape. Panic flared and the crowd swayed and surged.

Dane pushed forward, no longer bothering to be deft, shoving people out of his way as he headed for the Security-clad people spreading out with stun-sticks across the corridor. The woman clearly in charge spun to face him as he approached, her stick up and ready, then halted as he spoke rapidly, shaking her head, their argument rising. Finally she turned to the car she'd climbed off of, spoke over some kind of link.

"Hold!" Dane's voice rose over the babble of voices, ringing with authority. "I got a promise from Security. Only the people who did the fighting are in trouble. The rest of you can leave in a minute or two."

The small group of natives, men and women in equal numbers, Ahni noted, hustled their snarling captives through the crowd, their faces grim. The Security chief turned away from the car, her expression just as grim and clearly dissatisfied with whatever instructions she had received. She raised her wrist to her lips, her words suddenly loud above the crowd murmur, clearly amplified.

Remain where you are until an officer takes your bio-ID. Then you can leave. We will not charge anyone who was not actively involved with the disturbance. Remain where you are. Those of you involved in the brawl, we got a positive vid-ID on every one of you, so you remain here.

That raised a growl of protest. "Hey, they started it!" A small, squat Latino-faced native stepped forward. "They started the whole damn thing. Weren't you watching?"

Cries of agreement rose from the mob and it closed ranks once more. But a slight, Asian-mix native with an intricate network of braids decorating his scalp, touched Latino-face on the shoulder, shrugging and speaking rapidly to the men and women around him. Ahni had seen Dane talking to him before the fight. In fact . . . she reviewed her memory of that moment . . . she had noticed him talking to a couple of the others in the group, too. The sudden tightening of the crowd relaxed. People moved apart, the razor edge of violence blunted now, replaced by worry, fear, concern in a rainbow of shades. Ahni scanned the faces. Yeah, the two others she had noticed in conversation with Dane were talking to clustered natives, and clearly urging calm. Dane had faded into the crowd and she noticed him get one or two people past Security although reinforcements were arriving and in another minute, no one would be able to slip away down the corridor. He veered toward her. "Do you have a guest pass for your room?" he asked urgently.

Without a word she slipped it from her pocket, thumbprinted it to activate it, and handed it over. Dane vanished.

The cordon was complete now. The tourists were being loaded into a cart, two of them threatening legal action, but sobered and subdued now. The third man, the one who had started the brawl with his punch, stood patiently, never once saying a word. Curious, Ahni edged closer. He wasn't afraid or upset at all. Or drunk. Dane appeared just then at her side.

"Ready to go?" He nodded toward a forming stream of bodies at one point in the cordon, where Security was reading and recording ID.

"He's a pro." She twitched her chin in the direction of the third tourist. "Hired to do this."

"I caught that." Dane nodded. "I know Carrie—the woman in charge. She's going to see what she can trip him into."

"You and Laif run this platform, quite well, you know," she murmured.

He smiled.

They had turned onto the main cross corridor where her hotel was located. The doorman was a woman today, with the look of a native, and she lifted her chin to Ahni as she approached. "You have a visitor." Her skeptical expression said a lot.

"It's all right." Ahni nodded. "I gave him the pass."

"Okay." She disapproved.

"Question," Ahni said. "Clearly bumping is rude or even a challenge up here?"

Dane nodded.

"When that tourist passed gas . . . that is taboo, too?"

"Oh yes." Dane shook his head, sighed. "We can't get the tourist PR people to include that in their intro vids for visitors, but I wish they would. It's not just rude, it's sort of like spitting on everyone around you. Made a nice trigger didn't it?" He gave her a crooked smile. "He must have biological control like yours."

"Maybe." Ahni thought back. "Pause would explain his timing and his reflexes."

"Does it bother you to have machines in your head?" He was looking at her curiously.

"Does it bother you that you couldn't go down to Earth today and walk around comfortably?"

"That's just muscle." They had stopped beneath one of the flowering trees in the courtyard. "I can fix that by spending more time in the gym. If I want to. It doesn't change who I am."

"Nanoware doesn't either." She smiled. "It's not like some sort of AI mind. It doesn't affect who I am or how I think. It's just having a really fast computer is all. Don't people use it up here?"

"Not much. Tourists bring it up. How do you know that it doesn't affect how you think?"

She shrugged. "Well, I guess I don't really know if it affects me, since it was installed before I was born." She smiled again. "I'm just me. The nanos are just data access hardware, switches, instant connection to the net no matter if I have a link or not. It's not like I hear voices in my head."

Dane shook his head. "If you say so."

"What's going to happen to the people in the brawl?" she asked. "I saw you talking to the natives who were part of it." She raised an eyebrow. "Did you get them off?"

"Sure." He shrugged. "They got set up. I had Laif tell Carrie to bring the tourists in by a different route, and as soon as they were out of sight, let the natives go. That'll cool off the Con. There's a convenient stretch of corridor with a faulty cam in it, so there won't be any permanent vid record."

As they approached the room door the room voice murmured *You have a visitor waiting. He had a pass.*

"Thank you," Ahni said, and the door slid open.

The man, scruffy in a grubby overall that had once carried an insignia on the front zip pocket and showed the scar where it had been effaced, sprawled in a recliner, a glass of beer in his hand from the refreshment wall. His face had a leathery, weathered look, although how you could get "weathered" up here, Ahni had no idea. As he grinned and lifted the beer in a toast, she noticed that his teeth were all synthetic implants and that he only had a thumb and forefinger on the hand that held the beer. The deformities repelled her. Why, when it was so easy and cheap to get reconstructive surgery using cloned tissue?

"Nice company you keep, Dane." He grinned up at them. "Thanks for the nice soft place to hide. I hate having to come down here looking for you. Heard some rumors that say maybe mining looks good again."

Ahni eyed the man, wondering what his age was in years. His bones were about as diminished as Koi's and the heave of his chest suggested that too much time in fullG would kill him for sure.

"Kyros, Ahni. She's okay, Kyros." Dane amiled. "Ahni, meet Kyros. He's a miner . . . asteroid miner . . . so he doesn't have any manners to speak of, but he's harmless."

Lot of affection there. Longtime friends, Ahni guessed.

"What were you *doing* down here?" Dane dropped wearily onto the end of the bed. "Not even I can save your butt if Laif gets hold of you." He sighed. "You're lucky Ahni was there with her pass."

"Dane, you asked me to keep an eye out." Kyros sat forward. "I seen something. Somebody's tooling around out there where they don't belong."

"Not just some new competition?" Dane's eyes narrowed.

"Nah." Kyros shook his head. "It's Swat-Prala's old ship . . . that bucket of bolts that'll get any fool killed who trusts it too long. And whoever is using it is a crappy pilot. Damn lucky one of the rock jocks hasn't holed him, just to get him out of the way before he hits someone. Or one of Darkside's catchers. Jazmin's just about hot enough to do it. He nearly clipped her, bringing in a load of ice."

"You ID the pilot?" Dane asked softly.

"Nope. I don't run around with a chip reader. Somebody told Jazmin he's a wildcard. I think that's why she didn't scuttle him, but why would a wildcard buy a crap heap like that ship of Swat-Prala's? They're all filthy rich."

Ahni met Dane's eyes. "What's he' doing out there?" she asked the miner.

"Nothin'." Kyros shrugged. "That's what's funny. He's just kind of scootin' around. Driver's ed?"

"You hear any other rumors about him?" Dane asked.

Kyros shook his head. "Nobody really knows anythin' much about him. Or cares. Rocky's selling him ice for the ship and she gave the guy a few pointers. Wants to keep him alive to keep buying, I guess. Heard another bit that might or might not have somethin' to do with this." His eyes, dark and sly as a dragon's moved between them. "But I'm doin' all the givin' here, Dane. I'll tell you what else I hear when you tell me what's going on. You know me." He chuckled. "Just gotta know everything."

"It's blowing up, Kyros," Dane said slowly. "CSF is on the way. I need the guy who's in Swat-Prala's ship. He's the only bone Laif can throw this dog." He smiled mirthlessly. "And if he doesn't throw it something, it's going to eat us both."

Kyros leaned forward, his manner suddenly, deadly serious. "Dane, you don't need to end up the bone. This is Laif's game, not yours." He glanced fleetingly at Ahni.

"She knows, Kyros."

"Okay then. This is what's gonna come down, Dane." Kyros tilted his glass, drained the last of his beer. "CFS pops on up to the hub and all hell breaks loose. You're smack in the middle. 'Bout time you headed back out to the Belt before you get busted for those pets of yours."

Ahni winced at Dane's reaction. Watched Kyros's eyes darken. "Damn," the old man said, and drew a deep, labored breath. "What you see in them, I don't know. But then I don't, do I?" He levered himself to his feet with difficulty. "I'll go catch up with Jazmin. She's picking up a load and it's slow coming in. She's got time on her hands to go lookin'. You want him alive?"

"If possible," Dane said evenly. "It would be better to have him talking, but I don't want people dead who don't need to be." He didn't look at Ahni.

"Will do." Kyros shuffled toward the door, paused to look into Ahni's face. "Too bad you got mixed up in this. Dane's good at watching your back for you."

"Yeah." She gave him a faint smile. "I bet he is."

Kyros gave a cackling laugh and left the room.

Dane got Noah out of bed between shifts. Not sleeping, Ahni guessed from his tone of voice. But he agreed quickly to head down to the admin offices and work on the medallion's data dot. "Should be a piece of cake," he said.

"Tell him that Taiwanese will be the base for the encryption," Ahni said. "Not modern, but classical." Noah sounded stressed.

Dane passed on the information, closed the link, and stood, more gracefully than Kyros, although it clearly cost him an effort, too. For a moment he looked down into her upturned face, then leaned down and kissed her gently on the mouth. "Now we need to visit Li Zhen" he said. "We'll use my ship and see if you can get us in."

You have a message, the room broke in. *From Li Zhen, Chairman of Dragon Home.*

"Speak of the devil," Dane murmured.

It was prerecorded. Li Zhen would be happy to speak with her and would send a Courier. "You can't come," she told Dane. "A bonded courier won't take you without an invitation. And Laif needs you here," she answered his frown. "I'll convince him to meet with you."

He agreed, reluctantly, because she was right, took the guest pass she gave him and left. "Be very careful," he said from the doorway. "Please."

When the door closed behind him. Ahni dropped into Pause. Time to lay all her puzzle pieces out and see how Kyros's new piece fit.

FIFTEEN

THE SAME NATIVE COURIER WITH THE CANTONESE FACE arrived at Ahni's hotel room. He greeted her with a respectful bow and that quicksilver glimmer of an internal smile that she remembered from her previous trip with him. They didn't speak as the Courier led her to his ship, and in seemingly no time, the Courier docked his craft in the familiar bay and popped the winged hatch for her. "Thank you," she said as she climbed out of the craft. "I hope you can bring your family up here." She bowed to him.

He returned it with a smile.

The antechamber beyond, with its eggshell colored walls and embroidered silk hanging was empty. Ahni slipped off her shoes, her feet caressed by the woven carpets. The room gave her no message as she crossed the room to the inner door. She wondered if something had detained Li Zhen or if this was some sort of interesting test. The door opened for her, admitting her to the garden beyond. Today, the sky was streaked with thin white clouds and a flower-scented breeze kissed her cheeks. A gold and crimson dragon kite danced on the wind and she admired the reality of the holo for a moment, before she realized that it *was* real, that she was seeing a small kite up there beneath the artificial sky. It must have some kind of propulsion system, although the delicate construct of silk and light wood might have been one of the kites she had flown as a child. She followed the barely visible line of the string down to the other end of the small garden.

A woman sat lotus-legged on a mat of woven bamboo, laughing up at the boy who held the kite string. About five, maybe, he watched the kite, rapt. Chinese, she noted absently, and felt a tiny shock of recognition as he followed the kite's dance with milky, blind-looking eyes that seemed to shine in his too-long, tawny face. A cap of embroidered crimson silk covered his hairless scalp, and his arms and legs seemed a little too long for his body, too thin and delicate to be human. They . . . curved. Just slightly.

Another Koi. Not just in New York Up, then.

As if she had spoken out loud, the child turned to look at her. He smiled, and she felt the pressure of his curiosity. She smiled back, summoning a vision of Koi shooting through the NYUp garden, wondering if he would catch it.

The woman spied her and leaped to her feet, full of alarm and dismay. She grabbed the boy's arm and started to pull him away, the kite abandoned now, dancing erratically beneath the sky that was really a ceiling. But he twisted free and ran to Ahni, awkward and coltish on his too long, too fragile, bendable legs.

"Where?" His Mandarin was whispery, raspy, a bit like the sound of wind through grass. "Can I play with him? Is he here?"

"We have to go. I am sorry." The young woman . . . a native by her looks, but not nearly as extreme as the child . . . tugged at his arm, a metallic tinge of fear edging her words. "I apologize. I did not know that Li Zhen expected company, please excuse us." She had a grip on the boy's arm now, but he resisted and she seemed reluctant to use force.

"It's all right." Ahni smiled reassuringly. "I don't mind. I am pleased to meet you. Your kite is very wonderful," she said to the boy.

He shrugged. "Where does he fly like that?" he asked in his papery, grass-wind voice. "I want to do that."

"I am so sorry." The woman's resolve hardened. "He is . . . as you see . . . a tragedy." Her expression challenged Ahni to disagree, but near panic still surged beneath her apparent calm. "Come *now*," she said to the boy, "And I will take you flying."

That got his attention although it was tinged with skepticism, and the woman hustled him away, vanishing through a small door hidden by a pair of miniature cypress trees. Ahni stared thoughtfully at the kite bumping along the 'sky' and the woven mat where the woman had sat. She reached for the dangling kite string, gave it a sharp, short tug. It tumbled instantly to her feet, the red and yellow silk tails fluttering like broken wings, to land in a puddle of bright silk at her feet. She picked it up, noticing the carved bones of real wood that formed it. Someone had made this, carefully and well. The propulsion system was small enough not to be visible to casual inspection. Electromagnetic, she guessed, interacting with hardware in the ceiling/sky.

"I apologize. My garden is messy for your visit."

She turned to face Li Zhen. He must have come in from some other hidden doorway and he was flustered. "How surprising to find a kite up here." She smiled at him. "Very ingenious."

"A touch of home."

A tiny spike of pain/anger with that word 'home'? Ahni put on her sweetest and most unaware expression. "How can one live here and not be homesick for all the things we so take for granted on Earth?"

"Please." He managed a smile. "Some tea? Huang Ahni, you are far more than a mere delicate blossom meant to beautify some man's garden. Shall we talk clearly?" He offered her his arm.

She masked her uneasiness with a smile. "Clear talk is always the straightest path," she said and allowed him to usher her from the garden and the crumpled kite. They entered his private chamber again, with its mother-of-pearl inlaid furniture and the bamboo growing in its celadon pot.

"I was charmed to find a child playing in your garden," she said as Li Zhen bent to pour from the pot that steamed gently on the low table.

The tiny jerk of his hand was almost unnoticeable. Anger? Fear? Love? A little bit of all of that? Anhi kept her expression unaware as he handed her an eggshell fragile cup of golden tea.

"Ah, the child," he said at last, as he filled a cup for himself. "Such a tragedy for the parents at his birth. He is the child of a friend, badly deformed and retarded, but simple things delight him."

Lie. An interesting one.

"So I allow her to bring him to the garden. Why should I keep something just for myself?" He smiled at her, more confident now, sipped his tea.

Anhi smiled, too, her face expressing her admiration for someone who was able to share with those beneath him, the flowery taste of the tea filling her mouth.

A young woman, her long hair braided into a tight knot at her neck, brought in a tray of sliced bamboo shoots and cooked green soybean pods along with two pairs of lacquered chopsticks. This was the woman, the native, who had been playing with the child in the garden. Ahni glanced at her and turned back to Li Zhen, but she kept her attention focused on the woman. She set the tray on the table, her eyes downcast, bowed stiffly and nervously, and withdrew, carefully not looking at Ahni.

Ahni weighed the value of asking him outright if the boy in the garden was the reason he had tried to kidnap Koi. But she would only have one question to slip past his guard. After that, his armor would be in place and they would merely fence. He was as good a fencer as she was. Even though she had the advantage of her E rating. "So you grow bamboo here, too?" She picked up the chopsticks and selected a fat, chambered slice. It crunched between her teeth, thick and crisp, as succulent as the best grown in Taiwan. "Very nice," she said. "I am impressed."

"It is a strain developed for shoot production." Li Zhen waved a hand, but her praise warmed him. "Bamboo in particular seems to thrive in a micro gravity environment. A taste of home." He lifted his cup.

Question there, not a statement. Ahni lifted her own cup. "Perhaps," she said, and the word caught her by surprise. But this was not the time to look too deeply into her unconscious responses. She picked up a soybean pod in her chopsticks, deftly sucking the fat beans from the pod. "China gains power against the NAA," She said. "What is it that *you* gain from the arrival of CSF on New York Up?"

He felt a moment of triumph, but gave her a face of innocence, his eyebrows arching. "I am sorry." He spoke in careful and precise

Mandarin. "I had not heard that the World Council intended to occupy our sister platform."

Ha. "My brother is your agent there, creating friction there between native residents and tourists." She let her Taiwan accent dominate. No formality here, just truth. "But his presence has been detected, so the usefulness of that approach has been blunted." She smiled. "The spear in the dark has the sharpest edge. Especially when it comes from behind."

"There is truth in that old saying." Li Zhen smiled, his face still fixed in an expression of innocent surprise. "Why would I wish your brother to evoke violence?"

"Because you can then go before the World Council and offer to stabilize the platforms. The history of Dragon Home supports your claim, and of course, China will muster its votes to back the proposal in the Council. I suspect you will work for the World Council, in name only." She smiled gently. "You will have two platforms to rule. Will this be your empire?"

He had himself under control by the time she asked her question, but he had not been able to hide his response to her words at the outset, and he knew he had given himself away. Irony tinged his smile and he bowed. "Your father has underestimated you," he said softly, his dark eyes on her face. "He has forgotten that performance can be as important as the pedigree of the race horse."

"Thank you." Ahni gave him a crooked smile. "I will not take that as an insult."

"It's praise. I know you feel that." He rose to his feet, supple and lithe. Half a head taller than her with his Northern genes, he looked down at her, his expression enigmatic, reflecting the complex shift and flow of his emotions. "You're right. I should not play word games with you." He grinned, his confidence bright as sunlight. "It will happen just so. We are separate up here. We need to rule ourselves."

"*You* need to rule," she murmured. He was not going to meet with Dane.

"I'm the best one to do it." He shrugged and touched her cheek with one fingertip. "Our child would have enormous potential," he said softly. "With our intelligence and your ability. It's not just my own power I want. I want dynasty, too. Why not? This world is *mine*. I would share it with you."

Now that was a forthright proposition, Ahni thought. Li Zhen's desire prickled across her skin and tickled between her legs.

"Why not?" His eyes fixed on hers, bright with desire and his vision of tomorrow. "I offer more than you will ever have on Taiwan, even as heir to your father."

"That is my mother's dream for me. She traded her life for it." Ahni shook her head. "I cannot walk away from that obligation, honored cousin." *She* stood behind the carved screen. The native woman, her pain sharp as a knife. Ahni met Li Zhen's eyes. "I do not think our paths lie together," she said softly.

For an instant anger boiled behind his eyes, then he banished it. Shrugged. "One cannot see beyond the curve of the road," he said lightly. "Paths diverge and then meet again." He turned away to pour more tea. "From what you say, the North American Alliance's platform will be a dangerous place, especially for a visitor." He offered her the full cup. "You will be safer as my guest."

"That is thoughtful of you." She made no move to take the cup. "But I will be responsible for my own safety."

He shrugged, a wealth of meaning in the lift of both shoulders. "I will have Jin An show you to a room. I look forward to showing you the gardens here, with our bamboo that grows so luxuriously and our fish pools. Waterfalls in minimal gravity are quite lovely."

Ahni stifled her anger, kept her face smooth.

"How intimate."

The words, knife-edged with fury, made them both start. Xai! Ahni turned to face him as he strode into the room.

"We had words over this before *esteemed brother*." He faced Li Zhen, fists clenched at his sides. "I assume you have forgotten them?"

"I have not, but perhaps you did not listen the first time." Li Zhen faced the younger man, the ice of his own anger pitted against Xai's heat. "You seem to have made your involvement visible. That was clumsy."

"It wasn't my doing." Xai sent Ahni a cold, venomous look. "But perhaps you know all about that. I doubt you, esteemed brother.

I doubted you before, but you were so smooth that I listened to you. I made a mistake. I do not make the same mistake twice." Turning on his heel, he strode through the door.

Li Zhen looked after him, anger and distress hidden beneath the mask of his neutral face. He looked swiftly at Ahni. "We can talk more later."

Ahni hurried after him as he followed Xai but at the door to the chamber, the same slender, native-looking boy appeared to block her path. She seized his hand quickly, lightly, prepared to twist him out of her way, use his surprise and mass against him. But he reacted with lightning speed to pull her just a hair out of balance. Before she could recover, he had spun her backward, so that she fell heavily against the wall inside. The door whispered closed.

Ahni rubbed her shoulder where she had hit the wall. She had let herself believe that the elongated native phenotype meant a lack of strength. Angry at herself, because she had walked knowingly into this trap, she paced the chamber. Spacious by platform standards, it offered only two routes out—the door by which Xai and Li Zhen had exited, and the small service door behind the screen. She tried her access, but the room requested a password in polite Mandarin. Her link did not work, either. A security shell. Of course.

Li Zhen's words suggested that Xai was working on his own, allied only loosely with Li Zhen's cause. Ahni thought about the careful planning of the riot that had killed the tourist. Xai tended to think and act like a loose dragon. The orchestration, the careful coordination that had gone into the planning of the infiltration of the Con, the careful agitation to create violent eruptions at just the right time and place . . . this demonstrated a subtlety of thought that her brother utterly lacked.

If not Li Zhen, who was behind this? And why?

She had to get these new pieces to Dane. Ahni closed her eyes, despair nipping at her, feeling as if she had taken two steps forward and now, three back. "Jin An." She drew a slow breath, making her tone conversational, relaxed. "It's up to you to let me out the service door."

No response. No sign that anyone was listening and why would she be?

"I am not going to become Li Zhen's wife, or lover, or breeding female. I have business in NYUp that will make that quite clear."

Still no sign of listening, but Ahni wouldn't feel her response unless Jin An was pressed to the door, as she had been while she and Li Zhen had talked. The room would certainly be wired for listening. Ahni drew another slow breath and dropped briefly into Pause, summoning the image of the boy and the woman from short term memory. She called up an image of Li Zhen and ran a quick comparison.

Ahni opened her eyes and threw the dice.

"He's Li Zhen's son. And yours. Children like him are being born all over the platforms. It's not deformity. Not mutation. He has . . . adapted. Li Zhen will see this if he only looks. I will show him. If you let me out now, I will make Li Zhen look at the other children . . . see them for what they are. If the CSF arrive on New York Up and I am not there, I may not ever be able to do that. And your child will always remain . . . deformed. And hidden." She loaded the words with truth.

No response except the soft breath of air moving into and out of the room.

Then . . . the door behind the screen whispered open. Ahni crossed the room in a few brisk steps, moving fast before the woman could change her mind.

She stood just beyond the doorway.

Ahni met the woman's dark, bitter gaze. "Have you taken him to play in the hub garden?"

She shook her head.

"You should do that. He'll discover that he is much better in microG than you or I will ever be. He's better," she said softly. "Don't you see? It's evolution. It just isn't happening the way it has always happened on Earth." She shrugged. "Why should it?"

Jin An looked away, some of the bitterness muted into thoughtfulness, the darkness unmitigated.

"Li Zhen has already glimpsed the truth," Ahni said. "He already knows. Why his son is as he is. He's just afraid to let himself acknowledge that. I'll make him do that." A promise. The woman heard it, lifting her eyes to meet Ahni's, a tiny spark in their depths. She nodded, gestured with her chin.

Ahni approached the door she had indicated. It opened and Ahni stepped through, adrenaline pumping now, heart beating fast. How long before Li Zhen finished with Xai and came back? Dropping momentarily into Pause, she summoned up the path from dock to private chamber. She needed a corridor to take her to the right. Doors lined the carpeted corridor, without traffic, private space, she guessed.

One door was painted a soft blue rather than the creamy tan of the others. She touched it and opened to reveal a corridor. Lucky guess. Now if it led to the main corridor she could find her way back to the dock. She didn't run, because Security might notice a running person. She reached the end of the connecting corridor. Main corridor? Maybe. She had nothing but direction to guide her, no landmarks at all to tell her where she was in the maze of linking corridors. Turned right.

And her luck ran out. Around the curve in the of the corridor in the distance, a figure appeared, feet visible first as he descended the 'slope' of the skin level corridor. Frantically, Ahni touched the doors on either side of the corridor. *Access? Access?* She had no password. Too late now. She straightened, adopted a casually purposeful posture. The clothes weren't Li Zhen's and didn't seem to be a uniform either.

The figure appeared fully, halted briefly, then waved and hurried toward her.

Kyros!

"Need a lift?" He reached her, his weathered and aged-ugly face crinkled into a thousand folds of laughter.

"How did you get here?"

"I saw you leave your hotel." He winked. "I know that Courier. Dragon Home's head dragon owns him. I figured it might just be easier to get in here than to leave. So I called in a few favors. Quite a few." Kyros had her by the elbow and was steering her down the corridor. "Good timing. We have about . . ." He glanced at a tiny screen inset into his forearm. "Seven minutes and thirty five seconds."

"Before what?"

"Before Security finds the problem in their system, fixes it, and sees us."

Somebody owed him some *very* large favors.

Kyros paused in front of a door which opened, admitting them to the garden where she had first seen the boy. The abandoned kite lay where Li Zhen had dropped it.

The boy knelt beside it. Waiting.

"Damn," Kyros muttered.

The boy smiled at Ahni—*you're slow*. Rose awkwardly on those too-long feet.

"Ignore him," Kyros murmured. "We don't want him yelling for help."

"He's coming with us." She swept her arm around him at the same instant he leaped, so awkward in gravity, up onto her hip. She didn't stagger at all, remembered the fragile, too-light feel of Koi's body in her arms. "Don't ask, we do this. Trust me, okay?"

"Who the hell are you to trust?" But Kyros was already striding on, urgency a sharp stink in his wake, heading for the door that led to the vestibule and the dock. She followed, leaning to balance the boy's weight, counting down the time he'd given her. One minute and twenty seconds left, as the lock cycled behind them.

The ship waiting was ugly, matte black, battered, and scarred. Bigger than the Courier's little shuttle, but not huge, squat and nothing sleek about it. A hole appeared in the side as if the metal melted away. She ducked through, slinging the boy onto the curved inside hull, looking around for seats or webbing.

"Sit. Over there." Kyros jerked his head, flung himself into a webbing sling like the one she had seen in Dane's ship.

She sat, pulled the boy against her as the ship quivered beneath them. Sudden acceleration shoved them forward and Ahni clutched the boy as he started to tumble, hung on as the direction of the acceleration changed suddenly. Now a hand flattened them to the hull and she felt the ship leap beneath them, like a horse leaping into full gallop. The boy gasped for breath and for a few moments, even Ahni struggled with the feel of suffocation. Then the hand let go.

Without webbing to anchor them, they drifted, Ahni still clutching the boy by the hand, struggling briefly with *up* and *down*. The boy gasped, but this was the sound of delight, not struggle. "Flying," he said, and his smile was like a small sun in the ship.

"Okay, we're hiding in a nice little shadow where nobody can see us." Kyros twisted around in his hammock, his face cold as a winter desert. "Explain to me why this is a good thing." His chin pointed at the boy who had pushed himself off from the hull and was drifting across the small space, radiating delight. "I can take you back and probably earn a fat payoff." His eyes narrowed as he regarded Ahni.

"This is Li Zhen's son." Ahni spoke in English. No, the boy didn't understand the language. "He's a lever. Dane needs it."

For a moment, Kyros merely stared at her, but his reaction made her wince. "He looks like Dane's pets." A shadow of doubt colored his tone. "He's right, then? About . . . them?"

"I think so." Ahni shrugged. "Got another explanation?"

"You sure act like you know what you're doing." Kyros regarded her thoughtfully, coldly. "Out in the Belt, there's a sort of natural selection about that. If you *do* know what you're doing, you're alive. If you don't, you're not." His eyes narrowed. "I think I'd feel a lot better right now if you were a Belter."

Ahni shrugged and didn't look away, although the cold of the void beyond that hull chilled her spine. He had options. Sell her back to Li Zhen. Toss her out of the ship and sell the boy back to Li Zhen. Or take them to Dane. She relaxed her muscles to readiness, drew a single calming breath and . . . waited.

Kyros finally looked away. "You might have made it in the Belt. Maybe." He turned his back on her, ignoring the boy who zipped past his head, surprised and delighted with the result of his sudden push-off.

Ahni snagged him, spilled his momentum with a rebound off the hull and held on as acceleration's hand gently added weight. "Relax, Little Brother," she said to the sharp bloom of his disappointment. "You'll get to fly all you want pretty soon."

Kyros made a short, sharp sound of disapproval. "Nobody's looking for us yet anyway. I'm dumping you into Dane's lap and then I'm heading back out to the Belt. Politics down here are too damn complicated. And I don't want to be around when Zhen discovers his kid is missing and starts looking."

"The boy's not missing." Ahni braced herself and the boy as the ship maneuvered. "He already knows where to look for him."

"I hope for Dane's sake you're really as right as you think you are. You scare me."

Ahni shrugged and didn't tell him that she hoped she was, too. They were docking. A gentle impact vibrated through the hull and they were drifting again. A few moments later, the hull melted open and Ahni found herself in Dane's private dock, the one from which he had ferried her to the Elevator.

Years, ago, she thought. In another life.

"Come on." She took the boy firmly by the hand and towed him from the ship. "Just let me do it for now," she said as he tried to swim, thrashing ineffectively. "You'll figure all this out really fast. I have a good teacher for you."

"Show me." He was quivering with excitement, his Mandarin sloppy with hurry. "He is waiting?"

Was Koi waiting? If so, Li's son was a whole lot more sensitive than Ahni was.

But no, when the lock cycled and opened to the green-white glare of light and plants no Koi drifted, grinning.

No reason he should be, but it bothered her. The boy was pulling off his embroidered slippers, his cap aleady lost, stripping out of his jacket to leave him naked from the waist up, skinny, his toes, yes, as long and prehensile as Koi's. He pushed off, clumsy, arrowed away to crash into a tube planted to something leafy and green. Shreds of plant tissue drifted away and a couple of the small frog-things skimmed away in upset. The boy squealed a high, thin note of pure delight. Undisturbed by his collision he caught the tube as he rebounded and pushed again, rocketing off in a new direction.

"Wait up, kid. You'll trash the whole place." Kyros zoomed after him, grabbed one of the boy's ankles and spilled momentum on another tube, managing not to do too much damage in the process. "Go slow," he said sternly and let go of the wriggling, protesting boy. "Easy!"

"He doesn't speak English." Ahni laughed. "Slow," she said in Mandarin. "Careful!"

Chastened, he pushed off almost timidly and drifted on a wobbling course between tubes, experimenting with hands and feet.

He'd get the hang of it quickly, Ahni guessed. Already his toes were spreading, grasping as he pushed off from the tubes.

"Zhen's son, huh?" Absently, Kyros snagged the drifting shoes and the cap. "God help 'em all. Especially Dane."

"Thanks," she said. "For coming after me. I'm not sure how I would have gotten off Dragon Home."

"Me neither." Kyros gave her a crooked smile. "Zhen keeps a really tight hold on things over there. Good Security. If you don't have a membership card."

"I'm glad you do," Ahni said, and meant it. "I owe you."

"Oh, yeah, you do. Don't worry." His face folded into a grin. "I'll remind you."

"Kyros—" Ahni caught a nearby tube to halt her drift. It had been newly planted and she couldn't identify the tiny green sprouts. "Is Koi Dane's son?"

"Not by blood, if that's what you mean." Kyros let himself drift, his expression thoughtful. "But yeah, Koi is his kid. That's why I haven't been able to pry him loose and get him back out to the Belt." He shrugged. "Although he could take the kid. Koi would love it out there, bet you. Nah." Kyros wrinkled his grin at her. "I figured he liked men, then I figured sex just wasn't much interest to him at all. Guess I was wrong." He leered at her.

She didn't blush and tried Dane's link. No response. "Contact me," she messaged. "Kyros, can you go look for him? It's critical." She pushed off, following Li Zhen's son, intensely aware of the time that had passed while she was on Dragon Home. Aware of Koi's continued absence. Where was he? "Maybe he can use this little lever of ours before the CSF get here."

"It's a big can." Kyros sounded doubtful. "I'll try."

"Kyros?" Ahni spilled momentum on a tube planted to tomatoes, waited for the Belter to turn. "You said nobody was looking for us, on the way over. If they had been . . . would they have found us?"

"Depends on how good the looker was. I was shadow skipping. I'm pretty good at it . . . but if someone's looking . . ." He shrugged. "You gotta cross the light once in awhile."

"Shadow skipping?"

"You got spots where the sensor net can't look." He moved impatiently, ready to push off. "You got a lot of junk in this orbit now. Real mess. Lots of shadow, but most of it too small to really hide in if someone's looking for you. But you can make it tough for 'em."

"What about rocks?" She tilted her head. "Could you drop a small asteroid down to this level?"

Kyros looked away. "You know what happens if you do that up here?" he asked softly. "You fall out of your ship. If Earth got to thinking Belters were riding rocks down, Earth would get *real* upset. So we sort of have our own little system for dealing with it up here. If you're clumsy enough to get caught. Natural selection, remember?" He still wasn't looking at her. "You could sure make a hot profit, bringing the whole dirty iceball down here. Bringing it down as refined ice or metal is like hauling the ocean in a bucket."

Well, now she knew why Dane couldn't square Kyros with Laif. "Don't get caught," Ahni said as she kicked off.

"Oh, I don't do it anymore," Kyros said with a laugh. "Dane tells me I'm too important to risk my butt. I haul . . . other stuff."

She didn't entirely believe him, but it wasn't important right now.

If the CSF hadn't landed yet . . . there might still be a chance to stop this. Once Li Zhen came looking for his son.

SIXTEEN

"YOU GOT ANY GLIMMER YET?" LAIF PACED THE CRAMPED admin space, came to a stop behind the skinny kid hunched over the holo-field. "You asleep or what?"

"What."

Damn smart aleck. Laif glowered down at the back of the kid's neck, really wanting to smack him one. The ticking of the clock inside his skull damn near deafened him and this kid just sat there like a lump. Not that whatever was in that data dot was likely to be the magic wand to save their butts, but he sure didn't have any other options. He glared at the tattoo circling the kid's skinny wrist. He was almost one of Dane's creepy kids. They were moving that way, Dane was right. He'd looked at some of the recent births and you could see that Koi kid in their skinny bodies and low birth weight. Best kept secret on the platform, he thought sourly. They bothered him, those kids. They didn't look human.

"You have thirty-three minutes," Laif rasped. "The Elevator's at the top. You countin'?"

"I figure you are." The kid looked up, his face showing strain, his dark eyes angry. "And every time you interrupt me, by the way, you cost me about two and a half minutes. That's a grand total of fifteen minutes so far. You want to go do something else?"

"All right, all right." Laif turned on his heel. The heads up from his informants at the Euro Elevator had come way too soon. They must have pushed the climbers past the limit of safety to get here this quickly. "I'll go see if I can't stall our visitors and buy you back that fifteen minutes. When we run out of time . . . go up to the hub, okay? Use Dane's system. It's separate and firewalled. They'll probably take the main system over first thing. Depends on how good their sappers are. They may firewall you out." He left admin, snapping his fingers for the Security cart standing by. Hopped aboard as it rolled up beside him. "Arrival and pronto. Carrie, we're out of time." He lowered his voice. "I need to stall. Can you set something up? Call Dane for a flash mob?"

The Security Chief nodded. "I'll see if I can do as good a job as that mob that Dane settled over in A3. That what you need?"

He nodded, a single hard jerk of his chin. "Make a show, but nothing that'll bring weapons out. We'll round everybody up nice and efficient and dump all but a couple. Get volunteers for that and give 'em a get-out guarantee."

"I don't know if I can do that," Carrie said slowly, her eyes on the corridor ahead, lips barely moving. "Don't know if I'll have the keys."

Yeah, stupid. Laif ran a hand over his scalp in frustration. Why would they keep his Security Chief in place? That was the first thing Arlin would do . . . dump Carrie. Arlin knew what she thought of him. She hadn't exactly hidden her feelings. "They might send someone new up here."

"You don't think they will and I don't either." Carrie snorted, her expression hard. "Arlin's the perfect puppet. Whistle and he dances. Laif . . ." Carrie hesitated. "After the shit hits the floor." She gave him a sideways look. "I figure the odds are fifty-fifty for a forced relocation."

"They can't do that. We've got permanent leases on our space."

"Laws can change."

"It'd cost too much." Laif laughed, but it had a hollow feel. Like whistling in the dark.

Carrie didn't answer and her silence prodded him.

Laif let his breath out in a long sigh. "Well, whatever is gonna happen it's gonna happen. I don't think we can stop it, but maybe we can keep it civil." The Arrival Hall opened before them, and Carrie passworded them through the security curtain. Laif hopped out as the cart slowed. "Gods know, we might get lucky. Go get your mob." He lifted a hand to her, got a grim faced nod in return before she whipped the cart around and rocketed back through the curtain and down the corridor. Laif hoped she'd put on a good show. Straightening his shoulders, he headed for the main doors, his skin creeping in the vast emptiness. Tourists had abandoned NYUp in droves. This much space—empty like this—bothered him. Been up here too long, he thought. Well, maybe not for much longer. Look up and see sky again, walk the Towers Plaza in Manhattan and get rained on while watching the jugglers and light artists work. Would be good to be back.

Yeah, right.

A pair of uniformed CSF appeared in Entry B from the shuttle dock, blue berets perched aggressively, eyes flicking as they scoped the Hall. Weapons invisible anyway, thank you very much for that. Laif straightened his shoulders again. He was too damn old to go back to living on Earth. Back straight, he walked forward, annoyance in every stride, aware of the surreptitious stares of the nervous Immigration staff. The vanguard of the CSF spotted him and fanned out . . . threatening in stance and position, but still no weapons in hand. One stepped forward, flanked by two more.

Captain? Not even a Major? Laif read the insignia. Scandanavian-euro mix, blonde, white as one of Dane's damn flowers. And younger than him. A lot younger. I don't like you, he thought. They gave you this as a training mission. "Major." He strode forward, doing a 'dumb yokel' smile. "Laif Jones Egret, Administrator of the North American Alliance orbital platform New York Up. Welcome. We've been looking forward to your arrival."

"It's Captain, sir." The young officer said calmly. "Captain Bugloss. I am to report to the Administrator of the platform."

I should be insulted, Laif thought. Clearly the CSF's commanders had figured this for a cakewalk. But false expectations make a potent weapon. "Allow me to escort you to our offices . . . although . . ." He looked back at the uniformed men and women spilling from the entry bay. Only ten? The rest must be waiting until the vanguard secured the area? "You realize that your large numbers will present . . . ah . . . a bit of a problem. We don't have large amounts of public space up here. Do you plan to commandeer private hotel space?"

"We don't plan on being here that long." The young captain looked nonplussed for a beat. As if Laif had just read from the wrong script. "I don't anticipate any difficulty in completing our mission within a few hours at most." He handed over a Security Sealed data sphere. "We don't plan to cause any unnecessary disruption."

Huh? Something didn't compute here. Laif looked at the sphere. "I'm sorry. Our communication has been down all day, so I've had no current report on your arrival." He glanced at the troops. They didn't *act* like an advance guard securing a beachhead. To hell with games. "Why exactly are you here?"

The captain's eyebrows rose only a hair, but he made his surprise at that question clear. "We are here to arrest a North American Alliance employee suspected of diluting the human genotype with transgenic applications. An employee named Dane Nilsson. You didn't get the arrest warrant?"

Sweet Mohammad, Buddha, and Jesus. "I told you." Laif's voice didn't quite squeak. "Our communication has been down." He forced a look of mild surprise onto his face. "I know that man. While he's not my friend politically, he certainly isn't involved in anything like human genetic research. He works in the Platform agricultural hub. Pushes buttons and watches dials. Does a good job, too."

The captain's eyes had glazed slightly. "Yes, sir. I'm sure, sir."

Laif itched with the need to call Dane *now*, plastered a smile onto his face. "We'll have to go to Admin and verify your authorization." He jerked his chin at the data sphere clutched in his hand. "Since I have received no notification."

"Of course." The captain didn't look happy. "Just a moment." He turned away, touching up his link, clearly checking to find out if indeed, the platform had received the warrant. Turned back, his shoulders slumping a bare nanometer and no more. "You can ID the copy I brought," he said with well restrained impatience.

Damn, damn, damn, if he hadn't shut down communications, Dane could be halfway to the Belt by now.

"Transportation?" Bugloss said.

"Well we walk everywhere up here," Laif said apologetically, back to bumpkin mode. "But if you have people who . . . you know . . . have difficulty . . . I can call for a cart. Or two." Laying it on too thick, he thought, but no, the captain's weary expression suggested he bought it.

Good. He needed time. And a link to Dane.

The captain nodded once, and the ten members of his unit fell in, eyes flicking, not missing a detail. Six women, four men. They looked utterly competent. Laif halted as they reached a public rest-room. "Excuse me just a moment." He did a very credible job of looking utterly embarrassed. "Sorry. I'm just getting over a really nasty stomach flu." Ducked into the restroom before the captain had finished nodding. One touristy looking man stood at a urinal, dreamily studying the colorful mosaic on the wall above the trough carrying the gently circulating water. The three showers were empty although a breath of steam in the air suggested they had been in use recently. Laif ducked into one of the stalls as the door whispered open. Uh oh. CSF blue showed beneath the door. The man didn't use the urinal stream, simply stood there in the middle of the tile floor, booted feet visible beneath the stall door.

The back of Laif's neck prickled.

Damn. So much for downsider stupidity.

He flushed, his muttered words lost in the brief *whoosh* of suction, unlatched the door and made a show of sealing up his single-suit as he exited. The man waiting, very young, with a shadow of scalp fuzz and a very discreet heart inlaid behind his right ear in red light, stood aside with a slight nod and no smile at all on his Mediterranean face.

Not good. Laif marched out into the corridor, a fixed smile plastered to his face. Maybe the flash mob—

It happened and it was perfect . . . just enough people to block the sparse flow of traffic along the skinside promenade, send the few remaining downsiders scurrying for shelter. It didn't do much good either. The captain looked to Laif for information and when

Laif told him Security would handle it, he pulled his people back and they let Carrie handle it. Laif discovered that he had picked up a shadow, a buzz-headed woman who never strayed more than a meter from Laif's side. And he hadn't told Carrie that he needed some space. So she did a great job of doing what he had asked her to do and it didn't do him one damn bit of good. But it sure made 'em look real good. Not that this bunch cared one bit. Clearly they expected Security to do its job.

After she had cleared the hall with a credible show of competence and control, they resumed their march to Admin. With every step Laif's heart sank lower. As they entered the main room, Bar looked up from his screen, and his eyes skipped from Laif's face to the captain's and back again. "Only ten?"

"Police action," Laif said heavily. Noah was gone. Up to the hub. "You need to get hold of Noah," he said in a carefully casual tone. "Tell him we're on our way up."

"No." The Captain stepped forward. "No communications to anyone until we've completed our mission." He jerked his head at one of the women, who stepped forward, eyes on Bar.

Bar started to ask what about, and then a slow surmise began to stir in his eyes. He looked frightened.

He had a newborn son, Laif remembered wearily. One of the more extreme.

It didn't matter that Bar guessed. The captain looked over his shoulder as he opened the data sphere and had Laif retina stamp the warrant. They had never set up any kind of emergency heads-up alert to the hub . . . not one that they could activate with someone standing over them. Big mistake, Laif realized. He clenched his teeth as the captain issued orders. They used a shorthand language, a mix of acronyms and one-word commands that Laif could only guess at. "Let me call Nilsson up to Admin," he said, trying for casual, hick-mayor helpfulness. "No reason for him not to come. I consult with him now and again."

"We need to do an evidence search." The captain was checking a very small and compact stun gun.

"I'm coming with you." Laif stepped forward, reading refusal in the captain's narrowed eyes. "Simpler than issuing you a pass.

You need an upper level security clearance to ride the elevator clear up to the hub . . . at least the agricenter part of it. It's closed." He dropped the useless act. "Damn it, it's my platform." For now. Until they had to reestablish communication or the real occupying force showed up. At least this crew hadn't brought a sapper.

The captain considered for the space of three seconds, nodded. "All right. You do as I say." He made eye contact with a small, tough looking woman with a semitic-mix face. Jerked his chin infinitesimally in Laif's direction. The babysitter.

The captain left the hard-eyed watch bitch with Bar. So much for Bar tipping Dane off. Laif wondered bleakly who had started this ugly ball rolling. Whoever it was had clearly implicated Administration in the mess, but not enough that he was under arrest. Arlin, he wondered? But Boone was so utterly in the dark about anything that went on above the skinside level that it wasn't likely.

At the captain's order, Laif expressed the elevator so that they wouldn't stop at any intervening levels. Didn't really matter. Dane would know the elevator was coming, and the kid would come to see . . .

They strapped in at the microG pause, then lifted the last stretch to the hub. They knew how to handle themselves in microG, Laif noted sourly. Probably trained over on New Singapore, where you could buy anything if you were buddies with the Prime. Competent bunch, but then they recruited kids from birth, he'd heard, bought up orphans, kids from permanent refugee camps, anyone who wouldn't have much of a future. They grew up with no allegiance except to the Force. Ideal soldiers. Lifetime of training, and you could put 'em in anywhere with no complications of family or national identity. The woman who had been assigned to watch him was doing just that, dispassionately and competently. He wondered what her history was, wondered how the hell he was going to fix this mess.

Sweet Mohammad, Buddha, and Jesus.

The door chimed and opened, and Laif narrowed his eyes against the flood of light, cursing himself because he had forgotten to grab his goggles. Every damn one of them had donned a pair. "You stay back," the captain said, indicating Laif but speaking to his watchdog. She nodded. Laif didn't. Pushed off, got about two centimeters before she grabbed him and killed his momentum, still anchored to a strap.

She didn't say anything and she didn't have to.

For a moment, Laif thought they had figured it out, that Koi was already off in hiding with his family, that it would work out after all. His com link vibrated. Bar? "Yes?" he murmured, activating it. Nothing. He waited for a couple of heartbeats, then shrugged. Bar changed his mind.

Two members of the team pushed off gently, drifting sideways, eyes on small, hand-held screens. Spoke cryptically. The captain nodded once. Sharply. One of the others raised a small, squat weapon, fired it casually, with no apparent aim.

Guided, Laif thought bleakly. By that scanner. A small explosion of motion among the tubes sent three of the team pushing off hard and fast. They disappeared into the greenery. Laif pushed off reflexively, was tackled by his watchdog, who slammed them both into the side of the elevator housing. The impact knocked the wind out of him and they rebounded, drifting slowly, stalling in the open space around the elevator. Laif gasped for breath, his ribs aching, as the three returned, hauling a limp form with them.

Not Koi, thank the gods. One of the females—Koi said they all had names, but he didn't know them. Her eyes were open, glazed and unseeing, her limbs slack. The small bright orange butt of the guided stun dart protruded from her shoulder. The leader of the trio spoke a couple of syllables to the captain, shook her head. The captain swore one very English syllable and pushed over to them. Grabbed her neck, his frown intensifying, snatched open a pouch at his belt and slapped a small patch onto her carotid groove.

Dead. Laif stared, stunned. "You shot to kill and you did it *blind*? What the hell are you up to?" He kicked off from the elevator, arrowed over to them. "What the hell is going *on* here?"

"It was set on non-lethal." The captain looked up, his own face reflecting shock. "Maximum, but not lethal." He looked back at the narrow face and long, skinny torso, her breasts flat as any boy's, her back gently arched, arms and legs drifting.

"My God, what is it?" The captain's voice grated with the revulsion visible on his face. "Who would *do* this?"

"More." One of the pair holding scanners spoke up.

Dear gods, the whole family might be coming, maybe hoping to save this one? "Get out!" Laif yelled it at the top of his lungs, no longer giving a damn what the consequences were. "Now! Get out of here!"

Too late. Koi burst from the leaves, his milky eyes wide, zooming like an arrow straight at the cluster of CSF. The young latino-mix with the weapon pointed it casually . . .

. . . and went tumbling wildly, weapon flying, as Dane hit him from the rear, shoulder first, slamming him into a head-over-heels tumble into the planted tubes. "Koi, *go!*" He pushed off a tube, ricocheted off another, oblivious to a dart as it zoomed past him, not guided, just aimed. Hit a woman with just the right angle to send her cartwheeling, caught another tube and pushed off, aiming like a thrown spear for the captain.

A spot of bright orange appeared on his side.

He spasmed, arms and legs flying out, back arching briefly and terribly, muscles all jerking at once. Began to tumble, out of control, spun by the captain and slammed into a tube planted to beets. Rebounded in a cloud of torn leaves and droplets of crimson juice. Like blood, Laif thought numbly. He pushed off, blocked his watchdog's grab almost without thought, eyes on Dane's slack tumble, head full of white noise and a howl of pain like an animal dying.

Koi?

Laif reached Dane a heartbeat before the CSF, slammed into his limp body, going too fast, arms going around him, tumbling with his limp sprawl into another tube, blinded by a flurry of ruined leaves. Feel for it, feel—He groped, fingers finding Dane's throat, searching for a pulse even as hands closed on him like claws, reeling him in.

"He's alive, Koi," Laif yelled. "Get *out* of here."

They hauled him off Dane and they weren't gentle. Hung for a lamb, hung for a sheep, he thought and wondered for a flickering instant where the hell *that* saying had come from. Then he got a foot planted on a tube, slammed his forearm into the throat of the woman trying to twist his arm behind his back and had the small satisfaction of seeing her do a backward flip, struggling to breathe, before someone got a choke hold on him from behind. They won at that point, and when the blackness cleared from his vision, his hands were locked behind him and someone had just finished strapping his ankles together.

"You just killed a person, a kid," Laif rasped. "Hope you can justify child murder here."

The captain spared him one icy glance. "That's not human."

"You haven't seen the DNA readout yet. Don't get too cocky." He didn't know if the captain heard, or cared if he did. They weren't going to look beyond that face, eyes and body. Not until they had the readout in their hands, and even then it was going to be hard.

He knew that well enough. *Sorry, Dane,* he thought. *I really tried.* He twisted, trying to get himself drifting so he could see how Dane was doing. But then one of the CSF hauled him into view, heading for the elevator. They had put a restraint collar on him and a moment later, another of the 'Keepers was locking one around his throat, too. The woman fit it snugly, not tight, making sure that they'd get good contact if they zapped him, Laif thought sourly. You couldn't take these things off without a key. Not if you wanted to keep your head.

They'd slapped a patch on Dane's throat and he was coming around from the stun. They'd hit him with the top setting on the dart, Laif thought. He could have ended up like the girl. He watched Dane's eyes focus, watched memory flush out confusion. A 'Keeper grabbed him as he groped for something he could push off from.

"Koi's okay," Laif said conversationally.

Dane's eyes flicked his way, his expression utterly unreadable. But he relaxed. A hair.

The captain was reading them both their status, that they had been taken into custody by the World Council, that they would be treated under the International Convention on Human Rights statutes for all detainees, that they would have access to legal counsel and so forth. Dane's eyes had taken on a glazed, faraway look and Laif worried silently about that high-level stun. He could see a couple of the CSFs sealing the girl's body into a body-bag. No sign of Koi. They hauled the two of them into the elevator, and when it halted at the micro point, the captain released their restraints and explained the action of the collar in graphic detail.

At least he didn't demonstrate it. Laif silently thanked him for that small kindness.

Dane didn't look at him, merely stared at the wall as the elevator dropped to skin level. He might have been any commuter on his way to a boring day job.

The skinside corridor was empty and the back of Laif's neck prickled. Even the vendors' carts were deserted, parked crookedly in the promenade, the shops closed, curtains pulled across display space. The blue-uniformed figures guarding the first major intersection confirmed Laif's guess. The CSF saluted their small force, their faces alert and incurious. One of them murmured something, clearly speaking over a link.

The group split and half of them hustled Laif down the intersecting corridor toward the alley that led to Admin. He craned his neck to see where they were taking Dane, but a sharp shove in the small of his back encouraged him to keep moving. Another pair of CSF guarded the entrance to the alley. This corridor was eerily empty, too, although in the distance, Laif could make out blue figures clustered about at least a couple of residents. Arresting them? Answering questions? It was too near the rise in the corridor and he couldn't sort out the scene.

Efficient, these guys.

Laif shuffled into Admin flanked by the captain and his babysitter. The rest of the team vanished, off to some duty or other. Admin was full of blue uniforms. Two youngsters, a pair of scrawny, freckled redheads that looked like twins worked on the controls. The sappers. Laif's shoulders sagged. Three other CSF conferred over a holomap of the platform, speaking in link-voices. The captain gave a short, chest-high salute to an older man with a major's insignia. Laif strained his ears, but his babysitter hustled him off with that hard and unloving hand above his kidneys.

She took him to the tiny conference room at the end of Admin, shoved him through the opening door, just hard enough to make him stumble. By the time he recovered his balance, the door had closed behind him. Unsurprisingly it didn't open for him.

"Welcome to the holding tank." Bar sat on the tiny conference table, swinging his feet. "These guys are really really good."

"So I gather. What the hell happened here?"

"They showed up right after you left. I guess they came up on New Singapore's elevator. You know how they are over there . . . if they want secrecy, they get it." He grimaced. "Private contract transport over here. They hit the dock with a Council Directive that overrides everything, I guess, had our internal communications shut down about two seconds after Immigration gave me a heads up. I called you when they walked in the door, but they shut me down before you picked up."

Oh yeah . . . that com-link prod. Laif's lips tightened. He should have checked, would have maybe been alerted when the system turned out to be down.

What did it matter?

Bar shook his head, his eyes bleak. "Man, next time some fool hotshot at a bar spouts off about taking on Earth in some kind of military head-on . . ." He laughed a short, sour note. "They just got to meet these guys. No wonder it's so damn peaceful downside. You should have been here when they busted in the door. I damn near wet my pants."

"I didn't see anyone in the corridors."

"They got the elevators locked down. No traffic between levels. Without authorization. And they shut down the Con." He shrugged. "That took their net geeks a little time. They crashed it just before you got here—that's when they stuck me in here. Hey, we impressed 'em a little bit there anyway. They didn't like me much when I said I didn't have a clue how to control it, but I guess they play by the rules." He gave Laif a weak smile. "At least they didn't do some of the things they sort of hinted they were thinking about doing."

And if they hadn't managed to crash it? Laif hunched his shoulders, because you heard rumors.

The door whispered open again. A young CSF stood there, a broad faced African-mix wearing a Sergeant's insignia, short and muscular, his posture a relaxed readiness that suggested good behavior was a wise choice. "You the boss man?" He spoke an easy

U.S. slang, no second-language stiffness at all, although his accent suggested he was more likely Confederated Peoples of Africa than New York.

"Yeah." Laif lifted one shoulder. "I guess."

"I guess you're not anymore." The man's grin widened a hair. "Orders from downside. I guess your assistant's running the show. Cooperative guy. So you don't have to stick around."

Laif glanced sideways at Bar. "We can leave."

"Not him." The Seargeant shook his head. "Just you. But we want you to stay home for awhile, you know? Just so we know that you're not causing us any trouble." He stepped aside. "Let's go."

Laif exchanged another brief look with Bar, who lifted one shoulder. Straightening, Laif left the small chamber, following the CSF through the now-crowded admin. Yeah, there was Arlin, practically bowing and scraping as he conferenced with the gray-haired Major. Laif kept his eyes straight ahead as he marched though the press of blue uniforms. Nobody paid any attention to him, and the comments that he overheard were cryptic at best, a mix of at least four languages he could identify, maybe more.

A security cart waited out in the hall, but there was no sign of Carrie. "What about our security people?" Laif climbed into the cart at the CSF nod. "I hope you didn't just treat 'em all like enemies. We're not a hostile country, Sergeant. If your people don't start something, nobody's going to attack you."

"That's not what we've been hearing." The sergeant swung himself into the driver's seat with an athlete's grace. "We just shut you all down for now. Simpler than dealing with a mess. Your Security people are assigned to quarters. For the duration. You all can have 'em back when we pull out of here." The cart leaped forward at the maximum safe speed for this G.

"Where'd you guys practice in micro?" Laif eyed the abandoned carts, spotted a couple of blue uniforms in the distance. "New Singapore?"

The sergeant didn't answer.

"What happened to Nilsson. The other guy you arrested?"

The sergeant shrugged.

You're on your own, Dane, he thought bleakly. Better pray they do a DNA test on the dead girl.

The sergeant knew where he lived. The elevator opened as they approached and he drove the cart into it, sitting relaxed, arms crossed as the elevator lifted three levels. "Hey, you're top dog here. Or you were." He chuckled as he drove out into the corridor. "How come you live up here? I can feel my muscles wasting away just coming up here."

"Skinside earns income." Laif shrugged. "What's the fixation with feeling heavy all the time?" He glanced at the sergeant's dense musculature. "If you want big muscles, you spend time in a G gym is all." The man was a bit awkward in the reduced G up here, but not as much as your average tourist. They had reached his door and Laif's lips tightened as the door opened before he could even reach for the lock plate. So they were controlling it from Admin. Nice demonstration, thank you. "You want to come in?" he looked at the sergeant. "Look around for weapons?"

"We already checked." The sergeant smiled, his white teeth gleaming against his dark skin. "We don't want to get rough with you folk. But we can do it just fine if we have to. Just so you all know."

"Don't worry," Laif said with only a tinge of irony in his voice. "You made a believer out of me."

"Nice to know. Turn around."

"How come?"

"You want the collar off or you gonna wear it as a fashion statement?"

Huh. Laif turned, felt a touch at the back of his neck, then the collar dropped into his hands. He turned, handed it to the sergeant. Surprised him, just how glad he was to be free of the damn thing. He rubbed his throat. "I thought I was under arrest for interfering with you guys."

The sergeant shrugged. "I guess you haven't pissed off anybody really big." His grin widened. "As for us, if you give us any trouble . . . we'll hurt you. Okay?"

Laif met his stare. "Okay."

"You stay home, like everybody else. We'll tell you when you can go about your business." He flipped his fingers in a salute, turned neatly on his heel, and headed back to the elevator.

Just like that. They were damn sure of themselves. Laif rubbed his throat again. They had good reason to be. He wondered what the hell was going to come down now.

"Door close," he said, and crossed his room in three strides, flung himself down onto the sofa bed. "Sweet Mohammad, Buddha, and Jesus," he said softly.

Now what? Laif got to his feet and crossed to the service wall to order up a juice. Thought about making it a shot of brandy, hell make it six shots, and just forget this mess. Paced to the door and glared at it. Bet it rang a bell in Admin. He opened it, stared into the corridor for a few minutes. Closed it. Drank some juice. Opened the door again. Flung himself down on the sofa again and closed it.

Well, hell, it gave him something to do. He wanted to contact Noah, find out what he'd discovered with that medallion dot—but did it matter at this point? "Door open," Laif snarled. They'd be monitoring his private link, his access from the room. He could appreciate what the wildcards had, right now. We lost, he thought. We don't even know what the hell the game is about, but we lost it. "Door close."

They could have installed a monitor to make sure he was in here. But why, when they could track him any time they wanted to? "Door open." This time, he left it open.

After a good half hour, he decided that they weren't going to come check on him. Maybe they didn't really care.

He selected a vid—a remake of a twentieth-century Italian western—and started it.

He left the room, heading for the service elevator, hoping that his pass card still worked, even if they had disabled his personal access, hoping that they were busy enough securing the platform that they hadn't assigned someone to watch him personally or watch these corridors. Made it to the service bay and slipped his card into the slot beneath the palm plate. The doors whispered open a moment later.

So far, so good. This particular elevator brought him up to the hub near the control center, but far enough away so that anyone there wouldn't spot him exiting. He sent it up at normal speed, since the elevators were supposed to be locked down. With any luck, the CSF were using the elevators and this might slip by.

If it didn't slip by, all they had to do was stop the elevator, lock the door, and send someone up here to pick him up. He had a feeling he wouldn't get sent home with a pat on the butt this time around.

The damn trip took forever, and half a dozen times, he was sure it had been frozen. But finally . . . finally . . . the door sighed open and that searing, wonderful light flooded him. He kicked off and arrowed into the deep green light between the tubes. Most of them were close to harvest here and leaves brushed his face and as he sped past.

Laif let himself drift to a stop, grabbed anchor on a tube, breathing hard, sweating as he listened for any sound of pursuit. They could find him with scanners, but the hub garden was a big place. Knowing he was there and catching him were two different things. And it would be dangerous if he was armed. Which he wasn't, but they didn't know that.

Better to leave him alone?

He sure hoped that was their conclusion.

A shape rocketed from the green shadows over his left shoulder.

Wrong guess!

Laif had time for a single searing instant of fury at yet another poor choice, and then the universe exploded in shards of green and white light.

SEVENTEEN

AS THEY MADE THEIR WAY TO THE CONTROL CENTER AND
Dane's bower, Li Zhen's son gained ability in microG at an amazing
rate. Ren, he told Ahni when she asked his name, but it went with a
complex mix of image and sensation that Ahni guessed was his nonverbal name for himself. Like Koi's family, he seemed to be more at
home with nonverbal communication and spoke rarely. His happiness in the microG garden bathed Ahni in a golden glow as they
made their way though the planted tubes. Good thing Kyros knew
the way, she thought, because she was lost.

They reached the bower at last and Ahni froze. Someone had
slashed through the woven network of tubes and plants, leaving a
gaping opening. Shredded leaves and bruised blossoms drifted,
alive with feasting frog things. Beside her, Kyros muttered an oath.
"Get out of here," he said softly. "Right now."

She didn't argue, spun, yanked Ren tight against her chest pushed
off hard. They would have scanners if they were there. CSF? Fear
filled her heart. Kyros was right behind her, breathing hard, his anger
and fear a sour reek in the air. Frightened, Ren had wrapped his legs
around her waist, his heels digging into her kidneys as she shot

through the thick leaves. The dense plantings wouldn't fool a scan and she felt naked, utterly visible.

Koi, she thought with a pang of fear. *What had happened to Koi?*

And as if in answer, a slender shape shot across her path, somersaulted off a thickly planted tube was suddenly streaking along beside her. Koi! She nearly shouted his name, flinched at the white-hot turmoil of his distress.

"Dane?" She let herself slow, a fist of pain clenched in her chest. "Koi, tell me what happened?"

"They killed . . . they killed . . ."

"Not Dane?" She whispered it, could not say the words out loud. But he was shaking his head. A flash of image and voice briefly filled her mind—a slender shape tumbling, limbs ugly and slack . . . "They took him away." Koi's words emerged as a howl of grief. "Down!"

A dozen shapes burst from the greenery, Koi's family, darting and spinning in agitation.

"Koi, where are the people who took Dane?" Ahni asked urgently. "Are they here?" He didn't need to answer. Images flooded her mind, glimpses of blue clad figures seen through a screen of leaves, flashes of motion and waves of fear. Dizzy, Ahni closed her eyes, sorting out the kaleidoscope of image. "Are they up here?" she gasped. "Koi?"

"Yes." His milky eyes were wild and blank. "That way. Far." He pointed with his chin. "They have nets."

"Kyros, they'll have scanners." Anchoring herself on a tube, she faced the miner. "We have to get them out of here. Safe."

Kyros was shaking his head.

"There has to be someplace they can go . . . not on the platform, Kyros. Outside!"

"Maybe, yeah. There is." His eyes narrowed. "Let's go. It's going to be damn crowded, but I don't think we have time for two trips."

Ahni looked around for Ren, discovered him hanging from Koi's waist as he pushed off to follow Kyros. The school of Koi's relatives darted along on either side of them, sleek androgynous shapes twisting effortlessly through the green jungle. Suddenly, with a single fluid motion, Koi stripped Ren from his back and slung him precisely into Ahni's arms. She barely managed to grab the kid and push off from a tube as his momentum slammed her off course.

Koi vanished and a moment later, she heard an exclamation.

Felt someone's shock.

Oh, damn. Caught? She stretched her awareness, feeling for that hunter's-focus, for searching CSF, felt only Koi and he felt . . . pleased.

A moment or two later, he appeared, towing a body after him. The Administrator.

"I'm okay," he was saying thickly. "Let go of me, Koi. I can swim."

Koi released him and the man floundered, grabbing for the nearest tube, still disoriented. Koi must have hit him hard, she thought, and felt a small satisfaction at that.

"Sweet Buddha, you're all here?" He was looking around at the hovering shapes of the Koi's family. Then he focused on Ahni. And Kyros. "You, huh? Well, I guess we're all on the same side for sure."

Ahni wasn't sure to whom this last was addressed, but Kyros grunted, and he wasn't at all happy about this.

"Let's go." Still no CSF close, but that could change in a heartbeat. "Move, Kyros."

"I don't know—"

"Look, the rules have changed," Laif said urgently. "I'm out, I'm not Admin anymore. Anything I see, I don't see as Admin. Or remember, okay?"

Kyros grunted, still not happy, pushed off. There wasn't time to argue. Koi scooped Ren away from her, which made the boy giggle, and they took off once more. The trip back to the dock seemed much longer than she remembered, with the fear of CSF breathing on her neck.

Together, they packed Kyros's ship like fish in a can. Squeezed next to Laif with Koi beside her, Ren still clinging like an infant monkey to his back, Ahni caught her breath. As the ship cleared the lock she twisted to face Laif. "What about . . . Dane?" Her voice caught on his name.

"I think they took him straight down," Laif grated. "And the . . . body. They killed one of them. By accident, I think."

"They'll do a DNA scan . . . that'll clear him."

"I hope so."

His doubt chilled Ahni. She fixed her eyes on the holofield in front of Kyros. It displayed their path as if seen through a window. The ship arrowed away from the platform and she kept her eyes on the angle of their path, the view of Dragon Home in the distance, the plant's bulk, storing it all in short term memory.

Just in case.

Thick silence filled the small craft, the only sound that of Laif's harsh breathing. Ren hid his face against Koi's shoulder, and his family merely . . . waited.

"We're almost there." Kyros's voice finally broke the thick silence. "It's pressurized, but pretty stark. Not a fun place but nobody's gonna look for us here." He didn't quite look at Laif.

"I have a very short memory for places," Laif said sharply. "And a long one for friends. Okay?"

Kyros didn't say anything, but he relaxed a bit. A moment later, a tiny jar suggested that they had docked and a brief vibration shivered through the ship as the lock pressurized. "Wait," Kyros snapped. "Be right back." He wriggled through the press of bodies to the hull, which melted open for him, giving Ahni a brief glimpse of total darkness and nothing more.

"How come you were in the hub?" Ahni asked Laif softly.

"Looking for Koi. I apologize for getting rough with you. We ran out of time, anyway."

The hull melted open again, a larger hole this time, and cold, dry air flowed into the ship. Weak light glowed in the distance but it merely accentuated the utter darkness. "I've turned up the heat, but it's going to take a while to warm up," Kyros said.

Koi went first and his family followed. Ren still clung to Koi, curious and unafraid as they passed through a wide lock door and into a cavernous space, made larger by the shadows streaking the spherical hull. The light came from a couple of emergency globes tethered to the hull. The air was cold—not freezing cold, but winter cold. Ahni made out odd, bulky shapes also tethered to the hull in nets, but couldn't make out the contents. A matte black plate on the hull radiated heat and they gathered around it, their breath visible. Ahni noticed Laif's eyes on the netted goods, saw him lift a shoulder in a shrug and smile crookedly.

Smuggler's warehouse, she thought. Kyros's stock?

"Well, there's some food here. Not fancy, but you won't starve. Water. Enough air." Kyros was looking at her, Ahni realized. "It'll even warm up eventually. So, now what?"

"I go back to New York Up." She glanced at Laif. "Unless there's a reason I shouldn't?"

"Don't know." The Administrator gave her a cold look. "I had no warrant out for you. What the hell can you do?"

"Li Zhen is going to look for me there. He's the only lever we have and Koi, he needs to see you again. He needs to talk to you."

Koi flinched.

"He's not going to hurt you. Or your family." She reached out to touch Ren's dark head lightly. "This is his son, Koi. He doesn't understand yet, and he needs to understand."

Koi looked down at the boy, who smiled up at him, his arm tight around Koi's waist. Looked back at Ahni, still scared, lifted one shoulder. Reluctantly. She touched him lightly.

"What is Zhen up to?" Laif grumbled. "He takes care of his own yard and doesn't mix with the neighbors."

"We're on the same side."

"I hope you're as right as you think you are." Laif clearly doubted that. "And how does this brother of yours fit in here, anyway?"

"I don't know. What happened to that data dot that I gave Dane?" She eyed Laif. "Was there anything on it?"

"Gods, I forgot about that." The Administrator shivered, drifting with his arms wrapped around himself. "A kid named Noah has it. I sent him up to the hub when the CSF boarded. I don't know what the hell happened to him or the dot."

"I can find Noah." Hopefully. Surely the CSF had no reason to arrest him. "Kyros?" She looked at him.

The miner . . . smuggler . . . shrugged. "Might as well try something." He gave Koi a grim smile. "You and your family would do real well out in the Belt. We just need ships for you is all. That can be arranged. Let's go." He jerked his head at Ahni.

"You are coming back, right?" Laif's face looked strained.

"Maybe."

Laif shrugged and closed his eyes.

Kyros relented. "There's a link. It's with the water and food." He jerked his chin toward one of the hammocks. "Don't use it unless you have to. I'll be back. I don't plan on getting dead." He turned and pushed off toward the dock.

"What was this?" Ahni asked as she pushed into the ship on his heels.

"They called 'em lighthouses. Ask Dane why, I don't know my Earth history. Early rock jock hangout, maybe. Way back when. Primitive. Rock jocks live good, now." The ship shivered as it left the dock. "You really think Li Zhen is going to do anything but take you apart slowly for stealing his kid?"

"I hope so." She made it light.

She had expected Kyros to take her to a new dock, but when the ship hull opened for them, she found herself on the hub dock they had left from.

"I know the CSF can't see this one," Kyros said, in reply to her questioning look. "The private elevator is close, so you got a good chance of getting down to skin without getting netted. Have a story ready."

He wasn't coming with her. Ahni wondered briefly if he would stick around or just take off for the Belt and forget that he knew anybody down on the platforms. No, she decided. Dane had considered him a friend. "I'll need to bring Li Zhen to the lighthouse."

"Yeah. Right." Anchored to a handhold, Kyros extended his hand. "Palm it."

She hesitated only an instant, laid her palm against his. Yeah, he was hardwired, too, and their hardware talked. She felt the tingle in her flesh as his system overrode her interface. That shocked her. She'd dismissed Kyros, she realized, as a peasant who only knew ice and rocks. Turned out his software was a hair better than hers.

She laughed out loud as the link surfaced in her personal interface. "You paid a lot for that upgrade," she said.

"Yep." He lifted one shoulder, turned back to his ship, hesitated, then looked over his shoulder. "Luck," he said.

"Thank you." She pushed off then, arrowing through the thick green light and the brush of leaves/fruit/seed to the small private elevator that Dane had used. Took it down to the level where Noah sold his grilled lunches.

The corridors hummed with tension. The marines had landed Ahni thought sourly and wished she could read exact thought and not just emotion. Knots of natives clotted the corridor space, their anger burning like scalding currents from a deepwater volcanic vent. She could almost smell the sulfur. The park was thick with bodies and the sour/sulfur stink of rage. No sign of Noah, but he could be right next to her and how would she know it? She pushed her way through the crowd, feeling as if the currents of rage coupled with the marginal gravity might bounce her right to the ceiling at any minute.

At least she hadn't been spotted as a downsider. Ahni reached the far side of the park. Turned back to try again. Why had she thought she'd find Noah blithely peddling his food to a normal crowd? Stupid. She thought about the scrum field, but he wouldn't be playing. She passed an artfully crafted carved-rock bench, heading for the elevators, thinking that getting out in one piece was an achievement at least. A young, skinny native was haranguing the crowd about the excesses of the CSF and Laif's government as well. While a lot of folk weren't paying attention to him, some were, and the crackle of their anger sparked through the crowd. Time to get out of here.

"Geeze." Fingers dug into her arm. "Are you nuts?"

Noah. He smiled into her eyes, his face a few centimeters from hers, his expression that of a man who has just encountered a long lost good lay. Scared and furious.

"You want to die? What the hell are you doing down here?"

"Looking for you." I love you, darling, she said with her body language, crooking her arms around him, pelvis tilted forward, head back, throat exposed. "Let's go somewhere."

"Damn good idea." He hooked an arm through hers, his smile totally believable while his anger/fear/grief burned her like acid.

Didn't say anything more as they strolled through the crowd, but he did a nice job, keeping up the fake of a man with his *chica* on his arm, worrying about her.

As they passed a public restroom, he did quick up-and-down to check the corridor, palmed them both in, then pulled a tiny black box from his pocket, stuck it on the door.

It would kill any security ear as well, she was willing to bet. Ahni glanced at it, then up at him. He knew about Dane, she felt his grief. Closed her eyes, opened them. "Noah, what about the dot?" She couldn't keep the urgency out of her voice. "Did you get it figured out?"

He hated her for not speaking of Dane. But what was there to say, and what would it do besides to fog the moment?

"Yeah, I did." He spat the words. "What does it matter now?"

"It might matter a lot." She drew a deep breath, because he had no intention of giving it to her. "Dane could end up a scapegoat. They're going to blame somebody for this and they *have* him. Historically, that has been a damn good way to end up the public spectacle everybody wants."

"He didn't do it." Noah's eyes burned at her. "He didn't make those people in the hub."

He didn't call them kids. Interesting. "That might not matter." Ahni held his stare. "They might not bother to mention that before they execute him." She said the words harshly, brutally, saw Noah flinch, even as she stilled her own reaction. Held out her hand.

He fished a small data disc from his pocket, slapped it into her palm. "What are you going to do . . . for Dane? You're a wildcard. You can do anything you want."

She ignored that. "If there's anything you can do to keep the situation from boiling over into violence, do it," she snapped. "If CSF starts shooting, nobody is going to be able to fix things." She met his glare, held his stare. "I think I have a lever, but it won't work if CSF are killing you all. It *can't start,* Noah. If it does . . . whether Dane gets out of this alive or not, everything that matters to him is lost."

Noah looked away, his expression tortured. "He's on there." He jerked his head at the disk in her hands. "The guy who does the agitating. There's a couple of other people on it, too."

Ahni tilted her head. Sensing guilt. "What about the Con, Noah? That was a lot of the problem. Is it still being manipulated?"

He jerked as if she had stuck a blade into him. "Cleo," he said softly. "She didn't realize . . . what would happen. Didn't think it through."

Cleo. Ahni blinked. The scrum player. His lover.

"I . . . we got it straight." He kept his back to her, his tone bleak. "They got used . . . the ones who were doing it. They thought Dane was . . . you know . . . too careful. And the guy who conned 'em was real slick. I should have caught it." This, bitterly. "But Cleo knows how I work. Too late."

"Not too late." She grabbed his arm. "Get everyone you can and work on keeping the lid on. Use the Con."

"They shut it down."

"Get it back up again. It worked to get everybody hot, cool 'em off with it. I told you—I've got a lever. If you give me time to use it—we have a chance to stop this." No time to argue now, she headed for the door. Noah was looking at her with the first faint light of hope in his eyes. He jerked into motion, scooped the lock from the floor.

Ahni shoved through the door and into the corridor, the disk safely stowed in her singlesuit, headed for the elevator, felt Noah's hand on her arm, his presence beside her. Convoy. But nobody bothered them, and at the elevator he turned away, vanishing into the crowded corridor before the doors closed.

She rode the elevator to skin level. Three CSF stood in the elevator plaza, stun guns at their belts, watching the elevators with narrow, cold eyes. Two unselected Latino-types, one unselect Vietnamese. The Vietnamese woman stepped forward, glanced at a small handheld reader. Her eyebrows rose and she gave a tiny shrug . . . stepped aside with a nod.

Ahni headed to her hotel. CSF blue filled the corridors. A slender African-euro mix approached, blue and white light fiber woven into his braided hair. "Ma'am, this level is safety-curfewed," he said with a heavy West Indian accent. "You need to return to your hotel." He radiated annoyance. "You did not hear the announcements? We will provide transport to the Elevator for you."

"I'm on my way to my hotel right now." She smiled timidly for him. The last thing she needed right now was to end up in protective custody somewhere. "I'm sorry. I was visiting an old friend and I didn't hear the announcements." She put on dumb blonde tone and body language. "Thank you for being here. I feel very safe now."

He grunted noncommittally at that, but she caught a whiff of belief in her story. Still, he walked with her, keeping an eye on her, which was all right. She didn't need to go anywhere else anyway. Li Zhen would come to her.

At the hotel, the doorman had been replaced by a CSF, a young female Private, who exchanged quick hand-sign with her convoy. The African-asian man nodded to her, gave Ahni a brief courtesy-bow. "You must remain in your room, ma'am. Until we can escort you to the Elevator."

"I understand." She watched another exchange between the pair. Probably instructions about making sure she stayed put. His belief in her story only went so far. She marched straight to her room, her attention focused on the CSF behind her, hoping that they didn't decide after all that she would be better off somewhere else. It wasn't until she stepped through the doorway that she realized the room hadn't greeted her. An instant too late, she started to leap back, but a hard hand caught her arm, spun her in the direction of her automatic reaction, then flipped her neatly onto the floor. She hit the carpeting hard, shoulder tucked automatically to roll, but the edge of a hand chopped across her neck. She went down again, red light flashing in her vision this time, going limp to let her attacker yank her to her feet, then pivoting to use his triumph and certainty to throw him across her.

He was ready for that, deflected the force at the last second and locked up her arm, slamming her back against the wall.

Li Zhen.

She recognized him through the haze of adrenaline and pain response just as the wall slammed the breath from her body. For an instant he pressed close, his forearm across her throat, cutting off her breath, his body pressed against hers, fury burning in his eyes. Then he yanked her away, twisting her past him and down. She didn't try to fight him, broke her fall as she hit the floor, gasped as he landed on her back, twisting her wrists behind her, binding them. He dragged her to her feet, flung her backward onto the bed and straddled her hips, breathing hard, rage burning in his face, his thighs quivering against her hips.

Almost gently, he took her chin in one hand, twisting her head up and back, while his other thumb stroked lightly, delicately across her face.

Laid his palm against her temple.

She sucked in a strangled breath as pain sheeted white across her vision, blurring out the room, the hardware in his palm battering her nervous system. Retreated into the center of her being to wait while it peaked . . . faded. Stared up into his face as her vision returned.

"You took him." The words came out as the gentlest breath. "I want him back. Now." He pressed his palm against her face again.

She breathed slowly, focusing on that muscle response, the rush of air into and out of the alveoli, until the white-out avalanche of pain passed through her, over her. Her muscles trembled with reaction as it left her. "I . . . came here to wait for you." She managed to get the words out nearly coherently. "To take you to him."

"You will do that."

Once more the pain avalanche crashed through her and she let it obliterate her. This time, as it receded, the trembling made her teeth chatter. Her eyes focused finally, and she stared up into his face, into eyes like black ice, read her death in them.

Good.

For a moment, he merely stared down at her, his lips tight, his face carved from stone. "Do not play games with me." The threat made Ahni shiver inside. He reached out with one finger, traced the line of her cheek and jaw, down the curve of her neck, then rolled off her abruptly, with quick grace. Hauled her to her feet.

Her legs barely supported her, but she forced herself to stand straight as he released her hands. "We need a ship," she said, her voice only slightly unsteady. "He's not on the platform."

Li Zhen jerked his chin at her and she left the room, dropping briefly into Pause to stabilize her biochemistry as she stepped into the courtyard garden. The CSF private on duty looked from her to

Li Zhen behind her, then looked away. They had their orders. Ahni walked past them, scorched by the furnace heat of Li Zhen's controlled fury behind her.

They passed the elevator, still locked down, and Ahni saw CSF escorting several people through the halls, their body language suggesting that these were arrests. She hoped Noah was getting the Con back up.

Li Zhen stopped her outside an unmarked door and palmed the lock plate. It was another of the small, private docks. The craft inside was small, but sleek and gleaming, an elegant cousin of the courier's craft. A port melted open in the hull as they approached and she climbed through at Li Zhen's sharp nod. Inside, he bound her hands again, and strapped her into one of the two seats, slid into the other and activated his control field. The small craft shivered as the lock evacuated and its hull faded to transparency. Smoothly, the ship drifted out into the darkness beyond the platform hull.

Li Zhen looked at her silently.

Ahni closed her eyes briefly, dropping into Pause, replaying the trip in Kyros's ship, running the memory image through her mind, fixing reference points, the platform, satellites, the planet, and moon . . . Opened her eyes and superimposed the map briefly on her view of Earth's blue and white vastness, the star-glitter and black, and glare of sun. "That way." She pointed with her bound hands.

She directed him, running a comparison with the view and angles she had called up from memory to the images that surrounded her. For a terrible instant she thought she had made a mistake or that somehow the lighthouse, as Kyros had called it, had moved, but it was there, just hard to see in Sol's harsh light.

Li Zhen's face didn't alter as she pointed out their destination, but she caught his flicker of relief.

The small ship slid neatly into the dock and as it pressurized, the hull blanked to opacity.

As the engine shut down, Li Zhen pulled himself over to drift above Ahni. She stilled her reaction as his palm brushed her cheek. "This is not a trap?"

"It's not a trap." She held his dark stare. "I want you to see something. I don't think you understand . . . about your son."

She braced herself at the white lash of his rage. But he did nothing, merely drifted lover-close above her until the white-knuckled clench of his fists on her seat had relaxed. Then he pushed away from her without releasing her, drifted toward the opening port, reaching for a racked piece of equipment as he did.

Some kind of scanning device, Ahni guessed, wondered if he would leave her there. Her heart sank as she ran the Administrator's potential reactions through her mind. But in a few moments, he returned, racking the scanner, pushing over to her to release the webbing that held her into the seat, leaving her hands bound. He wore a stun gun. She let him tow her, offered no resistance. Light from within the ship cast a path in the utter darkness of the lock and faintly illuminated the lock plate beside the entry door. Li Zhen studied her for a moment, then released her hands. "Open it."

She laid her hand on the plate, her palm tingling as her hardware overrode the lock ID.

"Light off," Li Zhen murmured, and the glow from within the ship winked out.

The door irised open releasing a breath of warm air.

The emergency lamps at the far side of the spherical space cast a wan light streaked with moving shadows. Koi and Ren played with two of his family in the dim light, diving, looping, pushing off from one another or the netted goods with breathtaking precision, no momentum wasted, every change in direction perfect. Among them, Ren looked clumsy, but his moves had improved dramatically in the brief time since Ahni had seen him last, clinging to Koi's back.

They were teaching him. Ahni watched Koi dive across the space, glance off one of his relatives, angle neatly off to somersault off a hammock full of bundles, spilling his momentum just enough so that he drifted perfectly back to where Ren waited with another member of his family. Ren kicked off from her thigh, gliding on a slightly wobbly version of Koi's path, body twisting as he tried to keep to the trajectory. He somersaulted as Koi had, but had lost too much momentum and began to drift before he made it back to Koi. One of the sisters zoomed past him, snagging him, flipping him into a driving flight toward the hammock again. This time, Ren's somersault was nearly perfect and he arrowed back to Koi, slightly off target, but close enough that Koi could reach out and snag his outstretched wrist with one long-fingered hand. The pair spun counter-clockwise, momentum spilling, slowing to drift slowly toward Ahni and Li Zhen.

Ren laughed a single crystalline note of pure joy.

Beside Ahni, Li Zhen flinched.

As if someone had called his name, Ren's head came up and he turned to look in their direction. With a wordless cry, he kicked off from Koi's thigh, sending him drifting backward as Ren arrowed toward Ahni and his father. Li Zhen made a small sound in his throat, stretched out his arms, and caught his son, arms tightening around him, tumbling backward to bump into the lighthouse wall. Koi and his two sisters followed cautiously to hover a few meters from father and son.

"Koi, come here," Ahni said softly. "It's all right."

Koi gave a complex shiver that sent him drifting slowly, gently nearer, until he was close enough to touch Li Zhen. Arms around his son, who was grinning and making small excited noises, Li Zhen fixed narrowed eyes on Koi. His glance shifted to one of the females, who had drifted close behind Koi, curious and wary.

"Make me understand this," Li Zhen said hoarsely.

"They're the new version," Ahni said softly. "Same DNA, not mutations, not engineered. Not birth defects. You know that, because you sampled Koi."

"Why?" He didn't look down at his son, who had wrapped arms and legs around his father's torso, the same way he had clung Koi before.

"Dane thinks because we need to . . . evolve. To live out here."

Li Zhen shook his head, darkness filtering into his thoughts. "They can't even talk."

"Tell him, Koi," Ahni said in English. "That you can talk."

"Yes." Koi spoke up finally, his voice reedy with tension. "We can. You just don't listen."

"I don't believe you." Li Zhen switched to English, his eyes narrowed. Koi's sister nodded suddenly, looked toward Ren. He shook his head, apprehensive suddenly, looked up at his father's face.

If this was a test, they were about to fail it. Then Li Zhen's eyes widened slightly and he stared at his son. Ahni picked it up easily—the visual account of his meeting with Ahni and Kyros, told in image, sound, the smell of Ahni's hair as he leaped into her arms, and only the occasional word . . .

The swell of Li Zhen's reaction overwhelmed his son's images. With a cry, Li Zhen clasped his arms tightly about his son.

Koi was right, she thought. *He hadn't listened.* Drew a deep breath. Laif and the rest of Koi's family were headed their way now. "The CSF found them," she said. "They shot one. It never occurred to them that this thing was a human being. That's how they would look at your son." She spoke harshly, felt his reaction and realized suddenly who had told the Council where to look. "The only way to keep them safe is to be separate. A nation with the power to protect its own."

Li Zhen looked at her and didn't speak. But Ahni's heart leaped. They had their ally.

EIGHTEEN

DANE SAT ON THE BENCH IN THE SMALL CELL IN THE desert of time that stretched between the arrival of his meals, weighed down by despair. The walls had been painted a dull dun color and other than the video eyes near the ceiling, contained nothing but the narrow, padded bench that served as a bed and a sink/toilet combination in one corner. The one piece coverall he wore was made of tough paper. And there was the collar. Dane leaned back against the wall and closed his eyes, the air heavy, thick as soup in his lungs.

He had counted meals for awhile, then stopped, had no idea how long he had been here. Or where here was, for that matter. They had used some kind of drug on him. All that remained of the time between the murder of Aliya, Koi's cousin, and his presence here were a few hazy images of hands and movement. He wasn't on Earth. The gravity here was about that of an upper residential level on NYUp, where the cheapest apartments were located. So he was still in orbit, but the sense of *spin* was greater than that of NYUp. Smaller platform he thought. One of the Council's military bases? Probably.

The reasons for not taking him straight down to the World

Council were probably not good ones, he thought. Which probably meant that the media on Earth didn't know he existed. Or the dead child.

The media could rend you, but in public attention lay some measure of safety.

When he was sleepy Dane slept. The man who delivered his meals didn't speak to him, felt nothing for him, neither hatred nor curiosity. The first guard had hated him, he wasn't sure why. Some rumor, he supposed. That hatred had the old, familiar feel of religion. He had used the collar until Dane passed out. Apparently someone had monitored the security videos because a different man brought the meals after that.

By now, they would have had plenty of time to analyze Aliya's DNA and to know.

The molecules of air in the room seemed to have sensible mass, pressing against him like a thick blanket. Aliya had been the joyous one, the one who played tag with Koi for hours, who zoomed silently up behind him to see if she could make him start and laugh. Her name for herself had had the feel of joy. *I am sorry,* he thought. *I should have done better.* And what now? He wondered if the CSF had rounded up the others. Or had they received orders to simply kill them, euthanize them like animals? Her death had been an accident, he had overheard enough from the CSF who had arrested him to know that much.

They were easy to kill, highly sensitive to a stun charge.

He must have drowsed because when he opened his eyes again, a new meal tray lay on the floor. Not hungry, he picked it up, set it on the bench beside him. Lifted the plastic cover to stare at the cold food. Forced himself to eat the cooked and too sweet chunks of fruit and some rice, then set the tray back by the door, and lay down on the bench, hoping to sleep again. Heard the door open as the guard retrieved the tray, didn't open his eyes.

"Visitor." The guard's accented voice sounded like a shout after the long silence.

Dane jerked upright, blinking, found a tall, slender Asian man standing inside the door, his expression intent.

Li Zhen. Chairman of Dragon Home. Dane swung his feet to

the floor and bowed slightly. "Hello," he said. Inane, but what the hell else was there to say? He glanced up at the video eye in the wall above him. "What brings you here?"

"They are not monitoring this. Or recording it."

"Then you have a lot more power than I guessed, "Dane said.

"I wish to hear from your own mouth what is the nature of these . . . children." Li Zhen's expression was severe, but his emotions quivered between fear, rage, and a point of bright, sharp hope. Dane regarded him thoughtfully. Dangerous mix, that. And he had no idea what this man wanted to hear.

"What did the CSF tell you?" he asked finally.

Li Zhen shook his head. "I wish to hear what *you* say. I need to hear it *now*."

Dane regarded him thoughtfully. Looked once more at the video eye. "They're not children," he said slowly. "Most of them are adult. They just look like children."

Li Zhen's eyes barely narrowed at that. "Tell me more," he snapped. "Quickly."

Dane drew a deep breath "Sit down." He gestured at the end of the bench. "I'll tell you."

Li Zhen sat, stiffly, angled toward him, his emotions simmering.

"I think they are . . . our evolutionary next step." He met the Chairman's unreadable dark eyes. "I am guessing that some squatters moved into the Hub during the dislocation during the early years of the Platforms. They managed to survive there, and even . . . had children. These children were conceived and born in micro gravity and lived in micro gravity." He felt Li Zhen's doubt like a sharp fingernail, but pressed on. "I'm guessing the phenotype must have changed within a generation or two, to judge from the few mentions of them I've been able to find in the axle log. They have adapted. Their bone marrow is fully functional, their bone density is quite good, although infiltrated connective tissue allows for plasticity. Cilia sweep body cavities and mucosa clear—no need for gravity. Perhaps our DNA is designed to adapt." Dane paused as the Chairman looked briefly away, his face taut.

"But it happens only in your center . . . your hub?" he asked, his voice low and intense.

"Oh no." Dane sighed. "It's happening all over the platform to the generation being born now. Here and there. Not to all and most of them are not as extreme as Koi's family. But a few are." Did Koi still live? "I . . . suspect another generation will see more and more children like the hub family. If . . . they are allowed to be born."

"Why would they be stopped?" Li Zhen's eyes bored into him, the crimson leap of his anger reflected in his eye. "They are human! Their DNA is human. How can anyone intervene?"

"They are not *us*," Dane said harshly. "You looked at Koi. What did Ahni Huang's brother think of him?"

That question scored.

And what of Ahni? Where was she? "Their DNA analysis won't really matter. We have a history of destroying those who are not like us even when their humanity is unquestionable. The records will be buried, the public will look at videos and see monsters, and they will all die. Look at the records, at the history of genocides that go back as far as we have records. Go walk on the Palestine desert or Jerusalem," he said softly. "I think you still need anti-radiation gear there."

"That was the past," Li Zhen rasped.

Dane thought of the first guard and the cold, depthless feel of his hatred. "I think you are naïve," he said and watched the Chairman of Dragon Home flush. "We wanted the stars, but they are going to be better at living there than we are. We, Homo sapiens sapiens have never faced real competition. Do you really think we will handle competition well? Were you able to look at a DNA analysis of that girl?" That was another score, although the man's face gave nothing away. "Why not?" he went on. "Why isn't it public? And she *was* one of the children, by the way. She was twelve." He looked down at his clenched fists. "If they have analyzed her DNA, they know that she is a normal human . . . genetically. So why am I here? Why the silence, Chairman? We can prevent them— restrict residency on the platforms to a year. Or require birth control implants."

"What was her name?"

Dane wondered where the pain in those four words came from.

Shook his head. "I named her Aliya. Her own name for herself wasn't a word. They don't use verbal language much, and their names are . . . images. Feelings. Hers translates to Joy. They're telepathic, Chairman. Built in, instant communication. They can learn language if they need to, Koi's family speaks English, but they don't use it unless they have to."

Li Zhen stood, lifted his wrist, and touched something there. "Let me out," he said.

The door opened, the guard's shape visible just beyond it. Without a word, Li Zhen strode from the cell and the door whispered closed behind him.

He should have asked where he was. Not that it really mattered. For a long time, Dane stared at the door, wondering what had just transpired here. The hours passed, meal trays arrived, the light never changed. Slowly, the tiny bright seedling of hope that had sprouted in his chest withered and finally it died.

His guess about the reasons for the Chairman's visit had been wrong.

NINETEEN

AHNI USED THE LINK THAT LAIF SHOWED HER TO SUMMON Kyros, who nearly dropped dead on the spot to judge by his sputtering fury. "Thanks a lot," his voice snarled over the link. "Kidnap his kid and then show him my hole. Why the hell did I get myself involved with you in the first place? That's what I get for listening to Dane. I almost hope Dragon Home security gets to you before I do."

"Your safe place is still safe," Ahni snapped. "Smuggling wasn't exactly on Li Zhen's mind and it still isn't."

"I hope Dane was right about you being an empath and I hope you're telling me the truth," Kyros snarled. "Not that Zhen won't probably remember soon as all this is over. But by then I'll be gone. I'll send you the bill for relocating."

"Do that." Ahni shut down anger with a moment of Pause. "And charge me for a ride back to NYUp, will you? I need to find Noah. Do you know him?"

"No." Kyros was calming down at least. "What does this Noah have that you need."

"A link to the real person behind this." She hoped. "Kyros, I've got to find him."

"What about the others?"

"They need to stay here for now."

Silence hummed across the link and she said a small prayer that Dane had trusted him for a reason.

"Be there in a bit." He sounded weary. "Be ready. I have to play hide and seek. I hear the system is on alert. Courtesy of the CSF. Throwing their weight around."

"I'll be waiting."

"So you're heading back and just leaving us here again?" Laif glowered at her, one arm hooked through the webbing of a storage net. He looked haggard. "And why shouldn't he just come back and blow the lock anyway? Get his stuff and get out?"

"Because if it could stand vacuum, he wouldn't keep it here."

"Thank you for your comforting words."

Ahni looked past him. Ren was playing with Koi's family. How many more like him, she wondered? She'd seen that couple in the scrum field park. Maybe they went to the hub garden, maybe that was part of Dane's secret world . . . playground for the new generation.

"Do you think Li Zhen can do anything?" Laif drifted close. "He really didn't say a whole lot. You're the one who seems awfully sure that he's on our side. I didn't pick up much on that band, myself."

"He . . . intends to do something."

Laif gave her a dubious look.

A silvery chime sounded in the cavernous space, saving her from a reply. "That would be Kyros." Ahni pushed off, hurtled across the dark beyond the light toward the lock. Heard Laif shout behind her.

Sure enough, the lock irised open as she approached, closed behind her, but not before she caught a glimpse of Laif hurtling across the lighthouse. No, he did not want to be left behind. Kyros was still cocooned in his webbing. "Hurry up."

She pulled webbing across her, had barely secured it when the little ship whipped out of the dock, pinning her into the straps. "Why the hurry?"

"Got clipped by a search beam on the way in. Means they'll have upped frequency of the sweeps in this sector. Happens automatically.

Think of hide and seek in a desert, sweetheart. We better hope we find the next rat hole before a beam picks us up."

Ahni stifled a gasp as the ship leaped sideways. Acceleration pinned her against an invisible wall briefly, then the giant's hand released her, and she hurtled forward a third of a meter, the straps cutting painfully across her chest as they stopped her from crashing into the forward hull. For the space of a few heartbeats she was weightless, adrift, then that giant's hand slammed her again, forcing the air from her lungs in a grunt. Her stomach knotted and she concentrated on not throwing up.

Without warning the acceleration ended. Once more the webbing cut into her chest and abdomen, sent her bouncing back and forth in her tether, like a ball at the end of a short elastic cord. Kyros blanked the holo-field and turned to spill her momentum. "We're there. Go find Noah. I hope a few important gods are smiling on us and the guy knows something." The hull opened.

The hub lock once more. Déjà vu. "Can you wait here?"

"Why not?" Irony bittered his words. "They're gunning for anything without ID out there right now. You don't know how close you just came to meeting vacuum, girl."

She stretched her senses to the limit, in case the CSF were still searching for Koi and his family and shot forward through the green light, aiming for the small private elevator. Her trajectory took her close to Dane's bower and as she neared it, she felt a stranger's attention. CSF! An instant later, Noah slipped from the bower, his pale skin reflecting the green light as he looked furtively around.

"Noah!" She shot toward him, reaching for him as she closed, urgency burning her, because she still felt the 'aha' attention. "They know we're here, let's *go*."

Without a word they rocketed through the leafy space between the columns. They reached the private elevator, shot through the open doorway. Noah slapped the control plate, yelled "four" as they both spilled their momentum with a thud of palms and shoulders against the padded wall. Ahni rebounded, felt Noah's hand close on her arm, stopping her sideways drift. They both hit the "ceiling" hard as the elevator dropped and Noah hissed a curse as he grabbed for a strap, missed. The small private car dropped fast and before either of them could react, the car halted.

They fell.

Ahni twisted, trying to drop feet first, didn't quite make it. She landed hard and sideways, felt her ankle give. Pain spiked up her leg and she curled protectively as she hit the wall. She heard Noah's explosive grunt, then a gasped curse. The elevator door remained closed as Ahni rolled to a sitting position. Noah was picking himself up, across from her, a rapidly coloring bruise on his face promising a black eye, rubbing his shoulder. "You okay?"

"I don't think so." She held out a hand, let him pull her upright. When she tried to put weight on her left foot, she hissed through her teeth, her leg instantly buckling.

"Damn." Noah caught her before she could fall, an arm around her waist. "Broken?"

"Maybe just a sprain," she said through clenched teeth. "Let's get out of here."

Noah scooped her into his arms.

"No," Ahni said sharply. "Might as well wear a sign *look at me* if there are CSF down here. Are there?"

Noah nodded, eased her to the floor. "Open," he said and the doors whispered open.

Just in time. The elevator chimed a warning as they crossed the threshold and the doors instantly closed behind them with the feel of snapping jaws. Some kind of override, Ahni thought. She drew a deep breath, pain like a white hot knife stabbing upward to her hip. "Just a second." Nobody in sight. The empty corridor suggested curfew down here, too, now. "Don't let me fall and don't do anything for the next minute." She closed her eyes as Noah's arm tightened, summoned Pause. She looked inward, assessing the damage. No break, torn tissue, hyperflexed ligaments, lots of minor and painful damage. Suppressed the pain response. With a sigh she opened her eyes, put weight on her damaged foot. Stood straight.

Noah was looking at her with a mix of curiosity and mild alarm. "Thought you passed out for a second." He looked down at her foot, now firmly on the ground. "What did you do? Heal yourself?" A hint of awe colored the question.

"I wish." She shook her head. "I can shut out pain," she said, "But it's dangerous. If I touch something hot, for example, I won't feel it."

"You're walking on a broken ankle."

"Bad sprain." She shrugged. "Where do we go and fast?"

"My apartment." He jerked his chin. "This way." He offered her his arm and she leaned on it, trying to spare her injured foot as much as possible.

"They posted a curfew," Noah said, as they made their way down the nearly empty corridor. "You're supposed to have a reason to be out or face house arrest. I got stopped on the way to the elevator, but I'm listed as a temp employee of Admin, so the woman let me go. Here." He paused at an unmarked door, palmed the lock.

"Nice and close to the elevator," Ahni said gratefully.

"Yeah. Convenient. Dane found it for me." He helped her across the threshold.

She hadn't been in a residential apartment up here. Noah's was spare, with the curved walls of the upper levels, painted a soft salmon color. Wall hangings in shades of bronze, gold, pink and green picked up the color of the walls, giving the space a warm, bright feeling. A folding futon bed stood open and a kitchen wall faced it with a low table and a pile of floor cushions in between. The lights set into the floor and upper walls filled the room with the yellow light of a summer afternoon.

"Sit here." Noah guided her over to the futon. "Get your foot up." He grabbed a cushion stuffed it under Ahni's outstretched leg, then turned to the kitchen wall. Her ankle was already badly swollen. "Here." Noah returned with a thin towel filled with ice. He set it down and worked her flat heeled slipper off her foot. "That looks bad." He wrapped the compress around her foot. "You better not walk on it."

Ahni brushed that aside. "What were you doing in the bower?"

"Looking for Koi. They're gone. I guess the CSF rounded 'em up. My fault. If I'd told him about Cleo and the Con in time . . ." He buried his face in his hands again.

"They're safe, Noah," she explained rapidly, fended off his eager questions. "Noah, all we can do for Dane at this point is to find the people behind this and prove that it didn't happen on its own. That's the only way to keep any shred of Dane's plans alive. And we're running out of time."

"Yeah, right, got it." He wiped his face on his arm, hard and angry now, edged with purpose. "You were right. It *was* classic Taiwan language, wasn't even a tough encryption. What did he think, that nobody would ever try to read it?"

"Probably."

"I think it's a blackmail file . . . it's got a ton of information on it. Hang on." He crossed the room in a single stride, picked up a holo-desk from the floor beside the low table, nearly threw it down on the futon beside Ahni. "On," he snapped. "Dot-file open. This is the asshole who talked Cleo and the others into diddling the Con."

A face appeared in the field, next to a full view of a skinny man standing straight and relaxed, his eyes seeming to focus on Ahni's face. Three dimensional letters glowed golden in the blue mist. As Ahni moved her head, the letters seemed to move with her so that they were always readable. Del Schriner-Gerard. Ahni recognized the narrow, mixed-Euro face with the hard, focused stare. He had stabbed the tourist and had started the riot near admin. An ID code icon shone silver beneath his name. "That's the one!" She clenched a fist. "We give the ID to the CSF. No matter how good he is, they've got to at least have DNA proof that he was involved with the murder. There's our wedge."

"There are two more."

The holo shimmered and reformed. The man's face, an African-euro face looked vaguely familiar, but the connection eluded her. Again the holo shimmered and re-formed.

Ahni sucked in her breath and stared, all thought suspended.

Tania's broad fair face smiled at her, the honey colored hair tossed casually over one shoulder. Her dark eyes seemed to look into Ahni's, and her smile taunted.

"You okay?" Noah touched her arm. "You know her?"

Ahni laughed a single, hard note. "I thought so."

In a flash of connection, she recognized the African-Euro man.

Xai had hired him as Security at the family compound. He was a Gaiist, she remembered. Xai had joked about it.

"Ahni?" Noah touched her arm again. "So what is this all about?"

"I don't know yet." But she had all the pieces now, just needed to see the picture. Ahni pressed the heels of her hands against her eyes until red light webbed the darkness there. "We need to go to the CSF commander with this and give them my brother's name as well." She touched the holo base, blanked it. "I need to talk to Li Zhen again." Because Xai was indeed playing a double game here, and Li Zhen didn't know it. And what the hell *was* the game? Two Gaiists. What interest would the Gaiists have in the platforms? It also occurred to her that Tania was quite capable of the meticulous planning that had gone into the agitation campaign on NYUp. Tania and Xai?

"So now what?" Noah asked. "We give this to the CSF commander . . . and then what?"

"Do you know anything about the Gaiists?"

"Oh. Them." Noah rolled his eyes. "Some. I surf the downside media for Dane. Did you know they don't like us? They're pretty quiet about that, but you can find it if you look for it. I don't get why. I mean their whole idea is to make the Earth all clean and pristine, right? So why not send a bunch of people up into orbit? But I guess they'd rather see births really really controlled and keep everybody down there." He shook his head. "Bunch of crazies if you ask me, but pretty harmless I guess."

Maybe. Ahni touched the holo base. "Just how much do the Gaiists dislike the Platforms?" They didn't have enough time to chase any more shadows here. "Noah, can you search this question from here? Maybe look at the last year of downside media?"

"Yeah, I can." Noah nodded, his brow furrowed. "I have a really good AI, so I can do a thorough search pretty fast. I'm a good Synthesist. I kept . . . keep . . . Dane up on Earthside media about the Platforms." He looked away, dismayed by his slip of tense.

"See what you can find out," Ahni said wearily. Holding pain at bay required a lot of energy. "You're looking for anything the

Gaiists have had to say about the platforms for, say, the past two years at least." She closed her eyes, allowing the pain to seep into her consciousness. Her foot throbbed with a dull red agony, and she leaned back against the cushions on the futon, forcing herself to relax, putting that pain into the back of her mind, making her body rest. Vaguely, she was aware of Noah speaking commands over his link, the hum of the ventilation system, the rush of blood through her veins. Where was Dane right now? For a moment, an image formed in her head; Dane sitting on a bench, his expression bleak. It vanished, and she wondered what machinery Li Zhen had put into motion.

"AHNI? ARE YOU awake?" Noah's voice jolted her from a state between sleep and waking and she sat up, stifling a gasp of pain.

"Here. I made some tea. And I thawed a couple of sandwiches from the kitchen wall."

He had unfolded a small table beside the futon. A mug steamed beside a sandwich on a plate. Ahni picked up the mug as he got fresh ice for her foot and replaced the soaked towel with a dry one. The tea helped. She didn't think she was hungry until she bit into the sandwich. Then, suddenly, she was starving, and bolted the soy cheese and sliced vegetable stack ravenously. The food made her feel a lot better. She drank some more tea and sighed as Noah ate his own sandwich. He was worried. "What did you find out?"

"The Gaiists say some scary stuff." Noah popped the last bite of bread and veggies into his mouth. "Not so much to the popular media, but to small, real local meetings. In person. Like our town-plazas." He shook his head. "Those transcripts are hard to find, too. Nobody much cares about those little grass-roots local get-togethers, so only the fringe media reports on 'em. And a lot of those reports that do happen seem to have been deleted from media archives. Good thing I already had some search paths set up, or I could have been at this for a week. But that's the kind of thing we keep an eye on up here—groundswell opinion. We've got some media connections, you know, and we can do a little nudging downside when we need to." He gave her a crooked smile that masked guilt. "How do you think Cleo and the others could do such a good job up here?"

"This is very organized." She eyed him.

Noah nodded, looked away. "We all share it . . . Dane's vision. We all know what our kids are gonna look like. And the Gaiists . . ." He shook his head. "I should have picked them up before." He frowned. "But I sort of assumed that they were a harmless environmental group and since we're not part of Earth, they didn't care about us. Boy was I wrong. And they're covering their tracks, too— blipping those archives . . . just in the past few months, looks like."

"What *do* they say about the platforms?"

"That we are going to suck Earth dry, drain the resources. Become enemies and take over Earth. Mine it. Ahni, it's not rational." Noah shook his head, his eyes dark. "Why would we take over Earth? We *left* there. And it's so much easier to drop stuff down from the Belt than drag it up from downside. Why would we become enemies? But you know what scares me? The major media never gets any of this stuff. Why not?" He frowned. "Why have they kept this hatred of the Platforms so quiet? And it's *hatred*, Ahni. They don't just want to see the Platforms controlled, or limited, they want us *destroyed*." He sounded shaken. "Their approval rating is really going up, too. They do all this community service stuff—right down at that real local level. They're the big community heros. I put it all on a data sphere. In case we need it."

"They're building popular opinion to blindside established politicians." Ahni squeezed her eyes shut. "If the Gaiists wanted to destroy the Platforms . . ." She bit her lip. "Noah," she said softly. "How would you make everyone on Earth fear us up here? How would you make them hate everyone? Not just Koi's family?"

"You'd drop a rock on 'em," Noah said flatly. "You drop a good sized rock, just big enough to take out a city, and they'll empty us out—if they don't just shoot holes in us." Horror expanded in his eyes. "That can't happen," he said, his voice hushed. "We've got lookouts everywhere. And the rock jocks can deflect anything in time. Or blow it up."

"Noah, could someone subvert the Con? Bring CSF up here if you didn't want them to?"

He paled. "Point taken. You don't really think . . . yeah, you do." He looked away, his face all sharp edges. "Ahni, there are a lot of safeguards in place. I just don't think it could happen."

He was pleading, not asserting and that scared her. "Kyros brought me over from his 'safe place'," Ahni said wearily. "He said that the security system had been alerted, that we had to be careful because they were running all kinds of scans to find stray ships." She let her breath out slowly. "They didn't spot us, Noah. And I think . . . he has brought rocks down here before. How big a rock would you need?"

Noah looked down at his hands, knotted in his lap. "I'd like to say no one would do that . . . not for all the credit there is," he said slowly. "But you know—the miners—they're kind of an odd bunch. You don't go be a miner because you want to get rich. It's a long way out there and it's . . . it's a long way. I don't know that . . . dropping a rock on Earth would mean all that much to some of them." He shook his head, like someone waking up from a nightmare. "I just don't think you could do it. We'd spot it, coming in. That's our whole argument for us bringing rocks down to orbit. We *can't* miss 'em." He glared at her. "Earth has warning beacons all over the place this side of the Belt. We've got rock jocks out grabbing every scrap of floating junk."

"Kyros will know." Ahni swung her legs over the side of the futon. "I need to talk to Kyros and then I need to find Li Zhen."

"The Chairman of Dragon Home?" Noah looked aghast. "Are you crazy? He's totally against secession."

"No, he's not." Ahni gathered herself, the pain threatening to break through her control. "He has a son, Noah. Like Koi. And my brother intends to betray him."

Noah stared at her, silent and considering. "It's all out the lock now anyway. I'm not sure anything we do right now is going to save Dane. So hey, why not knock on Zhen's door and ask him to play?"

Ahni put weight on her foot, fought down dizziness. Okay, she could make it. Took a cautious step. Another. Noah put his arm around her and she leaned on him, which helped. They made their way out into the hall. "We'll have to get back up to the hub without getting arrested," she said as they made their way down the hallway. "I want Li Zhen in on this before we go to the CSF commander. He has more clout here than I do."

They were lucky and met no CSF in the hallway. Clearly, the force was stretched thin and as long as no crowd gathered, they were probably content to keep track of this level mostly through the vid eyes. The few residents they passed neither looked nor spoke.

They reached the elevators without incident, and Ahni used her implanted hardware to override the lock and send the car clear up to the hub, as she had on that very first trip here. The diminishing weight on her ankle was a blessing, and by the time they donned the straps and Ahni floated free, she was able to relax some of her tight control. Pushing off with only one foot, she made her way back to Dane's private lock, her senses tuned for anyone who might be watching for intruders, felt a familiar prod of intent behind them as they neared the lock.

"Wait, Noah." She caught a planted tube. "We don't have to find Li Zhen. He just found us." She turned to face him as he arrowed toward them out of the green distance. As he neared, Ahni recognized the small, handheld tracking module in his hand. *Idiot,* she thought. *Of course he had planted a beacon on her.* She had never thought to scan herself for one.

He spilled his momentum neatly, drifting gently, two meters away. "This is the one who was to find the data for you?" he asked her in Mandarin.

She nodded. "Noah, meet Li Zhen."

Noah nodded, tense and nervous.

"Li Zhen, Xai is playing a double game with you," she said harshly. "He intends to betray you the same way he betrayed our father. He means to destroy Dragon Home and all the platforms."

"What do you know?" the chairman snapped. "Why should your brother betray me?"

"He serves another master, Li Zhen. The Gaiists. I have proof. They mean to empty the platforms. That proof is in public space, and I have the links."

"Show me."

She handed him the data sphere on which Noah had recorded his synthesis of his media search on the Gaiist movement against the platforms. Li Zhen pulled out a pocket desk, dropped the sphere into it. Minutes crawled by as he skimmed through the information. Finally he looked up, humming with reaction.

"I talked to Nilsson," he said in English.

Ahni's chest tightened and she drew a labored breath.

"Where is he?" Noah broke in. "Still on NYUp?"

"I do not find that our goals are . . . dissimilar." Li Zhen ignored Noah, switched back to Mandarin. "I will hear what you know about Huang Xai and what you suspect him of."

"For that we need Kyros." She pushed off, heading for the lock, flanked by Li Zhen and Noah both. The lock didn't respond to Ahni's palm when they reached it. "Kyros?" She felt a moment of fear that he had left after all.

"Who's with you?" Kyros's growl rumbled from the speaker.

"Li Zhen, Kyros. We need you. Fast."

Silence. Ahni held her breath, her eye on the small green telltale that indicated pressure in the lock, waiting for it to turn yellow, then red, as Kyros blew the lock and took off. Said a small prayer to her ancestors that if he had stuck it out this long, he'd stay.

The lock melted open and she let her breath out in a rush of relief. Kyros faced her, his expression hard. "You owe me a *lot*."

"Yes."

Li Zhen pulled himself past her and through the lock without a word. Kyros gave way before him, still nervous, keeping distance between himself and the Chairman of Dragon Home.

"We are here. With your miner." Li Zhen faced her as the lock sealed behind them. "Explain."

"Kyros." Ahni drew a deep breath. "I think there is a plan to . . . drop a good sized rock on Earth." She felt rather than heard Li Zhen's reaction. "Could someone play hide and seek with something that big? Like you played it coming over here?"

"A rock?" Kyros's eyes narrowed. "Why the hell would anybody want to drop a rock on Earth?"

"To shut down the Platforms," Ahni said. "All of them. Say

they dropped something less than 100 meters in diameter. It might explode in the atmosphere, but it would cause enormous devastation if it came down anywhere near a population center. And it's our worst nightmare. You'd have the world population calling for the end of the Platforms in one voice."

"Why, damn it, why?" Kyros looked shaken.

"Because to the Gaiists, the Platforms are an alien cancer, an enemy of the planet and the planet is their goddess," Ahni said. "They are behind the uprisings in NYUp." She turned to Li Zhen. "Elder Brother." She switched to Mandarin. "Did you know Xai was working with them? Did he tell you that?" She reached into her singlesuit, handed him the data dot. "This needs to go to the CSF commander. It is the data file of the others who are involved with this." And I will match you betrayal for betrayal, she thought. "Your agenda will be destroyed if their agenda succeeds. Which master does my brother serve here, Li Zhen? Where will your son grow up, Elder Brother? Will your father welcome him?"

Li Zhen took the data dot from her. Pocketed it. "I will examine this." His face and tone were cold and closed. He looked at Kyros, spoke English. "Miner, you have not answered her. Is it possible for someone to bring a small M-type asteroid into the gravity of Earth without our beacon satellites' detection?"

Kyros looked from Li Zhen to Ahni. "Yes," he said.

"There are some crazy folk out in the Belt," Kyros went on. "I guess . . . if you had contacts on Darkside, on the moon, you could find 'em. Even the real crazies have to come in once in awhile, and everybody knows who they are. We all sort of give 'em a wide orbit." He frowned, thinking hard. "There are a few I know of who could pull it off . . . get a rock through the screen. They . . . uh . . . do that already." He looked away from Li Zhen. Swallowed. "They're real careful about it—a few people have gone out of their airlock because they got careless. But the money is real good if you do. Real good. A couple of the beacons . . . don't really work. Looks like it from this end, but it's a fake picture, you know? There's some real talent out there in the fringe. You got to stick with small rocks—under 250 meters. But if you know the screen . . . there are holes. You use hull mounted receptors and every time you come down to Darkside, you record when the scan beams touch the ship. You do that long enough, you swap your data around with like minded folk, and pretty soon you got a nice three D map of the sentry shell."

He gave them an uneasy shrug. "Believe me, it ain't the solid sphere they like to brag about downside. More like a big net and it's got a few good sized holes in it. It could happen. And . . ." He let his breath out in a long sigh. "I always listen to the close-in chatter when I'm down here, and a couple of days ago, I heard someone say they thought they saw a rock going through. Nobody looks too close. If you're towing a rock, your butt's on the line and you're carrying heavy hardware to deal with the curious. Everybody but the sentries steers clear of incoming—when it has a rider. And . . . this one had a rider."

"So there's a rock down here in Near Earth?" Ahni said softly. "All set to drop?"

"Dunno about all set to drop. Who the hell would drop a rock?" Kyros looked away. "I don't know where it is. Probably half refined by now."

"Find out." Li Zhen said softly. "Now."

Kyros bristled. "*Can* you find out?" Ahni put in quickly. "Kyros, could you ask people in the . . . the chatter . . . to tell you if they saw something? It's going to get dropped."

"One rock looks like another if you park it," he grumbled, his stare fixed on Li Zhen. "Folk don't talk about that kind of thing. Even between us." He sighed, looked at Ahni. "I can try," he said. "And I know a couple of local . . . parking places. Some big holes. Bounce from the Platforms makes 'em. Down here, it's a lot easier to hide a rock. The Platforms are looking for little local threats— junk and stuff that can bust a hole in the Platform hull or at least bang it up good. Everybody figures we'll stop the big stuff before it gets down here. Once you park the rock, you cut it up and move it. You move under power, you don't aim to hit anybody and you're pretty much invisible in the traffic."

He was worried, and that scared Ahni. "Can we go check out

the parking spots? Li Zhen, you can take the data to the CSF commander. Maybe they can pick up these people. They may be on Dragon Home," she said to Li Zhen. "At least some of them."

For an instant, Li Zhen's face tightened as if to refuse, his anger a lightning flash between them. Then he looked away. "I will look for them there before I go to the commander," he said.

"I don't think you have a lot of time." Kyros looked grim. "You bring a rock down here, you don't sit on it and have a picnic. While you're fetching the marines, I'd better start looking now. Damn, we need Dane."

"Nilsson, why?" Li Zhen narrowed his eyes.

"He was a miner for years and he still gets along with everybody. He's got an in with NYUp Admin and he pulls strings. People trust him and he knows the parking places, too. He has a ship and he could help us look."

Li Zhen considered. "Nilsson is Council property. From what you say, we do not have enough time for a Council argument. If . . ." he looked at Ahni, "you are correct about the intended course of events." He looked from her to Kyros. "I hope that you are not. Begin looking." He palmed the lock open and pushed himself through. It sealed closed behind him.

"So is he going to do anything or not?" Noah stared after him.

Ahni looked at Kyros. "I'm coming with you to look."

"No." Kyros turned his back on her.

"Yes." Ahni pushed off with her good foot, slammed into the ship's hull in front of him, killing her momentum with a slap of her palms that sounded like a shot in the small space. "I can hear them, Kyros. My brother. The Gaiist. I'll know if they're close, even if your instruments can't spot them. It's an edge."

Kyros met her glare for a moment. Then his shoulder slumped slightly. "You." He looked back at Noah. "You get this end. Here." He pulled a portable link from his suit, spun it toward Noah. "That's the link to the old lighthouse where your Administrator and Dane's kids are hiding out. They've got enough air and supplies for about ten days, okay?"

Noah caught the link, looking uncertain. "What should I do?"

"I don't know." Ahni shrugged. "Whatever you need to. Make sure Laif and Koi's family are okay." She pulled herself into the ship behind Kyros, grabbed the webbing as the closing hull cut off Noah's protest.

TWENTY

ANOTHER MEAL TRAY LAY ON THE FLOOR. DANE HADN'T even bothered to lift the cover. He looked up as the door opened, expecting the guard who would retrieve the tray and vanish without a word.

Li Zhen burst through, a small stunner in his hand. Beyond him, Dane saw the backs of two men in Dragon Home uniform. Their tension and exhilaration rolled into the room like a cloud of acrid smoke.

"Come, now." Li Zhen jerked his chin at the door.

Dane bolted to his feet, headed for the door. Paused as Li Zhen grabbed him by the shoulder. The Chairman of Dragon Home planted a small black disc on the collar around Dane's throat, then shoved him toward the door. An override? He'd find out soon enough. He burst from the cell, found himself in a small room with four CSF face down on the floor, hands clasped behind their heads, guarded by six Dragon Home Security.

Dane cast a glance at Li Zhen, but one of the guards was already shoving him toward the exit at the far side of the room. They ran together down the short hall, stepping over another prone CSF. The last two guards backed after them, tossed a gas grenade that burst at the end of the hallway. The guard in charge of Dane said something that clearly meant "hurry up" and shoved Dane through an opening door and into a small lock. The final two guards burst in after, letting their breath out in desperate gasps, a faint sickly sweet scent clinging to their uniform singlesuits. Dane felt briefly dizzy and the small, slight guard closest to the two swayed and nearly fell. Potent stuff. Hands propelled him through the lock of the small docked shuttle, everyone crowding in, bracing feet and hands against the bulkheads as the hull closed and the lock instantly cycled. The small, dark woman at the controls said something sharply and they blasted out of the lock.

Acceleration shoved at them all, but they were packed in so tightly that there wasn't much room to fall. The elegance and cleanliness of the shuttle's interior and the comfort-padded webbing and jade Buddha mounted above the control center suggested that this was Li Zhen's private shuttle.

He was speaking rapidly, in Mandarin. His speech was angry, with a hint of subservience that didn't fit Dane's impression of the dominant head of Dragon Home. But the rhythm of the conversation, punctuated with brief pauses, suggested that Li Zhen was speaking to someone downside. It occurred to him that he was speaking to his father, the Chairman of China.

Acceleration slammed them all sideways and then the shuttle braked hard. All up and down vanished in an instant and they floated in microG. Li Zhen faced him as the lock cycled and their ears popped slightly. "We are at your axle. Where is your ship? Quickly."

For an instant Dane hesitated, but the raw edge of Li Zhen's urgency decided him. "Private lock, here at the axle."

"Good." Li Zhen nodded. "I was correct. Take me there." He pushed himself away from the control panel, the hull opening as he soared through.

The Chairman was skillful in microG. Dane pushed after him, a little lightheaded from the gas. Recognized the main cargo lock at the NYUp hub. His ship was next door. He activated his direct link, waking the ship-core, ordering warm up and standby.

"This way." Dane pushed through the lock as it opened, into

the thick, familiar breath of the garden. He stretched his senses to the limit, searching for the bright echoes of Koi's people.

Silence.

His heart sank.

"Hurry," the Chairman snapped.

"Not yet." Dane stilled his momentum on a tube of peppers, faced the Chairman. "Details first." He held the man's glittering black stare. "What is going on?"

"The Gaiists have managed to acquire a rock and some assistance." Li Zhen bit the syllables off, his accent barely noticeable. "They will drop it on Earth in order to provoke closure of the Platforms. This must not happen."

A rock? "That's crazy. It would take a lot of careful coordination and people who know what they're doing, up here."

"Your friend . . . Kyros?" He pronounced the name carefully. "He believes it is could be done. Ahni Huang says it will happen."

Ahni . . . "Where are they? I want to talk to them."

"They are finding the rock and the ship that guides it."

Dane closed his eyes. If someone was really doing this they'd carry serious weaponry. Kyros knew that.

"I have gambled much on Ahni Huang's correct projection of the situation," Li Zhen said precisely. "We must prevent the catastrophe from occurring and . . ." he paused, "I must have proof of what we have done here. You will obtain this." He held Dane's eyes. "If you do not . . ." He shrugged. "None of us may have much influence on the immediate future. Huang believes that this matters to you. Does it?"

"What happened to the people who lived here? The one you kidnapped? The others?"

"They are safe. You have no time."

Dane heard truth and pushed off. As he arrowed between the planted tubes with Li Zhen and his team at his heels, he stretched once more to search the hub. If the CSF had been keeping watch here, they were gone now. He reached the small, private lock where he kept his ship with the Dragon Home team still at his heels, palmed the door.

His ship greeted him with a system check summary across their private link. All ready and on standby.

"This is what you do." Li Zhen had spilled his momentum on the lock doorway, hung motionless, a small compact unit in his hand, very much like a tracking unit, but slightly larger. "Link your ship sensors to this. It is already set to search for the transmitter beacon I planted on Huang. It is a sophisticated hacking-nano designed to divert a copy of incoming sensory data from her bio-ware directly to this transmitter, and from there, the data will come to me. But its range is very limited. You must be close to her transmitter." Li Zhen shrugged. "I need records of the rock and records of the successful intervention. That is critical. The miner indicated that you know where illicit asteroids might be safely parked. The unit will alert you when it has connected with Huang's beacon and will begin to relay."

"What's in this for you?" Dane held himself still beside the open hull, although every nerve in his body screamed *action*. "You do nothing for free, Chairman of Dragon Home."

Li Zhen stared at him, anger leaping behind his black-hole eyes. "A future for my son," he said softly. "I have already gambled far more than you know."

Dane nodded and toed himself neatly into the familiar confines of the ship. *You're carrying trackware,* Miriam told him.

"I know. It's a deal. Don't mess with it." He brought up the control field as the hull sealed. "We're looking for the signal the trackware is looking for. And don't try to block it. The trackware needs to hack your sensor net."

Hack me? Miriam could express outrage as well as any real-human voice. *No way.*

"Do it. We're going to sweep the rock holes. Spiral outward from NYUp." They would choose a hole near the platform. For ease of access. Still, he could wander aimlessly out here for a week, second guessing himself. He didn't have a week. The trackware hacked his ship and he felt the shiver of the connection through their link. Well, Li Zhen and whoever he directed the stream to was going to know all the rock holes in the system . . . or at least all the holes until they found the missing rock. And Ahni and Kyros. If they were still in one piece. "Listen to the chatter," he spoke to the ship out loud. "See if anyone has reported an explosion or a debris drift, will you?"

Nothing so far.

"Keep me posted." How in the nine hells had Ahni convinced Kyros to give away all his trade secrets? He would have said her entire family didn't have enough money to meet that price.

They passed the first hole, a nice little shadow created by the interaction of a rock jock station and the end of the NYUp platform. Nothing. No signal from the trackware. No sense of Ahni. What would happen if a rock came down? It couldn't be too big, not if it was coming down through the sentry net and the hidey holes of the rock trade. But you could drop one big enough to flatten a major metro area, set up your entry so that it hit where you wanted it to hit. Someone would have to ride it down, keep it on course. Grimly, Dane glanced at the blue and white disk of Earth. There had always been people willing to die. The Gaiists, Li Zhen had said. He drew a blank on that one.

Next hole, coming up, a funny patch of blank space right out in the middle of nowhere.

Nothing there, Miriam echoed his awareness. A security sensor-beam touched him, carried on a brief conversation with the ship's auto-ID, and moved on. Whoever was moving that rock would have to have valid ID. Kyros might be able to skip from hole to hole in his ship, and dodge the security beams, but you couldn't do that pushing a rock. The rock collectors hacked the beam patterns and came straight in through them. Once they hit a hole, they didn't move around, they just carved the rock up there and shipped it to the refineries on barges. Usually took 'em a matter of hours.

But this person would have to move the rock into orbit. So a security beam would certainly catch it. But the beams weren't designed to supply visuals or even a mass quotient. Lots of stuff of all sizes moved around inside the security net. As long as you weren't on a collision course with anything and you had a legitimate ID, you weren't going to set off any alarms. Unless somebody eyeballed you and blew the whistle. But the holes that got used were all outside normal traffic lanes between the Platforms. Residents didn't joyride around out here much. Vacuum was real, you went out and worked in it only when you had to. The tourists all had to look at the Platforms from the outside, skim the lunar surface, look at Earth from a tourboat, but they kept to safe, regular routes.

Only when the rock braked and started a reentry would alarms start going off, Dane thought grimly. And then it would be too late. It wouldn't be like the early space platforms that started a slow lazy spiral down to a fiery death, giving the rock jocks plenty of time to cut them into chunks or blow them apart. This would be a fast drop, like the ancient shuttles that had lifted people to orbit before the Elevators.

Earth had a huge hole in its defenses, Dane thought. He leaned forward because they were approaching the next hole on their spiral sweep.

Nothing. His ship's voice sounded as tense as he felt.

Big stuff wasn't supposed to get inside the net. Fast and maneuverable as they were, a dozen jocks would have to work together to bust a killer asteroid and they didn't have the heat shielding to take atmosphere. They'd have a limited time to react.

And if the ship doing the pushing was armed . . .

Two more holes came up blank. And then . . .

. . . he felt her. Ahni. Lost her. Dane strained for that whisper of contact, that faint echo of her thought. He had never really figured out the range of empathic contact. It seemed to vary quite a bit.

He groped until his head ached, couldn't find her. Just as he was beginning to think he had imagined it . . . he felt it again. A brief bright flicker of 'aha' came and went. They were out there, she and Kyros. And they had found the rock.

He called her, eyes closed, straining to reach her until he thought his head would explode. Wasn't sure if he had made contact or not, lost her again. "Start looking hard," he told his ship. "I think they were in the next hole. Plot a trajectory from the hole to orbit . . . something benign that won't wake up a security probe."

Plotting, the ship murmured. *They could pick up a tourist trail and end up well inside Platform orbit. They'd look like one of those big luxury liners.*

Bingo! Someone had put a lot of clear thought into this. The luxury liners were big floating hotels for the high-end paying guests who wanted to play at living in microG for a couple of days in utter comfort. They offered rooms with satin-lined padded walls and special features to let honeymoon couples do downside sex, water rooms, where you wore a breather and played among flying spherelets of water, fancy viewing rooms. The rock would be bigger than a liner, but if it behaved like a liner, in all probability, nobody would notice.

"I assume you're listening, Li Zhen," Dane said out loud. "I think we found it."

He's listening. Miriam gave a very human sniff.

"I think it's following a tourist liner trajectory. That will take it well inside Dragon Home's orbit and that much closer to atmosphere when it starts its descent. Looks like our rock dropper picked your turf, Zhen. I might be wrong but we're close. Better call out the guard."

They passed the next hole. "Can you access the nearest liner route?" Most of the operators reserved routes with the platform traffic departments. That way, they had right of way over random traffic.

Got it, Miriam said cheerfully.

Nothing. They slid along beside Dragon Home's curve. It was a lot longer than NYUp, with a larger population. It blocked out the sun and Earth's blue disk and the stars blazed coldly. In the far distance, Dane caught a glimpse of New Singapore's solar collectors gleaming in the sun.

There they are.

Dane suppressed a moment of nausea as his ship zoomed in on the tiny image in the distance. It resolved into a rock that looked like a pebble. Until you noticed the small matte black ship body next to it. The dull sheen of a second ship, smaller than the tug anchored to the rock, caught his eye. "Closer zoom," he snapped.

That's all you get without losing resolution, his ship sounded huffy. But it was enough. He recognized Kyro's green celtic-knot glyph on the hull.

Kyros' ship, Miriam confirmed. *His ship just answered my ID call.*

At that moment, light winked on the tug.

Missile, Miriam said sharply. *It got 'em.*

White light blossomed and his ship's eyes zoomed out, filters darkening the glare instantly. Dane blinked, red blotching his sight. As his vision cleared, he squinted, trying to spot Kyros's ship. Praying that his ship had been wrong.

Nothing there. A few bits of debris drifted. One jagged chunk bore a green streak . . . part of the hull and the celtic knot.

Dane put his face in his hands.

TWENTY-ONE

"OKAY, I BOUGHT IN." BREATHING HARD, KYROS LET THE ship rest in the fifth hole they had checked. "You believe somebody is gonna drop a rock and I believe you. But I want to know who's going to be shooting at me."

"They might not shoot." Ahni winced and rubbed the purpling bruise across her shoulder. They had been playing hide and seek with the security beams because Kyros didn't have an updated Low-Orbit license, just an up-and-down permit. Something to do with forgetting to pay transport tariffs on some merchandise he moved between Dragon Home and New Singapore he had told her. At least she barely noticed her ankle any more. Everything else hurt a lot more. "They might figure nobody would guess until it was too late."

"You don't know squat," Kyros growled and fished a water squeeze from a net above his head. "You don't push a rock around without a shipkiller."

Nice name. "Can I have some when you're finished?" She snagged the squeeze as he sailed it her way and gulped the tepid water, trying not to think that it tasted like old sweat. Her stomach was having enough trouble. "It's my brother. And . . . my friend."

"You keep nice company, kid" Kyros shook his head as she sailed the empty water bulb back to him. "What do they get out of it?"

"The end of the Platforms." She sighed, and stretched her senses, feeling for any echo of Tania.

And there she was.

Ahni turned her head. "That way." Eyes closed, she pointed at the source of that contact, the fuzzy, rich, tactile sense of Tania.

Kyros grunted. "You sure? ID is a luxury liner. You maybe feeling that?"

"No."

"Well, at least Security won't be combing the tourist track. Not as much anyhow. Although if that's really them, then maybe a Security hit or two wouldn't be a bad thing."

Ahni kept her eyes closed, focusing on the magnet-tug of Tania ahead.

"You're right. It's not a liner." Kyros laughed dryly. "That was a cute trick, using the tourist trail to slip down inside Platform orbit. He gambled that nobody inside would look our direction, but heck, most of the 'windows' in the Platforms are fake anyway. The sun could go nova and you wouldn't know till the wave front fried you."

A big patch of hull went transparent. There it was, straight ahead, a big chunk of rock, gray and battered in the harsh light from Sol. It didn't look big until you spied the small ship anchored to it, pushing it along.

"That's a tug," Kyros said absently. "Moves the balloons around once the miners drop 'em, moves the barges around, in Platform orbit. Lots of power, not a lot of size. Sort of a big engine with a pilot onboard. No frills. They'll brake, I guess, using the bulk of the rock to keep Dragon Home here from noticing that kind of hard burn this close. I guess they'll bail out before they get into the atmosphere too far, use escape pods, probably and have somebody pick 'em up. Let the rock and tug go down on their own from there on out. Time to suit up, girl. Just in case." He pulled a slick wad of fabric from a net and tossed it in her direction.

Ahni caught it. "Won't somebody see them and shoot them down?" She started pulling on the vacuum suit. The flimsy, thin feel of the nano-fabric made her skin crawl, never mind that she knew it could do the job. "Somebody has to notice something this big falling out of the sky."

"Oh sure." Kyros pulled his own suit on and sealed it in about thirty seconds. "But the rock jocks won't have time to intercept before they get into atmosphere and start to heat up."

"So what do we do now?"

"Call in the marines." Kyros touched shimmering icons, his scarred fingers glowing faintly blue-green in the light from Earth. "I'm sending a mayday. That'll get us somebody's attention, probably on Dragon Home since we're in its shadow. Good thing you speak Chinese. Let's hope Mr. Chairman remembered to tell the crew manning communications that we might be yelling for help here."

"Kyros, she knows we're here."

"The tug couldn't have seen us yet. Here we go." He broke off as the holo of a Cantonese-faced woman in a Dragon Home appeared in the cabin in front of them and briskly asked Kyros what his problem was.

Before Ahni could speak, the woman's face fractured into a million bits of light, then winked out.

"Damn, damn, damn." Kyros swiped a fist through the empty holo-field. "Tugs don't have that kind of hardware. Somebody thinks over there. You're right. They did see us. They've got a tight beam silencer like the pirates use and they just wrecked our communications. They want to make sure we don't tell anybody."

Incoming. A voice spoke urgently. *Three minutes to impact. Evasive maneuver initiating now.* Ahni grabbed for the nets as the ship shied like a frightened horse, then veered again. *Evasion failure, closing, four minutes to impact.*

"Four?" Kyros looked baffled. "They're slowing down?"

Hello, Ahni. Tania's sultry voice filled the cabin. *I'm controlling the missiles. You have one minute to climb into an escape pod. I have just sent a nav-file to the ship-mind. Have your pods set it as the default and I'll pick you up. Do anything else and I'll hole your pods. Your ship is going to die and if you wish to remain on board, that is your choice.*

Kyros swore softly in a language Ahni didn't recognize. Then he grabbed her arm, released her webbing with a practiced wrench.

"Let's go." He hauled her with him across the cramped space, slapped a palm against the hull. The hull melted open to reveal two narrow, padded spaces. A plastic bubble seemed embedded in the top of each. Escape pods. She had seen vids on the climber ride up about how to use them if needed.

"The helmet seals to your suit automatically," Kyros was saying. A blinking red light on a tiny control screen bothered her.

"That says the bitch really did ram a download into my system. Let's hope it takes us somewhere besides the sun."

Ahni scrambled into the narrow space, ducking her head into the helmet, the padding pressing against her. The hull melted back into place and the padding pressed harder against her so that she couldn't move. A sudden warmth and pressure at her neck and shoulders startled her and then a breath of cool air on her face tickled the sweaty space between her breasts. That must have been the helmet sealing into place. How much longer before they ejected? She stilled a sudden wild urge to struggle, claw at the padding. Summoned Pause until her heart rate began to slow. Felt a prick on her throat.

Oh yeah. She had forgotten. The pods put you out until you were picked up. "No," she said sharply, but the pod didn't respond.

Vibration shivered through her and a sudden rush of acceleration made her think of the giant roller-coaster in the huge floating amusement park in the bay off of Hong Kong. Nothing to see. Gentle, directionless light filled her helmet space, and the injection caught her like an unexpected roller on a flat beach, sweeping her up and over and away down a long dark tunnel.

SHE WOKE FROM dark things that leered at her just out of sight. Blinked crusted eyes, smelled metal and sweat and . . .

Remembered missiles, the pods, the needle prick as the pod anaesthetized her. Her throat itched where the needle went in. She tried to rub it, tried to sit up, couldn't bring her arms up. Netting held her fast. She twisted, looking for Kyros in a moment of panic. Found him next to her, his wrists and ankles bound with webbing, both of them held to the wall by a cargo net. His eyes were closed, but he was pretending unconsciousness.

Xai and Tania hung in hammocks beside them in the tiny cabin. As if Tania felt her gaze, she released the webbing and pulled herself around to face Ahni.

Ahni closed her eyes, summoning control. When she opened them, Tania floated in front of her, a handful of centimeters away. The familiar scents of ginger and coconut made her shiver.

"I wish you had listened to me," Tania said sadly. "Why did you have to get mixed up with this?"

"I don't understand." She looked beyond Tania, found Xai grinning at her. "How did *you* get involved in this? You're no Gaiist."

"No, but we do share some goals." His grin broadened. "I told you our father is never going to see me as anything but a spare part, and as long as he functions, I'll sit on the shelf. I've been keeping an eye on the bio-tech research—the stuff that doesn't come out in the media. The high-end private labs are on the verge of a breakthrough, Little Sister. By making use of stem cell implantation and a little genen retrofitting, you can replace worn out parts and keep those telomeres from measuring out the end of days. Within a decade, our esteemed father will have the option of living forever. I suspect he will embrace that option." Xai's grin had the look of a tiger's hungry snarl. "What does that mean for the spare part on the shelf, Little Sister? Do you have an answer for that?"

"Do you have to have it all, Xai?" Ahni looked away. "Never mind. You do. You are your father, after all."

"Yes." Xai's smile was pleasant, but the red churn of his emotions was not. "And let me tell you how I will get it."

"Not from dropping a rock onto Earth," She hooked her fingers through the cargo netting, her body language distressed, but feeling for the fastener that held the net, for a hint of weakness that would give if she braced against the wall and really pushed.

"Oh, yes. Just so, dropping a rock." Xai chuckled. "Li Zhen made a nice ally. Talk about someone blinded by his own ambitions." He laughed outright. "Tania introduced me to the Gaiists. You never realized she was my lover, did you?" He grinned. "I thought not. Our mother had no problems with *that* arrangement." He looked over at Tania and grinned. "The Gaiists are as power hungry as I am but it's a big planet. They had already laid the groundwork to fear the

Platforms and NYUp's little riots brought the media in to spread the word. Now we will confirm that fear, and in the meantime destroy the World Council." His grin broadened. "So many obstacles will be simply . . . removed. Even when the rock is discovered, no one will expect it to have a target. And by the time the exact trajectory is plotted, it will be too late to entirely evacuate the population of the Council Island. Our father is there. So is Li Zhen's. I am not sure he would approve of this, but it is never wise to share the entire picture. That is best kept to oneself. In the ensuing chaos, the Gaaists are positioned to claim a very large share of political and economic power courtesy of the anti-space backlash."

He looked like a shark about to take a belly-bite from a fat tuna.

"With the Huang money and machinery behind me, and with our mother's help, I will be able to assume a leading role in the power vacuum left by Li Zhen's father. She has been quietly laying the groundwork for this takeover. Li Zhen will be assassinated by a tourist crazy with grief. So he won't be a problem."

Our mother. Ice filled her. "I think you are wrong, Little Brother," she said softly. "I do not think our mother will share with you." Or anyone.

"Don't worry about that." Xai bared his teeth. An alarm chimed. "Ah, rescue has arrived." Xai scanned the icons. "I wondered if you had managed to warn anyone before we neutralized you. Or perhaps someone was watching from Dragon Home. Care to watch?" A holoimage formed against the curve of the hull, stars against blackness, the huge curve of nearby Dragon Home with its clusters of solar collectors and communication mirrors. A bright swarm of fireflies glittered against that matte black bulk, resolving slowly into a half dozen tiny oval shapes, gleaming silver and white.

Rock jocks. Just large enough for the single pilot, they picked up the system alerts and either vaporized or removed the floating trash or small rocks that threatened the Platforms and the in-system traffic. The little scooters converged on the tug like a swarm of bees in the holo image, veering off suddenly.

"Either somebody warned 'em or they saw me blow the miner." Xai was smiling gently. "They underestimate. Ah."

The scooters exploded in an expanding wave of small bright,

brief suns. In seconds, the holo showed nothing but a scatter of fine glitter as bits of the machinery caught the sun's light.

Ahni looked away, sickened by the creamy satisfaction on her brother's face. In an instant she was swept back to a hot, humid afternoon before the season's first monsoon. She had come upon her brother squatting at the edge of the tide pools, watching a fish flop out its life on the hot rocks. He had flicked it into the water as soon as he had seen her, but she remembered his expression in the instant before he heard her.

"There are some very nasty little booby traps out in the Belt." Xai chuckled. "That's not a nice place, is it, miner? You can stop pretending to be unconscious. The hibernation drug in the pod is very precisely calibrated to wear off when the unit is opened."

"We found your blood in that private cabin where you were supposed to have been kidnapped." Ahni looked at her brother, cold with horror. "It was your blood, your skin on the ropes. The forensics people said you had been beaten."

"Oh yes." Xai grinned. "Can't fool a forensic sweep. I was there. I paid one of my better operatives to play the role of interrogator." Xai's grin was cold as ice. "He enjoyed it a little too much. But I suppose that added a bit of verisimilitude."

"Someone was in that personal shuttle . . . when it blew."

"That was him." Xai's grin widened. "He didn't even suspect it when I put my hand on his shoulder. I woke him up once I had him strapped into the pilot seat, just used a local motor-blocker to keep him from messing things up. I told him just what was going to happen. If he hadn't had so much fun, I'd have let him sleep through it." Xai laughed softly, his perfect teeth just showing. "But instead he got to sit there and count the minutes and know about all that plastic stashed in the tail. I put a beacon on him, so I could listen to him." He licked his lips.

Ahni turned away, her belly twisted with nausea. Realized Tania was looking at her with amused pity. Rage rose up in her like lava and she wrestled it down.

"We'll be entering atmosphere in fifteen minutes." Tania waved at a shimmer of holographic data readouts floating in front of her, scattering the icons into glittering dust.

"That's when we bail and leave you to your fate." Xai chuckled. "When you develop a good method, don't change it. You'll get a nice ride . . . until the tug melts down in reentry. You know, there's a slight chance that the rock might actually impact whole."

"Who's staying behind to bring it down on the Council's head?" Kyros opened his eyes. "I thought that was part of your plan?"

"We don't need to stay for that." Xai shrugged. "Auto control will take it in on target."

"Who's your expert?." Kyros sneered. "Auto won't last that long."

Ahni caught a flicker of emotion from Tania.

"You're staying, Xai." Ahni didn't look at Tania, but her skin crawled at Tania's response. "Didn't Tania tell you? You're going to ride it in."

"Oh yes." Tania smiled at Ahni, her eyes windows into an endless dark. "How else can I atone for wounding Gaia? She will forgive me and welcome me into Her arms. I had the tug retrofitted so that it can survive reentry. I will make sure that it comes down on the Council island. We have all our people in place." She smiled a dreamy smile that raised the hair on Ahni's neck. "Within a month of that impact, we will very quietly control a near majority of world politics. Not openly, you understand. But we will be in control. Then we can begin to make the world in Her image. Once the population is sufficiently reduced, we will turn Her world into the Garden it once was."

"Feel free." Xai gave Tania a brief look over his shoulder. "How noble of you." He turned back to the controls. "Takes that last little margin of uncertainty right out of the equation. Give my thanks to your Goddess when you meet her, Tania."

"I will." Tania smiled and turned, her motions as smoothly controlled as an orbital native, stretching gracefully and silently across the meter of space between them. Xai started slightly as he felt the cool touch of her fingers on his neck, started to turn, to ask her what she wanted. Then the drug patch stuck to her fingertip finished dumping its contents into his bloodstream and his eyes rolled up in his head, limbs loosening, a single crystal bead of saliva detaching itself from his half-open mouth to drift across the cramped cabin. Tania maneuvered him neatly into his webbing and pulled it tight around him, closing his half-open eyes with one fingertip.

"I loved you, Ahni. But he was useful. And he confused sex with submission. She will appreciate his sacrifice, willing or not." Tania turned her smile on Ahni. "And yours as well. We will meet Her together."

"Tania?" Ahni said softly. "It was my mother who came between us."

"I know." Tania's gaze shifted for a mere instant.. "But I told you . . . we found later that we had similar agendas, she and I. She is a latecomer to the Goddess's arms, but she is a willing one. She will play a very important role in our future."

"She will betray you, too. Eventually." Ahni worked her hand through the netting, touched Tania's arm and felt her response. "You should have been more open with me. In my apartment." She stroked Tania's arm. Slowly. Sensuously. "I have always been afraid of the strength of . . . our feelings for each other. I have been wrong. I know that now. I would like . . . to ride this rock down with you. Willingly. I—don't know Her yet, but I—I will trust you, Tania." Her voice caught on those final words. Tears burned her eyes and they were real. She closed her eyes, drew a shuddering breath as Tania brushed away her tears, scattering crystal droplets.

The net relaxed.

Ahni untangled herself from it, felt Tania's arms around her.

Love, she thought hazily. Perhaps the sharpest weapon of all . . .

Gently, she turned to meet Tania's lips, shivering as Tania's hand caressed her back, sliding her palms up Tania's arms, over her taut shoulders, up the long curve of her neck to cup her face, their mouths together.

. . . and the most treacherous.

Ahni discharged the entire power core for her bioware into Tania's nervous system. It was the same energy that Li Zhen had used to punish her for taking his son, but at a much higher intensity. Tania spasmed, back arching, arms and legs straightening violently, a hoarse cry erupting from her throat as all her muscles convulsed. She hit the wall, rebounded, slack and drifting rearward, her eyes half open, whites gleaming.

Throat clenched tight, Ahni caught her and awkwardly webbed her into the other hammock. Flung herself across the space to release Kyros. He pushed across to the control field, making noises to himself as he called up holos, ran a flickering progression of images through the air in front of him. "Damn, they've jerked this old boat around. I don't know if I—okay, yeah, that's what I need." Fingers darting and stabbing he swore for a handful of seconds. "We can break this rock out of orbit and jack it into a trajectory that should take it sunward and miss the Platforms with luck. That gives time for the rock jocks to rope it and put some navigation power aboard if it's needed. Or bust it up."

"Do it!"

"Go check the escape pods for this boat, will you? We can't reuse ours."

She made her way over to the red escape icons glowing above the now-familiar slots. But when she touched the door, nothing happened. Neither opened. When she touched the small inset control screen it remained dark. "Any reason I can't open them?"

"Main control say's they're working." Tension edged Kyros's words. "Try again. They're never locked."

"The control screens are dark."

"Damn." He pushed over to join her, tried the screens, then the doors, then the screens again. "Neat little trick that." He glared at Tania's unconscious form. "She was making sure her Goddess was going to get her sacrifice for sure. Too bad we couldn't watch your brother's face when he went to bail out and realized there was no way to bail." Kyros laughed sourly. "Course we're stuck, too. Oh well." He pushed back to the control holos. Red glowed among the icons.

Not good.

"We have to push so hard so fast that the engines probably can't take it. We could slow it down and maybe delay reentry until the marines arrive, but we've got no communication, and we don't know they're coming." He looked at Ahni. "Here are our options. We delay, hope Li Zhen gets somebody out here to boost this thing to a higher orbit before it decays into atmosphere. But we only have enough fuel for that to slow it for about . . ." He glanced at the images again. 'Fifteen more minutes, damn. She cut the fuel too close, probably wouldn't had have had enough for maneuvering either. Bitch didn't know as much as she thought she did." He sighed. "We could end up in reentry anyway. It just depends. Or . . ." He looked at her. "We boost it out of orbit. But we're here if the ship blows."

Ahni closed her eyes. "Well, if we're going to die, I'd rather it be for a win than a loss."

"Me, I'd rather not die. Don't know if that's an option." He stabbed fingers into the field, scattering icons like drops of blood.

A shiver started deep in Ahni's bones. It grew stronger, spreading through her flesh until her teeth began to vibrate. It had the feel of nails dragged across a blackboard, but the blackboard was the inside of her skin.

"We'll make a safe orbit in seven more minutes." Kyros had to shout to be audible over the wail of the ship's dying. "I'll cut the power as soon as I can."

They weren't going to make it. She could feel the end coming in the increasing shriek of the tug's power plant. It wasn't so much audible noise as something she *felt,* as if the very atoms of the universe were being pulled apart here, stretched slowly to the breaking point.

The hull melted.

For an instant she stared at it dumbly, wondering why the exploding atmosphere hadn't dragged her through the hole yet.

"Go, go, let's go!" Kyros slammed into her. "I've got the system locked in, it'll push until it blows."

Another ship? Docked to them? She dove through the opening, the death scream of the tug vibrating through her bones. Kyros shot through on her heels. Ahni found herself staring through the contracting hole in the hull, at her brother and Tania. Still alive.

She pushed off, would just make it through before the hull closed, traced her trajectory coolly, a part of her mind screaming *no,* ignoring it.

Kyros yanked her backward, wrenching every joint in her body. "No way." His thumb pressed into the angle of her jaw, compressing the artery as his other arm clamped around her. She struggled as darkness closed in over her head.

SHE SWAM BACK to consciousness still fighting him. Bit. Because nothing else much was working yet.

"Damn it, ouch! Ahni, it's me."

Dane's voice. She focused her eyes. He looked awful, gaunt face, shadowed eyes.

But alive. She clung to him as his arms went around her.

"The tug?" she whispered.

"It blew. Four minutes after I picked you up."

She closed her eyes, his arms tight around her. Her tears floated away, tiny perfect spheres. In the sterile womb of this ship they were nothing but waste water. She squeezed the last waste droplets of tears from her eyes. "How did you get here?" She drew a breath. "Did they let you go?"

"Li Zhen busted me out, I think. He . . . put a beacon on you."

"I know." She struggled to catch his meaning.

"It was really a link. He hacked your bioware. You were transmitting."

She stared at him, openmouthed. Hacked. Couldn't happen. That meant that everything she had seen, heard . . . it had all gone over the link. To Li Zhen.

"He put it live on the media-net." Dane let his breath out slowly. "Upside and downside. I carried the booster. A little reality show," he said bitterly. "Great ratings, I'll bet. I'm sorry, Ahni. There wasn't any other way to do it."

Her brother. Her mother's role in this.

Her kiss.

"You're right." She looked up to meet his eyes. "What other way was there to play it?"

"You want to talk to your ship?" Kyros interrupted. "We've got a CSF escort with an arrest warrant for all of us, in case you thought we were the good guys here. You want to explain to Miriam why she shouldn't fire on 'em?"

"She won't fire on a CSF ship. She just doesn't like you and never has." Dane pulled Ahni close, his lips brushing her forehead.

Pushed gently away, without so much as stirring her from where she floated. "I'll surrender."

Arrest warrant. Some heroic welcome. Ahni let her breath out and looked around the neat ship interior. It occurred to her that her father would perhaps have rather died on the Council Island than have the world get to witness the details of his clone-son's betrayal. "What is the arrest warrant for?" she asked as she pulled herself forward to where Dane and Kyros hovered.

"Most likely escape," Dane said mildly.

"Nah. It's for trying to drop a rock on Earth." Kyros rolled his eyes. "Go figure."

TWENTY-TWO

THE CSF TROOPS BOARDED AND ARRESTED EVERYONE. Hard eyed and efficient, the squad put all three of them into restraints and towed them onto the armed patrol vehicle they had docked to Dane's reluctant ship. Nobody asked any questions or spoke to them at all beyond the commands necessary to secure them. During the trip back it occurred to Ahni that Li Zhen might have seen a way to use them to his advantage. She was getting used to betrayal.

She had no idea where the CSF took them. The opaque hull provided no views and her query to the woman wearing the Captain's insignia didn't even earn her a glance. Neither Kyros nor Dane said a word, although Kyros grumbled to himself in what she decided was probably Greek. The grumbling sounded surly, but beneath it, he was afraid.

Not so, Dane. His resigned calm made her angry.

She wanted to hit someone. Hard.

They finally docked, were towed into microG and separated. She felt Dane's touch diminish as her captors hauled her into a small, barren room and left her floating. A cell? The spherical chamber had no corners, no features at all to mar the bland white walls, except for the door. She tested the restraints that strapped her arms to her sides, but they had been well designed and she couldn't get her arms free or even gain any slack. The fabric seemed to tighten whenever she strained against it. Marooned in the center of the space, she contemplated wriggling enough to get over to a wall, where she could launch herself if needed, but to what purpose? Any escape here would come officially or not at all.

After a long time, a pair of CSF privates entered, fitted her with a control collar, released her and handed her a squeeze of tepid water. When she had drunk he handed her another squeeze full of some thick, faintly fruit flavored liquid that she guessed was a complete ration of some sort. It tasted awful. She handed it back without a word, the silent treatment contagious, she thought wryly.

The solid wall of the cell was comforting, she found. After awhile, she drowsed, waked, and drowsed again, although nightmares haunted her sleep.

The two guards took her to the lavatory after awhile, gave her more water which she drank, and more of the syrupy liquid which she did not drink, then towed her back to the cell again. This happened twice more, although with a different pair of guards. Ahni finally dropped into Pause where the nightmares couldn't reach her. Unlike the NYUp guards, nobody panicked and rushed in to check on her. That, at least, was good.

She was deep in Pause, hibernating, when the door opened. Too soon for another visit to the lavatory and water squeeze, her time sense told her. She had already marked that rhythm. She opened her eyes as two new guards entered, one man and one woman. All senses on alert now, she feigned indifference as they towed her down the corridor and through a dock portal and onto another shuttle.

This time, when they docked, she had weight, and she recognized NYUp. The smell, she thought as they marched her out of the lock and into an empty corridor. Sure enough, she recognized Laif's office as the door slid open, although the men and women in the space all wore CSF blue.

Nobody paid any attention to her as she crossed the room with her guards at heel. Just business as usual, Ahni thought wryly, and wondered just what was coming now. An inner door slid open and she stepped through. A man with unselected Mediterranean features and a Major's insignia sat behind a desktop, his arms folded, radiating restrained irritation. The cause for his irritation was immediately apparent.

Her father sat in the single chair beside the desk, seething.

Ahni stopped still, one pace inside the door.

"Ahni Huang, your entry visa to the North American Alliance territory of the New York Up orbital facility has been revoked," The Major said. "We are releasing you into the custody of Wen Huang. He will accompany you to the shuttle that will transport you to the Elevator."

"Honored Father." She bowed at him, speaking Old Taiwanese, aware by the Major's prick of interest that he was fluent in Old Taiwanese. Of course. "The two arrested with me saved my worthless self from death." She switched to Mandarin, used the convoluted Han syntax of supplication. "It would be impossible for one so worthless as I to depart this place without confirmation that these men have received a just reward for their intervention."

"And what reward would be appropriate for such an action?" Her father spoke through stiff lips.

Ahni kept her eyes downcast. "Their release from this place," she murmured. "A small thing for one of your stature."

"Did you need something?" The Major, who had surely spent time in someone's diplomatic corps, pitched his voice to innocence, chuckling deep inside. "Is there a problem?"

"Their names?" Her father's snap would have left a bruise had it been a physical blow.

"Kyros." No reaction from the Major. "Dane Nilsson." Ahni's heart sank at the Major's reaction.

It took her father a full fifteen minutes to negotiate Kyros's release, which he had to do now, or lose face in front of his daughter. And the Major extracted his pound of flesh in the process, clearly enjoying his power here. Wen Huang's anger had turned to white-hot coals by the time the last concession was granted and the Major gave him a nod that would have been a deadly insult at a Beijing business dinner. He did not speak to her as another CSF, a woman this time, removed Ahni's collar and had her thumbprint a release form.

As they left the office, Ahni turned to her father, bowed once more. "Thank you," she said, meaning it.

He didn't answer her, pushed past her into the corridor and halted.

"There. There she is!"

"Hey!"

"Nice catch! Not bad for a downsider!" People, dozens of them, milled in the main corridor watched by four or five nervous CSF. A vendor sold skewers of fruit and filled mugs with juice, as if it was a party. As Ahni stepped through the door they closed in, leaving her a wide ring of respect but reaching into it to flip fingers at her, grinning, or pump fists.

"Downsiders thought they could play games with us."

"Thought we were blind up here, huh?"

"You want to move up here, you do it, girl. You're no downsider, not really."

Laif appeared at the edge of the crowd, head and shoulders above the grinning men and women. They parted for him, sweeping aside into a formal path that led straight to Ahni. Her father actually flinched as the tall, dark man strode up to them, an impossible lapse that revealed his fear of this alien place.

"You're quite the hero, you know." Laif swept her into a bear hug that squeezed the breath from her lungs. The small crowd cheered and waved food and mugs of juice. "Your friend Noah hacked Li Zhen's link downside and dumped it straight into the Con." Laif was grinning. "Nothing like hacking the hacker. Talk about setting everybody straight all at once. You, Dane, and that crazy miner are everybody's heroes right now. You want it, you got it. Everybody heard on the Con that you were getting out. The CSF got a few leaks inside and they can't shut the Con down for more than a few hours at a time. Hi." He turned to her father, nodding down at him. "Pleased to meet you."

Wen Huang stiffened. "What is this?" He stepped forward, chin out, insult in his posture to cover fear. "We must hurry to catch the shuttle."

"There are many shuttles, Father. Laif, this is Wen Huang, my father."

The people in the corridor called greetings and compliments some of which Ahni hoped her father wasn't able to translate. Someone pushed a mug of juice at Ahni. She took it, drank and accepted the skewer of strawberries someone handed her. Dane's fruit. She swallowed a pang, ate one of the sweet, luscious berries. Her father shook jerked his head in a sharp *no* as food and juice were offered to him. He took a brisk step forward, clearly expecting the crowd—which was increasing to the unease of the CSF guards—to move aside. They didn't.

This was not turning into a good day for Wen Huang, Ahni thought wryly.

"Everybody heard you'd been kicked out." Laif spoke casually, but he had tensed up. "A lot of folk here feel you got the right to stay if you want to. Just so you know."

And he didn't want her to, and if she chose to, it would mean a new confrontation between CSF and upsiders. "I need to go downside." Ahni pitched her voice for the crowd, felt Laif's relief. What did you think I was going to do? she thought crossly. Start a riot? "Dane Nilsson—most of you probably know of him—he's been falsely accused by the World Council." The crowd's reaction told her she was right, and she lifted her hands before the mood darkened any more. "I mean to appear before the World Council on his behalf. He has done nothing wrong, and I'm a witness to that. The situation is critical." She raised her voice a hair as silence settled over the crowd. "The Council will judge him as a resident of New York Up. They'll judge him, in part, by your behavior up here."

"Oh, don't worry." A young man with a dark red celtic cross light-fibered into his naked scalp grinned at her, winked one green eye. "We're gonna be model citizens up here. We know we just won ourselves the jackpot of brownie points. We're not gonna screw it up." A chorus of affirmations followed his words.

"Get Nilsson back up here and we'll sort out or own affairs."

"Just let us know what you need."

"Quite the Joan of Arc, aren't you?" Laif put one arm around her waist, one around her father's. "Bless you," he whispered.

"Don't push him away," she said sharply to her father in Old Taiwanese.

He did not. Which said a lot about his fear of this place.

"I hope not Joan of Arc." She looked up and sideways at Laif as he strolled them toward the Arrival Hall. "I've read my history."

"I didn't mean *that* part of the story." Beneath his smile he was grim. "By the way, it's still dicey downside. Some folk still want us shut down and they're using Dane as a reason. I really hope you can help him. I hope that wasn't just for the crowd."

"They sent him downside already?"

Laif nodded. "Koi and his family are on Dragon Home. With Zhen's kid. Dane'll want to know. I don't know what's going to happen, but something. Some of the smaller Council members are all of a sudden calling for debate on orbital independence. There's a media feeding frenzy over that live link Li Zhen opened. Every second of your time on the tug is bouncing all over the place, upside and downside, and nobody has been able to shut it down for long. Everybody downside got the shit scared out of them and I kind of get the feeling a bunch of folk would be shooting at us . . . if the pilot of that tug hadn't been a downsider. Thank all the gods for that."

"We must leave." The Huang stepped firmly from beneath Laif's arm, finally recovering his downside presence as Head of the Taiwan Families as they reached the bustle of the Arrival Hall. "You may go." He spoke English, his tone putting Laif neatly in his place as something equal to a dog's accident.

It was the most insulting tone she had ever heard her father use.

"Yeah, I know. In a minute." The insult went right past Laif. "I'm almost done."

Ahni winced at her father's reaction and stifled a smile. Nobody had *ever* talked to him like that.

Laif's gaze shifted to a spot behind her, down the corridor. "I think you're about to get an escort to the shuttle," he murmured "Guess they think you might want to stay. Skedaddle, will you? Before the crowd gets protective."

"We are going," her father snapped in Old Taiwanese. "Now."

"Of course, Honored Father." She let him propel her forward. "So what's going to happen if the Council makes you independent?" she called back over her shoulder. "What then?"

"I'll get myself elected to run things." Laif didn't follow them. "I'll grant you the first immigration visa when it happens. Get Dane back up here, will you? I need him."

I'll try, she thought. But as her father propelled her through the corridor and into the Arrival Hall, his anger buzzing though his grip on her arm like electricity, her confidence ebbed.

It was an old pattern in global politics. If you had to cede a battle, find a scapegoat. Memories of the ugly human engineering years still lingered like nightmares in the global subconscious. Dane had scapegoat written all over him.

THE ELEVATOR TRIP seemed to take a month. Her father believed that Tania had been the would-be assassin, that she had brainwashed and destroyed Xai. He could understand a woman betraying her lover. It made sense to him, and he also believed that Ahni had attempted his rescue.

Her mother's doing, Ahni realized, although her father's approval of his daughter's actions was tempered with anger that she had brought this family disgrace to world attention. Her mother's spin on events and her father's willing belief disturbed her enormously, but Ahni remained silent in the face of his misinformation. Let her mother believe that she had given in to the temptation of *heir*. When the enemy holds the knife and you are weaponless, it is not time to fight.

And Dane came first.

She spent her time checking the news media. Xai's face was everywhere, and so was Tania's kiss and the glimpse from the link's view, of the edges of her hands as she cupped Tania's face to betray that moment of trust. Ahni had her link excise those images automatically, but she found them everywhere she looked, their absence like a missing tooth, inviting the tongue over and over again.

The planet was in turmoil, a host of fanatics demanding the destruction of the orbitals as a place of demons, another host of fanatics claiming them as wise keepers of Earth, probably with divine powers. Those fanatics pointed to Ahni's deadly touch as proof of the divine. Her first encounter with that interpretation of events left her full of nausea.

Dane's image was absent and so was any mention of the girl the CSF had killed.

That frightened her more than anything else.

She had only one doorway to Dane and that was through the gates of the Council island. She could only negotiate that doorway as daughter of The Huang. She had sent Li Zhen a message as they left the platform. *I want to be there.* He had so far sent no response. That worried her. She wasn't at all sure they were on the same side anymore.

On the surface, nothing had changed since she had left the compound a handful of weeks before. Servants came running to carry luggage, when they arrived, to bow to her father, usher her to her apartment with its pool. Ahni stood in the doorway, for a silent moment. "I will sleep in another apartment," she told Fan.

Her servant-relative murmured acquiescence, bowed, and hurried ahead of her across the courtyard to the tiled entry of a spotless, principal guest room. Barely able to contain her curiosity, Fan hurried through a list of apologies for the bed that was not aired, the room that was surely dusty (although it had the look of a dusting within the past hour) and the lack of comfort.

"I am not a guest," Ahni finally snapped at her. "I apologize," she amended, instantly guilty. "I am tired." Fan assured her many times that there was no problem, and scurried about to straighten and polish for what seemed hours and Ahni couldn't tell her not to, because she had been wrong and they both knew it. Fan finally left, her eyes downcast in a silent rebuke of Ahni's behavior.

Ahni stripped off her filthy singlesuit and tossed it into a corner. She hadn't washed since her arrest. Her skin and hair smelled of old sweat, the tug, of Xai and the platform. Of Tania. She crossed the room naked, stepped into the tiled bath. This one had a deep, square tub with a shower. The shower turned on as she stepped beneath it, just warmer than blood. It fell with the gentle rhythm of a spring shower and she scrubbed with soap scented with sandalwood, let the water sluice away the smell and memory of Tania's kiss, let it wash away the tears as they came. "Cold," she said finally. "Cold, cold, cold," until the rain pelted her like liquid ice and her teeth chattered.

She stepped from the shower and the water shut off instantly.

Dripping she stood on the cool, glossy tiles, her skin thick and ridged with goose flesh.

Her mother stood in the doorway.

She wore a sleeveless dress woven from raw silk and dyed the color of milky jade. She stood straight and still, her arms relaxed at her side, her face tranquil.

"Why are you here?" Ahni asked softly.

"To greet you." Her mother smiled silkily. "Surely you did not think my husband and those who know me would credit any ranting of desperate criminals. My son was misled by that evil woman. I grieve for him." She smiled and her smile was genuine. "It is not against the law to belong to Her, daughter. Your father is angry . . . but at Xai, who disgraced him. You are his heir. *I* do not matter." Her eyes flashed.

"But I know the truth. About you and others in your *cult*." Ahni spat the word, "You stood behind Tania, didn't you? Those were your clever plans, not hers."

"Your anger is to be excused after your brush with death. I feared for you." Her mother's smile softened. "Not one shred of evidence ties me to this *cult* as you call it. One uses the sharp tool at hand. Our paths have converged, child. We walk together, now. You will see the rightness of it in time. We will rule this planet, you and I. You are *my* heir, not his."

Ahni stood still, nearly dry now, still naked on the wet tiles as her mother vanished through the doorway. Her mother's *certainty* frightened her. The first scents of evening stole in through the open window and transported her back to that homecoming after her first trip upside. I walked into the spider's web, she thought, and then, *no. I was already there.* Shivering, she pulled a silk robe from a convenient hook beside the shower. The air from the garden caressed her, thick and humid, as she sat crosslegged on the low bed and accessed her link.

She accessed Jira, the family synthesist and one of the best, a woman with an impeccable reputation for predicting trends and compiling pertinent information. Ahni expected her formal interface. But to her surprise, Jira's torso materialized in front of her in realtime, her sari a soft gold that made her skin glow.

"Ah, I wondered if I would hear from you." She twinkled at Ahni, the dimple beside her mouth making her look childlike and innocent. "I wish to congratulate you on your father's announcement of your status as his formal heir. How may I help you?"

"I need a solid forecast of the Council vote on platform independence, Jira. Who is going to vote how, and their leverage points, if any suit my profile. And I want a forecast on the Judiciary decision on Dane Nilsson. Double fee if you can do it in less than six hours."

Jira's glazed look grew more pronounced and a sitar played softly in the background as she left a virtual placeholder to run a quick assessment of what information she had on hand "Doable." Her gaze refocused. "Can't cut it finer than six hours. This topic is up in the air right now and I suspect half the delegates don't know for sure which way they will vote yet. The deals are humming." She chuckled. "Gonna take a lot of AI hours. I'll need advance payment. Even from you, honey." Her speech had shifted from formal English with a trace of Bengal to something more like North American city-street.

Ahni had never entirely decided what Jira's personal history might be. Not Bengali upper middle class, the pose she wore for clients. Possibly not even female. Whatever the nature of her . . . or his . . . flesh reality, she delivered a high quality information synthesis. For a price. "I'll send it to you directly from my private account. I want something else, too."

Jira, about to exit, paused, one perfect eyebrow rising.

"I want solid proof of Gaiist influence on national coalitions. Past two years only. Look at local-focus media for a start."

"Your shift in interests intrigues me." Jira smiled politely, back to Bengali formality.

A new data point for Jira to add to her syntheses. Ahni wondered how much money it would earn for her. "Time bonus," Ahni said shortly. "ASAP."

"It is, as always, your money." Jira's smile turned creamy and feline.

Anhi blanked the connection, opened a new one, to Noah's private email. "I need one last thing," she said. "Go through what you found on the Gaiists and find me proof of Michelle Raud Huang's involvement with the Gaiists. It will be difficult to find. I need this, Noah." She ended the link and flung herself on the bed, her eyes on the ceiling. That, she dared not trust to Jira. One more task. She levered herself from the bed, opened her link again, highest security, diplomatic. "Li Zhen, Chairman of Dragon Home." She smiled, imagining him looking up, mental alarms going off at the expensive security level of the message. Just so, Chairman. "I wish to thank you for your assistance in the recent matter of orbital security." She used formal, diplomatic Mandarin. "I hope our goals are still aligned." She paused to let his tension rise a bit. "I wish to discuss the plight of Dane Nilsson with you." Another pause. He would be waiting now to find out just what she thought she could use in leverage against him.

"I was quite impressed with your son. He is charming, and represents a powerful future for the Zhen name in the universe. I am sure that his grandfather will share this opinion and it occurs to me that I should congratulate him on this continuation of his DNA into the future." Ahni broke off, let the silence hum for several heartbeats. "I will speak with you before the Committee meets to judge Nilsson, Chairman of Dragon Home. I look forward to our mutual support. End message," she instructed and stared at the delicately carved and painted screen that decorated the room. This was her only hope to save Dane. Translation: Make sure that Dane doesn't become a scapegoat or I will take DNA evidence of your son to your father. Perfection was expected of a Zhen heir. Imperfections did not come into existence. The price Li Zhen ultimately exacted from her for this blackmail would be . . . significant.

DNA. Something nagged at her. It came to her suddenly, a sudden memory of Dane, returning with the proof she needed that Xai was alive. *Check them,* he had told her and he had not realized that the DNA belonged to her half brother. That should have been obvious to him. Frowning, Ahni searched for it in her email, found it, unopened, archived and waiting.

It was standard report, a direct readout from the sequencer, stamped and legal, titled 'Huang, Ahni', the second titled only 'subject'. Ahni accessed the family archive, called up the birth registry for both herself and her brother, security stamped and encrypted. Curious, Ahni ran a comparison between Dane's sequence and the sequence from her birth registry and from Xai's.

Stared at the results, thinking furiously.

No wonder Dane had been puzzled. Ahni called up the very secure directory that contained the DNA sequence of all Elite members, alive and dead. It confirmed her guess.

Still numb, she tried Jira's access again, this time got her wide-smiling, "I have a message for you." face. Opened it. *The media has forgotten Dane Nilsson,* Jira's image said. *That is not by accident. I would suggest that his is a lost cause. I seriously doubt that sufficient media momentum could be built in time to motivate the Judiciary members. The crime he is accused of carries illogical, emotion-based baggage for a majority of the voting members.*

Ahni accessed Security. "I need a skimmer to take me to the Council island. Private pickup, top priority." There were advantages to being The Huang's heir, she thought bleakly.

Security had the skimmer at the private dock within half an hour. Ahni sat silently as it whisked her across the ocean, her mind circling back on itself again and again as she watched the sky lighten.

In spite of the early hour, a private Courier met her on the Council Island, with a greeting from Li Zhen. He was watching her. Ahni smiled bitterly. She still carried his beacon, hadn't bothered to search it out and destroy it yet. The sun was just peeping above the horizon as he delivered her to the small but luxurious hotel suite occupied by Li Zhen.

He greeted her formally, his icy anger carefully restrained. Without speaking he poured tea.

Ahni shook her head. "I did not come as your guest. I meant to blackmail you with your son, as you surmised." She faced him in the cluttered little European-furnished room. "I apologize." And she bowed. Felt surprise and disbelief dilute his anger.

"You would not throw away such a lever, Huang Ahni," he said at last. "You are very concerned about this man, Nilsson."

"I am tired of levers." Ahni drew a slow breath. "Dane Nilsson does not deserve to die, and I cannot save him." Bitterness twisted her lips. "I have a gift for you." She handed him a data sphere. "You will find my DNA scan on it. You will discover that I am your sister."

"What?" Li Zhen said softly.

"I am as much a created tool as was my brother. I was meant to be a lever. My mother found a better lever in the Gaiists. The existence of your son is between you and your father." She bowed again. Deeply. "I will not turn your son into a lever." And she turned and left.

TWENTY-THREE

THE ACCOMMODATIONS ON WORLD COUNCIL ISLAND were a lot more luxurious than the cell upside, wherever it was the Council Security Forces had held him. Dane prowled the carpeted suite, gravity leaning on his shoulders. Carpeting, a small, limited refreshment center, and a video screen with a library of popular vid selections in English softened the space. The bedroom with its sliding door offered an illusion of privacy that didn't fool him. The camera eyes were well disguised, but they were there. He made no effort to keep track of time, and the unchanging light didn't help. Meals came and were taken away. Sometimes he ate, mostly he didn't. The drag of the planet turned food to stone in his belly. He drank juice from the refreshment center. It said a lot about the security of this place, that they could be this generous.

A legal counsel had been appointed to his case. She arrived soon after a meal, dressed in a natural-fiber power suit, hair a crisp inch long, unselected-Scandinavian by the look of her fair skin, and pale hair. Had she expected a genetic countryman? He watched her take stock of his face and reconsider.

She tried hard. She had the formal charge and wanted him to read it and to retina that he had done so. He refused. She laid out various strategies for defense with their pros and cons, and he told her he had no interest in any defense. Let the gene scan speak for itself, he told her. She spent a lot of time explaining in carefully simplified English just why this wasn't a reasonable defense.

He let her work it out for herself . . . that he wasn't reasonable. She finally left, after delivering dire warnings about his future, and he was impressed that she kept her simmering fury at his uncooperative behavior utterly buried behind an impassive demeanor.

Dane completed his circuit of the carpeted space, aware of the mass of bone and muscle with every step, pain twinging through his joints and up and down his limbs as ligaments took the strain of gravity's pull. It had been a long time since he had lived in measurable gravity. Longer still since he had set foot on the planet.

He threw himself down on the bed. It offered a small relief from the endless drag of his leaden flesh. But it wasn't the physical discomfort of the overtaxed ligaments and joints that bothered him. The sense of weight brought with it . . . memories. Memories of life in the refugee camps, and an older brother who seemed so old at twelve.

Dane levered himself to his feet and began to pace again, the discomfort providing a focus, a way to avoid the memories.

They would come back as dreams when he finally slept.

Nobody had punished him here, or treated him with anything but the impersonal scrutiny of a professional. Nobody would answer his questions either. What was happening? How had the media portrayed the live link as Ahni faced her brother and the Gaiist? What had the reaction been?

He had to stop pacing again, give his aching body a break on the bed once more. What about Koi and his family? Had they already been rounded up and euthanized? Li Zhen would hand them over, if he had to. There was nothing he could do about it.

He got to his feet, pain preferable to the endless circle of his thoughts. Halted as the door whispered open. A man and a woman in CSF blue stepped into the room. "Put this on." The man tossed him a folded wad of cloth, dyed the same brilliant chartreuse as the jumpsuit he was wearing.

Clean clothes? "What's happening?" he asked, not really expecting them to answer.

"You're scheduled for the Committee."

The casual answer shocked him. He knew it was coming, but it had receded from reality to a "someday" event that loomed on a distant horizon. He stripped in their presence, staggered a bit as he lifted a leg to step into the clean jumpsuit, felt the sharpened attention of his guards. But he steadied himself. Once he had moved effortlessly here, he thought with a thin amusement.

Dressed in clean clothes, he walked heavily between the two guards. Their curiosity pricked at him. No hostility, just curiosity.

Even if they exonerated him from illegal alterations, would they let him go back upside?

That would probably depend on what happened up there. Dane swallowed a surge of frustration, wishing they had let him have access to the news media.

An elevator took them up to the Judiciary Committee chamber. Dane stepped out and his guards halted with him, saluting smartly. A horseshoe shaped table made of something that looked like a slab of agate curved before him, a single, comfortable chair in the center of the curve. Three women and four men faced him along the outer curve of the table, a range of ethnicities and genetic histories in their faces, their expressions unreadable, their emotions a broad spectrum from a flicker of envy to the disgust one might feel at an ugly spider crouching on your pillow. That last didn't bode well.

"Dane Nilsson, formerly resident botanical engineer for the orbital platform operated by the North American Alliance?" A tall, spare woman wearing a one piece suit of gray silk, her face either geneselected or naturally pure Masai, nodded to him.

"I am," Dane said.

"Please be seated." She inclined her head at the central chair, her eyes bright with intelligence. Her hair, silvered with age, had been clipped to a short, thick cap. She was thoughtful, but not hostile at least.

Dane walked over amidst a thick silence and sat down in the chair. The psychological effect of the chair and no desk was one of . . . nakedness. The person seated in that chair had no defenses. The Judiciary Committee surrounded, barricaded behind that slab of stone. Crimson letters in glowing script floated in front of the

Masai woman. *Ms. Mallolah Engoko, Chair.* None of the other members were named.

"Mr. Nilsson, do you understand why you are here?" Engoko leaned forward on her palms, her dark eyes on his face.

She wanted him to understand. What was it that was important to her, Dane wondered. Justice? Or simply that she be understood? "No." His voice felt rusty and unused. "I do not know why I am here."

She frowned. Looked down at the desktop between her palms, and Dane guessed she was reading an eyelid screen. "You have not signatured the formal charges presented to you. Did you read them? You were appointed a competent counsel who is capable of defending you adequately before this Committee. Did she not present you with the charges?" Her English was gently accented.

"Don't blame the counsel you assigned me." Dane said. "She was very competent and tried very hard. I would not do what she asked."

"Why not? Do you want to die? Do you realize you are charged with the only capital crime that exists in this day? Do you have a reason to choose death?"

She was *asking* him, the Committee members forgotten, asking him this question with urgency and personal focus. She wanted to *know*.

"I don't need a defense." He spoke to her, not to the Committee. "You can look at the evidence and see what is true. That's all that matters. If the outcome of this depends on anything else . . ." He shrugged. "Then it doesn't matter to me."

Someone down the curve of the table started to speak, but Engoko raised a hand.

"And you would die merely because you did not try to defend yourself?" She would not let it go.

"If it depends on anything other than the truth," he said softly. "Then I have no interest in playing untruth against untruth, Madam Chair. Yes, I will die, if that is what you decide."

His answer angered her, but he wasn't sure that her anger was directed at him.

"For the record," she said, looking right and left along the table.

"Our defendant, Dane Nilsson, has stated that he does not intend to defend himself in this case." She glared at him. "In certain cases, this might be grounds for reconsidering the mental acuity of the accused. I do not think that it is applicable in this case. If that is your position, Mr. Nilsson, we will proceed."

He bowed his head, accepting her anger.

"Mr. Nilsson has brought up the genetic evidence in this case." A small, round faced man with unselected Gallic features broke in from the end of the table. A nanosecond pause indicated that his words were filtered through translation software. One of the radical Catholics from the New Irish Republic?

"We have all seen the raw data." He spread small, thick fingered hands. "Which, fellow committee members, I am quite willing to admit, I cannot understand to any great degree of certainty. However, I am quite willing to abide by the scientific experts who appended their analysis to the data. I see no reason to extend this session any longer than necessary."

He believed Dane guilty. The certainty of his conviction chilled Dane. A murmur of assent rose from the table, but at least two of the committee members shook their heads in disapproval.

"I want to hear his explanation, Madam Chair." A small man with a Vietnamese or perhaps unselected Cambodian face spoke up, shooting the Gallic member a withering glance. The translator software gave his words a clipped, staccato rhythm as it synchronized the translation to his mouth movements. "A human life is at stake here. It does not seem humane to end it without query, based on the assertion of a handful of people we have never met, based solely on our assumption of their expert knowledge."

"They *are* experts." Gallic man glared down his nose. "We would not have hired them if they were anything but the best."

"Even the best of experts may be wrong," the Vietnamese man murmured gently. A small woman wearing a gold and orange sari with a blood-colored caste mark on her forehead nodded agreement, but said nothing.

"Mr. Nilsson, did you read the final report submitted by our panel of experts?" Ms. Engoko's eyes were on his face.

"I did not."

"I would like you to read it now."

She was not ordering him to read it, she was asking him to do so. Dane regarded her for a moment. This was a woman to whom justice mattered for its own sake. "I will," he said.

Silently a small table unfolded from the arm of his chair, opened out in front of him, much like the tables contained in the Elevator's passenger seats. The tabletop shimmered and turned white as a holofield activated. Letters appeared in a clear font. A pair of crimson scroll-arrows glowed at the right margin.

"Do you need assistance with the document?" Ms. Engoko asked.

"No." Dane smiled at her. "I have a Ph.D. in Botanical Engineering."

"I apologize." She bowed slightly.

Dane concentrated on the text, scrolling swiftly down the page. It said what he had expected it to say, that the DNA scan had revealed no overt insertion of non-human DNA, and neither had a more extensive, allele by allele study. However, the report continued, the phenotypic manifestation clearly revealed that non-human DNA had been inserted. The conclusion? Dane skimmed through the paragraphs of supporting arguments. Their conclusion was that Dane had simply perfected a method for inserting non-human DNA in such a way as to disguise it from scanning technology.

He looked up from the virtual page, met the Chair's eyes. "So they find no evidence that I did anything, but conclude that I must have."

Engoko sighed. "We reviewed the videos of the autopsy of the creature."

Dane stood, pushing against the crushing weight of this world. It wasn't gravity, he thought. It was the accumulated weight of millennia of xenophobia and genocide. "That was not a creature," he said softly, aware of the collar around his neck, hands at his sides. "I named her Aliya. She had a name for herself, but it wasn't a word, rather an image and a feel. I suppose in English, I would translate it as Joy. She was twelve years old. She liked to play tag, and she loved flowers. She wove blossoms together into intricate sculptures. Just because they were beautiful and they gave her pleasure. I was there when she was born, and I watched her learn to get around on her own in the microgravity of the hub garden of NYUp."

He paused for breath, his eye traveling along the table. Some of the committee looked down, refusing to meet his eye. The Indian woman and Engoko both met his gaze.

Engoko nodded. "I would like to hear what you have to say about these people." She did not hesitate before the word "people."

Dane nodded. He began at the beginning, repeating the history of Koi's family as he had explained it to Ahni. He recounted his own doubts about their origins, his DNA scans, the rapid evolution he had observed. "In a handful of generations, they have changed a lot," he said thoughtfully. "They are almost entirely telepathic now, although they use speech if they have to. Nearly all of them will talk to me in English. They are highly intelligent and learn quickly when they choose to." He lifted one shoulder. "I don't know where the changes will end. They are biologically adapted to microgravity. Their circulatory system depends apparently on venous peristalsis and ciliated cells for fluid movement in non venous spaces. Their bones are to some degree cartilaginous and flexible. I don't have the equipment at hand to do molecular assays, but their circadian rhythms seem to run to a thirty hour cycle. From the notes I've kept, I'm guessing that the cycle is lengthening, that it was no more than twenty-eight hours when I first encountered them. They are . . . playful for the most part. I have never seen a single instance of interpersonal violence among them. If you transport them down to the planet's surface, they won't survive long." His last words dropped into a vast silence.

After a moment, Engoko stirred. "What is your opinion, Mr. Nilsson," she said, her expression severe. "What are they?"

He met her eyes. "The next evolutionary step for Homo sapiens."

The table erupted in a babble of conversation. Dane made no attempt to listen to the individual conversations. He didn't need the words to follow the flow of the debate. We do not like the *other*, he thought heavily. He raised his eyes, found Engoko looking at him, and the pity in her eyes confirmed the flow of the discussion. I am sorry, Koi, he thought. I am so sorry for all of us.

Engoko turned her head sharply, as if someone had called her name. Tilted her head in a listening posture, eyes narrowing, then lifted a hand. The room fell silent.

"I have just received a request." Her eyes slid briefly toward Dane. "Chou Zhen, Chairman of China has requested to present evidence before the Committee as an interested party."

A low murmur made its way around the table.

"He understands that this is outside of the usual procedures, but claims that the evidence he has to offer has only recently come into his hands." Engoko spread her hands, palms up. "I see no reason to refuse him."

"I do." Gallic man bounced to his feet. "China thinks it can throw its weight around any time it chooses. The rules of procedure are clear and they apply to all nations and alliances equally. China needs to abide by those rules the same as the smallest island state."

"Are we concerned with protocol here?" Engoko's tone was icy. "Or are we concerned with justice . . . which may be served by the evidence Chou Zhen holds?"

"Perhaps your country needs to bow and scrape to China, but we don't."

Engoko said nothing, but after a moment or two, Gallic man broke their locked stare and looked down at the desktop. "We don't need this," he growled. "I think we're all ready to vote." He looked around the table for confirmation, but only two members nodded. "Fine." He flung himself back in his chair, tight lipped.

"Please invite Mr. Zhen to bring his evidence into the chamber," Engoko said pleasantly.

A door slid open and they all looked toward it, expectantly. Dane's eyes narrowed as the Chairman of China's huge empire strode through the door. He was a hand's-width shorter than his son, and something about his face caught Dane's eye. He reminded him of someone—Ahni, he thought. It was something about his eyes and the shape of his cheekbones. The Chairman carried a small child, his legs wrapped around the Chairman's waist, sitting astride the Chairman's hip. He was dressed in a ceremonial jacket and pants of thick brocaded silk, a rich crimson embroidered with gold-thread dragons. An embroidered cap covered his head and he buried his face against the Chairman's shoulder.

The Chairman stopped beside Dane's chair and with a murmured word, the boy slid to the floor, to lean against the Chairman,
clutching his hand in both his small, long-fingered hands. Dane
looked at the long fingers, too long, eyed the delicate bones of the
boy's face and caught the faintest milky translucence of his corneas
as the boy looked curiously up at him.

The Chairman bowed to the Committee. "I have read the summary of the case before you that was published for Council members," he said in crisp, perfect English. "You do not have all the facts
before you."

"So you tell us." Engoko bowed her head a hair less than the
Chairman had bowed his. "What facts do you wish to present to us?"

"You have a limited data set as regards the DNA origins of the
female whose body was brought to the Council by the Council's
forces," Zhen said in crisp, perfect English. "I wish to add to that
data set."

"Proceed." Engoko inclined her head again.

Without another word, Chou Zhen bent and gently unfastened
the carved ivory buttons of the boy's silk jacket. He removed it, then
unfastened the stiff, brocaded pants and the boy grabbed his hands
and with a grin, hopped out of the heavy outfit. The crimson silk
folded to the floor and for a moment, the boy swung lightly from
Zhen's hands, wearing nothing but a pair of underpants as the Chairman lowered him gently to the floor. He stood barefoot, smiling
shyly, his dark eyes glazed with as if with frost. His limbs looked too
long for his skinny torso and his long toes splayed across the floor.

Soft intakes of breath punctuated a rapt silence.

"This is my grandson, Ren Zhen." Chou Zhen spoke quietly as
he lifted the cap from Ren's hairless scalp, but his voice filled the
well of silence. "He was born to my son Li Zhen and Jin An, an administrator in our orbital colony. I have submitted a detailed analysis of the DNA of both parents and the child for your examination.
There has been no contamination of this child's genetic material.
This child has had no contact with the man on trial before you today." He did not look at Dane.

Dane smiled at the boy. "I know someone who would play with
you," he said softly, thinking of Koi.

The boy looked at him and smiled, and Dane caught a fleeting image of Koi and one of his sisters somersaulting in a dark space. The images were a bit warped with a child's perspective, but he recognized Koi for sure. Felt the boy's happy smile. The boy tottered over to him, his steps uneven, clambered into Dane's lap. Dane felt Chou's brief, intent scrutiny, ignored it. The boy's curiosity cascaded through him. He probably didn't speak English, Dane thought, so he envisioned the hub garden, the tubes of peppers and bok choi and spinach. Felt a happy burst of recognition, and then the boy showed him the scenes back, but with Koi and his family present. He had been in the garden. Dane itched to know just what had happened. Realized suddenly that the room had fallen absolutely silent.

He looked up, found them all staring at him. Felt curiosity edged with anger from Chou Zhen, more curiosity than disgust from the Committee members. Engoko's expression was enigmatic. "Mr. Nilsson," she said, as Chou Zhen lifted his grandson from Dane's lap. "Clearly we have acted without all the evidence. In the light of Chou Zhen's information, we must review the situation and ask our scientific experts to review the new data." She waited as Chou Zhen left the chamber with his grandson riding on his back. Then she cleared her throat. "We find you cleared of all current charges involving the adulteration of human DNA with material of nonhuman origin. We will return you to the New York Platform. Until this case is fully explored to our satisfaction, the Judiciary Committee requires that you wear a locator link that will allow us to recall you for further examination, should the need arise. But once we have completed our study of the new data, if we have found no reason to reexamine you, the locator will be removed and you will be free entirely of our scrutiny."

"Thank you, Madam Chair." Dane stood up. "What about the people of the Platforms? The ones like Chou Zhen's grandson?"

"What about them?" Engoko tilted her head, a sly twinkle in her eye. "They are the citizens of the newly sovereign platform of New York Up, are they not? They are not our concern unless they feature in a case brought before the World Council." She looked around the table, her eye pausing thoughtfully on the sullen Gallic man. "If there is no objection," she said mildly, "I will declare this Committee meeting adjourned."

The Gallic man looked as if he wanted to object, but clenched his teeth and gave a tiny shake of his head.

"Committee is adjourned," Engoko said and a silvery chime sounded in the chamber.

TWENTY-FOUR

AHNI CLIMBED OUT OF THE SKIMMER AT THE FAMILY DOCK, feeling as if she had been absent for weeks rather than a handful of days. The thick topical heat, rich with scents of green and rot oppressed her in a way it never had before, smothering her in a blanket of memory. She made her way to her father's apartments. He expected her. Plates of delicacies covered a low table in his elegant rooms. Her father was waiting for her. Ahni accepted an eggshell cup of pale, clear tea from him, complimented him on the tea and the age of the pot and sipped it. The flowery fragrance brought the scent of home to her nostrils. They grew tea on the platforms but it would not taste like this. Every tea tasted of its growing place.

"I am impressed with your competence in the matter of the World Council vote. I have studied the small points of leverage you used to persuade uncertain voters." He nodded. "You used a minimum amount of force to divert a mountain."

Ahni bowed her head.

"I am pleased with my choice of heir. I am old. It is time to permit my successor to take over the family's business."

"Ah, but you will live forever, Father." Ahni raised her eyebrows.

"I have looked at the results from the private research that you so generously fund."

"They are not certain," her father said smoothly. "But you are well informed. Those discoveries are closely guarded. You are very good." He smiled and selected a small, plump dumpling. "I value the sharp tool."

Ah, she thought. Father, you overlooked the heir you wanted. You married her, and hung a sharp sword on the wall to rust. It cut you and poisoned your blood.

"I am sorry," she said gently. "I have another path to walk. I have committed myself to the orbital platforms."

"A child's adventure." He waved her words away. "Our family's path lies down here. Not in some castle in the clouds that has no future. Your duty is to your family."

Ahni swallowed a sigh. You never looked beyond the world you created, she thought. You did not choose to see reality. That made you a ready tool for my mother's hand. "I am sorry, Honored Father." She bowed, deeply. "I have chosen my path. I can walk alongside Huang family or I can walk it alone, but I cannot stay here and do as you ask." She pulled a data sphere from her tunic, handed it to him with a formal bow. "This is my final gift to you."

"What is it?" he snapped.

"The gift of clear sight." She stood and left his chamber and he did not call her back.

She crossed the courtyard to her mother's apartments. Her mother sat on the embroidered cushions before her low table, a pot of tea steaming gently on it. Ahni wondered suddenly what had happened to the priceless Qin teapot Li Zhen had given her. She had left it in the hotel room on NYUp. Her mother inclined her head without speaking and Ahni sat down across from her.

"The Council votes went as you wished them to." Her mother stressed the word "wished." She offered Ahni a cup with both hands. "Your talents have been wasted for too long."

Ahni turned her head aside, refusing the tea. Her mother set it down on the table, lifted her own cup thoughtfully. "Why are you still angry, daughter? You come here with the taste of power in your mouth. Tell me that you are not hungry for more?" She smiled slyly.

"Tell me first how you became pregnant by Chou Zhen."

"Ah." For a moment her mother hesitated, the cup at her lips. "We were young." She sipped her tea. "There was never the slightest possibility that I could leave your father and marry him. It was . . . an afternoon whim."

"Does he know? Chou Zhen?"

"That you are his? Of course not." Her mother's eyes flashed. "Did you think he would shrug you off? No." She shook her head. "He believes what The Huang believes. That an egg slipped into my womb after Xai had been implanted. My doctor knew, of course, but he had reasons of his own to keep this secret for me. And he died soon after." She smiled.

"How did you plan to use me?" Ahni asked softly.

"If you know this much, I have no doubt that you can surmise my intentions," Her mother said coldly. "You would make him proud. Did you inform him?"

"No." Ahni met her gaze. "Although Li Zhen knows. I do not know what he will choose to do with that knowledge."

"What is your price?" Her mother smiled gently. "I assume a price lies beneath this conversation."

"Oh, there is more yet to discuss." Ahni held her mother's gaze. "I had an agent acquire details of the Gaiists and their involvement with world politics. Enough to make their purposes clear."

"I told you . . . a ready tool." Her mother waved her hand dismissively. "Perhaps they do lust for world power, but what has that to do with me?" She smiled. "I am no member."

"Oh yes, you are." Ahni smiled gently. "A very talented synthesist uncovered your tracks. You were good but he is better. And your son was not the naïve tool you believed. His private blackmail file confirms it. The proof will be enough to convict you of conspiracy to commit terrorism before the World Council. It will be more than enough for Wen Huang . . . along with my DNA scan."

Her mother rose to her feet, pale. "I offered you the planet."

"Is that what you offered Xai?"

"Yes," her mother said simply. "But that was a lie. He was never more than a tool. Like the Gaiists."

"Did you send him into Tania's bed?"

"I suggested it to Tania." Her mother lifted her chin. "You will not do this. You are not a fool, to walk away from what I offer."

"I have ethics, Mother," Ahni said softly. "That makes me unfit to walk your path."

With a sudden, savage gesture, her mother flung her tea cup across the room, and as Ahni's eyes followed its shattering, she sprang.

Ahni froze, the razor edge of a dagger's blade against her throat. "Killing me will not save you, Mother," she whispered. "He already has the data. He is reading it now. A skimmer is waiting at the dock, if you want to run. I will not stop you." A white-hot thread of pain crossed her throat as her mother's hand trembled. Ahni closed her eyes as hot wetness crawled down her throat and between her breasts.

Suddenly her mother laughed and stepped back. "You are so *prepared* to die. Like a Buddhist monk. You are weak."

"You are evil," Ahni breathed

Her mother spat on the table between them. She smiled, blood red lips stretching over her even teeth. "Live with my blood on your heart." She plunged the dagger into her throat.

Ahni stumbled backward as blood splattered her face, spraying crimson dots across the pale wall as her mother's body spasmed and fell, her heels beating briefly on the tiles. Ahni covered her face with her hands, her mother's blood and her own, sticky on her skin. Finally the tears came.

And tore her apart.

TWENTY-FIVE

PLEASE REMAIN SEATED UNTIL DOCKING IS COMPLETED,
the cool androgynous voice murmured. All through the cylindrical
cabin of the shuttle, seat-webs clicked and retracted. Business passengers plus a few tourists smoothed wrinkles from their singlesuits
and pulled bags from the storage bins beneath their seats. Ahni
shouldered her own carryall and let the stream of passengers carry
her into the Arrival Hall. It wasn't nearly as busy as it had been on
her last trip up here, but she spotted tourists among the business
travelers. *Good,* she thought. They were coming back up here more
quickly than she would have guessed. The native woman at the
Customs and Immigration desk scanned her new travel visa and
smiled at her, eyes widening. "Wow," she said. "How cool to really
meet you."

"Thanks." Ahni returned the smile, thinking that her arrival
would be all over the Con as soon as the woman went on break. *So
much for arriving anonymously,* she thought.

She reclaimed her bag and headed for the main corridor, but before she had gone more than ten meters from the Arrival Hall, a cart
zoomed up. Laif leaped from it and scooped her into a bear hug
that lifted her from the ground. "About time you came back up

here." He grinned as he set her down, his emerald flashing. "My first act as official Mayor of the independent territory of New York Up was to send you the very first immigration visa we issued. I told you I'd do that. So what the hell took you so long?"

"I had a . . . family tragedy to deal with, Laif." She closed her eyes briefly. "I had to get a lot settled . . . before I could come up here."

"I'm sorry." He peered at her. "Rough, huh?"

"Yes. It was rough." She summoned a smile for him. "So are you enjoying being Mayor?"

"Hey, I get more complaints . . . This independence thing has headaches not even Dane saw coming." He handed her into the cart, tossed her bag into the back seat. Looked at her sideways. "You want a lift to the elevator, I bet?"

"Of course." She smiled at him. "Where else? Are things working?" She studied him as the cart zipped along the corridor. "Is it going to turn out like you and Dane planned?"

"Yeah, I think so." He sighed. "Lots of growing pains and we were a little off on some of our estimations, but we brought down the first few rocks, let a lot of downside celebrities come up and see just to sooth the jitters downside, and that's going to tip the balance on supply up here. Tourism is coming back faster than we thought. Koi and his folk." He shook his head. Laughed. "Can you believe it? We got to watch out for the religious nutcases—they figure they're either devils or angels—but the rest just come to look, you know? I think Koi's family kind of likes it, now that they're used to it. We can really start building, once we get things stabilized and get our trade balance established. We've already got residency applications piling up." He pulled up at the elevator.

"I'll let Dane fill you in on all the important details." He leaned across the seat to hug her once more. "I'm glad you're back," he said. "Dane's been missing you. I may not have much of an E rating, but even I can see that." He laughed and handed down her bag. "Get up there before the Con finds out you're here. If you want any privacy."

"I'm on my way." She smiled up at him. "By the way, I'm here as the Huang heir to open a branch of family operations on NYUp.

With my father's blessing. For good, Laif. If you want to grant me permanent residency."

"Sweet Mohammad, Buddha, and Jesus, the stiff old goat has a brain after all." Laif grinned. "Never would have guessed it when I was pissing him off in the Arrival Hall." He clasped her wrist. Hard. "I didn't grant you a travel visa, sweetheart, I granted you an *immigration* visa. If I thought I could have kidnapped you, I would have. Welcome home and go see Dane." Laif spun the cart away from the elevator and headed down the hall with a flip of his fingers.

Welcome home. It felt right.

The climb to the hub seemed to take forever. The familiar flood of gold-green light made her squint as she pushed off from the elevator, towing her bag.

A familiar, slender shape zoomed out of the leafy shadows, missing her by a hair. Koi rebounded off the elevator, somersaulted, and in a second, had wrapped his long limbs around her. "I knew you'd come back up, I told Dane you would." He released her and pushed off from a tube, darting like a swallow through the leaves. Finally, he halted himself a handspan from her, grinning. "I didn't tell him I saw you coming." His grin widened. "You can surprise him."

"I hear you're a celebrity, Koi." Ahni laughed and took his hand. "You and your family."

"Yeah, we've been going to the park to meet people. Dane asked us to." Koi snagged her bag and towed it, drifting along with her. "It's fun. We're better at scrum than anybody." He laughed. "Li Zhen took us to Dragon Home after we left that lighthouse thing. They've got a really cool garden, too." Koi plucked a couple of ripe strawberries from a tube, passed her one. "Some of my family stayed there. Ren likes to play with them." Koi smiled. "I like Ren. He taught me his language," he said in Mandarin.

"Nice accent," Ahni said, impressed. "That was fast."

"It wasn't hard to learn."

She barely heard his response. Up ahead, in a clear space among newly planted tubes, Dane was checking plants, a handheld scanner of some sort in his hand. A couple of Koi's family drifted along with him. Emotion swept over her like a tidal wave.

"I'll take your stuff to Dane's place," Koi said, radiating a smile.

"He has your stuff from the hotel there, too. And that ugly pot. He said it's so old and ugly it has to be valuable. How come 'old' is valuable downside, Ahni? Old is just old."

"I'll explain about history," Ahni said absently. "Another time."

He had felt her. Turned. Let the scanner drift.

They met in the bright light of the open space, spilling momentum against each other, his arms going around her, the heat of his body warming her clear to the center of her being.

"What happened?" He pulled back to look at her, concern in his eyes.

"A lot. I'll tell you later." She laid her cheek against his chest, drifting with him. Koi's relatives zipped around them radiating happiness and welcome, finally zoomed away. "I'm up here to stay, Dane. For good." She pulled back a bit. "You got room up here?"

His mouth met hers and he answered that question with his body. It took a long time. Eventually, they drifted among blooming pea vines. Ahni plucked a white blossom and tucked it behind his ear. "Koi says they play scrum now."

Dane's deep chuckle carried happiness. "And they're all talking now . . . English. That helps."

"Koi's speaking Mandarin, too. Courtesy of Ren. That's amazingly fast, to pick up Chinese."

"Quite a few stayed on Dragon Home," Dane said thoughtfully. "They learn very fast, Ahni. When they want to. It seems that . . . living with us more openly . . . they want to. They mix really well with folk at the park."

"How's Kyros?" Ahni pushed back so that she could see his face. Touched his cheek lightly. "Did he run for the Belt now that I've totally exposed his businesses?"

"Nah, he's catching rocks." Dane chuckled again. "He's an expert after all. He's using my ship."

"I need to get hold of him." Ahni smiled. "I owe him a rather large debt. I did some research. The best ship outfitter on Darkside seems to be Outsystems, Inc. Is that a good one?"

"Oh, it's the best. Why?"

"Kyros has a ship waiting for him there. They'll custom fit it . . . whatever he wants."

"I'd say you've more than repaid any debt." Dane laughed and pulled her close, sending them drifting into the leafy shadows of the mature tubes. "He'll bankrupt you. Kyros is going to want every upgrade they have."

"I owe him that." Ahni smiled at him. "We're going to make this work, up here."

"You say that *we* with conviction." His pewter eyes held hers as he brushed a fingertip along her cheek.

"Don't start again." Koi popped out of the leafy shadows. "Li Zhen just showed up with Ren. I think he's probably looking for one of you."

"How is that going?" Ahni pushed herself away from Dane, looking for her singlesuit.

"Cautiously. We have different agendas," Dane said thoughtfully. "He and Laif butt heads. You might be able to smooth things out there. But I think we have the same ultimate goals, so we get along."

They met Li Zhen at the elevator. Ren had already zipped off to play with Koi and Li Zhen drifted, obviously waiting for them. When they emerged from the leaves, Li Zhen pushed gently away from the elevator, drifted to a stop a meter from Ahni. Bowed. "Welcome home, Little Sister," he said.

"Thank you," Ahni murmured, returning his bow.

"I wish to tell you that . . . I informed my father. That you are his daughter." Li Zhen's face gave nothing away, but he radiated only calm. "He will visit Dragon Home in a tenday, to celebrate Ren's birthday. I hope you will both do us the honor of being my guests."

"We will be honored." Ahni bowed again. Watched Ren zip past in pursuit of Koi. "Your son shines," she said.

"He is very smart." Li Zhen smiled. "I thank you . . . for opening my eyes. And my father's." With that he turned away, called the reluctant Ren to him, and returned to the Elevator.

"You are Chou Zhen's daughter?" Dane's eyebrows rose. "Is that why he showed up at the hearing?"

"Yes, I am. And I don't know if he knew, then. I think his arrival was purely Li Zhen's doing." Ahni took his hand. "Do you think we could officially disappear before anyone else comes up here to say hello? The Con has to know that I'm here, by now."

"Noah will be on his way. And a lot of others most likely. You *are* a celebrity up here." Dane laughed and pulled her close. "And Laif is going to want to plan out the next decade of business matters with you. But it's a big garden. We can disappear, even from Noah and Laif." He pushed off a tube and they arrowed down the aisle between tubes of eggplant and peas. He turned to face her as they drifted, his hands on her waist, his eyes on hers. "Welcome home, Ahni," he said.

She pulled him close. "I *am* home."

Truth.